RES

LIMERICK CITY LIBRARY

Published in 2004 by

ASHFIELD PRESS • DUBLIN • IRELAND

(Second Edition)

© Simon W. Kennedy, 2004

ISBN: 1 901658 36 8

A catalogue record for this book is available from the British Library.

Typeset in 11.5 on 14 point Dante
Designed by
SUSAN WAINE

Printed in Ireland by
ßETAPRINT, DUBLIN

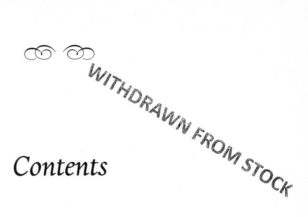

Contents

Acknowledgements

It took me ten years to write this book with the assistance of a great many people some of whom I am almost sure I will forget to acknowledge. I beg that they please forgive me in advance. I would like to acknowledge my Publishers, Trafford and in particular Deirdre and Marlow from Canada who have been of such great assistance to me. The cover is based on a Watercolour of my own duly enhanced technologically by Stephen Saleh of Helios of Cork. The script was edited by Isabel Cartwright of Carlow and subsequently proof read by Therese Carrick.

Great encouragement was given to me by a great many friends too numerous to mention but who kept me going when I received disappointment after disappointment. Now that it is published I wish to thank them, especially Will Sutherland and Angela who read, re-read and advised.

Brid Richardson, Mary Bailey, Jane Duignan, Laura Ryan, Rosemary Whelan and Pauline Maher, who typed and retyped, corrected and recorrected and who continually tolerated my moods, frustrations and disappointments.

Under this heading I particularly want to thank my family, Sinead, Patrick, Brian, Niamh, Grainne and Niall who put up with their sitting room being taken over, the continual drone of "Dad's boring voice" from the dictaphone transcribers which my wife Lillian used, early at morning, late at night between school, teaching, football, hurling and camogie matches (involving each of the kids), running a household and maintaining her good humour (most of the time) as I continually broke her heart with change after change (all of the time). I hope you will all benefit from all their input and efforts as much as I appreciate it.

Author's Note

I was born and raised a Catholic and more than likely will die one. I studied to be a priest for three and half years, "chucked it in" halfway through, half starved myself through Law School and three years after that I qualified as a Solicitor and got married. I practised law for eighteen years and then I hit a really bad patch. I lost everything and found myself in my early to mid-forties on the dole.

In the middle of darkness and confusion I discovered a principle of life; if you want to find great life, look to where there is great death! One of the reasons that farmers put animal dead waste material (manure) on land is to bring life into it.

What I have to tell is based on truth, but is, I believe a parable. Things seem to happen the way intended, not neatly, not comfortably, but real. Life is a paradox but I believe that I have found the answer to it! The answer to life, it seems to me, is a question. The question is, "What is the answer to life?" As long as we keep asking ourselves this question, and believing the answer will find us, we leave our minds open to wonder. As long as we can wonder we leave ourselves available to the stimulus of life and the baptism of a richly imagined and fruitfully realised life. However, as soon as the answer finds us, we want to keep it, mind it, own it and control it. We love the power of the answer and hate the notion of losing it. We want to be God – now – and the devices we invent to administer fear in order to preserve our answer defy the question and remove the astonishment and wonder of our lives that was intended by an imagination greater than ours. Everything alive was imagined by someone, somewhere, sometime. It is with that thought in mind I offer you this story of truthful imagination.

The more intently matters are scrutinised the more obfuscated they become. The truth is all around, but where is it? It's like trying to examine the Sun without being blinded. The most graphic portraits of it I have seen were coloured by children with crayons, something in the Van Gogh style. Colour, dashed on and splashed on with yellow crayon and an intensity revealing primeval dazzle, but allowing imaginative perception. The more mature and sophisticated, the more this ability becomes diluted and the Sun becomes more and more pale.

Sun is seen, through shadows and silhouettes, in hues of colour, shades and illuminations. Like the real Sun, the truth is dazzling – and so dazzling that it can be awful. It strips veneer like acid, the acid burns – and so can telling the truth. Remembering the truth is like recalling how the keloid scar of the burn was caused – the memory of the trauma, of the hurt and the pain, of the dazzle, will cause us to wince. But the truth frees, and once the veneer is removed, reality is palpable. In order to accept reality it is necessary to imagine it.

I remember reading that the magnetic North Pole rocks on an axis of 21.50 to 24.50 every 42,000 years, and the earth's path around the sun changes from an ellipse to a circle every 96,000 years. Is it any surprise therefore that in the cognitive certainty of mathematics, measurements are invariably reduced with the last decimal place of the measurement recurring to infinity (e.g. $\pi = 3.141666666$). It becomes clear therefore that nothing is certain, everything defies precise definition and it is not possible for us predetermine or preplan anything with the certainty of its accomplishment or achievement or completion. Was this why the Church was founded by such a wise man on such a wobbly undependable rock as Peter, but who had such a huge heart. I remember being told that we end up where our heart is and life is spent trying to unravel its mysteries.

Probably, historically, the most dramatic yet telling truthful one line sentence that I can recall is "But the Emperor isn't wearing any clothes" from the fairytale "The Emperor's New Clothes" There, is a lesson here in truth. Everyone present was astonished.

An aunt of mine who died at one hundred years of age last year told myself and my sister the story of a single woman who committed suicide by drowning herself at Hook Head lighthouse in the 1930s. This was not the first suicide committed at that spot, nor the last, unfortunately. The girl was pregnant and the thoughts of social ostracisation and the grim reality which it offered were less harsh than the alternative she chose. She was unable to imagine her life or her child's in that circumstance, in that place, at that time. She sacrificed herself and her child to the deep. These thoughts were revealed in what she did before she drowned herself. On the mossy grass verge before the rocks the local sergeant found a small-feathered bonnet which had been pierced through its heart with its hatpin, securing it to the earth. Initially he did not recognise it, but took it to be a wounded bird, eventually it was identified. The metaphor, for me, was powerful and struck home. What care and reverence this "wounded bird" displayed. Unable to save herself she secured the bonnet so it would not be blown away and scattered and wasted, by the "piercing" of its heart with pointed steel and securing it to what she imagined was secure and certain. This was the rubric she performed preliminary to the destruction of her life – a ritual of correctness and precision – a pathetic fallacy. The metaphor continued in reverse. Nine days later, not unlike the biblical Jonah, the sea vomited up her body and offered it back to the people from whom she had come, to bury her in the earth, to which she had secured her bonnet and where she belonged. But the notions that had put her in the sea were also belonging to the people who buried her and in doing so they continued the same pathetic pattern – they buried her outside the wall of the churchyard which was not consecrated ground, as if, having disowned herself, they would also disown her, and by so doing revealed their own enslavement to the same tyrannical principle that life would not be accepted unless it was kosher to culture. This happened twenty years before the story I am about to relate.

A Story

I call for your
Attention
Now
To listen
In singleminded fashion
To this story
That means so much
To me.
It happened once
And only then
Since had it happened
More than
That
It would not be
Unique
And hold me
As I now hold you
Nor would I
Tell you
For the bother,
I did not make
This up for you
But it did so
For no one
But itself
And I was told
It
In hushed
And dreaded
Tones
In fear.
And then
Upon

Another time
A dreadful
Happy person
Blurted stone deaf
Facts
To blinded minds
Who hoped
That hurt would
Never happen
Afraid it
Someday might.
And then the
Story hid.
Searched it yet
For time
And searched it
Still for place
And searched
Each mind
Each soul
Each face
To find
A soul
Wheron
To spill itself
As conflict does
With pain
And thereby
Wreak its change
Upon
Internal sight
And thrill our deep
Enthralls,
Where dragons eat the fairies.
Experience
Lurks in the shadows

Searching
For
A time
Upon which
It would be,
That time
comes once
And when it does
Its entrance
Makes
Down
To us
Through to the sod
From where
It first began.
And there it
Rests.

A reading from the prophet Ezekiel
34:11-12. 15-17

As for you my sheep, I will judge between sheep and sheep

The Lord says this: I am going to look after my flock myself and keep all of it in view. As a shepherd keeps all his flock in view when he stands up in the middle of his scattered sheep, so shall I keep my sheep in view. I shall rescue them from wherever they have been scattered during the mist and darkness. I myself will pasture my sheep. I myself will show them where to rest – it is the Lord who speaks. I shall look for the lost one, bring back the stray, bandage the wounded and make the weak strong. I shall watch over the fat and healthy. I shall be a true shepherd to them As for you, my sheep, the Lord says this: I will judge between sheep and sheep, between rams and he-goats.

This is the word of the Lord.

(Extract for Year A from the current *Roman Catholic Lectionary for Liturgical Readings*)

PART I

The First Summer of Fifty-Six

I

The Pecking Order

"You can laugh through the whole of a farce,
You can laugh through the whole of a play,
But you cannot laugh through the hole in your arse,
Because it's not built that way."

JOHN LEACY SNR., 1956

My father, from whom I inherited a healthy disrespect, used to recite this doggerel to show that there were some things you could not change. My mother, from whom I inherited a healthy respect, used to say; "Man appoints and God disappoints." It was the same principle but from a contrary disposition. My father had his feet firmly planted on the ground; he knew life was messy and would regularly remind himself and others of this fact by mischievously telling funny, vulgar stories. My mother who tolerated these vulgarities with a resigned raised eyebrow and shake of her head had her feet firmly planted beside his.

In 1956 I was 13 years old. I was the middle sibling of five, an older brother and sister and two younger brothers. My father was a shopkeeper and my mother, a teacher, gave up her job when she married. I lived in a little village called Coleman. It overlooks the Waterford estuary. It was always called "Waterford Harbour" a fact that I resented as I felt it reversed the natural order of precedence by putting Wexford second after all, our half of the coastline belonged to Wexford. Matters of this nature are important when you are thirteen and interested in tribalism and sport. My father's name was John Leacy and I was called after him; to differentiate I was called Jack.

Sometimes to get me going the boys in my class would call me "Lazy, lazy Leacy." This was because they knew I was the opposite

One particular Saturday morning in the month of May 1956 I sat in my father's garden looking down on the wide placid river below. The sea was a fresh calm blue. It was 10 o'clock. The Mailboat from Waterford was steaming down to the open sea. The sky was clear except for the presence of a light yellowy glow on the horizon. Occasionally a foghorn went off giving a muffled echo.

I had retreated to the garden for the purpose of going through a selection of comic books to decide which were eligible for swapping. Eligibility boiled down to a number of considerations; chiefly, decisions would be based on what the market could bear. You could have a "full swap," in which case the swap was "for keeps." You could have a "lend," in which case you loaned for a stipulated period in return for a like consideration.

The best comics were 64 pagers. They divided into three broad categories – "Westerners," "Wars" and "Classics." *Kit Carson, The Kansas Kid, Buck Jones, Lashlaroo* and many other gun totin' daredevils, redskins and cowboys made up the "Westerners'" library. I did not care much for the "War" comics because the British were always winning. My father used to say this was all British propaganda. He did not approve of the comics nor indeed, the British. He had one comment for them both, "they'd give you the shits!" He used to tell me that I would turn into a comic one day and that it would match me better to go out in the fresh air and have a run around for myself.

I picked out two comics, a 64-pager and a "Classic" ("Classics" were illustrated famous stories such as "Ivanhoe") and headed off to Michael Larkin's to do the business.

Larkin was a year older than I was. We served Mass together on a Sunday. During the week I served on my own because our house was the closest to the church – it was also the closest to the school. Larkin was a better footballer than I was, as good a hurler, but I was a faster runner. We both played on the parish team. My father, John Leacy, the Curate, Fr. Williams, and the schoolteacher, Thomas Byrne, were in charge of the football team. I played right half-forward, where my father played in his time, and Larkin was now playing in goal because he had slipped on the ice in the street during the winter and had broken his leg. When we were in school during that winter he played in goal with the plaster on. Not surprisingly, it had to be replaced three times before it finally came off.

When I arrived at his house he was drinking tea and eating bread with his father in the kitchen. It was dark. Larkin's mother was dead almost ten years and the absence of the female touch was palpable. Everything was clean, spartanlike and frugal. What was the point of putting out plates when you were only eatin' bread and there was a perfectly clean oilcloth on the table. Matthew Larkin looked up when I entered having been called from the front door in response to my knock.

"How a' ya' young Leacy?" he enquired.

"Not too bad thanks."

"Well, are yiz goin' to win next week?"

"I hope so."

"Well bejaysus yiz 'ud better make a better shape than yiz did in the simmy finals. Five points up ud ten minutes to go, an' yiz let them get within a point of yiz."

Michael blushed. He had let in the goal that nearly sank us. He told me that for three nights afterwards he dreamt he had been playing in the goal in Croke Park with ninety thousand people looking on and the goal posts had been the width of the pitch apart. He said he had woken up in a lather of sweat. I told him that if he had let in another goal he might never have woken up after the match. He knew well enough, and his father said to my father that he was "raley kilt about it."

We left the kitchen and his father told him not to be long because the cows needed to be let out again. After we had swapped comics he asked if we would play hurling in the evening in his father's field. I told him that there was a crack in my hurl and I was afraid that if I used it, it might split.

"So yer never goin' to hurl again is that what yer sayin'."

"Don't be so stupid, I'd take it down to Hiawatha to fix but I'll have to wait until tomorrow before I get a tanner from me uncle Martin to pay him."

"Are ya goin' to the matinee in the Hall then tomorrow? Captain Marvel is on again – an' after last week! 'Chazam'!" he said in the marvel mode and made as if to fly, and ran off shouting he would see me at Mass the next morning.

⌒⌒

Here was a dilemma. It was four-pence to go to the pictures and tuppence for a "flash bar" – chocolate coated toffee – it was six-pence to have your hurl banded by the blacksmith, Henry Isaac Watchorn. They called him Hiawatha. He was a strong handsome seventy-year old man who looked to be in his mid-fifties. As he said himself, "he was as fit as a fiddle." He also played one and he smoked a black pipe, but not while he was engaged with work. He was bald and the top of his head was shiny and polished. He was about five feet ten inches tall and always wore his shirtsleeves rolled up. When he was sixteen he ran away to the United States as a stowaway. He joined the American Army, first becoming a member of the Eighteenth Infantry, before eventually joining the famous U S Cavalry. Some had a story that President Teddy Roosevelt praised him for his horsemanship. Whilst in the cavalry he befriended an Indian who had enlisted. He met and married the Indian's sister. He subsequently settled in Spokane in Washington where they had a child. He was twenty-seven years old and married five years when his three-year old son and wife were knocked down and killed by a motorcar. Some well-to-do young university students had too well celebrated their examination successes and their motorcar had mounted the sidewalk where mother and child were walking.

They said he got a fortune from the compensation. Others said he got a fortune out of the IRB to come home during the Troubles to organise flying columns. He was a trained sniper. He kept forty Black-and-Tans pinned down for two days on the bridge of Waterford while Liam Mellows, the Republican leader, made good his escape by the ferry from Passage to Ballyhack and the relative freedom of Wexford.

His family had been Presbyterians from Antrim. Apparently, his great-great-grandfather had joined Henry Joy McCracken during the 1798 Rebellion. He went to church three times in the year: Christmas, Easter and the Harvest Thanksgiving. He wore a full moustache that was once black. He had kind, bright eyes and was a great whistler and fiddler. He wore a leather apron when working and he invariably whistled a reel or a jig. He never remarried but was seldom short of female company, yet he was not a womaniser. His forge was located convenient to the

Ballytarsna stream and regularly he would throw in a bucket with a rope tied to the handle to draw out such water as his task required.

⌒⌒

The forge consisted of two rooms – "the space" and "the office." "The space" was where all the work was done and "the office" – in which there was room for two people to stand sideways and face each other – was where payment was delivered, out of the gaze of the vulgar and inquisitive. He had good stories from the Wild West but he was slow to divulge. He loved the life he had lead but his memory trips hurt; yet, he appeared to increase the excursions as he got older. I only once heard him mention his wife and when he did his eyes welled up. It was that same Saturday afternoon.

I decided I would get the hurl fixed and look for credit and thereby resolve my sixpenny dilemma. At the forge, Hiawatha was putting a shoe on Sean Hanlon's horse. Mr. Hanlon was not there. When he saw me with the hurley-stick he looked up and smiled.

"More business," he said to the horse. "We'll have oats for a week."

I saw my chance.

"Could ya hold off on the oats for a fortnight or so?"

"Ho! Ho! Me boy. Live horse and ye'll get grass – is that it?"

"Somethin' like that."

"Aye, surely, we'll see what we can do. Stand back ou'-a-da space until I wheel out this fella."

"Hub off!" he addressed the horse.

"Hub off ou-a-da."

The horse moved around in a led circle, Hiawatha holding the bridle. He secured the reins to one of several rings on the outside of the stone forge wall. It started to rain lightly and he moved the horse further down the wall to the shelter of a sycamore tree which stood at the back of the forge near the stream. When he returned he removed the red kerchief, which he always wore in the cowboy fashion, from around his neck and rubbed his bald head dry. The corrugated iron roof was beginning to make noise for the rain.

"Show me here," he said. I gave him the hurley. He looked keenly at the split. It ran parallel to the back of the hurl from the toe, to the bas and almost a third of a way up the handle.

"Major surgery governor!" he said to me.

"Will I be able to use it?" I asked.

"Not for hurling matches I'm afraid."

He saw my disappointment. Nevertheless he was adamant. He explained he would put a narrow thin band at the toe and a much wider sheet of about four inches just above the bas going up the handle and it might hold. It could not be used in games because the four-inch sheet might cut the hurler or an opponent.

"You could take it with you when you're driving in yer uncle's cows" he said, and, as if to validate himself, added "Aye, surely."

His northern accent was not obvious, but this colloquialism had survived, but barely. It emerged when nothing more needed to be said, a kind of full stop.

He commenced his task as I watched him.

"Mr. Watchorn?" I innocently asked.

"Why do they call you Hiawatha?"

He froze for a moment. He blushed a little and laughed. He could see I was perplexed and he laughed some more, shaking his head incredulously. Initially, I tried to laugh a little as well, and then I became a bit self-conscious since I did not know what I was supposed to be laughing at. When he stopped, he gazed into my eyes and said,

"Do you know, you're the first person who ever asked me that to my face?" I felt a right eejit. He smiled, "That's why I love chaps."

He tossed my hair. I tried to smile but it only ended up as a sheepish grin. He worked. After a while he spoke fitfully and quietly at first.

He explained that he had received very little "schooling" as a child, and when he was recruited he was asked to write his name. Unsteadily he wrote his first initials "H." He had started to write "I" for "Isaac," but was misspelling. He had written "A" beside "I." He got as far as the "C" of "Watchorn" and as he said, he realised he was beat. So he stopped. The recruiting officer was presented with "H-I-A-W-A-T-C." He asked him if that was his first name or his second name.

"'Sure,' sez I 'tis all of 'em.' And he looked me up and down and said 'Well Mr. Hiawatha, you sure don't look like no redskin to me'."

We both laughed. He shook his head and left down the hurley stick. I felt the closeness that goes with sharing a privileged secret and here was a real red roaring honest-to-God, genuine no bullshit character from a Western standing right in front of me.

"Aye, surely," he laughed. He laughed again as he visualised his memory in the manner of the recollection of a faded innocence.

He rubbed his head with his hand and rested the other on his hips, "That's a name that belongs to the Iriquois Indians, you know. It means 'Wiseman' ." The Iriquois were friends from my "Westerners" library.

Then his expression changed and his eyes welled up.

"My wife was Iriquois you know."

He removed his kerchief from his neck and rubbed his head with it as he turned his back to me momentarily.

"It's warm," he explained. It was not that warm.

⋙⋘

In less than five minutes the hurley was banded. The skill of the blacksmith was impressive. The four-inch band on the throat of the stick was braided as if it had been cross-stitched in lace. He admired his work.

"Be careful there," he said. He pointed to the band and rubbed the front of it.

The band would flatten with use and the edge could sharpen, he had advised, insulating tape would make it safer.

At that point Sean Hanlon stepped into the forge.

"Well Hiawatha!" he said.

"All shod," the blacksmith replied.

The two men stepped outside. The smith was gently patting the horse's rump with the hurley as they talked. My father knew Sean Hanlon. He always wore a black beret. He was a fine good-looking man with a twinkle in his eye. His uncle was Dean Hanlon who was parish priest of Coleman up to his death at the age of eighty-six the previous year. His uncle had been a very important man in the parish and the diocese. The nephew was thirty years of age and was married with two children.

I remember the first night I ever saw him. He was at an interparish football match and I remember he took a photograph of the team. I was barely seven years old at the time and I remember some people at the match saying he had come home at last "with the Whitney wan." The disparaging remark related to Mrs. Hanlon, who was a Protestant. For a long time afterwards, whenever I would see him, my gaze would stay on him longer than usual. I think I was looking to see if I could see "the bad" in him, or if it was coming into him on account of having married a Protestant.

We were not allowed to go near the Protestant Church and we were not to bless ourselves passing it. Anthony Molloy did once when he was going home from school with the Meylers and he immediately fell and bled his nose. Whether there had been miraculous divine political intervention or whether the intervention was more human and more conveniently located was never disclosed by Anthony. Neither God nor the Meylers were offended.

We had been told in school that you could only get to heaven through the one true church. Everybody else was damned. Working from this unassailable position of being one of the saved it was going to be pretty tough going for the poor damned. There was only one shepherd and he had only one flock.

∽∘∾

Hiawatha came back to "the space" as Sean Hanlon led off his horse. He handed me the hurley and reminded me once again to apply insulating tape to the four-inch band. I cycled out of Aughadreimne back to Coleman on my older brother's bike to my father's shop where I immediately acquired and applied the insulating tape.

The shop was located on the crossroads of Coleman. When we were young we thought the name had something to do with coalmines. But the "priest" Doyle said that the village had been given its name by St. Colman. St. Colman had been the Bishop of Lindisfarne in Northumbria in the seventh century. He had adhered to the celtic customs of christian worship. The celtic christians were very conscious of the presence of God in nature and operated out of a sense of wonder. The feelings were important. The Roman church was more conscious of organisation and administration. The rules were important. When King Oswy of Northumbria took a Roman princess for his bride the clash between the two traditions became pronounced. They both had different dates for the celebration of Easter. A major Royal court battle ensued, which ended with Colman and the Celtic church being defeated in argument. The young Monk Ronan contended that the Beloved Disciple had bequeathed his tradition to the church of Rome but Colman maintained he had faithfully followed Columcille and the Celtic church. Lest, however, he be disowned by St. Peter at the pearly gates, the issue was decided by Oswy against Colman (Ah, fear! – how pervasive is your influencing cowardice!). Easter would be celebrated by the Roman calendar. Colman left Northumbria and on his way to Inishboffin stopped to rest at a little hamlet in South Wexford and left his name behind to mark the spot where he rested. I always found the story a remarkable one. It illustrated to me how people could behave when they got it into their heads that they were right and others were wrong. For this alone, if nothing else, the little village was aptly sponsored. Fear would play a big part in its history.

∞ ∞

The "priest" Doyle knew all the local history. He was called the priest because he had almost been ordained. He left the seminary a month before his ordination date and took up a position as bookkeeper/accountant in the Shelburne Co-Op. Shelburne was the name of the Barony. He was fifty-five years of age. He hated to be caught out, and seldom was. Although he was a know-all, he was seldom lampooned by the vulgar. He had an incisive mind, a hot temper and a sharp tongue, which could deftly reduce an assailant.

He was not well co-ordinated and had no history in sport but because it was such a central social outlet he participated by refereeing, which suited his authoritarian demeanour. He was bald and had a big head and tended to be plump.

He could be debonair and charming and was in his element during formal occasions when the rules of etiquette and social manners were required. He had notions of himself as a legal authority ever since his Canon Law results placed him continually at the head of his class. Whenever a football club in the district required assistance in drafting an objection or defending one he was invariably consulted. He was Fr. William's right hand man and was a type of voluntary sexton. He loved to give orders to the schoolboys who served the High Mass and Benediction. He was more wary of me because my father and Fr. Williams were friendly. He was what everyone referred to as "a spoilt priest." I did not like him. He always wanted his own way. On occasions, he would be upset if his advices or his admonitions were not observed and he had a tendency to carry grudges and sulk. He was a good singer, however, and loved to sing solo. Traditionally at Christmas he sang the "Adeste Fidelis" with the choir joining in the chorus. One year, before Christmas, when the choir were practising their hymn singing, an incident occurred. All of the hymns had been picked for Midnight Mass and preparations were about to commence when he was noticed to be silent. It dawned on Fr. Williams that the "Adeste Fidelis" had not been included. In their enthusiasm to pick a few different, more unusual hymns, it had been overlooked when the traditional ones were selected.

Fr. Williams stated it would not be Christmas in Coleman if William Doyle did not sing the "Adeste." His initial reaction was to give the impression that he really did not wish to sing, which he subsequently diluted by suggesting that someone else might, and ultimately, and very painfully, he allowed the coaxing persuade him on the basis that if there was nobody else prepared to, he would practice a little. If he was satisfied he could attempt it he would let the choir decide, providing they were prepared to be honest with him and tell him honestly, if he was good enough or not. I nearly puked. I would dearly have loved to have told him what everyone felt, but there was no permission to do that. Honesty was not allowed for adults and required dilution and so resided safely within the predetermined wisdom of centuries of tradition and convention.

As I was applying the insulation tape to my hurley the "priest" Doyle came into the shop. Saturday afternoon was his half-day from the Co-op. He had his grocery list. His wife had died some ten years previously from consumption, otherwise known as tuberculosis. She was buried in the graveyard in Coleman convenient to the road. Without doubt, it was the best kept grave in the cemetery. He took great pride in the fact and loved to be complimented on it, and his devotion to his departed spouse. He was a great mourner and was always quick to volunteer his services carrying coffins at funerals. In extending sympathy, he was sure to point out that he knew all about the pain of the bereaved. I had not known his wife but I once heard Hiawatha remark that the priest was afraid of her. He said that it was just as well since otherwise he would have been "eat, beat and spat out." She apparently was of a large constitution and in the partnership was the commanding, if not the demanding, presence. She reminded him of the priest's mother, Hiawatha said.

At that point the telephone rang and my father told me I was to go to my uncle Martin's to bring in the cows. My uncle Martin was a bachelor who lived in Rathroe about three miles from the shop and Coleman. It had been my grandparents' home. I never knew my grandfather, who was a farmer of some thirty acres. He had been to America as a young man for a few years before marrying into my grandmother's family farm. He was the District Chairman of Sinn Fein during "the Troubles." Canon Sheridan told him once, if there was trouble in the parish he would hold him directly responsible for it. He replied that he would be responsible for himself and his family and nobody else. Canon Sheridan told him to remember that he was taking on the might of the British Empire. My grandfather told him they were taking on the might of the Irish Race. They were like hammer and anvil.

My grandfather, I felt, had spunk. That was where my father got it, though, come to think of it, my grandmother was not exactly the servings of weak soup herself.

My uncle Martin lived with her, a spinster sister and another bachelor brother, James, who was the youngest. She had buried my grandfather twenty years previously. She was a formidable force to reckon with. She once challenged a girlfriend of my uncle Martin what business she had with her son. The poor girl fled the scene intimidated and embarrassed. Martin was very upset for a long time but continued working. He had fought during the Troubles. He was jailed during the Civil War by the Free Staters. When he was released at the end of the War one of his thumbs had been broken. It had set without medical intervention and functioned awkwardly. When he broke his other thumb some years later playing football, it healed in the same way with the same result. I found this attitude difficult to understand having regard to my own experiences. Whenever we were ill or injured we always got the best of medical care and attention. My father explained that in those times each family had regular bereavements. Oftentimes, babies and mothers would die on birth. One in two children would die from consumption. There was a lot of physical hardship. In this type of environment scant regard was given to minor injuries, particularly those acquired on the football field. His thumb was diagnosed by one of the mentors as being "out!" When it was discovered the diagnosis was wrong, he had more or less got used to the way it was and so neither interfered with the farming or the football, nor was it let.

I arrived at "the house," which my father referred to as his ancestral home. It was the new replacement for the old home, now an outoffice. I reported for duty and was told which field the cows were in by my aunt Pauline, or Poll as we called her. They were in a nearby field so I left my bike and proceeded through the haggard on my journey.

Three months previously, Poll replenished her fowl stock after she had sold off most for Christmas. She bought in about twenty pullets. She had about twenty Rhode Island Reds, six ducks and about ten turkey hens. The turkeys were a new venture. She also bought a friggin' turkey cock. From the moment he arrived, Rathroe lost half of its appeal for me. Everytime I arrived at the house I would scan to make sure that the haggard gate was shut. If it was not "God, man nor the devil would not get me out of the car," as Martin would say, amused at my private terror. The first encounter happened as I was looking for eggs in the hay shed for Poll. As I was coming down the ladder with sixteen eggs in a sweet-can, I saw all the other fowl running away. I thought Ponto, my uncle's sheepdog, was having fun. When I reached the bottom and turned around I was facing the turkey cock some twenty feet or so from me. His face was as red as a devil's poker. He pulled his head into his arched back, fanned out his black and white tail, stiffened his white wings until they were scraping the ground and when it appeared as if every sinew and feather could not be bound much tighter, he uncoiled with such speed and ferocity in my direction that I almost filled my britches. I dropped the sweet-can and was out of there, as Martin relayed afterwards, "like shit from a goose." I barely got the haggard gate shut. Of frights I had in my life to that point, this rated number one. After that there ensued guerrilla warfare. When nobody was looking and I was sure the coast was clear, I would get a few stones and, from the fortified security of an upturned horse's cart on the yard side of the haggard wall, I would give the "ould hoor" what grief I could by throwing stones. I was greatly taken by heroic stories. One story which appealed, related to how the ancient Irish hero CúChulainn got his name, which every schoolboy knows. His original name was Setanta. One day as he approached Cullen's Fort he was hitting a ball with his hurley and catching it. Cullen had a vicious watchdog. As Setanta approached, the dog ran to attack him. Setanta struck the ball with such strength that he killed the dog from the blow. Thereafter, as retribution, Setanta filled the role of watchdog for Cullen, and in the process acquired the nickname "CúChulainn" or Cullen's hound. Whenever I felt brave enough, I would venture inside the haggard gate with a few stones and belt them at the turkey cock with the hurley. I never could get a decent shot at him. Gender distinctions in fowl were not always obvious to me and, although I was well aware that cocks were male, I always referred to the cock as "her" or "she." We were taught by the nuns and one of them in particular had a very nasty temper, her name was Sr. Ignatius. As a tribute to my dislike of both I christened the turkey cock "Ignatius!"

So there I stood in the middle of the haggard with the fast dawning realisation of my exposure. Looking straight ahead of me were chickens and hens like Romans at Nero's Games. A glance to the left of the dung hill to the fowl house, for a way out, a glance to the right.

As a justification of raw and naked cowardice, I decided caution was by far the better part of valour. I convinced myself that I was not so much retreating as reversing in order to contemplate my situation more judiciously. Just before I moved, I heard the telltale sound of the wing feathers scraping the ground behind me. I was a good runner as a youth. I had won two County Medals in the County Wexford School Boys' Sports. I was second the first year and first the next. I ran good races and fast races. I can tell you with all the sincerity my heart can muster that the fastest I ever ran in my life was that Saturday afternoon in my uncle's haggard with my wellington boots on and Ignatius after me. I ran over the dunghill with such fleetness that Fionn MaCumhaill, CúChulainn and the entire of the Red Branch Knights would have been proud of me. Out of respect for the urgency of my case the other farmyard fowl withdrew from my path, feather after cackle after dust. At the bottom of the haggard was a small ditch with a barbed wire fence and a stream at the other side. With one leap I cleared the fence and never in my life before was the water of the stream more welcome to me.

Ignatius glared at me through the fence and gobble-gobbled some cautionary fowl advice and withdrew with a swagger of disdain. I looked at the state of me. I tarried a little before going back through the field to the yard to get my hurl to fetch the cows home. When I got back I got a lecture at the state of me "and the Yanks coming."

Poll went back to the kitchen where she listened to the rest of "Mrs. Dale's Diary" on the wireless as she prepared scones for me. I would have these, ritually, with a cup of tea, before I would go back to the shop with a "tommy can" of milk and a pound of farmers' butter, the result of Saturday morning's churning, for my mother. I dreaded further inquisition, so when her radio programme finished I moved to change the topic. I asked her to tell me about the Yanks. She told me they were the Kellys. There were three, Johnny and Maura and their daughter Melissa. She was fourteen. This did not rest easily with me. They called her "Mel" for short. At thirteen years of age, I was beginning to notice girls while quite strenuously denying it. I got plenty of opportunity to do this because my bachelor uncle loved to tease me about them. Poll told me that my grandfather had stayed with them in Boston as a young man and they were children of his aunt.

Johnny Kelly was a political correspondent for the *Boston Globe*. My father used to refer to him as "the reporter." They had come to Ireland one other time for a visit after the War, for a holiday. Johnny Kelly had served in the Navy during the War.

They would arrive in Rathroe with my uncle Peter who had driven to Shannon that day to meet them at the airport. They would stay with him as he was also a bachelor living in a farmhouse about two miles away in the townland of Kilhile. They were staying for six weeks. Staying with Peter meant they could pursue their own agenda without disrupting too many lives. Peter was a politician, farmer and butcher. He had played football for Wexford in the 30s and 40s and was elected a member of Wexford County Council ten years previously, just after the War. He was an enzyme of energy. He was five feet eight inches tall, two inches shorter than my father, and a year younger. They were not identical in features, but quite regularly my father would be mistaken for him. Peter was clever, bright and full of enthusiasm. He could be very serious and believed passionately in Fianna Fáil, as did my father. Because Peter had so many meetings to attend, this meant the Yanks could be left to their own devices and could come and go as they pleased.

When I arrived at the shop my father was serving Thomas Whitney. He was a farmer and son of Thomas Whitney Senior, who was the biggest "cattle dealer for forty fairs" as they said. His daughter was Thomas Junior's sister and married to Sean Hanlon. He was a handsome, fair-haired twenty-five year old bachelor.

My father told me to give Tommy a lift with a bag of coal onto the back of his tractor. This meant a sack of coal had to be filled and weighed. As Tommy drove his tractor into the shed, I noticed a scooter drove up to the shop. As I weighed the coal we spoke about films. He asked what films I liked best. He liked the travel pictures. I used to dread those, I told him. He never played football or hurling but was a good handballer. I told him I loved *Captain Marvel* and the adventure films. He told me *Frankenstein* was "the big picture" for Sunday. He told me it was a horror movie. I got excited at the prospect of being frightened.

I used the ball of twine provided to tie the sack and cut the same with my bare hands, very proudly displaying the shopkeeper's skill of cutting the twine off of itself by means of a loop. It was taught to me by my father and I can still do it today. This intrigued Tommy and he asked me to demonstrate it again, which I was delighted to do. He tried it and nearly broke his finger when he pulled the twine. We both laughed. He tried again and again – and I helped him – until eventually he succeeded. But when he tried it once more, he failed! He threw the twine away in exasperation – but he did not curse. (Protestants did not curse nearly as often as Catholics!) With one heave, he hoisted the bag up on the back of the tractor. I tied the bag to the hydraulic arm and cut the twine once more, with a flourish. Tommy philosophised, "To every cobbler his last – old habits die hard and it's hard to learn good ones." It was one of those statements that trips off the tongue without being noticed and yet sticks.

Tommy had dawdled since the scooter arrived. He was concealing his interest with the nonchalance of the awkward. He leaped onto his tractor and drove out of the shed to park. I arrived in the shop, and went into the meat room to wash my hands in the plastic basin provided, which was beside the water bucket. My father was in the office, which was the room adjacent. Agnes Maher was with him. She was the young school teacher in the Protestant school though a Catholic. She was beautiful with jet-black hair. She had a light complexion which revealed a very soft skin. She had the look of a film star and was quite shy in ways. She was not yet confident in who she was. Her father was dead almost from her birth and she lived alone with her ageing mother whom we used call "Mother Goose." In our mind her kindness and desire to see good was as unrealistic as the matron from the fairy fables. Peter had helped her when times were bad and both she and Agnes deeply appreciated it.

I went to the bucket. John was cutting a roast of beef on the block and was tying it, having inserted a skewer. It was a small cut. There was no water in the bucket.

"Where's your customer?" he enquired.

"He's parking," I replied.

"Tell him to howld on for a minute before he goes, I want him."

When I went out Tommy was dismounting and his eye caught the scooter. He asked me to bring out the groceries he had left on the counter. This was unusual for a man to request. I let the bucket down as if to go back. Then I told him that my father wanted to speak to him. I thought he would not want me to bring out his messages but he just grinned and musically said "Does he now?" The penny dropped with me.

My father loved practical jokes and teasings. He loved inventing situations in which people had their romantic concealments revealed. This was carried out in a spirit of great fun and good humour. No finer sport would take place than if two suspected lovebirds presented themselves in the shop at the same time. The stories of situation comedy hatched out and enacted on the shop floor were legendary. Its reputation was well known for teasing and so was John's. It did not even require them to be going out together and nearly all the better if they were not, since the denials that would emerge would be taken as defensiveness. It reflected the embarrassments of the times. I grinned back at Tommy. He grinned me out of it, knowingly. I ran off to the stream laughing, hurrying as fast as I could. Then I saw the tractor moving off. He had gone without his groceries rather than risk the embarrassment of confronting the suspect of his romantic and sexual ambitions on the open shop floor. As if in telepathic religious response, the morality police alert appeared to have been activated. Fr. Williams arrived, his car door was open and he was running towards the shop. He saw me coming with the water

"Run in there and get me twenty "Gold Flake" like a good man, I'm late for confessions," he handed me a ten shilling note.

"Tell your father I'll be in touch."

I ran in quickly and got the cigarettes. My father came out when he heard the door opening and asked where Tommy was.

"He's just gone off."

"Feck it!" he said revealing his disappointment.

"Who?" asked Agnes.

He ignored her mischievously. "Who's there now?" he asked me.

"Fr. Williams, he's in a hurry for Confessions." I quickly got the change.

When I came back I was carrying the bucket and Agnes was at the counter her face buried in her hands blushing, my father was grinning from ear to ear.

"John you're the limit," she said, "and now he's gone without his groceries."

"Sure maybe you'll bring them over," he laughed.

"Yid have a right opportunity to meet the mother."

She laughed and laughed and could not bring herself to make eye contact. I could sense her pleasure in her discomfort. Then her expression changed to semi-serious:

"And nearly in front of Fr. Williams too – no wonder he took to his heels."

More laughing.

I went inside to the meat room and whilst there I could hear them whispering. When I had washed and dried my hands my father asked me to place the teacher's box of groceries on her scooter. As I did so, I again proceeded to perform my little ritual with the twine on the carrier. She told me that I was a great man and that I must be a great help to my father and then she redeemed herself by giving me an English thrupenny bit for my services. When I came back in my father told me we had need to hurry.

We had to now detour to bring Whitney's groceries. We had to fit in Confessions and there was a Fianna Fáil Cumann meeting on that night.

At Whitney's there was no sign of Tommy. Mrs. Whitney took the messages and said she did not know what had come over Tommy since he had fallen in love, that he would forget his head only it was tied to him. She went in laughing. As my father drove away smiling he remarked, "They're gas."

The Yanks arrival, I reminded my father, would clash with the meeting? It would not, he said, since all the business that needed to be done was to organise for the National Collection at the church Gate in a fortnight's time.

∞ ∞

There was also some talk of a possibility that my uncle, Peter Leacy, might be elected Chairman of the County Council because there was a split coming in the Coalition. At County Council level in Wexford, Fianna Fáil were in the minority by two seats. As a matter of form there was an Annual Meeting of the Council at which the position of Chairman would be voted on. There was one independent member and in the current climate of increasing government unpopularity there was a distinct possibility his vote would change, in which event there would be a tie. In such an event the issue would be determined by drawing lots.

Fianna Fáil had two TDs in Wexford. Dr. Ryan was Shadow Minister for Finance in the Opposition. (Peter was his right-hand-man in the Constituency). Aidan Harpur was the other. He was in the North of the County and was a brother of the Parish Priest of Coleman, Canon Harpur. Seamus Greene had stood for election and been beaten. He was a member of the County Council. He was also Chairman of Wexford County Board of the Gaelic Athletic Association. Because of his profile I thought he would have been the one to be nominated by the party for the Chair, but as John pointed out, a deal had been done between them. When Peter agreed that Greene would stand for the Dáil the deal was that Peter would be proposed for the County Council Chair. Political deals were sacrosanct.

I suppose the political climate in which I grew up was the coming of age of the new nation. Going back to Daniel O'Connell, you had Old Ireland. Then you had Thomas Davis and Young Ireland. After the 1916 Insurrection and the 1922 Civil War you had the New Ireland. In the 1950s you had Adolescent Ireland. It was beginning to lose its innocence. Ireland was only beginning to emerge and a lot of it was still stuck back in the War of Independence and the Civil War. At political rallies shouts of "Where were you in 1916?" were the ultimate disparagement. In Wexford the memory was longer. It went back to 1798. One of my uncles on my mother's side told me that his father had called him to the parlour one

Sunday from play when he was a boy. Sean Hanlon's father Dan was there. My uncle was told to sit down and listen. Dan Hanlon told him that when he was a boy serving Mass in Coleman he remembered a man who always wore his cap in church. The fashion was for men to doff their hats in the presence of the Blessed Sacrament. When he enquired from his father why this member of the Faithful was not conforming, his father told him that he had been pitchcapped as a rebel in 1798. This was a reference to that cruel and ignominious torture practise, of applying boiling pitch to the head of the unfortunate victim. Such lessons and stories burned into the folk consciousness and emotion far more deeply than any sermon. In some people it prolonged bitterness – in others it deepened identity. However, it never failed to affect.

The memory of the men of 1798 was invariably invoked by politicians to endorse a campaign or policy. In 1955, Wexford beat Galway in the All-Ireland Final. Wexford had a great team. In the winter of that year they set out to add the National League Trophy to their collection. One fine winter Sunday in Enniscorthy, they were drawn to play Kilkenny, the 'ould' enemy. They were expert stylists and great exponents of skill. (That is not meant to take from their ability to wield the timber in more physically threatening ways as well!) A neighbour of ours, Fr. Devereux, was a member of the House of Missions in Enniscorthy. He invited a couple of characters from the County Nursing Home to the match. In the course of the game Wexford went into an early lead and there was little to be heard from the Kilkenny crowd. The Wexford crowd were making the most of it whooping and roaring. In the second half, however, the tables were beginning to turn and the Kilkenny crowd started to come to life. Fr. Devereux was a great prankster and thought to take a rise from his cohort.

"Why don't you shout?" he teased.

"Sure dammit father what can we shout?" they enquired.

"Blast it, sure shout something," he entreated. One looked at the other in desperation and then, hoisted himself up, looked and turned around to the crowd and shouted, "Who pissed on the powder in '98?" This was a reference to a tradition in Wexford that not alone did Kilkenny fail to respond to the call to arms but, prior to one important engagement during the Insurrection, the Kilkenny contingent present discharged the contents of their bladders on the gunpowder to render it impotent and then left the camp and the rebels to their doom. In response to the jeer the crowd responded with shouts of "Sit down ou' a' da' an' take yer batin,'" which was telling, since it indicated the barb got home.

Politics and religion were very much intertwined. In Croke Park on All-Ireland Day, "Faith of Our Fathers" was sung immediately prior to the National Anthem. At political Cumann meetings, votes of sympathy for deceased members would be responded to by the gathering reciting an "Our Father", "Hail Mary" and "Glory Be" for the happy repose of the departed soul.

The virtues which this environment required were rectitude, certitude and hard work. There was little recognised tolerance for play. Gaelic games only were advanced as the proper Irish way to recreate. Dancing was also politicised – it was fine to waltz or foxtrot but rock 'n 'roll, which was just emerging, was entirely too free and suggestive. Control and restraint were the key words in rectitude. Deviants from these conventions were put down by remarks. Those who were in positions of high social standing were said to bring disgrace on themselves and their families. Of the others, it was said, "Sure what could you expect?"

There were many clever little devices employed to preserve and keep the pecking order right. Coleman was shortly to learn one more.

2

Frankenstein, Ignatius & Co.

The summer of 1956 was not a bad summer. It was not as good as 1955, but it was not a bad one. We got the summer holidays that year in July and that was when we really regarded the summer as starting. Before then, however, three significant events occurred in my life: Wexford beat Laois in defence of their title in the opening round of the All-Ireland Hurling Championship; we played the County Under 14 Football Final of the Nicky Rackard League, so called after the hero of the hour of Wexford hurling; and I started to dislike school.

It used to start at nine o'clock. I used to like to get there before then so that we could have play before the serious business of the day commenced.We were taught by three nuns. The principal was Sr. Ignatius. I was in fifth class where she taught. Nuns appeared to me to be ageless and sexless. Their long black dresses and underskirts went to below the tops of their shoes. It gave the impression they had no legs. Their veils were like black shrouds over white starched cardboard, like facial honeycombs, revealing nothing except the front of the face They arrived at school reciting prayers aloud. They started school with prayers. They started each subject with prayers. They very nearly started prayers with prayers. Every subject was taught through Irish. Regularly, prayers were said in Irish. The Rosary and the Angelus fell into this category. However, Catechism was taught through English. Emphasis was laid on being proud of being Irish. Explicit resentment of the English and an intolerance of the British were nurtured. To achieve national intellectual independence in the world required discipline. Discipline was defined as toughness. It was brought about by punishment for being wrong or doing things that were wrong. Teachers therefore had a licence to inflict corporal punishment in order to implement this policy. However, I never remember punishment being delivered in the manner which suggested a dispassionate execution of duty. Invariably anger was present. On occasions, the anger blotted out reason with significant and frightening consequences.

⣿⣿

That particular Monday in school I was inattentive. I was tired as a consequence of an experience the previous day. Nine-pence was riches on a Sunday. Six-pence I had received from an uncle and a thruppenny bit from Agnes Maher. Fourpence secured a seat for the "pictures," tuppence the dietary essentials for gastronomical fulfilment, tuppence for a lucky bag and the remaining penny for gobstoppers. Gobstoppers were large, hard, round sweets which required a lot of sucking and could not be chewed. Fortune favoured me with the lucky bag. Mostly these bags of sweets and toys contained rubbish but, occasionally, one would contain a better value toy rather in excess of the price paid, if you were lucky.

Having made my purchase on the way to Colman's Hall, which was the acting cinema, I discovered my lucky bag contained the envy of every boy in my class. It was a small metal aeroplane. It was solid. It was heavy. It would not break easily. It was painted green – and it was mine.

The serial of *Captain Marvel* was great, it showed how he got his power, I think from an Ancient Egyptian magician called "Chazam." On the recitation of his name, Marvel changed from being an ordinary mortal to a superman with the legion of immunities from destruction and an even longer list of other magical powers. Each episode would present an enormous source of evil threatening calamity to defy the captain's capacity, just at the end of the current showing. For a week we were left guessing. The next episode resolved the issue easily by the invocation of the ancient eastern wizard. In this way our sense of excitement was titillated by whipping away the answer just when the question was being put.

The "big picture" was *Frankenstein*. Although I read a little bit when I was young, horror publications were deemed unsuitable. Surprisingly, the censor did not deem this particular offering offensive. The body-snatching was scary and the graveyard nights made me uncomfortable. As the plot unfolded it emerged that the mad doctor intended using the elements during a thunder storm to kick-start the spark of life into the perpendicular corpse which was secured by bands and straps to an edifice of wires, coils and gadgets.

As the clouds gathered for the impending tempest, so did my worst fears. At thirteen years of age I had served enough funeral masses and burials to have acquired a strong dislike for the process of death. At the first rattle of the lightning conductor my anxieties increased, manifested by sweaty hands and a racing heart. The minute the lightning charge sparked and lit up the dials and the lights, the imminence of the impossible was palpable. The corpse glowed, motionless, like the luminous statue of the Blessed Virgin which my uncle William brought my mother back from Lourdes. The first thing to move was the corpse's hand. It went rigid and straight. I was out of there "like shit from a goose" as my uncle Martin had said on my meeting Ignatius. Admittedly there was competition. I swept up the Main Street of Coleman like a "Shee-gee." (Sí gaoith or Fairy Wind.) Speed came naturally to me on occasions like that!

I never saw the strange car outside our house and when I burst into the kitchen I was in a state of considerable excited anguish. I was looking for stability and reassurance – mother and home. I was surprised by the strangers. I repressed my need to explain my plight. My confused quietness was mistakenly interpreted by Johnny Kelly as the natural innocence and shyness of Irish kids. Mel was there. A fourteen year old female. The situation needed to be weighed carefully. My sister Marie was still at the film. Had she been there she would have been paired automatically with her. My father was anxious that she feel at home so he immediately moved to ordain a friendship between Mel and myself.

"Take Melissa out there and play," he exhorted. I was of two minds about her. On the one hand, she was a dreaded female, and a year older into the bargain. On the other hand, she had an alluring eye and a sense of adventure. As we went outside I was feeling self-conscious and awkward. By contrast she was very relaxed, smiling and self-confident. If she had a hang-up about boys, it was well concealed.

Chatting to her was like stepping into another world. She said "I guess" a lot. Because it was unusual, it amused me, but I would not say anything about it. However, when I said "begor" on one occasion, we had an interesting discussion. She said "Wat?" which meant "What?" I looked puzzled and she repeated,

"Wat was that word you just used?"

"You mean 'begor'!"

"Yeah! Wat does that mean?"

What did "begor" mean? I had never thought about it.

"I'm not really sure. It's just a way of speaking."

"I guess it's like a swear word."

"No. No it's alright to use it in public."

"Hoh?"

"I mean they won't chastise you if you use it."

"Hoh?"

She was beginning to get to me.

"What do you mean, hoh?"

"Chastise?" She did not know what "chastise" meant. She needed to go on an orientation course. This would be tough going. When I eventually explained it she said, "Sure seems to me you should say what you mean in the first place, hoh?"

Was she being female or Yank? I could not make up my mind. It never occurred to me that my own reaction might be other than right and proper. I liked her though; she was gutsy and interesting, not like some of the dumb girls I went to school with, always giggling and fussing and giddy.

She said she missed TV and since I had only read about it or maybe seen one occasionally in the films or comics, I had many questions.

I told her about *Frankenstein* and she said she would have been scared too. She was becoming my friend.

I explained to her about hurling and football and although she asked a lot of questions about the games, I was disappointed when she said she did not have much interest in sport.

My two younger brothers, who were eight and four years of age, arrived home with my uncle Peter, who had taken them to buy sweets. My older brother and sister were still at the films. Peter had a white paper bag of "bulls eyes." He offered one, which I accepted. Mel declined on the basis that her "Mom" only rarely allowed her to eat "candy." This apparently had something to do with a dental injunction and, indeed, she had beautiful teeth. My older brother and sister arrived and proceeded to monopolise Mel. As the middle sibling, I was well used to this. I was not going to fight with them in front of our guest, however. They wanted to show her the new kittens. As they ran off excitedly I was slowly retreating into myself, when Mel stopped and turned and shouted "C'mon Jack – ain't you comin'?" Ain't you wha? I was there like a shot. When I remembered she was a girl, I steadied my excitement. Still, nobody knew how I felt, except me.

That evening after the supper Fr. Williams arrived to see my father and was introduced to the Yanks. My two younger brothers were packed off to bed at eight o'clock. At nine o'clock the three of us were called in from playing "Queenie-i-o who has the ball?" My older brother, Mogue, had been brought back to St. Peter's College by my uncle Peter, who brought him out for the day on very special permission. When he arrived back home he sat in around the open door cooker with my father and mother, the clergyman and the two Yanks.

My sister, Mel and myself were flicking through comics when the stories started. My bedtime was ten-thirty but there was always a good chance, if stories started, curfew would be extended. Everyone smoked cigarettes except the two Yanks and the children.

My father had the best stories, at least he was the best at telling them. They were very funny and, as he used say, "They were all true." Some of the stories had to be retold and explained to the Yanks. Fr. Williams adapted to this role easily. When the story was then explained with the priest's own slant he would take the applause of laughter and would wink at my father. I thought the Yanks were slow initially. It took a while for it to occur to me that they were simply different.

My father told a story about the devil in Loftus Hall. This was an old story going back to the eighteenth century. The landlord and his family were entertaining a handsome stranger with a card game. One of the daughters of the house dropped a card. When she stooped to retrieve it, to her horror she beheld a cloven hoof where the strangers foot should have been.

The Yanks were loving it. My mother was making the tea. The Yanks wanted to know how the matter was resolved. Fr. Williams took over and gave the profound version of how Fr. Broaders, his 18th century predecessor, had exorcised the devil. The Kellys were Catholic. They were fascinated. Mel was mesmerised. I was terrorised. I studied my father's face closely because his expression had changed. His eyes never left Fr. Williams while he was talking about the exorcism.

After my mother had dressed and set the table we all sat in and she served up tea and hot currant buns. The women had spoken little during the evening. My mother sat beside Maura Kelly and spoke a lot about children. Maura told her that Mel was a great singer. Mother acknowledged this by announcing to all and sundry. This meant party piece performances from the kids. My sister giggled. That used really get to me. Next she would be saying she did not want to sing – a real "priest" Doyle effort. Mel sang "The Battle Hymn of the Republic." Since the festivities were in honour of the Yanks, my sister recited "The Exile's Return" and, though I could sing, my mother insisted that I recite John Greenleaf Whittier's "Barbara Frietzsche." I liked this American Civil War poem about one woman's bravery in the face of the rebel Confederate horde. I liked spunk.

Fr. Williams was the first to leave at a quarter to eleven. This meant I was off to bed. On my lonely way up the stairs I could see nothing but Frankenstein sitting down to sup with the devil. I lingered outside the kitchen door and knew if I was caught I would get a lecture to act my age and go to bed. I could see most of them through the keyhole. I was delighted to see that Mel was not bonding with my sister but sitting awkwardly on her mother's knee. She was too big, but not too old, for this type of attention.

∞∞

When I did eventually go to bed I awoke twice with nightmares. My father said he would never let me go to another film. My mother made me a cup of hot tea. When I got up in the morning I was bothered and weary. The usual rituals were performed awkwardly. At Mass I missed the warning bell for the Consecration. At breakfast afterwards, I put the toy aeroplane on my saucer and the teaspoon in my pocket. My father remarked that between films and comics and getting up in the night I would turn into a fairyman.

It was a fine May morning in school. I was wearing only a tee-shirt and elastic waisted khaki shorts. The sun was splitting the trees. We were having an early summer.

Sr. Ignatius was in a foul mood since she arrived. She was in her mid-fifties. The square shaped headgear with black veil and heavy black dress emphasised severity. She was pale faced, but when she got excited she flushed profusely. Her countenance this morning revealed resentment. The dark furrowing brow of anger had not yet arrived.

She was teaching us Irish. There was a chart on the wall with a blacksmith, a carpenter, a cobbler and many other characters in the village displaying all their tools and weapons of trade. These were all indicated with Irish words. I was good at Irish. With the heat of the sun and the lack of a good night's sleep, my mind wandered to the toy plane in my pocket. I felt it. I could turn the little propellers. Suddenly she let a shout.

"Jack Leacy, stop fidgeting!"

My heart jumped and I blushed. In Irish she told me to stand up and recite the words she would point to. Then she turned the chart to face the wall and asked me to tell her the names of the instruments of the blacksmith. This was no problem to me since it was the one picture in the whole school that I loved. I was always welcome at the forge. When I recited the instruments perfectly she looked annoyed. She made me sit down and instructed us to get our maths copies.

She announced, after the prayer to the Holy Ghost for enlightenment, that we were doing fractions, probably the most dreaded word in a schoolchild's vocabulary. Internally I groaned, this could be grief. Worse still – money fractions!

She spent approximately half an hour explaining them. I stole odd glimpses at the plane. When she was writing on the blackboard, her back to the class, I placed it on the bottom ledge of my desk underneath the highly polished rigid top. She detected something and swung around. She was deadly.

"What have you got there?"

I blushed and hung my head.

"Speak up," she barked, again in English.

This was serious and no mistake. I handed up my prized possession. Triumphantly she seized it.

"I'm confiscating this," she said.

Anguish took me, but there was more.

"Out to the top of the floor." I obeyed.

"Hold out!" I held out my hand. She had a stick. It had been a three feet pointer in the style of a billiard cue. Due to exertions in its unorthodox use it had broken. There remained an eighteen-inch butt, or handle, which was used for punishment.

She struck me four times, twice on each hand. Her strokes were hard and very sore. Her face was flushed. Upper fourth class and sixth class, who shared the room with my class, were hushed. Sixth had been assigned poetry memorisation but the "to and fro" rocking motion, which pupils employed to mnemonically rhythm their brains to ensnare the quatrains, had stopped. Their heads were still and bent over their books. Upper fourth were just gaping.

"Back to your writing," she snapped at them.

They immediately corrected their gaze to their manuscripts and inkwells.

"Up to the blackboard!" she ordered.

I picked up the chalk, refusing to cry. I held my gaze evenly at her but not defiantly. The last thing I wanted to do was challenge her.

"Write this sum down 'One and six-pence ha'penny added to two and seven-pence three farthings' and add them up."

s – d

$1 – 6\frac{1}{2}$ (one and sixpence ha'penny)

$2 – 7\frac{3}{4}$ (two and sevenpence three-farthing)

(Four farthings in a penny, two ha'pennies in a penny)

I did as she said. When I had the sum written, I drew a line underneath. A ha'penny plus three farthings was a penny farthing. I knew that. There were three columns. Shillings, pennies and farthings. I knew I could put down the farthings in the farthings column, but how did you write down a penny in the farthings column. Due to my inattention I had missed the instruction to carry the penny forward and add it up with the other pennies. There I stood, unable to start.

"Well?" she enquired.

I shifted uneasily. Would I ask, or should I not? If I asked would she wallop me? Maybe I would get inspiration. I looked back at the board and tried to stare my concentration into inspiration. Nothing would come. I could sense the panic. My stomach was turning around towards my back.

In the next instant she swooped like a black draped demon. She hit me three times on the back of my left arm whilst holding my elbow.

"Now will you be so stubborn and not do your sums?"

She was clever. She pronounced my inability to proceed as wilful disobedience. Fear was in me now. I could not now ask her to solve my dilemma since it would seem as if I was either contradicting her findings of disobedience or else being doubly clever. My concentration had long since departed and I was enveloped in intellectual ignorance. She roared

"Answer, can't you?"

I thought her question on my stubbornness had been rhetorical. I moved immediately to defuse this explosive.

"No, Sister," I answered. She immediately twisted it.

"So you are refusing to answer, then."

She moved and caught my left forearm once more. She started to wallop me on the arm once again.

"You are a brazen ... (wallop) ... impudent ... (wallop) ... child ... (wallop) ... and I'll not ... (wallop)."

She moved to my left leg.

"Have you ... (wallop) ... treat me ... (wallop) ... in this fashion."

Her strokes were vicious. I was terrorised. I was reacting to each clout with sobs and cries. The pain from the bruises was numbing and stinging at the same time. She was flushed red and panting.

"Were you at Communion this morning?"

"Yes Sister," I higged.

She moved in again with her black mass – the demon was gone but the vulture had arrived, intent on indulgence. She moved to my left raised her eyes to heaven and said,

"Sacred Heart of Jesus, help me with this child."

She administered somewhere between ten and twenty strokes as she decried the presence of the Blessed Sacrament in such an unworthy body.

By this time I was hysterical. I had been trapped in that most terrible of childhood experiences – the powerlessness to answer, the inability to resolve. My dignity was leaving me and I was disintegrating into a higging and shaking, uncontrolled quivering jangle, unable to accept and deal with the brutish abuse she was giving me as a result of her uncontrolled anger.

Some of the girls in the class started to cry. She ignored it.

I was standing at the board shaking and shivering when my body came to my rescue. I wanted to go to the toilet. I turned to address her "Sister?" She lifted her head from fixing her long rosary beads which had become entangled in one of her strokes and had broken. In barely audible strains I asked her in Irish, as was the custom, for permission to go out.

"You most certainly will not leave here until you apologise to me and this class for your disgraceful conduct here today. First you disrupt the Irish class, secondly, Maths class, thirdly you stubbornly refuse to do a perfectly simple addition sum and then impudently confirm this attitude. And now you have the affrontery to look for permission to go out."

I was in great distress. I was in a black hole, a bottomless pit. Was there no escape from this torment? I cried uncontrollably and as I did, my dignity abandoned me entirely and flowed uncontrollably with my tears, down my bare legs and into a puddle on the black polished timber floor, wetting my trousers in the process.

"Take him out! Take him out!" she yelled. Michael Larkin came over and gently put his arm under my armpit and led me out, tenderly.

It took me twenty minutes to stop higging and when I did, it was half-past twelve and time to go home for dinner. Michael kept saying, "She's nothin' only a fuckin' bitch, she shouldn't be let teach."

When I got home my mother saw the state of me. She asked me about it and washed my arms and legs. I hated being a tittle-tattle and was reluctant to not "take yer batin' like a man." She told me I need not go back to school in the afternoon. No way. Back I was going. Ignatius tried to teach me fear, but I was learning fortitude.

That afternoon she ignored me and when we were going home at three o'clock I was being treated like a celebrity by the other children.

"Did you see his arms?"

"There's a big black wan on his left leg," a reference to the bruises.

"Are the red wans worser?"

When my father came home from work we were put out to play. Later he drove off in his Morris Minor motorcar. At a quarter past nine he came back. I was dressed for bed and was sitting listening to the "Clithero Kid" on the wireless. My two younger brothers were in bed and my sister had been taken back in the morning to the Mercy Convent. He asked me to turn off the wireless and sit on a stool beside him. My mother stopped her knitting. As he spoke he looked into the fire. He told how he had gone to Canon Harpur, the School Manager, who rang the convent and requested the Reverend Mother and Sr. Ignatius to come over. In her defence Sr. Ignatius said she was not able to teach without using corporal punishment. My father told her if that were so she had better give it up. I was proud of my father and I felt so restored and valuable that I welled up inside. My mother started looking for a knitting needle behind her, but they were both in the cardigan sleeve she was making on her lap. I did not know how to say thanks. He just put his hand on my head and said, "There now, everything will be alright. Get a cup of milk and a cut of bread out in the back kitchen and go to bed now."

As I was doing so, Fr. Williams came in as he was wont to do. When I finished, I said goodnight to them all and Fr. Williams said I would need to be in good form for the County Final on Saturday.

When I closed the door behind me I sat on the bottom step of the stairs to see if they would talk about my experience. I was not disappointed. I stayed there for a long time and only skedaddled out of it when my mother went to get the tea ready.

As I lay in my snug bed I could visualise my father letting her have both barrels. Fr. Williams was enthralled by it. He concurred with my father that they were frustrated. They knew nothing about children and had forgotten what family life was like he said. He told my mother that she must have been very upset. He said he would have reacted in the very same way himself if it had been a child of his very own. I thought that was a very odd remark for a priest to make. I fell asleep smiling to myself at the last remark my father made before I left the bottom step

"Well I'll tell you wan thing. She won't ever think of doing it again."

And he was right. Although it was far from the last time I was beaten by her with a stick, I never received a flailing again. The incident was never referred to after that, but the little aeroplane was gone. It was a symbol of how matters would stand, she knew she had no right to it but would not offer it back, and she knew it would not be asked for. It was another part of the land of nod and wink which was over-populated with blind horses.

∞∞

Blind or sighted, Mel loved horses. Because school was still open she would call to our house at evening and that was most evenings. She used to borrow my sister's bike (a matter that did not assist in cementing their relationship) and I would borrow my older brother's and we would cycle around Coleman or maybe go to Rathroe.

One evening we decided to go to Hiawatha, as she had never seen a forge before and there was always a good chance that there might be a horse there. As we sped down the hill to the forge I could make out Fr. William's horse in the distance tied to the forge wall. There was a man in "the space," as we cycled closer, I could see it was the "priest" Doyle. I introduced Mel and she was eyed up and down by both men. The smith was mending a small iron gate. It was from the railing which surrounded Mrs. Doyle's grave.

"May we go out to the horse?" I asked.

"Is this the girlie then?" ignored Hiawatha.

I blushed.

"She's my cousin from the States," I justified.

"You could still be married you know," quipped Doyle, "provided you don't come within the prohibited banns of consanguinity."

He had a poor laugh. I definitely did not like him. It sounded like "Heh! Heh! Heh! Heh!" but the laugh came on the intake.

"Eh?" said Mel as we went outside. I knew what he meant and I explained to Mel that when a couple got married, the banns of marriage would be announced from the pulpit by the priest inviting people to object to any wedding on any grounds, but particularly in the case of close blood relationship because inbreeding could result. She was astonished once more. Not at the genetic consequence but that it would be announced from the pulpit.

"Supposing a couple knew they were not related."

"There could be other reasons."

"Such as?"

"One of dem might have been married already."

"I guess," she was stroking the horse's front shoulder thoughtfully. "What else do they announce from the pulpit?"

"Most everything, I guess," I said and I noticed with mild surprise how I was entering into her way of speaking. "Mostly it's used for preachin' sermons an' announcin' t'ings like funerals an' weddin's an' readin' de Bishop's letters, ya know pastorals an' things. He read part of an Encyclical last Sunday."

Mel looked up.

"A wat?"

I concluded she must have had no religious training.

"An Encyclical – a sort a' declaration from de Pope."

"I guess," she looked at me and said, "I guess you must've a lot'a religious trainin'."

"I guess we do," I replied, aware again of my easy lapse from the vernacular.

I noticed Mel had been looking past me and now was straining her eyes.

"Jack, who's that?"

I looked behind and saw a small heap of rags and bags with a tossed and windswept hard brown puss in the shape of Miley Cassidy. I laughed at her anxious state and replied

"Dat's only Miley Cassidy."

"Is he a hobo?" she enquired.

Now it was my turn: "A what?"

"Ya know, a 'down an' out'."

Miley might be down but he was seldom out, unless he was lucky and therefore paralytic from drink. We used to call him a tramp. He walked the roads for miles calling to doors asking for "help" and blessing whoever gave it and reminding those who did not that all of their parental responsibilities did not necessarily reside under the one roof or, worse still, they were one of that ilk themselves.

Miley was in his late fifties, but looked seventy. He was five feet four inches tall and looked emaciated. For a man who walked so much, he was a bad walker. His gait was purposeless and he was more of a rambler. He wore a dirty black coat, mostly open, which was probably a cast off. His hair had been light brown and curly but was now thinning. He owned a set of false teeth, which he withdrew from his pocket and inserted in his mouth as occasion required. Mostly, he looked bleary because of the drink – he was either worse for it or badly in need of it! Generally he was very dirty.

In recent years, he had become dirty and smelly and, every so often, the Good Shepherd nuns in New Ross would get their hands on him and spruce him up. While he hated this, he knew he needed it and put up with it.

He seldom engaged in a relaxed conversation. Unlike his walking generally, his talking always had a direction. If the conversation was not perfunctory, it was sure to be leading up to something. Foolish people treated him with derision and paid the price for their conceit. He gave the impression he had no ability to concentrate. He almost used it like a lure. He never attacked his prey, they attacked him only to discover the trap. It was his best means of defence and he was a master of it. He had lost most of his dignity but that which he retained he treasured. He loved to receive help, but hated to be patronised.

Hiawatha enjoyed him and occasionally sought to take a rise out of him. He had compassion for him and often during the winter he would let him sleep in the forge on the back seat of an old scrapped Model 'T' Ford which was located at the side of the space. Its location invited use from passers-by who might stop to redden their pipes, or somebody's ears, before climbing the hill.

Hiawatha stuck his head around the forge wall and invited Mel to lead in the horse. She was delighted and brought around the graceful hunter. Miley had arrived in "the space" and was sitting on the well-sprung throne. This courtier was, however, recuperating. He coughed and spluttered and out of deference to the court leaned his head and body in a swivelling motion to the outside. He pinched and blew his nose with his bare fingers and slung his snot out on the road with the co-ordination of one of Caesar's Balearic slingers.

The "priest" winced in disgust as the slimy green extract slapped, splat, off the ground. His gate had been fixed and he was waiting for it to cool and also to discharge his account. He was foostering in his pockets for change as the horses hooves were being pared. Mel and I watched the master at work.

Miley wiped his hand on the leg of his trousers and then drew the sleeve of his forearm across his nose leaving a silvery snail-like trace on the cuff. He looked woe begotten right enough. The "priest" was taking it all in, uncomfortably. There was a perplexed look in his eye. He stopped rummaging, looked at Hiawatha who was busy, and then took in Miley again. He turned around, removed his cap and rubbed his big bald pate. He replaced it and stuck his hands down deep in his pockets and walked over to Miley.

"Miley, you're an awful man," he said. "There you are now with neither health nor heat. You could be up in the County Home with three square meals a day, a roof over your head and a dry bed, and you could go for a drink every night if you wanted."

Miley let his head come only halfway up from resting in his hands and then turned his head to look outside and spit.

"If it's so friggin' nice isn't it a wonder yer not in it yerself!"

Stuck him to the roots! He recovered.

"You're an impudent pup!"

Miley looked up.

"Howld on dere now Mr. Doyle," he said, "don't lose yer hair."

A second hit. I nearly snorted.

"Take it handy there, Miley," said Hiawatha anxiously and interrupted the flow.

"That'll be two shillings, please William," as he handed him out the cooled gate.

He laid it up against Miley's seat. The intrusion invited the tramp's notice and then a begrudging inspection.

"That's a mighty fine gate ye've got dere Mr. Doyle," said Miley. Doyle saw an opening and moved to get his revenge.

"It is," he said, "I made that one out of me head!"

"I'd say," said Miley, "dere's the makings of another wan left in it"

I laughed out and Hiawatha found it difficult to conceal his own mirth, but he did better. Mel did not get the joke, but she could sense the situation. Almost immediately Fr. Williams walked in. He had an ash plant under his arm and was paring off the shoots with a penknife. It would be used as a riding crop.

"God save the men!"

"God save you kindly, Father," said the "priest" Doyle.

The Smith told him the horse would be a little while still. The "priest"

Doyle lingered, with the gate under his oxter, waiting to get the Clergyman's attention.

"Mrs. Kent isn't well," he said.

"I must call over, is she bad?"

"A stroke I believe, according to Dr. Sheehan."

Hiawatha looked up. The doctor had been in the old IRA with him. He had the nickname of "Paxo." It was a corruption of the Latin for peace (pax) – which he had given very little of to the British when they were in the country – and it was also an ingredient used in the making of bombs. Nobody knew quite which was the correct reason.

They spoke about all the old people dying off.

When the "priest" had gone, Fr. Williams turned to Miley.

"What way are you Miley?"

"I'm poorly, Father," he replied.

Hiawatha looked up from shoeing the hoof with a grin. Fr. Williams winked at him.

"What do you think of my ashplant?"

Miley looked and said it was grand entirely. The clergyman winked and nodded again. He bent the plant, admired it and said, "When would be the best time to cut one Miley?"

"Begog, Father, when yid see it," he replied. The profundity was lost.

Everyone laughed except Miley. He was looking down at his feet. A big spider came out from under the seat. Mel touched me. Miley came down on it with his brogue.

"Ah Miley!" said Hiawatha. "What did you kill him for?" Don't you know it isn't lucky?"

" 'Twasn't lucky for that fella anyway," he said. More laughter.

When the horse was shod the clergyman put on the reins and led him off. Miley left to go the Presbytery for a mug of milk and bread. Before I left Hiawatha asked me to tell him "about school and all that." He had obviously heard about my being beaten. I knew that because of the way he said "and all that." He knew it was too painful to mention directly.

I blushed and looked down.

"It's alright," he said tossing my hair as he usually did, "we'll talk about it sometime." Mel had not heard about the beating and was surprised by the manifestation of discomfort in me. She looked at me keenly and puzzled. Larkin arrived with his bike in the nick of time to rescue me from her inquisition.

"Mrs. Kent is dead."

"May she rest in peace," said Hiawatha.

"We have to serve the funeral," he beamed. This meant money for the servers.

"Brilliant!" I exclaimed.

"It's an ill wind doesn't blow luck to somebody," said Hiawatha.

"The 'box' Whitney is dead as well."

He was Abel Whitney. He was a Protestant farmer whose granddaughter was married to Sean Hanlon. Tommy Whitney Senior was his son. The "box" was a man with a lighthearted disposition and whenever he would meet a young boy he would at some stage adopt a boxer's stance and ask, "Are you any good to box?" with a glint of devilment in his eye.

"The boxer" might have implied a more serious nature and if "the box" was to be confused with the soft cardboard containers, so prolific at the time, the purpose of nicknames would not have been entirely defeated in this instance. Normally I would have said, "God be good to him" or, "God be merciful to him" as I would have heard people say hundreds of times. But this was a Protestant and it appeared that God did not have any real choice as to where he was going. To utter the aspiration would be to invoke God pointlessly, which was blasphemy, and much worse than swearing. I felt I should say something in front of the non-Catholic blacksmith and all I could say awkwardly and arrogantly was "I hope they won't be too hard on him."

"Well they won't be too hard on 'the box' or if they do we're all in for a bit of a roasting," Hiawatha laughed. "Aye, surely."

I realised then that Hiawatha did not know he was going to go to Hell when he died. I felt I should start praying for his conversion. I thought at least some of the adults might have tried to make him understand. I began to develop a curiosity and fascination about Protestantism.

3

"He Fell Himself!"

Much as curiosity was aroused by stories like this, we still did not venture near the Protestant churchyard. Protestants were not of the One True Church and consequently their church and environs were off limits. Martin Boland and his wife Trissey (Patricia) used to clean this church and they were Catholics, but they must have had some type of dispensation. We used to ask their children about the inside of the church and what used to go on. They took full advantage of our ignorance by telling us seriously that some of them were buried standing up and others were encased in the wall of the church. They said you could smell the devil in it. We did not believe them but, for all that, we wondered a lot about what went on in there.

Mel wanted to explore it and I was sorely tempted. However, since my current preoccupation was with the County Football Final I did not wish to tempt God by being bold. I went to Holy Communion every day that week and prayed very hard for a just outcome to the match. We had been taught not to pray for specific temporal favours, instead we ought pray for God's will and the grace to accept it. I reasoned this was fair enough, on the basis that if He had only a modicum of "cop on" he would see the justice of our case. When the time came, however, the issue was far from clear cut.

The match was played in Tomcoole. Ballymore were our opposition. Their centre half-back caused a lot of problems for us from the start. At half time my father called Michael Larkin and myself to one side.

"I'm taking you out of the goal," he said to Larkin. "I want you to do something for me. I'm putting you on Scallon," a reference to their centre half-back.

"I want you to forget about the ball," and he turned to me and said,

"And I want you to forget about your man." He faced back to Larkin,

"Everytime Scallon goes to jump for the ball hit him with your shoulder your dead level best." He turned back to me, "and you get the breaking ball."

We did as we were bid on the resumption and by and large it worked well. We caught up with them and went ahead by two points. In the dying moments of the game there was high drama. Ballymore were awarded a fourteen yards free. A point for them was no good whereas if they scored a goal they would have victory by a point. Fr. Williams was beside himself with rage at the award of a free.

"He never touched him," he roared at the referee. "He fell himself."

Every Ballymore player moved down the field to the action. So did we. There were players everywhere. The free was taken. The ball hit the back of the net. There was a roar from the Ballymore contingent. My father ran into the referee and shouted,

"You're surely to God not going to allow that and fourteen of 'em on the square."

The referee was shaken. If there had been an infringement the goal would be disallowed and there would be a Ballymore revolution. He ordered that it be retaken because the free had been taken before he had blown his whistle he decided. The school teacher from Ballymore ran on to protest, followed by a large partisan contingent. There were angry scenes. I shouted at one man to get off the pitch. He had been a linesman and was carrying the white flag of the umpire. He hit me on the arse with the handle. Larkin ran over and shoved him. The official, who was a full grown man, lost his temper and, to my horror, hit Larkin a box in the face. He fell back shocked, his nose bloodied and his football jersey caught the tumbling, spurting blood. The crowd invaded the pitch and the match was abandoned. There was consternation. Fr. Williams' face was red. My father told the Ballymore teacher he did not give a shite for him or forty like him. Fr. Williams was insisting on getting the name of "the buck" that hit a child in his care for whom he was responsible to the parents.

Larkin's nose was bleeding and his lip was split and swollen. His two front teeth were gone. He was very pale and his green football shirt had dark brown stains down the front where his red blood had mixed with the green parish colours. He looked like a fallen patriot. When tempers had cooled a bit Fr. Williams told the Ballymore School teachers that by whatever means they would employ they had a responsibility to give the name of the culprit who hit Larkin. Everyone knew it was the umpire but that was not the point. Knowing who was wrong justified indignation. Acceptance by the others meant shame for their side and vindication for ours.

The "priest" Doyle was at the match and pronounced it the greatest display of ignorance and brutish behaviour he had ever seen. My father was being complimented left right and centre for standing up for the chaps. There would be more to do about it. An investigation would now take place by the County Board.

It would be at least a fortnight before the case would be heard. This gave plenty of time for the story to be told and retold and refined. Larkin's nose was not broken but he had a very thick lip. He now spoke with a lisp on account of his missing teeth.

Mel was not at the match but that evening her folks called to our house and I told her all about it. Fr. Williams called in to discuss the entire affair and it was mulled over and moaned over and what a terrible thing had been done to the chaps. The embellishments that were added were all justified by simply pointing out what had happened to Larkin. She expressed more concern for him than I thought was appropriate. This disturbed me slightly. Mel was good fun and good company for a girl, but that was it.

ᇮᇮ

The Kellys did not stay long and tea was served early as it was Saturday night and there was fasting from midnight for anyone who would be receiving Communion in the morning.

My sister and I were sent to bed at the same time. When she was in her room, I returned to the bottom step to see if Fr. Williams had anything further to volunteer. The topic had been exhausted and they were now discussing the two funerals which had taken place during the week. I heard a sound at the front door and scarpered without a sound. It was my uncle

Peter. When he walked in I could tell by the commotion that something unusual, but good, had taken place. Everyone was congratulating him. I returned to the eavesdropper's throne to discover Peter had been elected Chairman of Wexford County Council the previous day. I peeped through the keyhole. Fr. Williams was ebullient; Peter looked very pleased; I could not see my father but I felt very proud and I knew he must have been as well.

My mother made more tea. While she was out they discussed the match again. There would be an investigation Peter said. The priest thought that would be proper as did my father. Peter said he would have a word in Seamus Greene's ear before the hearing. Greene was the Chairman of the County Board and a member of Fianna Fail. Fr. Williams thought that would not be a good idea. He thought it would compromise the independence of the Chairman and it would be an unfair exertion of influence. "It's best these things be let run their course. It will work itself out." I felt this was very honourable and all that but, damn it, we had been cheated and badly treated and really what was the problem with making sure that justice was done. Peter agreed with the priest but my father was less inclined.

"Feck 'em to hell an' back – they tried to rob us."

But he did not pursue the point. The tea was in. The topic changed. "I heard you had right sport up in Kent's before she died," said Fr. Williams. My father's expression changed.

"Will you stop?" he laughed. He went on to describe the set up. Poor Tommy, Mrs. Kent's only son, sat up with him for almost ten consecutive nights before she died.

"She was there," he said, "with the flat of the sheet on her chest and that's the way she was going."

He placed the flat of his palm on his chest (representing the sheet) and closed his eyes (representing Mrs. Kent). He imitated a laboured haphazard breathing and raised and lowered his hand in time.

"I was sitting there for the fifth night just like that with Tommy when the next thing she sits bolt upright in the bed and says to the two of us 'Are yous goin' to gi' me nothing to ate or are yous goin' to let me die a' de hunger?"

"D'ya hear tha?" says Tommy.

"I do, says I. 'I do."

"What'll we do? What'll we do?" says he.

"Sure,'says I is there anything in it to eat?"

Tommy thought for a minute and says,

"There's a side a' bacon down below in the safe."

(This was a reference to an aluminium contraption on legs with a perforated shelf which was used for keeping meat fresh by allowing the air to circulate, keeping insects and flies out).

"Ay, sure maybe we ought to cut a rasher off it an' boil it," says I.

"Ay,' says Tommy, 'an' sure if she choke itself anyhow, ain't she dyin'?"

They all laughed heartily. The tears streamed down my mother's face from laughing.

"I'll tell you an even better wan," my father continued. "In the shop last week Tom Hanton came in and took up the paper to see what the arrangements for Mrs. Kent's funeral were. He was looking down along the column and says to me, 'Ah Jaysus, John, the poor ould Box Whitney is dead". "Begor he is Tom," says I.

He started to read the notice out loud.

"Whitney, John. (15 th May 1956)

At his residence Ballytarsna New Ross (suddenly)

Removal will take place to St. Mogue's church of

Ireland this evening at 7 pm. Interment will take

place tomorrow at 3 pm. House private.

Safe in the arms of Jesus."

He looks up from the paper an says,

"Well begogs lads, isn't poor oul' Jaysus well off with the Box Whitney in his arms."

Fr. Williams let down his cup of tea and laughed, half snorting it into his rushed-for hankie, coughing and spluttering. I sniggered myself. Tom Hanton was very droll and placid. When the laughing died down my father said there had been a big turn out at the funeral. Peter remarked that he was there and sure hadn't they been talking at it. But my father was talking about the Whitney and not the Kent funeral.

"Were you at that?" Peter asked.

"It was the first time I was at a Protestant service in my life."

"You mean the burial," asked Fr. Williams.

"No I mean the mass, or whatever the yoke is – ye know, the service."
My father detected the priest's discomfort.
"There's nothing wrong with that is there?"
"Well, I think it's more frowned on than forbidden," said the priest uncomfortably. "Personally I think it's the decent thing to do. The Canon, however, might be a different kettle of fish," he continued.
"Oh feck him," said my father with more courage than conviction.
"Curse a' God I couldn't wait to get out of the place the smell of …"
There was a noise behind me. I took a start. It was my sister.
"What 're you doin' there?"
"I couldn't sleep," I lied.
"I'm tellin'," she said.
"Here hold on," I said.
She barged past me in the door. I scooted to bed waiting for the execution squad to arrive. I heard her in the back kitchen at the tap. She was there a few minutes before I heard her return to the stairs. She went into her bedroom and closed the door. Had she snitched? I was in a dither. Eventually I fell asleep.

∞∞

The next morning at mass, I had to serve on my own. The injured Larkin had cried off. I looked out the Vestry window at five minutes to eight, as Larkin and I did every Sunday morning to see Tim Mallon, a veteran of the Great War, blow a snot from his nose with his fingers. He would walk around the back of the church tower out of the public gaze to perform this personal function. He did not own a handkerchief. He little realised he had a regular private audience of two every Sunday morning. He also left his blackthorn walking stick there – to be collected after Mass – doffed his cap and with a half gouged out eye, went into his God

In the pulpit Fr. Williams appeared off-handed in ways and he gave very entertaining sermons. This particular morning he appeared a little more solemn than usual. The sermon stuck in my memory.

He commenced by referring to the gospel which concerned the rich young man who went away sorrowing when Christ told him to go and sell all and give to the poor if he would obtain eternal life. He told a funny story about a pig and a hen who were both reading a hotel advertisement which showed an Irish breakfast of egg and bacon. The pig looked dolefully at the hen and said, "It's alright for you. With you it's only a token gesture – but with me, it's full commitment."

"Silks and satins put out the fire as do wealth and riches a spiritual one." He spoke of fashions and customs.

"This is a small rural Catholic Community," he said. "I see no need for anyone here to be sporting last year's Paris fashions. It's alright for those in other religions to engage in that type of vanity – they can make their own rules as they go along – but that is not the way in our church."

He then produced a document the title of which he read which he said was an instruction on the subject of female dress which had been issued by the Sacred Congregation of the Council in the Vatican. The document made it the responsibility of the Clergy in each parish to admonish women that they should dress modestly and chastely. Parents, schools and institutions should see to it that dress was "becoming" and inhibit and prohibit the contrary. Girls and women who dressed in an "unbecoming fashion" were to be refused Holy Communion and, if necessary, admission to the church.

The Diocesan Council would now require a report from parishes of methods and suggestions on how female modesty should be promoted. The first rule he felt was that ladies should not allow themselves to be affected by what other cultures and religions did. He was aware that the local Tennis Club, which had a mixed religious membership, had difficulties in making rules for attire which suited our church. He, however, had no such difficulty and he was now banning all from wearing those revealing short white dresses. He was giving a liberal interpretation on the instruction of the Council, since it said that parents should deter their youthful daughters from public gymnastic exercises. Tennis might come under such a heading but he was willing to allow an interpretation which permitted it being played, but modestly.

This was the first shock I got. In the previous week I had seen Agnes Maher with Thomas Whitney and a sister of his and her boyfriend all playing tennis in whites. The two girls had been wearing the white dresses that had been prohibited. I could see her in the congregation with her head bent. He went on to say that in order to assist his parishioners he would now give a description and list of various clothing items that were outside the bounds of modesty and decency.

My second shock came when he denounced figure-hugging apparel such as slacks and shorts. For the very young this injunction did not apply.

Mel had both slacks and shorts. Did she fall into the category of the very young? The rest of the sermon faded on me. I came back from my daydreams with a start when I realised the priest was addressing me for the second time. He was back on the altar.

"Jack! Jack!" I flustered and got to my feet. "Bring me out the 'Pius List' from the cruet table in the sacristy." I vanished.

He read out the list of his parishioners who had subscribed to the upkeep and maintenance of their church and clergy. The first name would be the donor of the highest subscription. There was always competition for this position between Fianna Fáil and Fine Gael. Invariably it fell between my uncle Peter and Thomas Byrne, the schoolteacher from Coleman, one of our team's mentors and the local Fine Gael party boss. This year Peter won, and no mistake. He had contributed six pounds against Thomas Byrne's five pounds. My father always disappointed me in the Pius List. He always gave ten shillings. Still, it was a consolation to know that Peter could do it. It was particularly appropriate that he should do so now since he was the County Council Chairman.

The investigation into the football match incident was a drama in its own right. Ballymore had taken the initiative by objecting to our team on the basis that we had players who were not from our parish. Larkin, who lived on the parish boundary, was the source of the objection. His father had land on both sides of the divide but the farmhouse was located in the parish of Ballyhack. He went to school in Coleman. He served mass in Coleman. He spent all his time in Coleman.

The "priest" Doyle was consulted. He examined the paper on which the objection had been written to see if it had the Irish watermark. When the paper was held to the light, the mark was visible. Had the stipulated objection fee been enclosed? It had. It was written in Irish, and in triplicate. "This would not be simple," he informed my father and Fr. Williams.

There was no obvious or technical loophole to defeat it. Every detail of semantic certitude had been observed as required. Two days later he advised that since Ballymore were making the objection it was for them to prove the parish boundary, not us. Fr. Williams thought this might be a poor enough dependence, but my father thought it had merit. The case was reported verbatim in *The Free Press*. Objections, appeals and investigations were reported in the local papers in scripted fashion, like the parts of a play. Most of what happened at these meetings entered local folklore.

At the commencement of the meeting my father proposed that the referee's report be adopted. His opposition, Peadar Murphy, disagreed on the basis that such a procedure ignored the objection to Michael Larkin. Peadar Murphy, said he had been asked to represent his club although he had not been at the match. Fr. Meyler who accompanied him had not been there either. Peadar Murphy was a schoolteacher, a know-all and as I overheard my father privately describe him, "an awkward oul bollix." Fr. Williams protested vigorously saying there was now nobody present from Ballymore who could now explain their behaviour on that night. The thrust and parry was revealed in the exchanges.

Peadar Murphy: "If we win the objection there is no need for an investigation since the match would then be ours."

John Leacy: "Unable to kill the boy at the match you come here now to try and take his character and ours when everyone knows he played with us all his life."

Peadar Murphy: "I am asking the Chairman to disregard this emotional outburst and rule that our objection be dealt with in the first instance."

(Seamus Greene ruled that the objection be dealt with in the first instance.)

Flushed by this initial success the Ballymore representative went on to say that Michael Larkin had lived in the parish of Ballyhack and this was well known to be the case.

Mr. Greene (County Chairman): "What proof have you of this?"

Mr. Murphy: "Everybody knows this."

County Chairman: "This is the hearing of an objection. I must have proof."

Mr. Murphy: "I will call Fr. Williams the curate in Coleman as I believe he, as a priest, will not tell a lie."

County Chairman: "You cannot rely on the opposition to prove your case. You must prove it against them."

Mr. Murphy: "In that case I will offer my own testimony against them."(Not as thick as I thought.)

Mr. Murphy: "I know the house where this boy lives and I am acquainted with the Diocesan boundary map and I say from my own knowledge that this boy lives in the parish of Ballyhack." (Bollixed now – definitely and decidedly bollixed.)

Chairman: "Does Coleman deny this?"

Fr. Williams: "Surely this is not proof."

Chairman: "It is unless it is contradicted."

Fr. Williams: "We will not tell lies." (When yer bollixed – yer bollixed).

Chairman: "Is this the case for Ballymore?"

Mr. Murphy: "We wish to call no other evidence."

County Chairman: "What have Coleman to say?"

Mr. Leacy: "They have not proved their case." (Hello?)

County Chairman: "In what respect?"

Mr. Leacy: "They may have proved that Michael Larkin is illegal to play with our team, but they have not proved that we played him." (Bejaysus!)

Mr. Murphy: "His name is on the list of players."

Chairman: "Do Ballymore have the list of players?"

Mr. Murphy: "No, Chairman. But the referee was given one at the match and he'll support us here."

Chairman:- "But at the outset you objected to the Referee's report being adopted, you cannot have it both ways." (Bejaysus he's right – we're right – fuck me – we were right all along.)

Mr. Murphy: "This is farcical." (Take yer batin'.)

Chairman: "It is not farcical. I have to go by the rules. I cannot allow your objection unless you show proof that he played."

Mr. Murphy: "Everyone knows that he played. It's all over the place. Not alone that, but he was injured in the match. Surely the referee's report will state that."

Chairman: "Mr. Murphy, surely you can see you cannot object to the Referee's report being in when it suits you, and out when it suits you, at the same time. Either it's in or it's out and you objected to its being in and I ruled it out at your request." (Ya thick oul' hoor.)

Mr. Murphy: "Would the Chairman accept a newspaper cutting that he played?"

Chairman: "No. I can only accept a list with the signatures. It is one of the rules that in a case like this it must be an official document or evidence given at the hearing."

Mr. Murphy: "Sure what is the point. If you keep going on like this you'll have no regulations."

Chairman: "I cannot prove your case for you. I know there has been a lot of talk about this case but I cannot go on talk alone."

Fr. Williams: "Poetic justice – 'hoist on your own petard!" (Bejaysus – St. Thomas A'friggin' Quinas.)

Chairman: "I have to rule the objection out for want of evidence." (Me oul' flower – I never doubted ya for a minute!)

After all this had taken place, the Ballymore delegation left the meeting in protest. The investigation into the incident was abandoned and we were awarded the match. A bad taste was left, however, when it was discovered later that Ballymore purchased a set of their own medals and presented them to their own team. At our celebrations they showed a film of "Laurel and Hardy" in St. Colman's Hall. There was a party with lemonade, orange and a wide selection of sandwiches, buns and biscuits. Larkin said he thought he would burst after it all.

Fr. Williams gave a speech about having the courage to stand up for what you believe in.

"There is no point in being half a man," he said. "The whole hog or nothing."

He pointed out the Wexford hurling team as an example.

"Fine stout-hearted men, none afraid of the struggle and this year they will go on to win the Leinster final against Kilkenny and beat the pick of Munster and Connaught after that."

We all roared and cheered.

"This is a summer you'll never forget," he said. "The summer of 'fifty-six, the summer you won the county title. This summer Wexford will win the All-Ireland Final, believe you me, and I don't tell lies. For a long time we have been struggling upwards. This is the year. This is the time. This country will become the place that Pearse and Connolly dreamt about. Like the football field and the hurling field, discipline and industry, strength and determination will be rewarded. Indifference, apathy and weakness will be routed. In years to come you will look back with pride at this time and when you will remember this summer, you will be remembering the blossoming of Ireland's manhood."

The medals were presented on the stage by Seamus Greene, the County Chairman. Peter was there, as well, in his capacity as Chairman of the County Council. We were proud. The stars and the planets were so astrologically aligned that the Irish dream could not fail but to emerge. It would only be a short time now before Ireland would be united. We were about to come into our own.

∞ ∞

The following day Larkin, Mel and myself went down to Hiawatha to show off our medals. He heaped great praise on us. He examined Larkin's lip.

"When will the stitch come out?"

"Nekth week."

"Hard to talk with?"

"Yeth."

"That must be a big penance entirely," he laughed.

So did myself and Mel. Larkin tried to resist a reaction because every time he smiled, the stitch hurt. Then we spoke about the match and the objection.

"We'll beat them nekth year too," said Larkin.

"Remember, boys, winning isn't everything," said Hiawatha. We had heard all that before, it was usually after we had been beaten. We must have looked a bit bored. He immediately followed it up by saying "Don't misunderstand. It's great to win and enjoy it fully but be aware of the danger."

Larkin and myself nodded, a little bit disappointed that he might have thought we needed a lecture. He saw our good manners. He seemed uneasy. He washed his hands and dried them in his apron. The talking had stopped. This was a little awkward. Larkin whistled, the fool. It grated. I nudged him to stop. He looked at me,

"Wha?" (Jesus!)

"I'll tell you a story," Hiawatha said.

This was going to be more embarrassing. Still, nothing was going to stop him making his point.

"On the northeast coast of the United States there lived a tribe of Indians," he said. "They kept slaves. Another tribe lived opposite them. About thirty of the first tribe embarked in a large canoe to raid their neighbours. At this time the second tribe were sending their best warriors on a hunting expedition. When they had just left, the others landed at a small island to conceal themselves. They intended to make slaves of the defenceless. They hid their big canoe, but not well enough. It was spotted by a scout who, with two of his friends, stole the canoe leaving the invaders marooned. After a few weeks the hunters returned. They went to the island. The slavehunters were in a state of weakness and starvation and were glad to see them. They were prepared to accept any terms instead of the certain death that faced them if they remained on the island. They lied that they had come to hunt and that their canoe had been stolen. They were taken prisoner and were made slaves. Some were kept in the village and others were sold to distant tribes. Things like that have a habit of backfirin'." said Hiawatha.

Larkin asked if any of them were cannibals. Hiawatha laughed. I think we got the point, but I am not sure if we learned it very well. We felt a bit unnecessarily chastened. On the way home we discussed him some more.

∞∞

It was a sultry July late afternoon heading towards evening. There was a heavy scent of new mown hay. The tar was soft on the road. The only sounds were the birds, chiefly the corncrake and the busy noisy tractors with their buckrakes of cocks of hay being ferried from field to farm yard.

As we walked we spoke. Mel thought he was lovely.

"He's just so kind and he's so gentle and sensitive."

(Girls!)

I told her he had been a sniper in the IRA.

"I just couldn't imagine him killin' anyone."

"If you're killing an Englith tholdier you wouldn't jutht be killin' anyone," Larkin offered.

We digressed to a major political discussion on the misfortunes of Ireland. Larkin said Hiawatha was related to his mother's people.

"He is not," I contradicted.

"He ith too," he protested.

I felt Larkin was inventing a fanciful connection to align himself with someone who was the object of Mel's admiration, not to mention a patriot. We talked about the Penal Laws and the way the priests had been hunted with a price on their heads just like rabbits and foxes. Larkin told her about the explosion that took place in Saltmills during the Troubles. He was able to name some of the men who had been killed.

I told her about Uncle Martin's thumbs. She stopped walking and was clearly shocked. She looked at me very intently and said, "He was really, in jail?"

"My Da would've been too 'ceptin he was too young," I apologised and bragged simultaneously. "But he carried dispatches and messages for the rebels."

"Really?"

Larkin's father was younger still, so he was only marginally in this conversation.

"Sure he did, several times. And the Black an' Tans raided his home several times."

"Who were the Black an' Tans?"

"They were right bathtards," Larkin swore for effect as he leaped in to explain about the army of thugs the British had let loose in Ireland at that time with instructions from General Maxwell to "Make Ireland a hell for rebels to live in." His lisp bothered him, but it was not going to stop him.

When he had finished his explanation I told of one raid on my grandfather's house which my father had told me. Since my grandfather had been the President of Sinn Fein in the area, his home was regularly subjected to checks since the British would have known that his was more than probably "a safe house for the men on the run."

He also received documentation and manuals on military manoeuvres, roadblocks, ambushes and the like. It was a magazine called *An Toglach*. and it was a treasonable offence to have these in your possession. One particular manual he had hidden in an out-office, used for pigs, behind a loose stone in an old fireplace. One morning, very early, before anyone was up, two Crossley Tenders arrived in the yard. With a great hullabaloo the *Tans* dismounted and went directly to the pigsty. My grandfather was sure they had been tipped off about the manual. He turned to my grandmother and said, "Stay here with the children. I'll do this on my own. The game is up!"

When he went to the pigsty, to his surprise, the Tans were admiring a litter of newly farrowed bonhams. These city boys had never seen them before. The distraction halted the search and saved my grandfather. They left almost as quickly as they arrived. Generally with a surprise raid, they would immediately rise their quarry from cover. When this did not happen they left to visit another "safe house."

"You have great stories," Mel told me.

"But they're not stories, all those things happened," I said, supposedly innocently, but chuffed. Much later it occurred to me this was how my father responded to the same compliment.

"It must have been awful," she encouraged.

"They were right fuckerth," said Larkin with the conviction of a battle scarred veteran. Mel did not like bad language and eyed him. I laughed and winked at him, – his indignation – her rebuke.

⚭

At this stage we had arrived outside the Protestant Church in Blackhill. He had stopped, to make his point. She stopped. I stopped a little further on.

"Well they were right bathtardth," he modified and added defiantly, "I'd love to have a go at them methelf."

I laughed at the obvious safety of his impossible wish. His lisp knocked the edge off of his bad language. His brow furrowed. His eye caught the church.

"Leth go in," he said.

He was going to show he had neither fear nor respect for British or Protestant and sure, dammit, after all, they were the same difference, were they not?

"It looks spookey!" Mel hesitated.

My curiosity had been getting the better of me about Protestant worship, and there was strength in numbers. The allure of the forbidden was compelling.

There was a clap of thunder and the heavens opened letting loose a torrent of rain. We were startled in mid-temptation and fell where invitation beckoned. We ran for cover scarpering around the side of the church away from the road and the direction of the shower. There was a porch there. Standing at the back we got almost total shelter, particularly when we stood back against the door.

The windows in the church were leaded glass. From a distance they revealed little of the inside. The rain started to lash. Larkin turned the handle of the door and, to our surprise, it opened.

The daylight inside was sparse. There was a heavy atmosphere.

"Turn on a light," said Larkin.

"Don't be such a friggin' eejit," I said.

He glared at me.

"Do you want the whole friggin' parish to know we're here?" I back answered.

There was a loud peal of thunder and a few flashes of lightning. (Shite.)

"I'm scared," Mel said. (Shite again.)

"Whathts there to be thcared about?" Larkin bostooned. (Gobshite.) Mel eyed him gingerly. (He really was acting the gobshite.) Another thunderclap. She held his arm. (I really wished that friggin' thunder would stop.) More rain. The thunder seemed to move away.

As our eyes became used to the darkness, I could make out an altar and some pews. There were lots of prayer books and hymnals. There was no sanctuary lamp but there was a tabernacle. Then, I got the smell that I recognised – it was must, and there was plenty of dust on the floor. That was no consolation. It summoned up images of decay, death and decrepitude. I was becoming more uncomfortable. There was an organ loft.

"Leth go up on the gallery," said Larkin. (For frig's sake, hold on here folks!)

"Let's get out of here," said Mel. (Thanks be to Jesus!)

Next there was a noise.

"Whisht," I said.

They both stopped and looked at me. I could hear footsteps outside. They were running to the church.

"Quick – hide!" I whispered.

Larkin ran for the gallery stairs. Mel and I hid behind the panelled face of an enclosed pew. We closed the door of it and we both sat huddled on the ground with our backs to it. The door of the church opened. Mel held my arm with both her hands tightly.

"I'm really scared," she whispered and I could see a telltale glistening trace on her cheek.

"Sshh!" I urged, pressing her hand to reassure her. (Holy Jesus make her whisht – keep her scared – but make her whist.)

Next there was laughter.

"Dammit, I'm really drowned!"

I recognised Agnes Maher's voice.

"You and your blasted flowers."

Thomas Whitney was with her.

"It's the least I could do," she said. "Wasn't he your Grandfather."

"I'm sure he'll be worried one way or t'other."

"Tommy! That's not nice," coyly (girlie mode).

"I didn't mean anything," he answered.

"That's okay Tommy." (Oh Tommy, you're some gobshite.)

They spoke for a while. After a little, they were silent. Then we heard Agnes sigh, "Oh! Mmmh."

Mel looked at me. I smothered a giggle. She smiled a type of inquisitive, sinful smile. The fear was gone, but the excitement remained. She placed a finger to her lips to indicate silence. She pulled her legs in under her and knelt. She very slowly raised her head above the elbow rest of the pew. Her eyes opened wide drenched with lasciviousness and ducked down again.

"They're kissing," she beamed.

Cynically, I edged around and like a submarine commander in enemy waters, raised my periscope carefully. They had just stopped embracing.

Then suddenly she darted off.

"The rain has stopped, c'mon."

There was a noise from the organ loft. We ducked.

"What was that?" she stopped.

(Larkin! The friggin' eejit!) I wanted to malafooster him. I could hear Tommy going to the loft.

"Who's there? Who have we got here? C'mon out."

No sound. Eventually he found him. (Curse a' God – you could depend on no one.) There wasn't a word to be got out of Larkin.

"That's Michael Larkin," she said.

"Well me boy, what's your excuse for breaking and entering."

"I came in out of the rain, Thir," (Sir! Sir? Jesus!)

"And what did you hear?"

"Nothin' Thir."

"Let him go, Tommy," she said.

"Go on, ya chancer," said Tommy.

Larkin crunched his way out on the gravel. They said nothing until the sound stopped.

"What d'ya think?" said Tommy.

"He'll say nothin'," she replied. "He won't want it known he was caught in the Protestant Church."

"C'mon let's put the flowers on the grave. We'd best lock the church in case anyone else tries to break in." (Hold on! Jesus Christ. For frigs sake who'd want to break into a Protestant Church. You'd think they'd encourage it. It wasn't exactly bursting at the seams with an overpopulated congregation or an'thin'.)

"The keys are across the road in Bolands, I'll get them," he ran off. When he was gone we could hear her walking up to the altar. She was having a good gawk as well. She lifted her skirt to straighten the elastic in her knickers leg. She ran her finger around the circumference of the leg, and then pleated and flattened her skirt down again. (Fuck me!) Tommy was back. "There's one in the door." I could see a look of panic in Mel's eyes as they locked the door. Click! I could feel it in my own heart. We could hear them. They locked the door. We stayed in the pew until we heard them coming back from the grave to the road. Mel looked at me.

"What now?"

"Let's look around."

With the disappearance of the thunderstorm the church filled with sunlight. It looked pleasant, almost. It was past teatime and the sun was developing an evening hue. Missing tea at home was not a good idea. It was like informal assembly – absence was glaring. It was also a serious misdemeanour. Still, if we could get out and get home a stiff rebuke might be its extent. There were three doors in the church. The porch door was now locked. A huge gothic double door was at the western end under the organ loft. The vestry door was located on the northern face. The vestry had an empty fireplace. The room was damp and the plaster had bulged and fallen from part of the wall littering part of the mantelpiece. There was a single crucifix hanging over the fireplace. There was a predieu, a table and chair. I tried the door but it was securely locked. All of the windows were gothic. Two thirds of the way up there was a small restricted vent with an opening for air. Every window in the building was the same.

Our only hope was the big double door. This had a great big horizontal bolt which was also twin bolted at the top and bottom in perpendicular fashion. I pulled back the big horizontal one with great difficulty. We carried the table from the vestry and placed a chair on it. From this perch I coaxed and cursed the stubborn small rusty shafts from their housing. The bottom bolts came more easily. When they were all removed I placed my hands on both doors and pushed. The doors still resisted. We both pushed. We could then see there was a bolt on the outside of the door as well.

"We're trapped," Mel said.

It was difficult not to agree. It appeared our sin of curiosity was going to be severely punished. The desperation we were both in increased as the sun became redder. Soberly and silently we brought the furniture back to the vestry.

"Maybe Larkin will come back," she said.

I knew he would not say a word – why should he, the door was not locked until after he had gone? He would assume we were coming behind him.

"Maybe we should break a window?" she said.

I had heard of boys who had been brought to court in Ballycullane because they had broken windows in a derelict house. To do so in a church might be regarded as a much more serious matter. What were we going to do? We were trapped in a crucible of the blackest most poisoned, potion and not alone were we being forced to swim in it, but we were being made drink it as well. Shortly we would drown.

I thought of the advancing night. All of the stories came flooding back. The accounts of blood drinking and devil worship that had already gone on in the middle of the night here. Scenes of drunken debauchery that had been enacted within this very building. Their dead were not buried in consecrated ground. The bodies of dead heretics were much more prone to mischievous evil spirits. I could feel the pressure in my head. How could we get out? We had to get out. Mel must have noticed my anxiety for she looked at me and touched my arm tenderly saying, "It will be alright, really."

Her care touched me. I started to cry. I took out my hankie and sat bawling in the pew.

Left alone, I could be tough. Once I was touched I was shagged. The red sun was streaming in through the big circular window overlooking the organ loft. As I sobbed Mel sat beside me with her arm around my shoulder, sobbing as well. She felt soft and tender. She put her other arm around me and held me to her. I felt a bit flushed and my anxiety was receding. The sun was shining on my face. I noticed she was breathing more deeply. She stroked my hair with her fingers. I was starting to glow. I lifted my head to look at her. Her eyes were beautiful. I could see straight into her soul. I thrilled all over. She smiled and moved to me, slowly. We kissed. I closed my eyes. She was wearing scent. I thought I was fracturing inside of me. I wanted to never let her go.

There was a movement on the organ loft. I jumped back. My eyes riveted on the gallery. "Look!" I screamed and pointed. She looked. A black demon draped silhouette was rising up from the organ. The cadaver of cadavers. It was framed in the brilliant red, illuminated by the setting sun of the circular west window. Its arms were stretched up and out as if they were soaring. The shadowy substance floated towards the front of the loft. Mel ran to the porch. Where were the lights? My nightmares had all arrived together. Mel pushed at the door crying "Let us out! Let us out!" She slapped and banged and knocked with both hands screaming and shouting until she started to cry. She was almost hysterical. I fumbled the wall for a light switch. I felt weak. I could feel my bowels beginning to move. I heard a belch. I was sure I had farted. But it was not me. It certainly was not Mel. I felt a light switch. (Jesus, at last.) I turned it on. The front of the church lit up. I pressed all of the switches. Momentarily we were shocked from the light. The whole church lit up.

"Curse a' Jaysus Christ," a voice shrieked from the loft. "Jesus we're haunted – Mother a' fuck. Hagh! Hagh! Jesus! Fuck!" (Holy fuck meself).

I nearly died. By turning on the lights I had succeeded in frightening the living shit out of Miley Cassidy and myself into the bargain. There was a crash in the porch. I turned, Mel had broken a window by using a weight which had been left in the porch to keep the door ajar when opened.

"It's okay," I told her. "It's only Miley Cassidy." She was trembling and higging from the scare. "It's okay," I repeated again.

She virtually collapsed into me. Then we started to laugh and laugh and as the fear departed it left an hysterical relief. Miley had fallen asleep in the loft of the church. He made his way down. The organ loft was as good a place to shelter as any barn or byre. Miley had no religious prejudice when it came to need. He had recovered his composure.

"Who're you young fella?"

"I'm Jack Leacy – she's me cousin."

"Are yiz after turning Protestant?"

"No. We came in out of the rain and we got locked in."

Miley took a penknife out of his pocket. He went to the door lock and prized back the housing. The screws jumped out of their mouldy home and fell near the broken glass on the ground. The door opened.

The look of relief on Mel's face reflected my own feelings.

"You gave me the fright of me life," I said invitingly.

"Begod thass a fright," he quipped.

There was no answering that. He trundled off into the evening. The sky continued its reddening to a brilliant crimson.

As Mel walked home with me I remarked:

"Red sky at night is shepherd's delight.

Red sky at morning is shepherd's warning."

I was full of philosophy again. She was more settled now and asked where I had heard the rhyme. Hiawatha I said. He told me the sky was divided into four quarters.

"You mean north, south, east and west,"

"Not really. He says that if you look in front of you into the sky it will be different than what's behind you and the same goes for the two sides. He says it changes every twenty minutes and you'll never see two skies the same – ever."

We tested his theory all the way home and we arrived there before we knew it. When we did get home I got a verbal lambasting. My father brought Mel home to Peter's. My mother was close to tears when we arrived. I sang dumb about being in the Protestant Church. I decided to face one charge at a time and maybe, if fortune favoured me, I might successfully conceal the others. Unfortunately, this principle did not work for me then, nor after. It never stopped me from believing it might.

Mel's holiday was coming to an end. She gave me a present of a writing pad and a pen with instructions to write. I was uncomfortable. This was a token of love and no mistake. We never mentioned the romantic incident in the Protestant Church. I thought and believed I had committed a sin. Mel wanted to publicise and compound it by sending love letters. I just wanted it all to stop. Life was getting too complicated. I wanted to tell my sin in confession but I just could not bring myself to do so. I had learned all about company keeping in Catechism class. I decided to carry the darkness around with me and hoped I would not die in the meantime and go to Hell. I promised God I would never do it again and I prayed that Mel would go away and stop forcing me to go astray.

$$\text{\textcircled{o}} 4 \text{\textcircled{o}}$$

Hard, Tough and Grummock

W hen Mel went back to the States, my father brought me to work in the shop for the summer. I could do a lot of little jobs. I was not allowed to tot up customers' accounts, however.

The shop was an emporium of some importance to Coleman. It consisted of a pair of haysheds made of corrugated iron. They were side by side. One was the store and the other was the shop. They were built at the bottom of a hill. The result was a split level effect. The top half of the first shed could be approached at road level. The floor of the shop acted as a ceiling for the basement in the bottom half which was concealed by the road. The outline shape of the shed was concealed by a cement facade, which bore the name "LEACY" in block cement capitals painted red.

When my father filled out forms that required "Occupation" to be inserted he would write "Merchant." I associated this title with wealthy mediaeval traders in exotic produce with foreign cultures. With a lofty title of this nature, I perceived my father as a man of considerable substance in business and the community.

I had not been working in the shop very long when the local Sergeant of the Civic Guards called. His name was William Thorpey and was a known Fine Gael sympathiser. Mostly Guards kept their political views hidden but Thorpey was known to have supported General Eoin O'Duffy in the 1930s, when the fascist Blueshirt movement was formed. On the surface my father passed him off but tried to have as little to do with him as possible at the same time.

He purchased a tin of tobacco for his pipe and since the shop was empty he settled himself to have a smoke and a chat. My father had a customer's grocery list which had been left in that morning. He got the groceries and ticked off the list as we went.

"Wexford had a good win on Sunday," said Thorpey.

"They had."

"Close enough in the end."

"It was."

"You'd never get the end of Kilkenny."

"That's true."

"Who are they playing next?"

"Galway."

"Didn't they beat them last year?"

(I was amazed he was not sure.)

"They did, indeed."

He drew a long drag on his pipe and the flame of the match disappeared into the bowl, and reappeared and disappeared with each suck. My father watched him without looking at him.

"The government aren't going very well," Thorpey was teasing.

"So they say." The eyes left the list for a split second.

"Ah, they made a mess of it the last time they were in as well with the 'Mother and Child Bill'." He was arse-licking now.

My father refused to be drawn, content with the admission.

"Religion was always strong in the country," modified Thorpey. "The people have great respect for religion."

"They have indeed," observed my father.

"Which reminds me," said Thorpey, "you didn't see Miley Cassidy around by any chance?"

I stopped taking the sugar out of the big sugar bag. I had been filling pound bags from the bulk. My father looked at him now.

"Is Miley in trouble?" asked my father.

"He broke into the Protestant Church last week, smashed a window and forced the door. I'd say he was after the altar wine."

My heart stopped and then started racing. Keep the head down, I told myself, keep the head down. I kept the head down.

"Ah!" said Thorpey. "The drink is a scourge. You didn't see him around then?"

"No indeed," said my father.

Thorpey walked out to his car shortly after this. He was puffing away on his pipe looking around over the village, he pulled up his trousers, the lord of all he surveyed.

My father regarded him through the glass panelled shop door.

"That's the biggest bollix ..." he trailed off shaking his head in exasperation.

My conscience and my fear started to work. Miley might do a stretch for something he had not done. But against that why should I get involved for something I had not done. Worse still, Mel might be implicated for something she had done. If I told my father he would be furious with me, particularly now. I had to think this out slowly and carefully. Maybe Larkin would have an idea. (Jesus, did Larkin tell the guards? How did they know Miley was in the church? Holy Christ, would he hang us all?) I resolved that a visit to Larkin was urgently required.

But that evening after hurling practice he denied it. He had heard a noise in the organ loft and that was what gave him away when he was hiding. He had not seen anyone there. I thought he had made the noise at the time but he was only on the stairs.

I never slept a wink that night and, if I did, I have forgotten. My memory is of worry and anxiety and I remember the washed-out feeling I had in the morning. My father told me I looked like "a stewed fairy." I prayed about it, but that only made matters worse. Everytime I called on God I kept thinking he was punishing me for committing the sin of company-keeping and (uh) kissing! Everytime I mentioned the word to myself, I winced. How could I bring myself to say it out loud let alone tell someone else. I would have to tell it in Confession. Life was just so difficult and complicated. I felt miserable. I knew I could not carry my load around with me indefinitely. "Truth will out," Sr. Ignatius used say.

When I finished serving Mass one morning Fr. Williams called me back. He had two oranges.

"You'd hardly be able to eat two I suppose?"

"I'd do me best," I responded.

"Are you going to see Wexford beat Galway on Sunday week?"

"I don't think so," I said. "Daddy says we'll go to the All-Ireland if they win."

"I might even cadge a lift, would you bring me?"

"I suppose you'd better ask me father," I replied. He was familiar.

"Well there's a politician for you. You'll be as good as your uncle Peter yet."

"I have a grocery list here," he said. He searched his pockets for it. He could not find it.

I started to look around the sacristy with him.

He continued to fooster in his clothes.

"I'll run in and ask Mae," I volunteered.

"No, don't do that," he said. "I'll go myself. It may come to me on the way," he excused. "I won't be a minute."

When he came back he had the list in his hand.

"I'm getting old, the old brain is seizing up," he laughed.

My father supplied the priest with his groceries. Because we lived beside the church he would bring the clerical provisions home and one of us, usually me, would be despatched with them, usually straight away. The priest was a chain smoker and hated to run out of cigarettes. He used to smoke "Gold Flake." These and "Players" and "Sweet Afton" were the strongest cigarettes. The "Woodbines" were the poor man's fag and the young boys learning to smoke bought them in ones and twos for tuppence apiece.

The priest's housekeeper, Mae Brennan, was sixty years of age. She was stooped and walked with the aid of a walking stick. Her right leg was shorter than her left and her right shoe had a platform sole. Whenever I would call she would talk to me endlessly. I liked her nevertheless, but it was impossible to keep a visit short without being rude. She was a chain smoker also and she smoked "Players." She looked seventy-five. She suffered from goitre and her neck looked like a turkey's in the way her throat had become disfigured. As I walked away from the presbytery I studied the list, which was longer than usual. Head of the list, as usual, 200 Players, 200 Sweet Afton and then, unusually, 200 Gold Flake.

When I delivered the messages that evening I thought Mae was a bit distracted. As I was leaving she asked me to bring in some anthracite for the Aga Cooker. When I went to the coal house the shovel was not there. I filled the self-loading coal shuttle half full but I needed the shovel to top it up, as I was not strong enough to self-load it full. I went to the garden shed as the shovel would often be used outdoors and might have been hurriedly put back with the garden implements. I was surprised to see a black Ford Prefect motor car there. I finished my chore and went home. I had not seen that car before.

Next morning at ten minutes past seven I arrived in the Chapel to prepare the altar for Mass. Fr. Williams was normally in the Vestry reading his Divine Office. His routine would normally include unlocking the outside sacristy door and then he would commence his prayers. It would be left to me to unlock the door from the sacristy to the church. When I arrived the door opened for me in the usual way. Having donned the black soutane and surplice I proceeded to the church. I was surprised to find the interconnecting door unlocked. Having removed the altar cloth I went back into the sacristy to get the cruets and finger bowl. These had to be filled with water and wine. The door into the priest's vestry, where these items were located, was closed. As I opened the door, I heard a snore. There on the floor fast asleep was the one and only, Miley Cassidy. There was a strong smell of altar wine. Standing beside the outstretched beggerman was a corkless empty bottle. He lay there like a dying animal, snorting through his open mouth into the carpet. His raw state and unexpected presence frightened the guts in me. Fr. Williams arrived simultaneously. His face paled and darkened. He roared something. He hauled Miley to his feet. Miley was utterly bewildered. The priest's temper was rising. I was transfixed.

"Get out you pup," he shouted at Miley, "and don't you dare darken the door around here again – bringing shame into God's house. You're not fit to be put with the animals – bite the hand that feeds you and then spit it back in God's face. Out I tell you! Out!"

Miley was unsteady on his feet when he was put standing at first, but the priest roughhoused him to the door with such force Miley had neither time nor opportunity to make the adjustment from the horizontal to the vertical. The priest saw to that. Miley was wearing the great black coat. The priest had it gripped on the back and the collar from behind. There was a stench from Miley. The priest's face was red with rage. Miley looked confused. The collar was nearly over his head. The priest was a strong forty-five year old man. He opened the sacristy door with one hand and threw Miley out on the gravel with a strong hard push. The little tramp lost his balance and fell on his two hands and knees. The priest wiped the smell from his clean hands.

"You filthy beast – I'll have the guards on you," roared the priest.

I was shocked at the defilement.

"He's a blinkin' nuisance to have around the place at all."

He picked up the wine bottle.

"Drink! Drink! Drink!"

"Will I get a fresh bottle?" I asked. The priest looked at me for a minute.

I had meant for Mass. My innocent question was nearly mistaken.

I knew where the wine was kept in the priest's dining room. As a matter of course the altar wine would be replenished from a box of bottles.

"No. I'll get it now in a minute. Go ahead and get the altar ready."

As I walked out I looked through the window and saw Miley standing up shakily, looking at his two palms. They were both bleeding and the knee of one of his trousers legs was torn. He turned towards the sacristy and shouted at the top of his voice holding up both palms.

"Just like Christ Crucified! Yiz let him down and yiz're still doin' it. Yiz wouldn't do it to the big shots but yiz'd give the poor a toe in the hole!"

The priest came out and saw me looking. He heard Miley shouting. He was vexed. He looked sternly at me and said

"Didn't I tell you to be about your business. I'll deal with him. Now go on!"

I skedaddled.

"I'm phonin' the guards this very instant to have you locked up."

I could hear Miley shouting, "Judas Iscariot – thassall yiz are – Judas Iscariot."

"Get out of here now I'm warnin' you," said the half-vested cleric.

The sacristy door slammed shut. When I came back in, the door into the priest's house was open. I could see him on the phone in the hallway. Sergeant Thorpey would not like being called at this early hour. His displeasure would not be taken out on the priest, however. I went into the vestry to await his return. I was very quiet. This was a good time for obedience. I could still hear Miley roaring, "And yer wine is as wake as piss."

I caught myself laughing, but instantly checked it. He roared again, "Ya wouldn't turn that stuff into water if ya drank it for a week."

The priest came back in.

"Is that fool still out there?"

"He is Father."

"Who's in the church?"

I had been too flustered to notice and in any event we had been lectured against gawking into the church from the altar.

"Go out and see if Mr. Doyle is there. Tell him I want him."

Out I went and sure enough he was. He came carrying that troubled demeanour of interrupted adoration.

"William," Fr. Williams said, "will you go out there and keep that fool quiet whilst I try to say Mass, he broke in here last night and drank all the altar wine." The priest was dressing the chalice as he spoke.

"Certainly Father!" Doyle replied flushed by this anointing. "Certainly Father!"

When he arrived at the foot of the altar, Fr. Williams noticed he had forgotten the keys to the tabernacle. When a priest went on the altar to say Mass he had to stay there until the Act of Worship was over, or died in the course.

He genuflected and doffed his biretta which he handed to me. He walked up three steps and placed the dressed chalice in front of the tabernacle. He genuflected and as he came back down Miley was roaring at Doyle outside the church at the top of his voice.

"Referee me arse, ya wouldn't know a football from a snowball. Ya don't even walk like a referee ya awkward oul' bollix."

Fr. Williams bent towards the altar and intoned the monotonous Latin text.

"Introibo ad Altare Dei. Ad deum qui laetificat juventutem meam."

There were a few coughs in the church.

"Judica me, Deus, et discerne causam meam de gente non sancta: ab homine iniquio et dolorosa erue me."

And having entreated to be distinguished from the nation that was not holy, he petitioned God to be delivered from the unjust and deceitful man in the Roman tongue which was understood by few, if any.

At the same time from outside the stained glass windows came the bellowing roars of Miley which could be already heard and understood by all.

"Judge not and ya shall not be judged – ya big bollix. Leggo a' me coat."

"Confiteor Deo Omnipotenti

Beáto Mariae, semper Virgini
Beatae Michaeli Archangelo
Beáto Joanni Baptistae
Sanctis Apostolis Petro et Paulo
Omnibus sanctis, et tibi Pater,"
He struck his breast, "Mea culpa, mea culpa, Mea maxima ..."
There was a screech outside.

"Yeow! Well ya little bollix, I'll teach you to bite," said the "priest" Doyle, who never swore. Someone sniggered in the church. There followed the sound of footsteps on the gravel. The church was quiet. Fr. Williams looked pained as he finished his ritual examination of conscience. It was my turn now on behalf of the faithful. I motored through the Confiteor like an old professional.

The action now appeared to have moved away from the church. You could still hear commotion but it was incoherent. Then a lull came.

The Epistle was read and when it was finished I left my kneeling step and proceeded to carry the heavy missal and stand from the Epistle to the Gospel side. The priest retreated to incline towards the tabernacle to beseech the cleansing of his heart and lips through Isaiah before he would utter the Holy Word. I descended in diagonal fashion to the bottom step centre, as the custom was, to genuflect before ascending to the gospel side. I lost my balance holding the book and it and stand fell crashing and tumbling down the marble steps. What a morning. The priest stopped praying. He spurred me into action.

"Pick it up!" he resumed his prayerful, if exasperated, demeanour.

There were sniggers or gasps in the church, I believed. I gathered the book. One page had torn out entirely, another had torn almost completely across its middle but was still intact. I got the stand, placed the book on it, and carried them both in lumbered cumbersome fashion to the Gospel side of the altar. I was scarlet. The priest was white with anger. He found the spot.

"Dominius Vobiscum," he said, barely audibly. (It was one of those days.)

"Et cum spiritu tuo. Sequentia Sancti Evangeli Secundum Joannes" (Go into my coat pocket on the hallstand and get the keys of the tabernacle in my pocket.)

He was speaking to me.

"What? Oh, yes Father! Uh – Gloria, Tibi, Domine."

I bowed and departed to do my errand.

A chance to make up. The door from the altar to the sacristy was left open during Mass to allow Mae Brennan worship from a prie-dieu, off of the altar, on weekdays and the claustrophobic Mrs. Gillane on Sundays. There was a look of support and solidarity on Mae's face and she looked at me knowingly as I swept past. I raised my eyebrows in resigned acknowledgement. I went to the priest's hallstand and put my hand in his coat pocket. My face brushed against a fur sleeve. I realised this was not the priest's coat. I got the smell of scent. I looked underneath and there sure enough was the priest's black gabardine. I put my hand in the deep inside pocket standing on my tiptoes. There they were – right second time – relief. I heard the toilet flush upstairs. The toilet was located on the mezzanine floor. The slender figure of a young woman in a pink dressing gown stepped out and lightly walked up four steps to the first floor. She had a white towel wrapped like a turban around her head. Her presence only startled me because I believed I was in the house on my own. I raced back to the altar just as the priest was finishing the Gospel.

"Laus Tibi Christi," I said as I handed him the keys.

"Good man," he said soberly.

I was absolved.

The rest of the Mass was uneventful but I feared at one stage that we would run out of Communion wafer there was such a large crowd for the First Friday. I was relieved when it was over. Afterwards the priest examined the book where the page had been torn. I stayed very quiet.

"Accidents will happen, me boyo, accidents will happen."

"I'll get some sellotape from Miss Brennan?"

"No," he replied, "I'll get it. Stay there until I come back."

When he left I stood there looking at the large Latin text. It was mostly written in red and black. Although I could say the responses in Latin, I had no real idea what they actually meant. I knew the Confiteor was a confession to the saints and to God and to everyone of all our sins but the rest of it was wrapped up in a web of intellectual inscrutability and incensed liturgy. It was a labyrinth based on traditions, power and schism. Incomprehension was explained as ignorance and confusion as mystery education was authority. There was no questioning authority. There was a lot of confusion. No one was ignorant, everyone comprehended. I felt ignorant. One thing was for sure, what we had we held and there was no room for change.

The outside door opened and in came Sergeant Thorpey and the "priest" Doyle. Simultaneously, Fr. Williams arrived in from the house with the sellotape. They stood just outside of the vestry door in the hallway.

"Well?" enquired Fr. Williams.

"He's handcuffed in the car," said Thorpey.

"A proper scamp and an impudent cur," said Doyle.

"Do you wish to bring charges?" asked Thorpey.

"Do we have to?" asked Fr. Williams.

"He'll have to be taught a lesson, Father. Sergeant Thorpey just told me he broke into the Protestant Church no length ago and broke a window into the bargain."

"That's true," said the Sergeant.

I squirmed.

"Still – the poor oul' devil," said a relenting Fr. Williams.

"And he broke in here as well, Father. People will be afraid in their homes next if he keeps on getting away with it. You can't be too soft with fellas like Miley. They'd be up on your back in a flash. My advice is let the law take its course."

The priest pondered for a moment.

"What would he be charged with?"

"Burglary. You know, breaking and entering. He swears, of course, that he didn't break in."

"Oh he broke in alright. The doors were locked all night. I opened them myself this morning."

The door to the sacristy and the church had both been open when I arrived. All the priest's keys were in his coat pocket where I got them. Before I could utter or stutter, Fr. Williams asked,

"What are the Protestants doing?"

"Well I have yet to see Reverend Handcock but he'll probably have to consult someone else. If we're going to go on past performances, I'd say when they find out who did it they'll ignore it, but at their peril," said the Sergeant.

"I'll think about it," said the clergyman.

"Anyway, it's no harm to give him a bit of a shakin' up. Let him know what's what around the place," justified and excused the policeman.

When I came back in I knew I would tell him. He opened the book and inserted the torn page and pulled out a length of sellotape from the roll and bit it off with his teeth. He handed me the roll and with a level eye went about repairs to the missal.

"Not bad for a clergyman," he chuckled, "I might have made a seamstress."

When he had finished the last page I told him.

"Father, Miley didn't force the doors open, they were open when I got here this morning."

I could feel myself dying. He momentarily paused but kept fingering the sellotape as if to ensure full bonding.

"Is that so?" he said without looking at me. (I always knew I was a stupid bastard, now would I please kindly shut up.) Too thick to even listen to my own advice I heard myself say.

"I got the keys out of your overcoat during Mass."

(Did I say that?)

"Obedience, Jack, obedience!" was all he replied.

"Yes, Father," I answered, mystified and ignorant.

∞∞

That Friday we were busy in the shop. The forenoon had seen an array of motor cars, bikes and horses and carts there. Some women had bought in fowl to fatten for Christmas. Others had a sow, or maybe two, due to farrow. The demand for meal from the store was up. There was hay in the cutting and on their way from field to haggard the farmers and their helpers would stop occasionally to get a packet of fags or a bottle of orange, to slake their drewth. The day was fine in the countryside, everything was at its lusty zenith. Nature was letting its essence ooze. There was a buzz about, an atmosphere of happening.

At five to one, the last of the forenoon shoppers was seen off. My father lit a cigarette and smiled saying they were hardly as busy in "Healy and Collins" in Wexford. The postman, Jimmy Whitty, walked in.

The postman opened his bag and took out a bundle of letters which were tied with a soft fawn twine. He gave my father some brown envelopes and then he produced a bright blue envelope with a decorated orange edge, he handed it to me. My father grinned mischievously. It was for me from the USA. I blushed. Fortunately, Dr. Paxo Sheahan came in. They started talking hurling and football. I slipped into the meatroom off the shop to read the letter.

Mel told me how she missed Wexford and Hiawatha and how we had such great fun and how she remembered the fright in the Protestant Church. She said she had read that the American people were presenting Wexford with a statue of Commodore John Barry (the founder of the American Navy) who was a native of Wexford. She said it was happening next month and she really wished she could be there and how was Larkin and how she missed all the stories and lastly how she missed me. (Christ, on a bike!) I was chuffed but shaken. She had a postscript which said there was a chance she might get over next summer and was "really, really, hoping" that she would and really, really missed us all, "so cross my heart and hope to die."

I sat against the meat block and started reading again. The men in the shop were assessing the chances against Galway in the semi-final of the hurling when Canon Harpur came in. He was in his usual fuss.

Whitty went off straight away. Paxo lingered out of defiance. He had been refused the Sacraments during "the Troubles" by the Canon when he had been a curate in Coleman, a neighbouring parish. Being a doctor, he was well known. He had been at the Communion rails when the Canon simply blessed him and passed him by. This morning Paxo made him wait by keeping my father engaged in the match. They never spoke directly to each other.

"Pardon Me," said the Canon, "I would like a word with you, John."

Without averting his gaze, Paxo said, "Pardon me, but I am speaking, please"

The Canon, vexed, moved to the bottom of the shop. My father got very uncomfortable fearing a row. Paxo ordered a box of "Mick McQuaid" tobacco and a box of matches and while my father was getting them, kept talking about that "Cursed goddamn myxamatosis that's killing all the rabbits that could be hunted" and "that cursed goddam polio" that had newly arrived and was the bane of every doctor's life between tests and inoculations.

"There's always some goddam thing, if it's not TB, it's polio. It's impossible to stem the tide. It's nature's way I suppose of keeping us in our place. It lets us save a few and we keep trying to save a few more and then it turns 'round and takes us whatever way it likes whenever it likes, in the end. Still," he said pointedly, "it's an ill wind blows no good for someone. See you later" he said and then, pointedly, "Keep the faith." He was cheeky.

The Canon had a mission on his mind.

"I would like to speak to you privately John, I would," he said.

This looked serious. Serious conversations took place in the little office. The office was located adjacent to the meatroom at the back of the shop. The walls of the shop were constructed of timber frame, cladded over with tongued and grooved ceiling boards. The privacy this ensured was simply visual. They went in.

The office contained a clerk's desk. This was a flip-top desk, approximately four feet high resting on two pedestals, one of which contained drawers and the other, a little press. The desk was used for writing while standing and if the task was longer, there was a tall bar stool to sit on. The press, or cupboard, always contained a bottle of whiskey. Although my father was a member of the Pioneer Total Abstinence Association, he snook a drink and while we knew, we were really only concerned by his inability to acknowledge it. It was false.

My presence in the meatroom though accidental, was fortuitous. My father offered the Canon a drink but he was not to be deflected.

"I am here because I am concerned, I am," he intoned.

"I have always known you to be a decent Catholic family man with respect for the church and its clergy. I have to admonish you for your attendance at the service for that late Protestant gentleman, Mr. Whitney, I have. I can understand he may have been a customer, I can, or even a friend, yes indeed, even a friend, there's no harm in having a Protestant for a friend. But attending a Protestant service is something else – to them it is a ritual, it is not like the Holy Sacrifice of the Mass is to us. And then there is the scandal element of it, yes indeed, the scandal. If your presence is tolerated at a Protestant Service then why not others, yes indeed, why not? People in the position of you and your brother have a special responsibility for setting an example, yes indeed, an example. I understand one of the local vagrants, who was always afraid to go near the Protestant Church, became so bold as to break into it and use it as a type of dormitory no less, – yes indeed, a guesthouse. Just goes to show you can't be careful enough when it comes to giving bad example – we have to be very vigilant, yes indeed – ever vigilant."

I was stuck to the block inside in the meatroom. The ramifications of my own misdemeanours in the church were taking on a deeper and more sinister interpretation.

The Canon went on some more about the difference between tolerating and respecting the Protestant viewpoint whilst not condoning it. I do not remember the start of the conversation very well. It was only a long time afterwards my father reminded me of it. There was an incongruous suggestion that later appealed.

"Canon," he enquired "Did you ever walk into a ladies toilet by mistake."

The Canon was offended.

"I do not see the need for vulgarity or baseness."

"The fact I might end up in a ladies toilet doesn't make me a lady, and it never will."

"It's not the same thing at all."

The Canon got defensive.

"We could argue this John until the cows come home. The question is whether you are prepared to accept the authority of your church or not?"

My father was a fanatical follower of De Valera. He always admired the early stance that he took against it when the church was outlawing "the men on the run." Apart altogether from that, my father was a rebel.

"I follow my conscience, Canon."

I could see Canon Sheridan and my grandfather being acted out all over again when he told him off during the Troubles.

"But you have to be obedient while forming your conscience," said the Canon.

There was a knock on the shop door. By the time I got to the door which had been bolted, both of them were coming out of the office behind me. The atmosphere was hostile. The noise had interrupted them. The Canon knew he was not going to budge my father easily. I opened the door and there was Sean Hanlon. He was wiping the sweat from his brow with his beret. "Sorry to disturb," he said. "I was passing and I thought I'd get a paper." I retreated behind the counter and he followed me in. Unaware of the atmosphere into which he had arrived, he cheerily greeted my father and the Canon. My father responded, but the Canon said very coldly. "Mr. Hanlon" and walked past him to his black Volkswagen. I gave him the paper. He looked at the headlines as I fetched him a box of matches as well.

"Has herself got any eggs, Sean?" my father recovered.

"Crikey, but I'm not sure, d'you know!" he said.

"If she has we could do with a few dozen," said my father.

The Hanlons were thrifty. A lot of baking would be starting in order to feed the hungry hordes of men that would descend on the various farms to help with the threshings later on.

"I'm combining myself this year," he proclaimed. "I've invested in one with the father-in-law – a sort of partnership," he grinned. "If you know of anyone looking to save themselves the fuss of a threshing, I'll be happy to relieve them of a few pounds," he quipped.

"It should be aisey enough to buy the eggs from you so," said my father.

"You'll have to deal with the Minister for Domestic Affairs on that one, I don't think the Marshall Aid Plan extends that far," he laughed on the way out.

He was referring to the US Monetary Assistance which had been given to post-war Europe. Mrs. Hanlon was well known for her "busy bee" approach to farmyard enterprise. My father used to refer to her as "a toppin' bleddy woman" that would put half of her Catholic counterparts to shame. She had two children still at home but coming up to "school going" age and she could yet find time to milk twenty cows and make butter and bread for the shop. She kept hens, pullets and turkeys, supplied eggs, kept three sows (always had a litter) and could knit and sew – she could darn a cobweb into a handkerchief, she was that nifty with a needle and wool thread.

As Sean Hanlon was the nephew of the late Dean, it was no real surprise to see that Canon Harpur had waited for him. The Canon's expression had not ameliorated much, however, and shortly before he drove off I noticed Mr. Hanlon shrug, once, at least. My father said we would wait until they had gone before going for the dinner. He shifted stuff around on the counter and cleaned away imaginary crumbs and straightened newspapers.

"Close the window in the office," he said, "I don't want any of those feckin' birds getting in while we're out."

I did as bid and when I came back he pulled his gaze back from the crossroads and said,

"I think they're going now."

When we went out, the Canon had gone and, but for the fact that he had started the tractor, Sean Hanlon would possibly have spoken. Having locked the door my father turned around and the two men's eyes met briefly, hesitating between delaying and proceeding. Then my father raised his eyebrows nodded his head once in an up-and-down fashion. Sean Hanlon did likewise and they moved off.

That afternoon my uncle Martin brought me to the hay field where I was put in charge of "Dolly" and the Hayrake. Dolly was the pony. She was being used less and less on account of the arrival of the second tractor. I was put tumbling hay with her in one field while the men made haycocks in another. I was beginning to feel grown up. I was working with big strong sweaty men with a big strong sweaty horse (well, nearly a horse) with coarse smells and brute instinct that I could control. The handle to tumble the rake was made for a man's big hand. I had to use both of mine to hoist it but I developed a technique of leaving the reins around my neck at the critical juncture, in order to have both hands available to tumble it.

When the three o'clock tea arrived in the tommy can we all stopped and sat down at the same cock of hay. It was the sweetest tea I ever had in my life.

Martin was there, Tommy Murphy, Peter's workman Mogue, and my brother, who was driving the tractor, a position of alleged superior agricultural social standing than driving the pony. Peter and Jim Carley, Martin's workman, were also there. The atmosphere was great. There was the smell of hay, the quaffing of thirst, more sweat – a type of contended connection between effort, refreshment and gathering bounty.

Tommy Murphy was very funny. He was intense about everything he said and, as a consequence, he regularly overstated matters. His statements were often incongruous and added to this was a facility to use, or rather misuse, words he did not fully understand with hilarious results. Martin would try to draw him out.

Jim Carley was a quiet, inoffensive man who did his work and loved to watch the fun. He was a Protestant. Most Protestants were well off, but the Carley's had been labouring people all of their lives. Though they had little, every Friday they had fried rashers for the dinner. The smell meandered for miles and more over the countryside. Friday was a day of abstinence from meat for Catholics and the first Friday was a feast day. This meant only one full meal and two collations, and no meat all day. If these rules were not observed then both fast and abstinence would be broken and a mortal sin committed. These were the Precepts of the church and, in some dioceses, were reserved sins which required Episcopal Absolution.

Jim Carley had two buttered slices of white current bread. The butter was melting on the second slice.

"I must have a piss," said Carley.

As he got up he left his mug down with his teeth marks in half a slice but nobody else was eating on account of it being a First Friday. Tommy Murphy looked up away from the buttered slices and said to Martin under his breath,

"The curse a' fuck on fast days and Protestants. I'm raley starvin'," Martin laughed.

A horsedoctor* landed on Tommy's arms. He flattened it with a smack and rolled it between the thumb and finger of his right hand into a blob. Carley was still releasing his deluge behind the haycock. Murphy dabbed the dead insect into the molten butter. It looked just like another currant. When Carley came back he ate away on the bread. Murphy was delighted with his practical joke and kept smiling and making faces behind Carley's back, as he consumed every scrap and morsel including the dead horsedoctor. He could contain himself no longer and said,

"Bejaysus Jim, you sure broke your fast and incontinence today anyhow."

Jim looked around amused and confused. As he piked hay for the rest of the day Murphy kept singing "I know an old woman who swallowed a fly."

Peter had to tell him to whisht for a finish.

After I had tossed all the hay, Tommy Murphy and I went into the other field and started to bend the straight swards into circles, preparatory

*Stingy flies

to making cocks of them later. I unyoked the horse from the hayrake and Martin gave me a hand yoking a cart, with a sidelace, to Dolly.

Piking hay was hard work. It required strength, pace and effort. As with most things, experience was a big advantage. In approaching a cock of hay, the cart or trailer would be positioned down wind of the work. The first pike would be inserted near the cap and a "shkeal" of hay would be removed and hoisted over the pikeman, like a giant parasol, and carried to the trailer where it would be neither dumped nor tossed, but pitched. In the course of so carrying it, remnants of withered thistle, insects and dried weeds would drop from this lofty perch, atop the pike, down onto the sinewy gnarling and sweaty body beneath.

At thirteen years of masculine manhood, opportunity was all that was required to entice emulation. I laced into the day with a vengeance and reacted hugely to the alleged disbelief of my capacity for work by those whom I was now quickly regarding as my comrades.

My heart nearly burst with pride when I perched on the edge of the sidelace and was handed the reins.

"Do you think you could take her in?" asked Peter.

Could a cat drink milk?

"No problem," I assured.

My confidence reached arrogance when I was going out the field gate. My brother was returning with the tractor. "Engine give way to nature" is the country rule. He had to wait until the pony came out and it killed him that he had to acknowledge his younger sibling's relevance. He reduced the throttle as I approached. "Huboff," I shouted at Dolly, in as gruff a manner as I could muster.

"C'mon boy," he roared, "you're not at a funeral."

It stung, but I was learning that earthiness, ignorance and roughness were to do with survival and toughness, and it seemed to me then that they were double first cousins.

"Kiss me arse!" I shouted back at him.

I nursed a mischievous grin for myself. He reacted by opening the throttle whilst the tractor was idling in a neutral gear. Dolly was too used to farmwork and machinery to be troubled, and too engaged in her effort to react. The grin refused to be wiped.

"Gelang," I urged, in imitation of Tommy Murphy's carelessly strewn and course invitation to "Get along." This was an expression he used like "huboff," a swear word, with the belief that animals were brute and responded better to the vulgar and rough. The attitude was not uncommon. It sometimes carried over into personal behaviour. Hard, tough and grummock men were feared and enjoyed an envied respect by the more sensitive and less robust.

When I arrived in the haggard, I drew the cart alongside the hayshed and drew the reins back as I had seen "Buckskin" do many times on screen in *The Durango Kid*. I leaped down and proceeded to tie the reins around the pillar of the hayshed. Though I was tall for my age, even if I was wearing summer shorts, I was unable to lean in and reach the lugs on the collar on account of the pony's big belly. The horsedoctors were nipping Dolly and she hindlifted a stomp and swished her tail in blinkered annoyance. I slung the rope to the off side over the reach of the collar, in order to collect it and make it fast. The men on the rick had stopped piking. I let on to ignore them. I intertwined the rope in figure of eight style. The pony's rope was almost secure enough to stop her from wandering. Whilst in this process my concentration was totally absorbed. I was being scrutinised as if in the course of an examination and I knew I was getting honours. Just as I was about to receive my laurel wreath it was swept away from me. That goddam turkey cock struck again.

When the workmen initially invaded his territory, Tommy Murphy gave him a few belts with his pike and "a few nips in the hole" as he said, "to put manners on him." The turkey retreated and when a mealtime of grain increased his profit and his lustiness, he strutted forward with fanned feathers, only to be doused with a "shkeal" of hay aloft the rick to the mirth and merriment of the haymakers and the utter "sharoose" of the humiliated fowl.

Spotting me was a different matter. He homed in on me with the unerring instinct of a bully. Instinctively I leaped to get back on my perch on the sidelace. The turkey tumbled in under the pony's legs; she back kicked and pulled her head and reins loose. The knot was undone, but she couldn't run far because of her load. I fell off. The pony bolted about ten or fifteen feet from the hayshed and in the process broke a timber feeding trough for the fowl and the fowl bucket which Poll had left there to let the hens pick at. One of the split car tyres, which was used as a feeding trough, had been "tiddly-winked" on to the pier of the pigsty by the bruising cartwheel. The pike which I had been using had fallen under the cart and the handle was broken. The guinea hens had flown up into the apple trees in the orchard beside. Ponto was barking as if he had been told there was no tomorrow and was exacting the last decibel from his vocal chords. I cut my elbow in the fall, a matter for which I was grateful, since it distracted from the source of my injured pride and abject failure.

When order was restored and the turkey cock "hooshed" inside, Poll arrived on the scene.

"In the name of God what happened? Did someone get hurt?"

Sam Duffin who had been making the rick and who was about twenty-one years old had slipped down to the rescue.

"The ould turkey made "a fly" at the pony and she shied," he lied.

She came over to me when she saw the blood on my arm.

"Show me," she said.

I had now armed myself with the spare hurl that Hiawatha had fixed with the sheet of tin. It had been left beside the cowhouse door and was now being used by all and sundry to drive home the cows. The blood had run down on the handle and I stood there recovering, aided by the lie I had heard. I sighed a new significance into "I couldn't stop him." This was the truth right enough, but I presented it as if my injury had resulted from heroic intervention as opposed to fearful retreat. At that point, the others arrived from the field behind the five miles per hour tractor wobbling its wary way over stone and pothole. My brother was curious.

"What happened the lad?"

"He nearly killed himself trying to save the rest of us," explained Duffin and when my brother's gaze met mine I noticed the others react to Duffin's wink, behind him. My exposure was concealed. I was at least spared the ignominy of a jeering.

It was about half-past four in the evening. Peter could see I was shaken. He picked up the broken pitchfork and told me to go to the shop and get a pike handle and take it down to the blacksmith to fit. Though Poll's bike was what we called a "High Nelly," I was able to manage it, though not entirely comfortably. I secured the new handle like a crossbar from handlebar to saddle. On my way into Coleman I met Miley Cassidy trudging out, looking forlorn. I pedalled on to Hiawatha. He was rinsing out two mugs and a teapot. He looked at the implement.

"Needed yesterday, I presume?"

He took the pike handle and brought it to the bench. Whilst he was looking for his tools he started to whistle. His gift was brilliant. He was a warbling whistler.

"D'you know the name of that?"

I recognised it and replied "I think it's called 'Johnny Dubh' (pronounced 'Do')."

"The 'Little Beggarman' some call it," he said. "Aye, Surely." Miley had been with him. I thought about him as I waited.

The ghost of my conscience was back to haunt me, even though I had tried to explain matters to the priest. He had told me to leave it alone and I did not want to go against him. But I had not been consoled by his "wait and see" approach.

Hiawatha took out a big chisel and an oilstone and applied some oil to the stone. He rubbed the chisel on it, carefully and steadily sharpening it. He trimmed the handle in measured shaves and tried it on the head "for a fit." He repeated the process, his sharp eye gauging and judging.

"You never told me about the school that time."

I was jolted back to life.

"The time I got the beltin'?"

"The very thing."

"I got over it."

"Did you now?"

I looked at my shoes uncomfortably.

"Sure there's always slappin' and givin' out."

"Is that a fact?"

"I wish I was finished school."

"And what would you do?"

"I'd be able to do what I wanted to do – I'd be free."

"And are you not free now?"

"Well ya have to do as yer told all the time and ya have to do this and there's always somewan gettin' on to you."

"Things gettin' to you?" he asked. He was getting too close. I paused and looked away at the harnesses on the wall.

"Sometimes," I answered.

He had the handle fitting like a glove. He proceeded to mark the handle through a hole in the sleeve of the pikehead. When he retracted it he got a small hand drill and placed the pikehandle in the bench vice, he drilled a hole through. He occasionally whistled as his concentration eased. He replaced the handle this time and tapped the head on, tap-tap, tap-tap, until the hole in the pike and the handle met. He got a rivet and tapped it through. When it came out he turned it around and with a steady strong blow-and-a-quarter, Bang-tap! Bang-tap!, he belted and flattened the proud metal into a blob on the back of the pike. He tested it. It was solid. He admired it and said, "That's about the only place a beltin' works." He never looked at me.

I gave him the halfcrown which had been given to me for the purpose. He handed back one shilling.

"Are you going to the Fair in Ross tomorrow?"

I had not realised it was the first Saturday of the month.

"There's a tanner for some sweets."

He tousled my hair. I felt a lump in my throat. I went out and we fixed the pike on to Poll's bike. As we did a motor car pulled up and a man got out.

He had a big smile and was a big man with a greying head of hair.

"For the pikes must be together ..." he broke off.

The blacksmith looked up and grinned.

"Aisey known there's an election in the air."

I held the bike. They shook hands warmly and good humouredly.

When I arrived back at the farm they were all in the kitchen having their supper. Peter was in the back kitchen drying his hands with a towel. There was a single brass tap pointing into a big white square enamel sink that was swirling its soapy contents into a gurgling choke out the plughole. He looked at me

"Be up in the morning at eight o'clock. I need help with the cattle for the fair." I was delighted. At that point the car I had seen at the forge drove into the yard. Peter looked out.

"Ryan," he observed. "Go in and get your supper. Don't be late in the morning or I'll go without you," he teased. He went out the door.

Yessiree. I was afraid the invitation had only included my attendance to load the animals into the trailer but now it was confirmed, I was going to the Fair.

Halfway through the supper my father arrived to collect me. He was shown to the parlour where Peter had already gone with Dr. Ryan. Martin and Poll had come out to let both politicians talk but there was no way would my father leave without telling "Ryan" something about what Fianna Fáil should be doing and maybe have a yarn as well.

Much later that night Peter arrived at our house to talk to my father. Fr. Williams came in. They spoke about the credit squeeze and the way it was ruining the farmers. Dr. Ryan had earlier agreed with Peter. My father volunteered that Jim Dillon was only an eejit. "Didn't he suggest tearing the rocks out of Connemara one time, and sowing wheat in it. Did ya ever hear the like in all your born days?"

It was bedtime for me. "You'll be late for the Fair" was my cue. My mother rattled the cups and saucers in the back kitchen. They spoke about the match. "They'll hammer Galway," the priest volunteered. I closed the door having said goodnight. Now we could all enjoy the conversation.

"I'd say we'll have an election before we have an All-Ireland," said my mother as she went back for the kettle. They were all smoking as usual. Although it was August it was a windy cold night and the fire door of the Rayburn cooker was open. My father and mother sat at opposite sides of it, facing each other. The priest and Peter sat opposite the cooker itself and a backless kitchen wooden chair acted as a small table. There was a plate of currant buns, sugar, milk and tea. All the cups had saucers, even if they did not match. The odd crumb would fall on the lino floor. My father would "ferry it" into the grate with a neat flick from a small fender brush.

"I suppose the next step is the Senate?" Fr. Williams taunted Peter, who was much too quick.

"At the very least," he quipped. "They'll probably want to bring me straight into the cabinet."

"There's nothin' only eejits in it," my father said. "They'll never notice ya," and laughed.

They all laughed. My father seldom teased his brother and never in front of non-family. The priest was in.

"I heard you got a bit of a tickin' today."

They spoke about the incident with the Canon in the shop. It was the consensus that the Canon was getting too old.

"He got on to Hanlon about something."

"The young lad's going to school I'm sure," said the priest.

"Sure his eldest young wan is six and other lassie must be five. They should be started schoolin' ages. I have a notion it's not all a bunch a roses down there. I also have a notion his Reverence is putting the pressure on Hanlon to make them go. Elisha Whitney could be a scaldy lady, I dare say."

"Well, her father is a dacent man," said Peter.

"I never had difficulty with him once and I suppose I dealt with him as much as anyone."

"And certainly not a bigot. Still, they have their ways and we have ours," said my father.

"Protestants are fine ..." the ʄ commenced but before he could finish the front door of the hall of the house burst open.

I scarpered up the stairs.

"Are ya there, John? Quick!" a voice roared.

I looked around the corner of the banisters and there was Matt Larkin, Michael's father, and Sam Duffin carrying someone in a blanket who was obviously badly injured. It was my mother's brother. There was pandemonium.

"What happened?"

"He fell into the friggin' dock," said Larkin.

"He was goin' to look at the coal boat."

They bundled him into the kitchen. He was shaking and trembling. My mother turned white – she went for towels.

The arrival of the coal boat in Coleman was a sure signal summer was ending. My grandfather, my mother's father, was the manager of the local cooperative who arranged this timely importation of fuel for the cookers and fires of the Shelburne area for the winter. My uncle apparently had gone down to the pier to investigate and satisfy his curiosity. A foreign boat in the dock attracted onlookers from far and near. Once there had been a black man on board, but I only heard about that.

"Wan of the sailors grabbed him be the hair o' the head when he was goin' down for the third time," said Duffin.

Marie came out of her room and had her dressing gown on. The priest saw me.

"Run up as far as Mae as fast as you can and get the bottle of brandy."

I ran like a hare to the priest's house. Mae was tidying the kitchen before going to bed. My adrenaline was up with the drama and excitement. I panted my explanation.

"It's in the sideboard in the dining room," she said. "I'll get it."

But my uncle's life was at stake.

"I'll get it," I proclaimed, whilst eyeing her stick. "Come back!" she shouted.

I was venturing into the holy of holies where she only ventured with deference and not without reason. There lurked a darker reason which explained why the door from the kitchen to the hall was always closed and if by chance it was ever ajar it was promptly closed with the arrival of a visitor to the kitchen. I ran through the hall and burst open the door of the cupboard. I rummaged for the bottle without turning on the light. I heard another door open and footsteps in the hall. Somebody went to the telephone. I found the bottle and closed the door of the sideboard. The voice said, "Kilbeggan 75, please." It was a woman. My appearance in the hall startled the lady on the phone but I rushed back, focused with the intensity of my task, fearful a fatality might occur if the elixir was not delivered by the pony-express.

My return was greeted with acclaim. My uncle was a teetotaller. The introduction of alcohol into his system made him cough and splutter.

"That'll crown him," the priest said.

He was still shaking and unable to talk.

"Make some tea, Statia," my father, said to my mother.

The excitement maintained for a while and the saviours had to have some tea and something a little stronger was offered to Mr. Larkin, but because he was going to the Fair in the morning he said he would leave it.

The priest said he would have to go and a long time later Peter left in order to bring my uncle home.

"Go to bed you sparrowfart," he grinned at me. "You'll be stuck to the pillow in the morning."

The Hand of God, Communism, and "Big Mickie's"

The marts are taking their toll," Thomas Whitney Senior said to Peter the next day in New Ross. "They are indeed," he responded. "You have to move with the times."

The Fair was held in the Irishtown, that part of the town outside the town walls which the conquerors identified on Cromwellian maps as belonging to "The mere Irish."

It was the widest street by far, located at the top of the town. It descended in steep streets to the river. The Nore joined the Barrow just above Ross, flowed into it and brought out seafaring barques of every description in every age.

The Normans held the town under Earl Marshall. The Loyalists commemorated the 55th Anniversary of the Battle of the Boyne by inscription on the Municipal Mansion, the Tholsel, in 1745: "This stone laid the 12th day of July 1745 the Anniversary of the glorious Battle of the Boyne." To define and assert their supremacy, the nineteenth century Nationalists erected a bronze pike man in 1898 on the 100th Anniversary of the insurrection of 1798 by the United Irishmen. The bronze pike man stands there ever since, shaking his fist at the Tholsel door. If one hand could lay a foundation stone to declare superiority, another could be cast into a fist of bronze defiance against all claims of domination. The more the hands were used in this fashion and the longer time passed, the less likely it appeared they would ever shake each others'. They remain a metaphor to monuments everywhere – declarations cast in stone, eternal gestures cast in bronze – unshakeable. Monuments become icons to immutability. Life demands change.

The smell in the Irishtown was heavy with manure. Dogs were barking at the heels of the cattle. There were sheep in horseboxes. Pigs were in vans with no windows in the back. Some were in small trailers strewn with straw. There was a fellow with some thimbles who was doing a variation on a three-card trick. There were three thimbles and one pea. I kept guessing the pea was under the right one – when someone bet, I was wrong.

I saw the townies. They had Brylcreem in their hair. They were called Teddyboys. We were told some of them carried flick knives, so we gave them a wide berth.

Early on, I met Larkin. His father was bargaining with a man over pigs. He sold them for a figure which was nearly half of what he asked the buyer at the start. Each man spit on his hand and slapped the others to seal the deal. Hands were an important part in the bargain.

One man I saw who was trying to buy from another seemed to be forcing him to sell. The enthusiastic cattle jobber held his cupped right hand aloft, inviting the reluctant seller to hold his out in order to seal the deal with a slap. The would-be purchaser used his left hand to catch the right of the vendor, and held it out. When he excitedly moved to quickly seal the purchase, the other farmer pulled his own back and the bargain hunter tore his hand on an upturned nail that was securing the creels of the adjacent trailer. His hand bled. The incident stuck in my mind because I was impressed by the injured party who ignored his clearly painful injury in order to continue his haggling. People like this were called "tanglers" and virtually lived on their wits by buying at one Fair today and selling at another tomorrow.

Peter had sold six heifers which were in calf for the first time. They were called "Springers." He had bought six bullocks which were loaded into the trailer with the high creels which had been tractored in that morning. He brought myself and Larkin down to the Phoenix Restaurant where we had tea and buns to our fill. On the way down he pointed out to us the Three Bullet Gate with its Cromwellian overtones and showed us the streets where the blood ran down in rivers before mingling in the waters far below during the 1798 Insurrection.

It was nearly noon before we arrived back at the Fair. Larkin's father had bought a dozen sheep. Peter told me to give Michael a hand driving them home.

Sheep were stupid. Every lane on the way had to be blocked or they would run down. They were terrified of traffic and would face the ditch away from the direction of sound. Driving them required a shepherd in front and another behind. Since they were Larkin's sheep, he took charge from behind. It was a sultry close day as we trudged up Camblin Hill. At the top was an old lime kiln which we called "Nolan's Kills." It was in fact "Nolan's Kiln." Sitting in the eye of the kiln, like a leprechaun on a toadstool, was Miley Cassidy himself. Larkin nodded me over to him. He looked around at the countryside beneath him and, imbued with the sense of importance that travels with the responsibility for a flock of sheep, said grandly,

"Indeed and it's a very close day Miley and everything looks nearer in the haze."

"Indeed and it is boy," said Miley, "t'ed be a right day to go to Ross."

I sniggered and Larkin himself laughed. The sheep wandered off in the direction of Campile. Miley was looking at them and started to recite.

"Mary had a little lamb," and stopped. He looked off over the ditches into the valley below and repeated, "Mary had a little lamb," he got down from the Kiln and stumbled out through the thick luscious grass that the sheep were munching down the way. "Mary had a little lamb," he stopped to look at us both, as if for the first time, and said, "I bet she was a Protestant," and moved on. We looked after him bemusedly. Larkin laughed and so did I. I thought I knew why it was funny. Miley was like that the strangest things came out at the strangest times. We got talking about Miley and the trouble he was in. Larkin was not very sympathetic to me.

"Sure jays, you'll have to tell someone, you can't let him go to jail."

"Well I told the priest."

"Not about the Protestant Church you didn't."

He had me, and no mistake.

"Yeah, well, you were there as well!" I countered.

"I had to take me medicine," he replied.

When we rounded the next bend in the road, the sheep were nowhere to be seen.

"Shite for ya," said Larkin.

"Don't be such a gobshite, they're probably down the lane," I defended.

There was a gravelled avenue. At either side there were trees. They joined overhead. We ran down through this tunnel and came out into an opening revealing a very large period house. There were steps, about nine, up to the front door and a basement below. To the left was a large timber gate which was shut, and some stables and outoffices were revealed by their tidy slate roofs which could be seen over the wall. There was a weather vane in the shape of a cock on a tower.

On the right was a gate, which seemed to be the entrance to a garden. It was open. There was a smell of woodbine. There were midges everywhere. I kept scratching my head. The perspiration was rolling off us both.

"Fecking bastards!" swore Larkin.

"Try the gate," I urged. He looked through.

"There's the hoor – in the orchard."

The orchard was not being kept and the grass was very long and had grown wild. It was what we called scutch. I ran through it in knee high jerks to get to the other side and to drive them back. Larkin circled opposite. They hopped and jumped out through the gate we had come in. When they were out we knew we were alright because the road was straight ahead.

"Look at those." Larkin nodded at the apples.

"They're not ripe," I said.

"They're ripe enough," he answered. "There's nobody home."

He shinnied up the tree and picked, plucked and shook an ass-load of reddening green shiny apples from their perch. We stuffed them in our pockets and shirts until the elastic waist bands in my shorts were sagging.

"Who owns this place?" I asked, as I unbuckled my sandals to extract the gravel that was wedging my bare toes apart. We were back at the front of the house. He could not answer with his mouth full, he was chomping.

"You're like a horse eatin' a turnip," I interrupted my question.

"Go an' shite," he slobbered and sprayed, ignoring both question and correction.

"Say it – don't spray it," I wiped apple from my face.

We moved towards the road back through the dark avenue only to meet the sheep coming back. We waved our hands and shouted. There was a car behind them. It was stopped. The sheep stopped on seeing us. We shouted and flapped our arms. Larkin threw away the apple and blew the contents of his mouth back over his shoulder.

"Keep goin' whatever ya do," he shouted to me. The three bears had come back and had found two Goldilocks chasing sheep in their yard and eating their apples. The animals turned around, they all ran to the same side of the car. It was a priest, no, it was the Minister. He looked annoyed. He let down his window as we ran past. I saw him looking at me. He had horn rimmed round glasses. He looked dark.

"You boys – you boys!"

We were past him. I could hear the door opening.

"You boys, come back here ... You boys ..." (Gobshite.)

I shouted back, "We can't. The sheep."

When we got out on the road we started skitting and laughing until we heard the sound of the motor car coming down the avenue. The sheep were leathering it down the road for all they were worth.

"Quick," said Larkin. "Over the gate."

We scampered over it. We lay down in a deep dry drain which was overgrown.

"Yeow! Jesus! Me arse!" Larkin jumped. "Fuckin' nettles."

"Sit down ya fool, we'll be caught."

"I will in me hole sit down there again," he complained.

"Jesus! Give us a dock leaf quick."

He applied the wide leaf herb to the blotchy bubbles breaking out high up on his spindly thigh. The car passed by the gate of the field. He rubbed and rubbed and winced and cursed.

"We may wait," I said.

It was not to be. The first drops of rain started to fall almost immediately. We ran to the ditch which bounded the avenue to avail of the leaf shelter of the trees.

"At least we won't get caught in the rain," I volunteered.

"The friggin' sheep will be home before us," Larkin said, unable to conceal his disappointment that we were unable to control them.

"You're some friggin shepherd," I said.

"Oh Jesus – me leg!" he winced.

"Ah ye'll be alright. Ya mightn't be able to shite for a year or two, but ye'll be alright." My wit was ignored.

We ate apples until we thought we would burst. When the rain stopped we raised our camp. We caught up with the sheep at the church in Horsewood where they were lazily lying and chewing what remained of the recently mown lawn. Fortunately there was no flower bed and no priest around. We both bemoaned the lack of a bicycle. We were sweaty, having walked the best part of eight miles. The remnants of my swag of apples were accommodated in my pockets. Larkin had a lot more than I had. He was wearing the green uniform jacket (slightly faded green) of the FCA* which still had half of its brass buttons intact, plus a few piebalds and, of course, the ubiquitous safety pin. These jackets were of a worsted hard-wearing material and had a buttoned waistband. It was ideal for concealing apples, but was cumbersome and prickly.

"They seek us here, they seek us there, they can't find us anywhere. Yahoo!" roared the Scarlet Pimpernel laughing his head off with the rush of adrenaline the adventure had caused.

"Shut up you eejit!" I cautioned.

It was just so typical of him. He would always have to tear the arse in it and feck him to hell and back but he always got caught. I used stay out of trouble as much as I could on that account. For the same reason I ended up in a lot more than I ever planned. We were always the last two to get caught in the games of fisherman's nets. I was the fastest, but he was big and strong from the farm work. He was tough. He had warts on his hand which leant to his age and maturity. He bled them onto my hand for me so that I could get them too. It was nothing to do with blood brothers, we were almost too big for that, it was presumed I would want it done in the same way you might ask for the pull of a fag in a ditch or in the way one fella might tell another which girls were wearing what colour knickers. My voice was beginning to break and warts would fit in. No more the unblemished skin of the child.

*Forsa Cosanta Aituil

We ambled most of the way home talking about my uncle who nearly drowned, and then of course, the matches. Neither of us wanted to talk about school reopening in a fortnight.

"They says a girl in Fethard has Polio," I said.

"That crowd always have something," said Larkin.

"True as jayus!" I swore, maturely. "Peter said it."

"It's only bladder."

"But he says Fethard school won't open and the All-Ireland Hurling Final will be put off, as well."

"Go to God!" he reacted now as intended.

"It's only a chance if our school doesn't open as well."

"Wouldn't it be great if someone in our place got it."

I looked at him. As I said, there were times when Larkin could tear the arse in it.

"Larkin, how were you born such a gobshite – or did you have to work at it?"

"I only meant if the friggin' school was closed for longer."

"I only meant – I only meant – why don't you ever think before you meant."

There was a long pause as I let it sink in for him and he sulked. He came out of it shortly.

"I'm going to th' All-Ireland," he diverted.

"You are if we win the Semi," I condescended.

"Jesus! You can be an awful pain in the hole," he said.

"I'd say the nettles stung you higher up than you thought."

"Ya bollicks!" he laughed and ran after me.

The school reopened in 1956 on the first week of September. It was a time of excitement and tension. We changed classes and books and sometimes changed teachers. Unfortunately for me, I only changed classes. This was my last year in school. The last with Sr. Ignatius. September was a time of great excitement. There were the threshings and the newly arrived combine harvesters. A great agricultural debate had started on the merits and demerits of silage versus hay as a winter feed for stock. The credit squeeze was on again and was hitting fowl production.

"Two shillings for a hen and half a crown for a cock! Merciful hour!" was Poll's reaction.

On top of the usual seasonal excitements there were three extra calendar events. The first was the unveiling of the statute of Commodore John Barry the Founder of the US Navy who had been born in County Wexford. It was unveiled in Wexford town. The day was wet, but I got to see the President, Sean T. O'Kelly. He had a top hat and his chest stuck out. He looked cheerful. He always reminded me of a leprechaun. There was a frigate in Rosslare which had brought the statue over the previous week, and the local papers carried photographs of the uninhibited lively young sailors. Admiral Boon was at the unveiling with Mr. Tafte, the Ambassador. Mr. Costello, the frowning Taoiseach, was there, as was the gaunt and serious leader of the Opposition, Mr. DeValera.

Admiral Boon made a speech. He relayed how Commodore Barry of the US Navy and Commodore Sweeney of the Royal Navy broke off their negotiations before resuming war during the American Revolution of the eighteenth century.

"Adieu my countryman," said Admiral Sweeney.

"Not exactly so," corrected Barry. "You, Commodore are a Briton; I, an American."

"I am an Irishman," Sweeney responded. "So are you. You have too many of the strong features of a genuine Irishman for me to be mistaken. You're attachment to the country for which you fought and bled is both natural and highly to your honour; but Sir, you are too good a fellow not to be an Irishman."

The journalists would record it for posterity and I was receiving it with the conviction of an apprentice champion. But the real champions were taking on Cork in Croke Park on the first Sunday in September.

The wiley Christy Ring of Cork, the wizard of Munster who could conjure a score almost before he was given the ball, versus Bobby Rackard who could humanise Ring by saying, "Christy Ring without the ball was no better than anybody else on the field." True – but would he civilise him?

Wexford had mighty men. The three Rackards – surpassed only in fame by the O'Kennedy Brothers of an earlier football era – and here to emulate their feats. Ned Wheeler, the blonde-haired Adonis, Jim Morrissey, with shoulders like Collossus, and Padge Kehoe, the brains of the outfit. Ten of us set out from Coleman in an Austin van. It had three rows of seats and a space behind the last. Myself and my brother were located there on a fine Foxford rug. Peter was driving and Fr. Williams was with him in front. Then came Martin and Tommy Murphy. In the last seat was my father and Tommy Duffin. There was a smell of clay and binder twine in the back of the van. A tomato basket contained mugs and flasks of tea and a biscuit tin of assorted ham and tomato sandwiches and a few bottles of minerals "for the young lads." They smoked their way to New Ross after first Mass. Fr. Kehoe was home from the Missions, and he relieved Fr. Williams from his duty as Curate by saying second Mass in the parish church.

My father had brought us home a Wexford flag after the Leinster Final, and my mother hemmed it and emblazoned "1956" across the purple and gold. As we drove through Graiguenamanagh in County Kilkenny, myself and my brother roared and jeered at the Mass-going faithful whom we were now depriving of a day out.

"You wouldn't bate snow off a rope," he clichéd.

My father admonished him for jeering. Martin and Tommy Murphy laughed. Tommy Duffin said to "lave" him alone, "Hadn't we to listen to those hoors for long enough." Tommy Whitney said, "You can't bate breedin'," and they all laughed and joked.

It was my first time in Dublin. We went up O'Connell Street and I saw the GPO where the 1916 Rising took place and Nelson's Pillar. What really took my fancy were the double-decker buses. They looked as if they could topple over when they rounded the bends.

I saw Findlater's church and I was told it had more to do with business than religion. I knew it was not Catholic. It looked very ornate though and the fumes of the passing traffic had blackened it in places. I never saw such a mass of people. I held on to my father's coatbelt for dear life. Sometimes the crowd pushed and, being smaller, my face was shoved against peoples backs or arms. I bore it manfully, if uncomfortably.

We got in on the sideline eventually in front of the long stand. Perfect! There were hawkers with wicker baskets going through the crowd calling out "apples, oranges now or chocolates." Murphy shouted at one fellow "Hey boss, how much are the sixpenny bars of chocolate?" and laughed.

The streetwise Dubliner did him and said, "Mind now, you don't peel these like a banana!" Murphy was flummoxed. His confidence went and his own crowd involuntarily laughed at the display of wit.

The Artane Boys' Band played "Clare's Dragoons." I had no interest in the minor match, but when the Archbishop of Cashel threw in the ball after singing "Faith of Our Fathers" and the National Anthem, then the place erupted. I had never heard such a cacophonous explosion. Almost ninety thousand estimated fanatics, stripped of pretensions, vented their naked frenzied anxiety, ferocious and focused for vengeance and victory. Cork had robbed us in 1954; not today, no sirree – no way – not today!

Early on in play, Wexford scored a point and we roared, clenching our fists as we punched the air. Almost immediately, Padge Kehoe scored a goal for Wexford. I thought the air would rent in two. We leaped and roared. My father was delighted, but kept saying, "It's early days yet."

He was right. Cork scored a point, so did we; and then we scored another, so did Cork. The hoors! After Wexford attacked the next time, backs and forwards pulled with their hurleys, left, right and centre. Blood was streaming down Nicky Rackard's face. A Cork player went down injured. The ball was gone out wide. Rackard was claiming the ball had been assisted out by the Cork back. A sub was on for the injured Cork player.

"That's the stuff for those fellas," my father said with merciless partisan approval. "We're taking it long enough."

Fr. Williams laughed. Peter smiled but told my father to take it "aisey." Wexford began to steal away from them. Point after point went over for Wexford. We were cruising and clear ahead by four points at half time.

Tommy Murphy, who had been particularly quiet, got up and went to the toilet. My father told Tommy Duffin to go after him. A few minutes later, Tommy Murphy was back on his own, ashen faced. My father noticed him and asked whether he was okay, had he gone to the lav?

"I did John, but I was afraid to go. There was a whole hape a' big Cork fellas down there, and they had 'mickies' as big as pike handles and I was afraid to take out me own."

My father went into convulsions of laughter.

"This fella came up to me and says, 'Hello, I'm Jack Cody from

Duncannon, don't you know me Tommy? 'I do in me arse, 'sez I, 'an' I don't want to know you aither'."

Tommy was suspended between fear and desire. Out of his environment his independence departed. He was in his mid-sixties and what I had not realised was that this was the first day in his life he had left Wexford. It was difficult to believe the transformation that had taken place. The oracle of wit was now the epitome of the lost sheep. He ate his sandwiches silently in the concealed nervous manner of a grazing, suspicious rabbit, occasionally looking up. His interest in the match was reduced to observer, the excitement did not involve him. His preoccupation was expressed in his repeated enquiries to know what time it was. He was beginning to get on Tommy Duffin's nerves.

At the start of the second half, we were ecstatic. Wexford resumed their form sending over point after glorious point. This would be the greatest day of my life. (Oh God! Please, God! Please be on our side!) The chocolate Tommy Duffin had bought for me at half-time was beginning to melt in my pocket. I took it out and covered it with my hankie. The whistle was blown for a free.

"You blind hoor," roared my father. Peter was up and so was Fr. Williams. Tommy Murphy was the only one sitting. The Cork crowd shouted, "Sit down, sit down" and "Play the ref." My father was raging. A little Cork fellow in front was jeering. Ring took the twenty-one-yards free and stuck it in the net. We were stunned. The little Cork lad was up, prancing around again and shouting, "Up the Wizard o' Cloyne. Up the Rebels."

We could hardly look. Still, we were four points ahead. They scored two points; we scored one and then Paddy Barry of Cork scored the equalising goal. We were stomached. The little fellow from Cork was standing on his seat roaring back at us and when the noise dropped he jibed, "You can't bate the bacon and cabbage."

Too much for my father, he shouted back, "Faith an' they must 've fed you on the graisey water."

It flattened him, but not as much as the guffaws from our quarters.

"Take your batin'," he roared.

Ring had the ball again. He raced forward and hand-passed a point for the lead. Padge Kehoe got one back. Barry got one for Cork. Rackard caught the ball in front of their goal – he lashed – we rose – it must have stripped the paint from the post – it went wide. We groaned and sat down in dread and despair. Wexford kept at them – they got a point and another and then Ring got the ball. What happened after that is history. It has been told and retold. At point blank range, Ring blasted for goal and victory three minutes from time. The impossible happened. Arty Foley, the Wexford goalman, caught the rocket with a felt hand, cleared his lines and Nicky Rackard stuck it in the net at the far Cork end for Wexford. The explosion of excitement was frightening. The ground shook, the sun vibrated. My brother and myself hugged and leaped. Fr. Williams kissed a woman beside him. Peter stood on his seat both arms waving.

"What do you think now?" Fr. Williams shouted to my father.

"I think our ass is in foal," he laughed.

Two more points were added for Wexford before Jim English came into the stand to get the cup for Wexford. Our Bishop, Dr. Staunton was there. Seamus Greene, Canon Harpur, the GAA President, the President of Ireland, the Taoiseach, the Cabinet, the Hierarchy and ourselves – the Leacys – all wrapped up in a roly-poly of molten lava and falling ash exploded from the caverns of historical deprivation to ascend the highest peaks of attainment and receive the laurels and acclamation that justice bestows on the righteous and victorious. It was the greatest day of my life. Our heroes indeed were champions. Bonfires would blaze from Bunclody to Ballyhack. A beacon to those who were blessed and baptised in the faith and tradition of fighting to the last puck of the ball, and trusting in God's mercy to offset the ill effects of blind referees and ignorant bostoons of bogmen. We whooped like yahoos, until we were hoarse and could yell no more. The tension over, our strength relaxed, we retreated home in the failing light and the candle-lit amber of the weak headlights of our Austin of England stationwagon.

For ages afterwards the exploits of the hurling heroes were recalled. In the immediate aftermath, and in the flush of victory, boundaries were lowered in a type of genuflection to greatness. Bishop Staunton conferred on them the status of paragons. At the victory banquet he congratulated them not alone on their victory in the contest, but also on the spirit in which they had played the game which had brought honour to the County and to the Association, which was doing so much good for our country and youth. The setting was Killiney Castle, a metaphor in itself. Where else would princes dine except in a castle. This was appropriate to the achievement, a translation of the Christian virtue "as you sow, so shall you reap." The metaphysical mingled with temporal success was a heady potion.

Some suggested the hand of God was at work in the manner in which victory was attained. The more wicked and disrespectful observed with acute astuteness that it might have had more to do with the hand of Arty Foley! That evening very few could tell the difference. The chivalry exemplified by the legendary Ring rushing in to shake the Wexford goalman's hand after he had saved a magnificent shot and the magnanimous response of the Wexford team in chairing the same Cork man from the pitch when the game was over was the stuff of legend.

A song was composed about "Nicky Rackard" to the air of the popular American ballad "Davy Crocket." My father thought it unfair to immortalise him before his death. The pedestal, he felt, was being raised far too high for any one man to stay on.

The nuns took little active interest in sport. Their reaction, or rather lack of it, was a frustration to the exuberance of their scholars. However, when Fr. Williams came in for Catechism, it was different, he forgot religion entirely and made myself and Larkin relay what had happened at the match to the whole school. Larkin had gone on the train with his father and some others.

We vied with each other to relate each dramatic happening after another. "Tell them about the save," he encouraged and then, "Tell them about Rackard's goal," we outdid each other. Everyone entered into it. He laughed and joked having aroused our passions. The nuns acknowledged the priest's enthusiasm. What remained with them, however, had no great depth. It was a continuation of the '98 spirit, but it neither replaced nor enlarged it. This dry approach almost devalued the experience of the victory for me. Everything was so friggin' virtuous. At lunch time we played football every day. Nuns felt hurling was too dangerous. The adrenaline recharged by the priest was potent. Although it was football we were playing at lunchtime each "man" on the field was one of the hurling heroes of the day before. Padge Kehoe's goal was rescored with the aid of ageing sandal and a soft-pumped weary football. Each time a save was made, it was Arty Foley's save and the challenge was whether a goal at the other end could be immediately scored by another "Nicky Rackard."

Sweating and panting we reluctantly resumed our desks at the bell. The secret to life was success. We felt it without knowing it. Success was attained by effort. Everything was earned. Winning the County Football Championship was great. Winning the All-Ireland Hurling Senior Final was the greatest feeling known to man. By these means would we live successful lives; consequently, we would have happy lives; and in this manner we would save our unworthy souls under the direction and guidance of those who knew.

After school, Larkin told me about the train journey. The way Thomas Whitney and Agnes Maher were caught courtin' in a dark corner between the carriages on the way home; how they put whiskey in the "priest" Doyle's orange and made him sick; and the way Hiawatha got merry and sang "Oft in the stilly night" and started crying; and how two Cork fellas were so drunk they got on the Wexford train home by mistake.

☙ ❧

After a week or so, the hullabaloo died down and the routine of home, Mass and school took over once more. Next year was Confirmation year. More than particular attention would be given to religion. Answers to questions in the Catechism had to be learned off by heart.

"What was the Real Presence?"

"What was meant by transubstantiation?"

We were instructed on the heretic Martin Luther and how he had nailed his articles of religion to the door of Wittenberg Cathedral, and how Henry the Eighth had eventually espoused his heresy to facilitate his own lust and greed for power.

When she was in good humour, Sr. Ignatius would tell spellbinding stories about the Devil; how certain Irish girls who lapsed in their prayers when they went to England became possessed; how Communism was the way of the Anti-Christ; and how we should pray for the conversion of Russia and Black Pagan Africa. She told of the church's Mission to many parts of the World and how, ultimately, the Catholic Church was being, and would be acknowledged as, the only One True Church of Christ. There was only one fold. This was because it had the four marks, it was One, Holy, Catholic and Apostolic. If she was in the humour, we might enter into a type of quizzical pursuit with her. She might on occasion concede to some other religion, two of the true marks or, at a push, three, but there was no way was she ever going to concede on the fourth. The third point, Catholic, was a very difficult one to budge her on. How could you say any of the other religions were Catholic without seeming to concede the argument to start with. But when she teased us with an explanation that "Catholic" meant "universal" this opened up possibilities. If a universal church could be identified as being within this concept, like a magician pulling a rabbit out of a hat, she would show how one of the other three marks were absent.

The challenge of the argument used to intrigue me and like a moth to the light I followed her lure. Larkin berated me for being such an eejit: "Sure you couldn't win with that wan. Are you a fool or wha'?" If there was only one fold there was also only one shepherd, and she was carrying the crook. Larkin, however, had his own views on who his shepherd was.

Yet, she kept our interest and attention with stories of how the Sacred Host had reacted to individual indiscretions over the centuries. She had one story about how the Host bled when shot through its centre in the course of Consecration by a Pagan sniper in a Communist country where they were repressing the Catholic religion. Another story told how after shooting the Host, the assassin, when leaving the church left red blood footprints on the aisle in his sacrilegious wake as he departed. The power of God was manifest in His clergy, and neither He nor they were to be disrespected, except at the risk of dire and grave personal consequence. The public house in a neighbouring parish that left its premises open during Mass on a Sunday were denounced from the pulpit by the priest. He cursed them and said the grass would grow green outside their door. Within twelve months yellow buchalans were sprouting from the base of the door jam, whose flaky paint was cracking in the winter sun. The fact that in the course of the sermon he denounced any would-be patrons as heretics and sinners without a hope of salvation probably assisted with the prophecy and the curse. The real shepherd would protect the fold.

During the last century in the parish of Coleman, Fr. David O'Hanlon

Walsh was agitating with Canon Doyle and others for Agrarian reform for the cottiers and labourers. Some of the more substantial Catholic farmers took exception to what they perceived as a threat to their position. Though Catholics themselves, they secured and bolted the chapel door at Toberboy against him. For three Sundays he attended and said the rosary with the Faithful poor outside the doors of the locked church. On the last Sunday, he rose from his knees and cursed:

"The Clohessys to the hills from the streets of Coleman;
the high seas for Jim Barry in the dead of the night;
and the roar of damnation eternal from the lips of Laurence
Growther."

These were the hands that had secured the doors against the cleric. Within twelve months, Laurence Growther's coat got caught in a mill wheel and he was slowly crushed to an agonising death. The miller and his son succeeded in stopping the mill-wheel for a few minutes only to trap him underneath screaming before crushing the poor unfortunate to death. The year after that, Jem Barry's crops failed for the second year and under cover of darkness he fled his debtors by horse to Waterford and Steam Packet to Liverpool. The same year the Clohessys put their store for auction and moved to Sliabh Coillte in an effort to relieve their father's "galloping consumption." Sliabh Coillte was the highest point in our district, and the most windswept and barren.

I remember my father telling how "the Dummy Ferguson" went to Confession to Fr. Ned Doyle one time. The mute handed in his written confession on a sheet of paper and when the priest handed it back after Absolution, the writing had disappeared from the note.

"They have the power alright," people said. My father had an instinct for draiocht, but if he had, it was tempered with the Rebels dislike of clerical authoritarianism. On one occasion he told how he was refused Absolution in Waterford and when the priest asked him what he would do then, my father matter of factly replied that he would go and get it at home – and did!

 ❦

That winter, a lot of old people died. Between the first day of November 1956 and the last day of February 1957, over fifty people had died and were buried. Myself and Larkin served all their funerals and when we noticed the volume, we began to keep count to see whether a record would be broken.

The first of these funerals I will never forget – nor the last one! Mrs. Jones was 89 years old when she died. She was bedridden for some time as a result of a weak heart. For a finish, she had some type of haemorrhage in the middle of the night. When I arrived to serve Mass the next morning, her son was standing around the corner of the church tower. It was dark when I was walking past but when he moved from the shadow and spoke, I got a start.

"Tell the priest me mother is dead and to pray for her at Mass."

I got such a fright I felt like telling him what to do with himself and his mother. They were very old and furtive people. Normally the priest would have been sent for on the point of expiry, but not in this case, since she was "ould an' they all knew she was dyin'." She had Holy Communion every day almost, on the priest's sick visit, in any event.

That night my mother was going to the wake and since I had never been to one my curiosity was aroused. I was seven weeks after my thirteenth birthday and had been wearing long trousers since the winter had started. I wanted to go. My father's instinct was to resist, but my mother caved in.

I walked directly behind my mother into the wake room. She was wearing a black coat. Standing in front of me, as she was, I could see nothing. She paused in prayer and blessed herself and then immediately knelt to the floor revealing the corpse with a half-blackened face from internal bleeding, the result of her terminal trauma. Her countenance was of a dark death, dismal and awful. I was shocked, transfixed. I could not urge my gaze away nor could I dare to look. My mother turned and touched me, indicating I should kneel. I responded and was momentarily earthed. I looked away from the coffin to the eight legs of the four men sitting on the bench to my left at the wall.

The pain in me was numbing. I felt slightly faint. It was my first experience of the ruthlessness of nature. My innocence was violated – my soul was raped by a female corpse. That night as I went to bed, all my demons had a picnic. Ould Nick and Frankenstein had Mrs. Jones for a houseguest and there she remained for many years.

Dr. Paxo was at the funeral with Hiawatha and they had both called into our house afterwards. I was sent to bed, the two younger ones already asleep. I was on my own. Everywhere there were devouring demons of gigantic proportions. The upstairs of our house had three rooms and a landing. Because of the cost of electricity there was an empty light socket dangling from the dark ceiling in our room. In addition to the waste of electricity, my father believed we would spend the night reading comics "and not be worth a curse in the morning." I shared a room with my two brothers who were fast asleep. I sat in the light of the landing on the window box. I was beginning to shake and shiver. My pyjamas were located under the corner of the eiderdown on my bed. The distance from the end of the landing light to the edge of my bed was six feet. It was like six miles. I gathered my courage to try to run from the security of the light through the evil darkness to retrieve my night-clothes and return to my refuge. My courage failed me. I stole down the stairs to be near some life. I sat on the step. The hall door suddenly opened and in walked Fr. Williams from the Wake. He saw me.

"Not gone to bed yet?" he enquired.

"Just going," I lied.

"Funeral tomorrow – High Mass – you'll be on the thurible."

Later that night, Peter came in and I was caught on the stairs still dressed. My mother was despatched to attend to me amid great noddings of my father's head. "I knew I should not have brought you," she remonstrated as she waited for me to get into bed. As soon as she was gone I covered my head with the clothes, knowing I would hate the dark and going to bed for the rest of my life.

Mrs. Jones' coffin was draped with the black covering provided for that purpose. Larkin and I had placed the six black stands with their six black shields (bearing the three gold initials IHS) and their six tall white candles around the catafalque which held her coffin. Larkin was to carry the cross and Michael Thorpey assisted me with the incense boat. Doyle and Byrne served the mass. While the mass was being sung, I reddened the charcoal by igniting and fanning it with flame and breath alternatively. I had done it many times for benediction. The sacristy door had to be left open for the housekeeper, Mae, and her claustrophobic friend.

Mrs. Jones was mother to a farmer, a fisherman and a clerk who worked for CIE in Waterford. The girls all married well, it was said, apart from Stasia who remained a spinster having stayed at home to mind "Mamma." They had a shop and between that, mamma and the Fine Gael Party she preserved an active, narrow interest in life.

As Mrs. Jones had been a woman of substance it was a High Mass. While the clergy were were chanting in Latin, chanting the psalms and antiphons of High Office, Larkin and I started guessing what we might get paid. There were about twenty priests in the front of the church in the pews. They were the choir, and distinct and separate from the Celebrant, Deacon and Sub-deacon on the altar. I saw Hiawatha in the Congregation. The singing was awful. The priests in the church wore black soutanes and white surplices. They donned and doffed their birettas with an awkward yet relaxed indifference. They never started all together and the croaking betrayed leather vocal chords, coarse, aged and dry. Some sang with their hands in their cassock pockets, looking about nonchalantly in the manner appropriate to veterans. The awesomeness of the Solemn High Mass was no longer their focus. This was the liturgy and the rite that led the deceased to paradise, a path they had led many times for many people. They were the weary ferry guides across the abyss. Where others feared to venture, they had been and back. They had buried babies barely born, pardoned letchers, thieves and killers. They were the spiritual morticians who embalmed their faithful with the spiritual ointment that would immunise them against the wiles of the Devil and for this the populace was grateful.

"ET LUX PERPETUA LUCEAT EIS" – and Eternal Light would shine, and each would get a share in the High Mass purse and ten shillings from the willing Christians who wished to secure the salvation of the deceased with the priest's signature on the Mass card which would verify the event. This certificate would then be presented to the relatives as the ultimate consolation. Such Masses as the priest could not say would be delegated to missionaries, who would receive the stipend for the Mass. In foreign climes clergymen would offer masses for the dearly departed of some family in Ireland, unprayed for but paid for.

"Dies Irae, dies illa,
Teste David, cum Sibilla"
("Day of wrath and Doom impending,
David's word with Sybil's blending")
chanted the hoary voices in a swirl of incense and heavy-browed latin,

leading the now naked coffin away from its incandescent 65 per cent beeswax amber, flickering beacons into the bowels of decay and decrepitude. The assurance of life hereafter with its accompanying panaplea and all its paraphenalia was intimidating, impressive and important. It provoked misgiving and unease in the laity whilst providing a mystique which was incomprehensible to the unscholared and therefore unquestioned and unanswered. A sense of wonder was created and whilst open-mouthed, were invaded for conversion. The right to Divine knowledge required sacrifice and sanctity and was the preserve of higher beings. Their patronage was available and accessible in all and every form, from charitable alms to cures for ailments, physical, spiritual or temporal. All that was needed was a pure and receptive heart, the courage and grace to ask and the willingness to obey. Obedience required the bending of the neck. The removal of resistance at critical, vulnerable and emotional points in the lives of the people. The church neutered reactions to distress by replacing human expressions and celebrations of lamentation with ritual and religious incantation and ceremony.

We got two pounds from Finbar Jones for our trouble – eight bob a man. I bought 72 bubble-gum golf balls, which were forbidden us, and hid them in a box in an outoffice and told my mother a dirty lie that we got five shillings, or five bob a man. She let me spend a shilling on two bars of chocolate. I was in bubble-gum until nearly Christmas unknown to anyone.

Week in, week out, there was funeral after funeral. High Mass, Low Mass and Black Mass we served. The Low Masses were for people who were low and the High Masses for people who were high. The Black Masses were celebrated on the anniversary. That was the order of things. Mostly, only the priest got paid for the Low Masses. The coffins were poorer and very highly varnished, unlike the smooth matt finish of the paler more substantial variety at the High Masses.

I dreaded evening funeral arrivals at the church, when Larkin might be off for the evening somewhere with his father. I had to wait until the last person had left the church before walking down the centre aisle to the front door of the church to bolt it, turn off the lights, extinguish the large coffin side candles and retreat heart thumping to bang the sacristy door shut tight and secure. The expansion and contraction of church furniture and joists was always loudest when the congregation had departed. Inevitably, I imagined a hinged creaking coffin lid opening or an internal scratching by some misdiagnosed unfortunate, trying to claw its suffocating escape.

Each funeral brought visitors to our home because of its convenience to the church, apart from anything else. Such visitations brought their own atmosphere and subjects generally commenced with references to the deceased.

"Not a bad poor hoor."

"Poor Liza." (The widow.) "Didn't she look awful?"

"Still, time and patience 'ud take a snail to Jerusalem."

"God be good to him."

"Aye indeed."

"Jays, I was only after saying ..." and the story that sprung to mind at the time of the news of the demise would be told and retold until it was acknowledged that his departure was fact and his life mattered enough to be worthy of the memory. The community listened patiently to whatever aspect impressed, and then made tea.

In the late winter of 1956 the price of fowl did not improve coming up to the winter. I was sure "Ignatius" was for the chop, but he escaped with his neck. "Ignatius" would have to earn his keep for another while.

That Christmas I got a present of my last toy. It was an air rifle which propelled one inch diameter hollow hard red plastic balls. The gun was nearly four feet long and was plastic. It was called a "Frontiers-man" after the style of weapons of the early American settlers. The balls were stuffed through a rubber flange at the top of the gleaming steel barrel. There was a bolt to retract, in the eighteenth century mode, to compress the air preparatory to discharge.

My brother got a present of an air rifle which had lead pellets. It also fired very small stones. In his absence, unknown to him, I borrowed it one day. I made my younger brother hold a straw between forefinger and thumb in order to test a comic book theory. Kit Carson had severed the moorings of a rope bridge with rifle shots to cut off a band of marauding Redskins. Proportionately, I felt a pellet should sever a straw. I never fully answered the question, because when I fired the pellet, it did not hit the straw but it lodged neatly in the pulp of my younger brother's finger. It struck him just in front of the nail. This was something I did not discover until considerably later, because at the time of the incident he ran in buck-jumps and yelps into my mother. Having removed the stone and calmed him down and bandaged him, she dealt with me. I was sent to bed – I was too big to be slapped.

Shortly after this, I noticed she was going to the doctor a lot. Early in 1957 she went into hospital. My father looked very grave and he was not telling many funny stories now. I was sent to my uncle's where there were other children. He was my mother's brother. Fr. Williams called for me every morning to serve Mass. 1956 was left behind. I would start boarding school in September 1957. This would be a big year, I was sure.

ᘓ6ᘓ

Iníon, Coinín and the Blind Ould Hoor

1957 started with political turbulence. The IRA attacked an RUC barracks and two of their members were killed. *The Free Press* carried a short report of the incident the following week. One of the fatally injured was from Limerick. An account of the note he had left for his mother was reported in the daily papers. They also reported he was a member of the Legion of Mary. The IRA were recommencing their campaign to retake the Six Counties from the Protestant-planted Loyalists' control and drive out the British once and for all. Some were for them, some against. This division was reflected in the Coalition Cabinet and Clann na Poblachta, one of the smaller parties, indicated their intention to withdraw support. John A. Costello advised the President, who dissolved the Dáil, and an election was called.

The shop became a debating ground for Fianna Fáil protagonists. The Fine Gael cohort knew to hold their whisht in certain locations, and this was one. Some of them liked to provoke and the deep wounds of the Civil War of 1922 would be irritated once more.

Up to 1949 Fianna Fáil and 'Dev' had been in power for sixteen years. Since then, they had managed only two and a half years. This time, however, there would be no mistake. They had two big issues. Coalitions did not work and led to political instability and secondly the credit squeeze imposed by the Government had stunted growth and kept the small man down. The Six Counties issue was submerged with Fianna Fáil asserting it would not support private armies on any side of the political spectrum.

Every Sunday after mass there would be a political orator on a trailer, stand or some type of platform to appeal to voters. Each party claimed that their cause was in the National interest.

Peter supplied us with blotting paper for school which had glossy photographs of the three Fianna Fáil Candidates for the Constituency of Wexford complete with embossed slogan. Thorpey went around in school with a badge which said FG and we jeered him that it meant "Friggin' Gutless" because, we maintained, they would not fight the British and caused the Civil War. Most of the school supported Fianna Fáil.

One Saturday night, a Fianna Fáil Cumann meeting was called for Coleman. Peter was there. Dr. Ryan was coming. Afterwards they called to our house for tea. Ryan would stay the night with Peter and canvass the area over the next few days. The Register of Electors had been marked, remarked and notes added. Everyone in every townland was considered.

I sat on my usual perch on the stairs taking it all in, or at least as much as I was able. My father was telling Dr. Ryan they would have to come out much stronger on the credit squeeze – the people were fed up with hard times. People found it hard to get loans and that meant they could buy very little – at least so I believed. I more easily understood about the Border. My father insisted that the only way the British would ever go out of there would be in coffins.

"Wasn't it the same down here? Wasn't it the same everywhere? I never heard tell a' the British leaving anywhere because o' the 'cowld or the haet.'"

Ryan would not be drawn, but listened and listened.

"How is the Missus?" Ryan asked.

"Still going for tests," my father replied.

Because it was Saturday and since my father would not be working on Sunday I was taken down from my uncle's, after the Fianna Fáil meeting, to spend the night at home. I made the tea for my father and his guests and Dr. Ryan told me I was "a right man." "Make him join the clergy," he advised my father, and they all laughed, just before I left for bed. When guests arrived, I departed shortly afterwards in order to remove the inhibition which my presence would impose on the adults' conversation. My absence would allow them to speak more easily and I could learn all the more. I knew, however, that most adults preferred children would not be seen either, particularly when it came to exchanging the news that shocked. My father seldom commented on gossip and used berate my mother on occasions for believing stories from "such as that feckin' eejit." Duly subdued she would impatiently but resignedly accept the admonition by saying, "Very well, then, but we'll see" and she would continue darning or knitting and he would respond by reading the paper or putting coal in the cooker. A few of the Fianna Fáil Cumann had come home with my father, including Matt Larkin, Michael's father, Jim Byrne and Pat Shanks. When the Shadow Minister left with Peter to get some sleep, the residue fell to considering the register in more personalised detail than even the Cumann Meeting would allow. Pat Shanks said, "I think the Browne wan is wavering, whatever you do, don't let Francie Cummins canvass over there."

Mrs. Browne had previously voted for Fine Gael but because she had been badly affected financially by the poor price of poultry, my father had been "working on her" when she called to the shop for the last while. Francie Cummins' dog reputedly had worried her sheep the previous week – though he flatly denied it – and they had words on the road, she from her bike, whilst he continued driving his three cows home.

"Begog ma'am," he said, "my dog isn't that hungry or cowld' that he'd go to a Blueshirt to aither feed or exercise himself chasin' yer ould wethers!"

They guffawed at the notion of the prim widow being even loosely associated with anything as overtly sexual as a castrated ram.

"Faith," said McGrath, "I was coming down from Confessions last night and who was wheezing and puffing his two walking sticks in front of me only Leonard Black."

Black had been gassed in the trenches in the Great War and as a consequence had an airways disability.

"He turned an' he says to me, 'I suppose you'll be heading off to the Six Counties with your Smith and Wessen one of these days to frighten the British home'."

Shanks was cleaning his glasses.

"I towld the ould bollix 'twas a wonder he didn't go with the hoors when they were l'avin' here."

He put his glasses back on. They laughed and laughed and eventually went back to the pink register, lane by lane, house by house. All the Protestants were ignored. No point in flogging a dead horse.

Before the election day arrived, my mother was allowed home from hospital, but she would have to go back within a fortnight for tests. She looked tired and drawn. Her hair had a lot more grey in it now. She was spirited though and good humoured and went to Mass every morning.

In school, Sr. Ignatius was back to her old tricks. She took advantage of the election fever to hold a political debate. The motion was simple and straightforward: "Fianna Fáil would make the best Government." I was put in charge of one team and Thorpey the other. We were given one night to prepare. Consistent with the perverted twist she put on things, myself and my team mates, all Fianna Fáil protagonists, were appointed to oppose the motion. Initially, we had been looking forward to it. When we realised we would be handing each other sticks to beat one another with later, we were less enthusiastic. The mistress of dilemma had scored again.

My mother advised me to simply admit the arguments of the proposer. I was wise enough to know a technical compliance would attract a substantive response. I entered into the debate in the same harried state that one might cross a field with a bull in it. She deliberately interpreted my animated arguments as conviction and complimented me on how convincing I was. For days afterwards, whenever a teacher, priest or any adult would arrive in the room, she would recount how I nearly came to blows in the debate in defence of Fine Gael. I nearly puked. Thorpey was equally unenthusiastic. Larkin told Thorpey it was all the same which side of the debate he got, he still "talked through his arse." That same evening they fought. Larkin hit him a box in the puss and when the blood appeared the row was over. Thorpey went home crying. It was the first time I had seen anyone being hit in the face, and it both shocked and frightened me. We all told Larkin he would be in for it now when the Sergeant would hear. He started it," said Larkin, "he called Dev a blind ould hoor."

The following day when I saw a big uniformed Civic Guard walk to the door of our house and ring the bell, I felt my bowels wanted to shift.

"I would like to speak to Jack in the presence of his parents," he told my mother. "A matter to do with the law."

My mother was beside herself with anxiety. What trouble had I been up to now? She could not let me out of her sight for five minutes. I had her worn out. What would my father think, and in the middle of an election too. I sang dumb. When Sergeant Thorpey arrived back at 7 pm he was taken by my mother to what, as I said before, she called "the parlour" and my father "the front room." My father joined him and after a quarter of an hour or so I heard the door open. My belly sank. The outside door opened and the Sergeant said, "Well goodnight then." My father said simply "Goodnight." My heart rose, but only a little.

When he came into the kitchen he put some coal in the cooker and asked my mother to put my two younger brothers to bed and to leave the washing up. He would finish it later. I was not sure if he was upset, yet he appeared to be calm.

"Did Michael Larkin break into the Protestant church?" he asked.

"No," I said.

"Are you sure?"

"Yes."

"Because he was seen there you know."

"I know."

"How do you know?"

I paused

"He said so."

"Did he tell you he didn't break into it as well?"

"No."

"Well how do you know?"

He was intent on finding out and was getting impatient. I could feel the tears welling up inside me. I knew I was going to be such a disappointment to him.

"Well?" he waited.

I started to bawl.

"Don't be crying, come here," he said. He was sitting down and put his hand around my waist to reassure me. "There is no one going to do you any harm. I won't let them. Now please tell me what happened."

I told him I was with Larkin when we went in out of the rain and the door had been open and that he had been discovered by Thomas Whitney and Agnes Maher, but I had stayed hidden.

"That's all I wanted to know," he said.

It was as if once the truth had been revealed to him, he needed no more. I did not tell him about Mel and the window.

The following day I told Larkin what happened. He knew who had squealed.

"Thorpey! Well the little bollix, I'll kick his arse up his neck."

"You're in trouble enough," I advised. We gave him a wide berth and he us. He did not play football for a couple of weeks after that because he knew well enough what would happen.

A few days later the school was closed to allow the election take place. My father brought me with him to put up posters and run errands. Larkin was to come later after he had seen to his father's cows.

The polling station opened at 9 o'clock in the morning and my father had gone to Ballystraw and was back marking the voting paper for Will Devereux, who was "voting blind." I was outside at the big table which Fianna Fáil had covered with posters. There were two timber laths nailed to hardboard, smothered with more posters than any of the others parties, proclaiming the party's slogan and candidates. They were stuck on with sellotape and thumb tacks and flapped briskly in the fine chilly air.

In the polling station the meticulous-minded members of the various parties jealously guarded their interests by pencilling the register with reminders of times to collect individual supporters while keeping a weather eye on the names of deceased opposition supporters not yet removed from the list of voters lest impersonation take place.

My father came out having assisted his voter and was off to get "the dummy" Chapman. He used to attend the shop, and although he did not have sign language, he could communicate with him where others were confused or embarrassed.

Pat Shanks and Matt Larkin arrived with more Fianna Fáil posters and waited. My father told them "the Jones wan" was inside for Fine Gael and Pat McDonald for Labour. Patsy Prendergast arrived with his battered up Ford Prefect festooned with Fine Gael posters, like a circus car. He had a loud speaker on the top and was broad casting to vote for Esmonde and the other Fine Gael hopefuls. Shanks looked at the car while Prendergast was passing in and sardonically enquired of him,

"You wouldn't be travelling for Duffy's Circus be any chance?"

This was supposedly a clever reference to the famous circus family and the more infamous Fine Gael General O'Duffy of the Blueshirt Fascist in the 30s. Prendergast paused,

"No," he said, "Unlike you fellows, I don't think we have clowns enough."

"T'ed be hard for yiz, to find clowns that foolish." (Guffaws.)

The stage was being set for a humdinger of an election in Coleman. Sergeant Thorpey arrived about the same time as the school-master from Ballyhack, Tom Byrne, who would represent Fine Gael as a personating agent outside the booths. He had a few Fine Gael posters and there was only one Labour poster.

My father arrived back about half past nine with the mute just as Sergeant Thorpey was ignoring his way past Larkin and Tom Byrne. My father took stock of Prendergast's colourful car as he came up to the polling station and said, nodding at the car rustling of breezy posters, "You'd want to mind t'wouldn't blow away in the wind." The men laughed heartily. When my father went into the room an argument arose. The first person out was Mary Jones, she was red in the face; she was followed by Prendergast who was telling her to cool down. Shortly afterwards an uncomfortable Sergeant Thorpey walked towards the car. Prendergast looked at him, "You'd want to start waking up," he said and drove off.

The Sergeant was blushing. When Peter pulled up in his Volkswagen, Thorpey quickened his pace away from the scene. Peter came to the Fianna Fáil table as my father emerged with his two voters.

"What happened?" asked Shanks. We were all curious.

"That gobshite of a Jones wan objected to me voting for the 'dummies' because they didn't need assistance and they were well able to write, an' I had been there already today to vote for somebody else."

"Well?" said Shanks.

"That big gobshite of a Thorpey said she had a point, and I ought to leave the voter alone, in accordance with the electoral law."

"Well?" said Larkin.

My father had asked the dummy if he could write. When he indicated he was unable my father rounded on Thorpey.

" 'T'would match you better,' says I, 'to go out and summons the owner of that car with the posters. There's no tax on it for the last year and a half – and if you want to uphold the law, that's the place to start'."

Peter shook his head.

"What did he say?" asked Shanks, warming to it.

"He never said a word," said my father. "What could he say? He damn near shit himself and so did Prendergast. They nearly got stuck in the door in their hurry to get out."

"Did they vote?" asked Shanks, keeping his eye to the practicalities.

"Wan more for the doctor," beamed my father.

Mrs. Jones came back with a book under her arm and a dark frown. The book was prominently displayed, and read "Canvassers Manual." The men went quiet as she was passing in. She went in through the door and closed it and immediately reopened it. She looked at the men and nodded at all the Fianna Fáil posters.

"National purse minders indeed – a fine lot of monies worth there gone to waste – I ask you?"

Before she could shut the door, Shanks answered "I dare say there's not a whole lot of it out of your pocket."

She disappeared.

"That's the stuff for that ould wan – feckin' ould bitch looking for trouble," said my father.

"I'd better get out of here," said Peter laughing, "before I end up in jail."

Talk continued after he had gone.

"A good start's half the battle," said Larkin.

"There's only wan language that crowd understands," said my father, "Put 'em up the lane an' the dog after 'em."

It was the opinion if you scratched a Fine Gaeler, you'd get a Blueshirt, a Unionist or a Protestant; if you scratched a Fianna Fáiler you'd get an IRA man at heart.

The tide of voters ebbed and flowed all day and the tensions decreased as the day wore on. That night Peter called down and I was allowed to stay up longer than usual as acknowledgement of my involvement. After the conjectures had finished, the tea was drained. They got tired of politics and turned to local gossip. My father had been speaking to Sean Hanlon who said the Canon and Elisha had fairly strong words about why her children had not started school, and apparently "the man up above" – a reference to Fr. Williams – was now in on the act. At this point my father gave me that look that indicated I should say goodnight.

Outside, I waited, but they whispered. I moved up the stairs sufficient to give the impression I had gone. I came back down again when their voices raised a little. They mentioned something about Easter being the limit. It seemed the Hanlon children would have to start school under the Catholic regime, management of Fr. Williams.

Having rescued my pyjamas from under the eiderdown, I undressed and without creaking the stairs I stole back down to the door.

"You'd want to be awful careful with him," I heard Peter say. They were talking about the priest.

"Do you remember that time with the chap's objection – do you remember – Jack's team – that time?"

"I do."

"And he was saying for you not to approach Greene because it would compromise him as chairman of the investigating committee."

"I do."

"Well he didn't approach him himself – but he got his message to him!"

"Go to God! Who?"

"I can't say out loud but he 's a member of ..." he trailed off.

"Fianna Fáil?"

"No!" he replied. "He's a great friend of the Bishop and is involved…" And just as he was giving his answer my mother turned on the tap at the back kitchen. When the noise subsided they were talking about Thorpey and Larkin. I had missed the best part.

"A bad hoor that fellow," my father volunteered.

"Oh a dangerous man!" Peter concurred.

Fianna Fáil won the election handsomely. My father was delighted. Three Fianna Fáil TDs were elected from Wexford. When the radio announced that Fianna Fáil now had seventy-seven seats the number assumed a mystical characteristic. Seventy-seven Republicans had been shot by the Free Staters in the Civil War. It was as if the number came back to haunt them and taunt them.

Just when matters appeared to be right, they went wrong again. Three days after the election, my mother went back into hospital. A few days later again a great tragedy struck Coleman when a fishing trawler went down drowning three of the crew. Two of them were from the little village. It was just at the start of Lent.

Myself and Larkin and the others of the servers team were back in

action. There had been little rest for us. Those were the fiftieth that year, Larkin remembered. It was sad because they were such young men. I was too young to understand it, but I felt it. The older and more mature cast off their differences when events like this took place and Fianna Fáil and Fine Gael, Protestant and Catholic helped each other and wept together. Inevitably, stories were told of how at the turn of the Century the crew of the "Mexico" were saved and how the lifeboat crew of mixed religions were drowned in the rescue attempts. Or how the "The Alfred D. Snow" was lost because of the reluctance of the master of the life boat to put out. His discredited memory lingers on in a few well-spun lines in a sea shanty of that name.

This was the biggest funeral I had ever seen in my life. The press were there. Dr. Ryan, who was now Minister for Agriculture, was there. One victim's father, Jackie Grennan, was a great Fianna Fáiler. I saw Thomas Whitney Senior and Junior near the front of the church with Hiawatha and Gerry Denn. Gerry was doing a line with Tom Byrne's daughter who was a Protestant. Elisha Hanlon and the Clarkes from the pub. Jim Carley was in the back with Sam Duffin. There were Protestants from other parishes. I could tell by their church manners. They did not know when to sit, kneel and stand, and generally looked a little confused. It was the first time I saw Bishop Staunton. The "priest" Doyle was dressed in soutane and surplice and walked, knelt and sat in the wake of his Lordship. He paraded like a peacock and primed his feathers with obnoxious stilted bows with a studied, stoic reverence in his walk – a cross between a ballerina and someone with a poker stuck up his arse. He never smiled and looked very serious. Both Larkin and myself were quite nervous from fear that we might make mistakes in front of such a large congregation. Fr. Williams told us jokingly that if we misbehaved the Bishop would probably not confirm us. Although we knew he was half joking about the Confirmation, we equally knew he was dead in earnest about misbehaving.

My father closed the shop for the day as a mark of respect and the school was closed. After the funeral, I came home. There were callers and I fulfilled the function of cook, steward and bottle washer and my father spoke to the visitors. It was then I heard him say for the first time my mother was going for a biopsy on the following day. Everyone he met asked him how she was, and though he said it was in God's hands, I knew by him he was more optimistic than confident. I had to ask him what a biopsy was and he told me. I asked him if she was going to be all right and he reassured me that of course she was, but he looked away when he was saying it.

∞ ∞

All the next day my mind wandered and wondered. Ignatius put me in charge of the fire. I had to make sure it was kept lighting and did not fall out on the floor. It was a cold day. She used to let us sit at the fire, six at a time, in turns. Four in front and one at each side. Generally we had to learn something by heart when we were allowed this luxury, but not today.

My uncle called to collect me that evening from school, and I heard him say to the nun there was no news yet. My uncle Seamus had a phone. That night it rang and I knew he was talking to my grandfather, as all of them, including my mother, referred to him as "Dada." I had a room to myself and I stared silently at the open door as I lay in bed listening intently to the voice in the hall at the bottom of the stairs. I heard him say "a tumour" and he repeated it a couple of times. It was in the brain. I had no idea what a tumour was and although I knew that any illness to do with the brain was not good, it was the disbelieving sound in his voice that convinced me she was dying. There was a pause.

"Is there anything at all can be done?"

A short time afterwards he put down the phone. I heard him coming up the stairs. He checked on his own children, my very much younger cousins. Then he came to my door. I had turned to face away towards the window. I lay still. He paused quietly for a moment and went back down into the kitchen. I felt very lonely and a short time afterwards I began to cry silently to myself. I had been told my father had enough on his hands and I ought not bother or upset him. I fell asleep. In the night I awoke with a shout and fell from the bed in a nightmare. I dreamt I was in an earthquake and was falling, falling, falling down into one of the cracks. My aunt turned on the light but I gave her the impression that I had shouted when I had fallen out.

"We'll have to get a bigger bed for you," she said. She tucked me in.

"I'll be telling your father the great man you are."

Heretofore they used always say they would tell my mother the great man I was when she got home.

Next day in school an inspector arrived. She wore a fur coat. She looked familiar but I could not think where I had seen her. She would examine us in Irish. Her name was Iníon Ní Breathnach. We kept calling her sister or "Shiúir" which was the Irish translation. Because of the difficulty we were having she said, "Very well then, call me "Iníon," which literally meant daughter or Miss. She started questions on grammar and immediately got into personal pronouns. It could have been worse – it could have been verbs. She took a shine to me because I was getting my answers right. The examination was oral. She took us out in front of the fire. She asked Larkin a question.

"Cá bhfuil mo cóta?" (Where is my coat?)

"Tá sé orainn," (It is on us) he replied. She looked displeased.

"Aon Duine?" (Anyone?) she invited.

"Tá sé ort," (Its on you) I corrected.

Ó, nach Maith an fear? Tar liom." (Oh isn't he a great man? Come here to me.) When I walked over to where she was sitting, she got up and gave me a hug. She buried my face in her fur-coated bosom. I was taken aback.

"Arís a Sheán, Tá se ..." (Again Jack, It is ...)

"Ort" (On you.)

"Maith an bhuacall!" (Good boy!)

And she stepped forward and hugged me again. I threw a wince at the rest of them, and the stupid girls were all grinning through their books. Larkin was scratching his forehead covering his eyes and I knew he was concealing a smirk. She kept me standing by her and when I answered incorrectly, she told me the right answer. When she repeated the question I then gave her the correct reply, she hugged me again and again.

"Nach bhfuil phóg agat liomsa?" (Do you not have a kiss for me?)

I nearly fainted. She immediately said, "Agat agus 'liomsa' ins an líona-céadhma" ('Your' and 'for me' in the same line'.)

She had been giving an example of the use of personal pronouns in the same sentence. The smell of perfume from her coat was familiar to me, but I could not recall from where, try though I might to remember. I felt ill at ease and embarrassed. I was glad to see her go and I hoped I would never see her again as long as I lived. But I knew that I knew that fur coat from someplace.

After school I asked my uncle if I could go to see my father, but he told me he would probably call around on the way home. Indeed he did and he brought with him a newspaper cone of sweets for myself and my cousins, but I was unable to get to talk to him on my own. I enquired about my two younger brothers. He told me they were fine, but I was secretly hoping he could see how lonely I was.

He told me he was going to see my mother with Fr. Williams tomorrow and to make sure and pray for her as she was going to have a big operation. I wanted to know if I could go to see her on Sunday, at which point my aunt left the room and my father said that we would see. I noticed him place his tongue on his inside upper lip as he looked away, but still I merely wondered in the confused way of early adolescence, guessing, afraid to really ask and even more afraid of being told.

The priest and my father went to Dublin from Mass the next mornng. It was the first time I had seen my father at daily Mass, because the shop opened at the same time as Mass started. People who went daily were pointed out to us as an example to be followed and I regretted that my father could not be included in their number. I knew he was the best man who ever lived, it was just that I was not happy that others might have had the opportunity to think otherwise.

The day passed slowly and the nuns prayed for Jack Leacy's mother, who was having an operation. The girls wanted to know if she was going to have a baby. They used really get to me. Larkin said nothing until Thorpey said, "Is she going to die?" Larkin asked him if one belt in the gob had not been enough for him. It was only then I realised what it must have been like for Larkin. He must have been wondering what it was like to have a mother all these years. He was only three years old when his mother died. And yet I knew he was feeling it deeply, because he could not let it be spoken about. He gave me a gentle puck on the shoulder and said that his father had said it was all right for me to go home with him after school, that he had said it to my father and uncle. I looked forward to that. I could be with the men driving in the cows and watch them being milked.

Immediately after school he brought me to the sand hills. They were the fields adjacent to the dunes which undulated down onto the beach. Here he had set snares to catch rabbits. They were made from fine brass coloured wire, trimmed off with a brown twine and were set on tracks which were regularly run by his quarry. These were obvious to the hunter's eye and Larkin showed me the narrow tracks of ruffled grass and how to set the snare. He took three snares from the cowhouse when we were going and we set them at the most strategic points in his judgement. As we came home through the "Martello field" which was located behind my father's house, we saw two of the Miskellas who lived nearby. One of them was standing in front of a briar that straddled the stone wall of the laneway to the Martello Tower. One of them was standing to the side kicking it. They called us. There was a rabbit in the bush, they said, and they were trying to frighten it out into the older brother's arms. Larkin went to the upper side and kicked and shouted. Out jumped the rabbit. Miskella grabbed its ears and chopped at the back of its neck with the back edge of his right hand. Three strikes and it was dead. They told me they would have stew that night. I was slightly shocked at the earthy reality. I had always regarded rabbits as quiet, fuzzy things. They retracted the lip of the dead animal to reveal two sharp white fangs which they assured me would have been sunk in them if they had not caught it properly. I had seen sheep and cattle killed in the slaughter house by my uncle Peter, but apart from these and rats and birds that I had seen dead on the road, it was the first wild living thing that I had seen being killed, and had assisted in killing.

When we got back to Larkins we helped with the milking of the cows and then we had our tea. We ate nearly a loaf of sliced white bread between the three of us. There was a spicey sausage which was bought in the shops and sliced and was simply called "shop-cooked sausage." It was delicious on the slices of white bread with hot tea and a hunter's appetite. Just after the tea my uncle Francis called and I was taken back. When we returned to his house my father's black Morris Minor car, KI-5334, was parked outside. I saw him at the door going in. He stopped when he was aware of my uncle's car. He was in the porch and was talking to my aunt. I saw her taking out her handkerchief as we walked the short pathway to the porch. I could feel my uncle hesitating about bringing me in the front way. He was saying, "Yes bedad – yes bedad – all home safe anyway. Yes bedad."

My father had stepped into the warm misty porch. He came out again. He beckoned to us. "It's all right, come on. Everything is all right. A real miracle," he said. "Fr. Williams blessed her before she went down and it was gone."

My aunt was still crying saying, "Oh thanks be to God! Oh thanks be to God and his Holy Mother!"

My uncle said it was great news entirely. My father kept telling and retelling how the priest had blessed her and when she was taken down to be X-rayed before the surgery began, the tumour was gone. They x-rayed her upside down and inside out, but there was no sign of it. It was truly a miracle. She was coming home on Sunday, and we could all go for her. I know I must have felt relief, but I cannot really remember. It was as if it had never been intended to happen, or maybe I had simply chosen not to believe it. It was like the false promise of a lie, in the end everyone knew what would really happen. With my father, however, it was different. I remembered seeing that look in his eyes before, the night the priest told the yanks the story of the devil in Loftus Hall. It was a look of wonder and disbelief. He had listened then and believed, he believed now as well. The priests had the power alright. This time, he had been present and he had seen the devil ride into his life on the shoulders of doctors with bad news, then he had seen him ride out again, banished and retreating in the face of Fr. Williams' spiritual confrontation. The priest had cured her and that was that. This was ritual incantation. This was the power of invocation. This was biting at a wincing level. Life and death could be subjected to the dictate of the anointed.

They came home that Sunday and all I can remember of that time now was my father telling her to "take it aisey, for Chris' sake take it aisey." I remember she fainted once in the following week, but it was what my father called "a little lightness in the head."

◌◌◌

During her convalescence, a girl named Kathleen came to help her with the housework. It was about three weeks from Easter. In school we were preparing for the Holy Week ceremonies. Latin hymns were taught and learned by heart, "Lauda Jerusalem," "Pange Lingua" and the "Kyrie Eleison." The litany of the saints was learned and answered in Latin, "Ora pro nobis." Shifts were organised for the Perpetual Adoration of the Blessed Sacrament on Good Friday. A team of servers and acolytes, the pecking order in the procession and choir had to be established. Positions of responsibility would be given to those whom, in the view of the nuns, had merited them. The position had to be earned. On the basis that I had served mass every morning for the previous two years, and since this was my last year, I assumed I would be given the task of thurifer. I had not bargained on Ignatius, however. She assigned the task to Thorpey. Larkin was delegated to carry the large crucifix. The incense boat was carried by Jim Doyle. Down through the ranks she went and I was passed over, even for carrying the candles! Ignatius informed me I would be a member of the choir – a goddam' foot soldier again. This was my last year and I would never have a chance as an officer. My disappointment was great and it reflected in my behaviour. Though I was asked by my mother what was the matter, I wouldn't tell her. Larkin said Ignatius had a twisted mind and she got uncomfortable if people were content or happy.

A week before Palm Sunday, Fr. Williams called to view the progress of the preparations for the ceremonies. We were lined out in the long corridor. It ran the length of the school. I took my place in the black soutanes, the liturgical attire of the male chorister. The girls had to be fitted with veils, blue capes and some had their gym slips revamped. The daily routine used take its toll on the girl's uniforms. The boys wore mufti.

When the priest arrived, he disappeared with Ignatius into the Seniors' room. The classroom doors had six glass panes, but they were covered with opaque cellophane. With the passage of time, the edges of this paper had frayed sufficiently to allow the tail end of the procession a squint-eyed view of the nun taking the roll book from her desk for the priest's examination. They spoke for a while and when he came out he acknowledged the congregated entourage. With the other two nuns, kitting out the girls and Ignatius was fixing a belt on the gymslip of Marjorie Hempenstall.

The priest inspected the troops and when he saw me in the choir his smiling countenance changed. He went to the top without saying a word.

"Who is going to carry the missal?" he asked her.

"I was going to get ..."

"Where's Jack?" he enquired. "Wasn't he serving me the whole year?"

(A Daniel come to judgement!)

"Young Thorpey there looks like a fine young strong lump of a man who could carry a missal under each arm." We all laughed. Thorpey swelled at this acknowledgement of his strength. Thorpey was fat and not in the slightest bit athletic. This seemed like a boost to him, though it was demotion.

"That's a good fellow," the priest patronised.

"Jack Leacy can do the Thurible, he's well used to it."

Ignatius was raging, but she knew her place.

"Very well, Father," she cast her eyes down. Her lips were like thin lines.

When the priest had gone she went back to Marjorie Hempenstall. She had been trying to make a further hole in the attached belt of her uniform. She had a needle which was not a sufficient awl to pierce the tough belt material. She grimaced as she pushed the point. It did not work. Her disgruntled humour was coming through.

"Come here!" she pulled the frightened girl to the hallway and into the top room to the side of where we were standing.

"Take it off," she commanded. The frightened best-looking girl in the school removed her dress in full view of the sniggering tail of the long liturgical queue. She was standing, blushing, in a green knickers. One of the children in the other class who was not involved rang the dinner time handbell. Ignatius was making no progress.

"Oh go to your lunch," she snapped. Robeless and confused, the exposed, undressed victim turned to walk semi-naked amongst the crowd. I noticed her slender shape and the dramatically descending lines of the elastic in the legs of her knickers, smooth and sheer.

"What are you gawking at?" one of her friends asked me. I flustered and cleared. I ran home for my dinner.

⌘⌘

My mind quickly returned to my elevation from the ranks and in animated gasps between fork full of potatoes and parsnip, I recounted my vindication to my mother. Thorpey was now angry. Although he was still "in the cabinet," he was no longer "the Taoiseach." For a day or two afterwards he did not play with us, but contented himself with watching, when he thought we did not see.

On the Friday before Passion Week he arrived in school full of glee. I had arrived in school with my own problems.

"What kept you mister?" Ignatius enquired of me.

"I had to help Fr. Williams get the Tabernacle for the altar of repose, Sister," this was accepted.

On Holy Thursday the Blessed Sacrament would be transferred from the golden-doored marble tabernacle to a veiled and fancily decorated portable timber structure which would be placed on the left-hand side of the Sanctuary. This liturgical metaphor was an age-old tradition. The end of the old and the start of the new.

This Tabernacle was locked away all year and as a consequence, it needed an annual dusting. Because I was supple the priest would send me into the big ground cupboard, an area of the sacristy sheeted off by carpenters to hold religious furniture the crib statues and so on. The door to the cupboard was locked. The curate and the "priest" Doyle were on the altar discussing details about the Palm Sunday procession. If it was a fine day, the traditional outside route would obtain, but if it was not, a different internal version would be required. They went to the gallery to get a birdseye view of the situation. Though the church was connected to the priest's house by means of a corridor, we had been well-lectured by the nuns and by Mae to proceed from the church to the house by means of the external route to the kitchen. In that fashion, respect for the priest's privacy would be observed and no unwarranted or surprising intrusion would occur. I went to the kitchen to see if Mae knew where the keys to the cupboard were.

"Unless he has them with him, they are in the hall stand," she said.

I knew the effort for her to go there was more than she needed. "Stay there and I will check," I said to her.

"No." she said.

"It's alright," I said, "there's nobody about."

This was a reference to the priest. In a moment of weakness her body spoke.

"Very well then, but be quick."

I proceeded quickly to the hallway and it was quite plain nobody was about. As I was checking the hallstand I got the smell. I knew I recognised it vaguely. And then I saw the fur coat of Iníon Ní Breathnach and I suddenly remembered where I had seen her before. No wonder she had seemed familiar to me in school when she examined us in Irish grammar.

The thought of it all came back to me and I fled from the priest's hallway. I had seen Iníon Ní Breathnach in the priest's house previously, when she had stayed overnight as a guest. When I got back to the church, the priest was still in the gallery and I had to wait. When eventually he came down he told me the padlock on the door was not locked. The thought of meeting the schools Inspector bothered me.

∽◦∽

At the 11 o'clock break Thorpey came out with the rest of the boys to the "jacks."

"What's the matter with you?" said Larkin. "Did you get out on the wrong side of the bed or wha'?"

"Ah nothin'," I answered. "Just things."

"Do you feel like mitchin'?" he asked.

"Whisht," I said, looking around, "do you want to get us into trouble?"

"Don't be such a coward – everybody does it goin' to school. I heard them talkin' in our house last night – the way they went off to Whalan's wood and cooked a rabbit."

"Jeez' we'd get into awful trouble if they found out."

"The hol'days are next week. Anyhow who's goin' to tell."

"Thorpey for one."

"We'll tell the nun the priest wants us to help him in the church. She's not goin' to question you on that."

The adventurer was wrestling with the rule maker within me. The last while had been tough. To hell – life was too short!

We hit on a plan. We told Thorpey the priest needed the three of us. He was delighted. We told him he had better tell the nun and with the naive confidence of the innocent he fronted for the three of us with Ignatius. It was plain she was annoyed. Salt in the wound from the priest, so to speak. This probably helped us to carry it off.

Outside the school we turned left instead of right. Thorpey suspected something was afoot.

"We're making an initial detour," said Larkin.

"But where are we going – we'll all get into trouble – I'm going back." There was a half-broken slate on the road. Larkin bent and picked it up.

"Do ya see tha'?" he threatened.

"I'll split yer skull wide open with it if ya open yer mouth – d'ya hear?" The two eyes were leapin' out of Larkin's head. Thorpey started to cry. Larkin looked at me.

"Did you ever see such a gobshite in yer life?" "If you don't shut up yer bawlin' I'll hit ya a kick in the hole – d'ya hear?" Thorpey stopped his keening, but was occasionally higging involuntarily. "I'm sorry" he apologised. "I can't stop (hig) – I (hig) – can't stop (hig) – (hig) – (hig) – (hig again!)."

"Mammy's boy!" Larkin jeered.

We walked the mile or so out of the village to the wood. We walked over the sandy banks, but all of the snares were empty. Larkin went to a burrow. He put in his hand and pulled out about a third of a rubber car tube, which had been folded over and tied. He untwirled it and from it took a big penknife, a box of matches and a piece of twine about two yards long. Pen knives were forbidden.

When we got to the wood we went in. We had kept away from the road and we wanted to keep out of sight of the farmers tilling the fields. Thorpey looked liked he was living through his own worst nightmare. It was a master stroke to bring him along; there was no way could he snitch. To tell the truth, I was none too happy myself, although my nonchalant demeanour was intended to convince not just myself what a great time I was having.

We arrived at a clearing in the small wood. The vegetation was only coming into leaf. The mucky wet was gone out of the clay and replaced by a firmer softness.

"We'll fish," said Larkin.

"With what?" I enquired, somewhat bemused by his absence of realism.

"Let's get a sally, I have some twine – and we'll make a hook," he sparkled.

"How will we make a hook?" I dulled.

He lifted his jumper to reveal a pair of braces which we called gallasses. At the front each strap had a forked leather tongue with a button hole to receive the buttons on the trousers. In Larkin's case, he had one button on the right and a safety pin on the left. He removed the pin.

"How are ya goin' to keep yer trousers up ya eejit?"

"No bother," he winked. "Thorpey, take off your belt an' sit down an' shut up!"

He started to cry again. Larkin went over to him.

"You shut up yer bawlin' or I'll use yer mickey for bait."

Thorpey stopped straight away and took off a red and white elastic belt and handed it to him.

"What will we use for bait?" I asked.

"Worms ya eejit – look for a stone, a big flat one."

That afternoon we made a fishing rod from a hazel twig, twine and a safety pin. Eventually we got a maggot and caught what Larkin called, "two fish." They looked suspiciously like eels to me, they caused such an entanglement with our fishing twine, we had to get new twine and cut the hook out of the slippery slimy catch. We made a fire after several failures and the smell of burning dead wood and old roots had a vague allure that eventually invited conversation. Our attempts at cooking only succeeded in convincing everybody they were not that hungry. The dinner ended up as aromatic fuel. The smell was strong, but not unpleasant.

"Bates school anyways," said Larkin.

"They'll be goin' home shortly," said Thorpey. "Then we'll be in shite."

"Nobody'll be in shite if you keep yer duck-house shut, d'ya hear." Larkin was taking full advantage of his supremacy with his fists.

"Thorpey, you're no fool," he used say, giving him credit for his scholastic achievements, "But yer an awful friggin' eejit."

"Wait 'til me father finds out," said Thorpey.

"Sergeant Keystone," hissed Larkin.

"You don't be such a gobshite," said Thorpey. "My father is loads better than your oul' father. My father can put people in jail."

"Would ya ever go an' have a lep' at yerself. When was there ever anybody in jail in Coleman for Chrissakes," swore Larkin.

"Miley Cassidy was locked up. I seen him with me own bare eyes."

I laughed. Larkin hooted.

"Miley friggin' Cassidy, the terror of the badlands, wanted dead or alive in twenty-five states. Five-hundred dollars reward."

"Very funny! Just because you were wrong," he countered.

"Why don't ya drink a bottle of cop on," said Larkin. "An' rub a bit on yerself as well. Nothin' big ever happens in Coleman. If yer oul' fella was any use of a cop, he'd be in the cities where the rale crime is, murders an' things, an' courts, not stuff like oul' drunk fellas, tinkers fightin' and movin' 'em on an' stuff."

"Well, Fr. Williams said he was the best sergeant that was ever here. He said he had more brains than the rest of them put together."

This opinion surprised me. Thorpey was an eejit but I never regarded him as a liar. Larkin said the rest of them must have been a herd of elephants if that was the case. I asked him what feat had been performed by his father to merit this compliment. He turned right around to Larkin in order to take full advantage of my question.

"Actually, Mr. high an' mighty, he said he had more 'cop on' than any of the rest of them."

"Why was that?" I pressed.

"Last week," he replied.

"I didn't say 'when'? I said 'Why?' dumbo"

"Okay jumbo, something to do with not bringin' Miley to court."

He flattened me. I started to feel a freeze coming over me.

"What's so friggin' brilliant about that?" said Larkin,

"Well father friggin' Williams said it was brilliant, didn't he?"

"Whatcha think he'd tell him, the truth or somethin'. Whatcha think he'd say to him?"

"Well he told someone else as well."

Larkin cut in smartly. "He told yer mudder. Ha! Ha! Ha! Udderwise she'd never a' married him – and then we'd have no you – an' jays wouldn't tha' be an awful pity?"

"He told Mr. Hanlon," Thorpey said defiantly.

"He told him wha'?" I asked.

"He told him tha' unless he sent the two Hanlon girls to school after Easter that he would have to deal with Sergeant Thorpey, who would be well able to take care of him."

"What are ya' on about?" said Larkin.

"There's a law in this country about going to school you know," said Thorpey.

"Yeah," laughed Larkin, "and we're breaking it."

Not for the first time that day, I got a sinking feeling.

"There's the crowd from school," Larkin pointed them out in the distance. They were coming out below the church, down the steep hill to the crossroads below where they would divide and scatter to their various homes.

"Get into the trees!" he ordered kicking out the fire embers like they used in the Wild West.

⚭⚭

That weekend there was not a mention about mitching or school. On Saturday we rehearsed for the Procession on Sunday. Nobody said a word. On Sunday, Larkin and myself starred. Thorpey had to hold the missal open for the priest. It was an awful weight, as only too well I knew. He had to hold it up, and lie it back against his forehead so the priest could read it. Larkin kept at him about the way he was taking after his father, the way he was "using his head." "I knew well you'd find a use for it wan day," he said.

My mother used to say that pride always comes before a fall and she was right. That same afternoon, I fell from my brother's bike when I was acting the clown with Larkin. I was taken to the doctor and he put two stitches in my knee. I was now obliged to keep my leg straight until the stitches came out or they would burst. This meant I could not genuflect and I could take no further part in the Easter ceremonies. I would only get the first two days of the week off school. The Easter holidays started on Wednesday. Such a waste of a genuine injury almost sent me into a depression. This would never happen during schooltime.

Thorpey was the only one of the truants in school on Monday. The other children told us that. Ignatius cornered him.

"Master Thorpey, stand up!" He stood.

"Where were you on Friday?"

"I was mitching Sister."

Thorpey could be clever and he knew when it was not safe to lie.

"And who was mitching with you?" He paused dolefully. She eyed him. He shifted and stopped.

"Integrity, Master Thorpey, do you know what integrity means?"

"Yes, Sister."

"What does it mean?"

"It means doing what's right no matter what."

"Not bad Master Thorpey – for a self-confessed truant. It is a quality I

—147—

believe every altar boy should have. I'll go further. It is an essential requirement and the more responsible the position the greater the requirement," she was hinting.

"Now, Master Thorpey, who was mitching with you?"

"I can't say sister."

"Well let me help you a little. A certain altar boy who carried the cross on Sunday and another who carried the thurible left this school with you on Friday, did they not?"

"They did sister."

"And tell me now, who was mitching with you?"

He still remained silent. After a longer pause he eventually said, "I can't say sister."

She looked at him disconsolately. "Well, Master Thorpey," she said, "you're either a very great man, or a very great coward."

Thorpey knew right enough that Larkin would kill him if he split on us. Ignatius knew as well. Thorpey got the thurible and Larkin kept goading him that he only got it because he was no good to use his head, and when the priest found out he sacked him from carrying the Missal.

The Easter ceremonies finished Lent and we could all eat sweets again. When the holidays would be over, my leg would be nearly better. I would be confirmed next term, my last in primary school.

Cardinal Red, Paxo and the Knights

There was a tradition in Coleman that hurling started in full earnest on Good Friday after the ceremonies. On account of my injury this was out for me. However, it did not stop me from going to watch. Larkin gave me a lift on the crossbar of his bike, my leg stuck out straight. Fortunately, the distance to the field was only a mile and a half and mostly uphill, so we had to walk a lot of it. Larkin had been "the cripple" two years earlier, so he had all the tricks that handicap reveals. He showed me how to walk with the aid of a hurley. You simply held it in both hands in normal mode placed the bas in the ground, leaned on it and swivelled a vault forward. The old hurl that Hiawatha had fixed was ideal for this purpose.

In the field, I stood behind the goal flicking back the balls that broke from play. As the players arrived in the field one was put marking another until there were more or less two balanced teams. Inevitably, there was an odd number and I was asked to stand in the goal in order to balance matters.

However, 'briseann an dúcais trí shúile an cait' (the cat's nature breaks out through its eyes). After about twenty minutes when the heat of battle arose, the ball broke loose in the attack on my keep. I deftly flicked the ball to safety after I had harmlessly lunged.

The initial inspection of the bandage revealed nothing but brown clay from the wellworn patch between the goal posts. But I knew the stitch was gone because it was stinging.

"Tis alright, 't'will do," I shrugged semi-disinterestedly, determined not to be a "cissy" or a "pussy-babbie".

When the hurling was finished there was a big red patch of blood on the side of the liniment.

"Ya gobshite, why didn't ya say?" Larkin remonstrated.

"It's alright," I said, "I'll wash it when I get home."

"I don't know who's the bigger gobshite, you or Thorpey."

"It's alright, stop fussin'," I said. They were all beginning to gawk.

"Wha's wrong with Leacy's leg?

"Eh Leacy, wha'ss wrong wi' yer leg?"

The focus of attention was getting to me and I told Larkin to come on.

"He could get friggin' gangrene," said Larkin.

I asked him sarcastically whether he had acquired his medical expertise in the course of his considerable veterinary practice on his father's farm.

"D' ya think he'll have to be put down," shouted Thorpey, taking advantage.

"Would be a change from having to put up with you," I quipped.

With difficulty I got up on Larkin's crossbar. I was in the precarious position of Larkin being nearly not able to carry me on his bike. As we rode out the gate they were shouting after us with a mixture of encouragement and derision at our efforts to get the bike going with both of us on. My knee was hurting.

"Go on 'peg leg'," someone, shouted at me, a reference to an outlaw with a cork leg who graced the silver screen of Coleman in the Western serials.

"Get yer mammy to rub it for you!" shouted Thorpey.

When we got on the road, Larkin was in his stride. I was none too happy at the prospect of descending the undulating hills overlooking scenic Coleman in the hands of my best friend. As we proceeded downwards we had to negotiate a sharp right hand bend.

"Mind yer leg," he said.

"Wha?"

"Mind yer friggin' leg."

He lifted his foot up off the right pedal and put it in on top of the front tyre just in front of the mudguard. Holy Divine Jesus, these were his brakes? We wobbled around the bend on the wrong side, my eyes firmly closed and a most sincere Act of Contrition in my heart. "Yahoo!" he roared as he released his foot. I just kept my head down and prayed. There was no point in trying to reason with Larkin when the blood was up. As we came down past the church and school, the bike passed from being a vehicle of transport to a projectile. As we sped through the stop signs at Glenduff crossroads, we were transformed into a missile. When he pulled up at our house, he knew he had frightened me and laughed it off.

"Jays ya must a' lost a lot 'a blood, yer as white as a sheet. Ye'd think ye'd seen a ghost."

I roared back at him in the safety of the yard. "Yer always tearin' the arse in it, ya big galoot. What sort of an eejit are ya?" It was the first time I had really turned on him in anger. He had frightened me. "Look at the state a' me leg." I blamed him for the blood now seeping down through my stocking. The leg of my trousers was stained. The blood stopped him saying anything by way of reply. "Ya better come in with me and say that I fell," I winced.

Being Good Friday, the shop was closed and my father was there. I had to go back to the doctor, the stitches were burst all right. My mother gave out "yards" and said I was not to go back near the field again. My father brought me to the doctor. Paxo dispensed with the necessity of anaesthetic. In the course of his ministrations, he spoke to my father. They spoke about the election for a while. He then asked how my mother was? My father relayed the full story of Fr. Williams' miraculous cure.

"Amazing, to say the least," said Paxo.

"Miraculous is the word," said my father.

"I have no time for that fella, nor the Canon – indeed I have more respect for the Canon – bitter oul' bollix an' all that he is."

"Begog Paxo," said my father, "you'd have to admit what happened to the Missus was fairly remarkable."

Paxo stopped at my knee. "Listen John, I don't know whether he can heal people or not, but I know he is well capable of acting the bollix."

"Well I'm not going to fall out with you about him," said my father. "But he has never caused harm for me, and I have cause to be grateful to him and you."

"He never harmed me either," said Paxo, "and fear for him. The Canon had a go at me one time – then he backed off, but still you'd know his point of view and he is man enough to do it himself."

"Well, I've had me differences with him meself," my father conceded.

"Indeed, I heard – the day I left the shop after I had a few words – something about the Box Whitney's funeral?"

My father retold the story, both of them caught up in it. My knee was secondary and got punctuated attention. Paxo listened to the story as he inserted the painful sutures. My father's hands were holding my shoulders as I winced my way through the operation. He stood behind me in the little surgery. Having listened, Paxo said he could still respect a man like that even though he might strongly disagree.

"But I don't like that other fella. I don't like the way he goes on. I'll tell you," he said, "the Canon went down to Sean and Elisha Hanlon to make them send their children to the Catholic school – did you hear?"

"Be the hokey," my father responded, surprised.

Paxo continued that Sean Hanlon was not there at the time, but Elisha "cleaned" him and ran him. He knew of the clergyman encouraging Sergeant Thorpey to prosecute the parents for absence from school. Reference to that unsettled me. The Canon had told her there was nothing she could do about the matter. Her children would be raised as Catholics whether she liked it or not. Paxo was amazed at how stupid the clergy were to involve the guards. My father remarked that they would hardly send anyone to jail. Paxo had an opinion that Fr. Williams was a dangerous man, and that was that. My father was uncomfortable. So was I. The priest had cured my mother, so had the doctor, and both were friends.

The sutures were over and the knee re-bandaged. It was put on tightly, whether as a medical requirement or a reflection of the doctor's opinion of the curate, I was not sure. To soften matters, he said to tell my mother he was asking for her. On the way to the door he told my father he had to go for tests himself after Easter. He appeared to be dismissive of his ailment.

My freedom during the holiday Easter week would now be restricted. Larkin called on the Tuesday after Easter and said we should go fishing. He had found an old fishing reel with catgut, hooks and lead in one of the out houses. All we needed was a rod.

"I know where we could get a bamboo cane," he gleamed.

"Up in the Reverend Hancock's, there's a whole hape of 'em."

"That's seven miles away," I protested.

"Have'nt we got bikes?" he queried.

"I can't ride me friggin' bike and I sure to jays am not gettin' up on your crossbar ever again as long as I live."

He paused for a moment. He would swap a dinky bulldozer for a farmset plough if I would come. This was a tempting offer.

"I don't know."

"An' two comics."

"What sort?"

"64 pagers ... a Kit Carson an' ... a Buck Jones."

More than the strength of man could withstand.

"Okay, okay, but we walk down the hills."

"Oh for frigs' sake."

"No deal, unless we walk down the hills."

"Okay we walk down the friggin' hills."

By the time we got to where the sheep had run wild on us coming from the Fair of Ross, it was three o'clock. We hid the bikes and strolled up through the trees. "Moose Doyle" was the gardener. He had a nose for chaps and a leather belt around his waist to use on them if caught. The bamboo grove was in front of the orchard wall, lavishing itself on the lawn.

"We'll get three each," Larkin said. "Just in case."

At the front of the house was a barrow with a rake and weeds. A large timber door to the out offices was open. There was no car. We needed to cross the lane. Like two Commandoes, we stole up through the trees to the front where cover disappeared. Quickly and noisily we ran across the gravel to the tropical Victorian spray.

"Get in to the middle, pick only good ones." I had only two plucked when I heard someone coming on the gravel. Larkin looked up. We waited silently to see if we had been discovered. Breath held – hearts thumping. If it was "Moose," we were in trouble, particularly me because I could not run. We peeked through the bamboos and saw two women. They were coming from the out-offices. One had a watering can and was wearing an apron. She was the Rector's wife. The other was wheeling a bicycle. I knew her. It was Elisha Hanlon. As they bade farewell, I could barely hear her say that she needed to see "himself" urgently. As she rode off, her host went back to the out-offices.

"Come on," I said, "we have enough."

"Just one more," said Larkin.

"Come on," I repeated, "we have enough, we'll get caught." Larkin had his penknife out and cut another.

"Will you for frigs' sake come on!" I urged. We ran back to where the bike was hidden and saw Elisha Hanlon as she went out on the road. We turned right. I sat on the cross bar. We had travelled about three miles and Larkin and myself were singing at the top of our voices.

"Hang down your head Tom Doo-ooley.

Hang down your head an' cry,

Hang down your head Tom Doo-ooley,

Poor boy, you're gonna die."

Between that and "Last train to San Fernando" –

"If you miss this one – you'll never get another one

id-a-mid-a-bom-bom!

To San Fer nando,

Lass traiaain to San Fernando."

– we shouted and sang the whole way home high on the adrenaline produced by the success of our derring do!

Coming along a straight stretch before the hills home, we met a car. I recognised it. It was the Protestant Minister's.

"Jeez," I said. "Look who we're meeting."

"Frig'em!" said Larkin. "Watch this."

As we were passing, he stuck out his tongue at the driver. The car stopped. Larkin pedalled like the devil himself, head down. I had to lean forward craning my face away from the road in front of us. The driver was out of the car.

"What's he doin'?" said Larkin.

"He's shoutin' after us, are ya deaf?"

I saw the driver get back in.

"Jeez – he's – turnin'," I stuttered. Larkin started to pedal harder.

"Let me off" I shouted. "I'm not goin' down those friggin' hills again."

"Shut up yer gob!" he roared.

Just as we came to the top of the hill the car was about thirty yards behind. We sped down the hill with me hoping to Holy Sweet Divine

Christ that nothing was coming. We rounded the right angle bend and sped on for the cross of Coleman. Down past the school and the chapel. I was collecting the tops of thistles with my shoelaces.

"We're goin' right," he shouted.

There was no sign of the car as we turned. We had lost him. Larkin yahooed again. I shook my head. Then we laughed and laughed with the sheer exhilaration of the release of nervous tension. We had eluded our pursuer.

∞∞

The following day was a cold miserable windy day. When I called to Larkin he was in the barn and had taken the nylon gut off of the reel that had been painted with silver paint, apparently to use as a decoration. We decided to seek the advice of Hiawatha and maybe his assistance: not alone had he the knack with metals, tins and irons but was previously a keen fly fisherman. He struck a deal with us that he would show us how to fish and fix up the rod and reel for us if we would let him have the pick of the catch if successful. We were partners, even partners, except he had the 51 per cent share – the right to call the shots. Larkin spat on his hand like they did at the Fair and held it out, I followed suit. Hiawatha smacked each of us on the palm. This was just like the Old West – "partners" in the frontier, Davy Crockett, Daniel Boone and Hiawatha. We were on top of the world. He told us to come back the next day with two jam jars.

On the way home, we started roaring our lungs out again. "Dayvee – Dayvee Crockett, King of the Wild Frontier." Usually we sang it to the words of "Nicky Rackard." We sang one verse from Davy Crockett and one verse from Nicky Rackard.

"Over the hills on a summers' morn.

Greatest man in the land, he was born.

He learned to hunt and so gifted was he.

He killed himself a bear when he was only three."

Chorus: "Dayveeee – Dayvee Crockett.

The man who don't know fear."

Aroused, we conjured up the celtic mystical heroes with our chanting of their modern replacement.

"Over in Killane on a summer's morn.

Greatest Gael in the land he was born.
He learned to hurl and so gifted was he.
He tipped it o'er the bar when he was only three."
Chorus: "Nickeeee – Nickee Rackard
King of the close-in-frees."

There was not a bird left in a bush as we terrorised the ditches with our roars and the buchallains and rag weed with belts and pucks and kicks, me with my crutch-substituting hurley, which hourly was becoming more redundant as a cripple's aid and Larkin, his sou'wester thrown back from his head, holding the string of it with his Adam's apple, his FCA jacket hung open, chest out, he wellingtoned the weeds to death that dared impede his passage.

That evening there was a great shock. News spread through Coleman like wildfire. Dr. Paxo Sheehan was dead. I had remembered when leaving him after my knee was sutured he had said to my father he was going for tests. I also remembered what he had said about Fr. Williams. I wondered would he be sorry now.

That night, Peter came in at home. They were all very shaken. My brother and sister were home from school on holidays now and were allowed to participate in the conversation now that they were growing up. I sort of blended. When you are in the middle of brothers and sisters on either side you get lots of opportunities to learn how to blend.

"He was sure he had 'the lad'," my father said, a reference to cancer.

"And it was only appendicitis," my mother said, incredulous.

Peritonitis had carried him off.

"If they had left Nurse Condon with him itself," Peter remarked. "He had confidence in her. He'd listen to no one else – he was too head strong."

"When is he buryin'?"

"Tuesday, in Coleman. They have to carry out a post mortem."

"Who's doin' the funeral?" my father asked.

"Pierce Power."

"Not the undertaker – who's doin' the Mass?"

"I suppose the Canon," said Peter. And after a short pause said, "I see what you mean."

This certainly was going to be a difficult funeral for the church to negotiate the burial of an excommunicant but a doctor nonetheless. That was the end of the conversation, however.

Next day, Larkin and myself spoke about it on our way to Hiawatha.

"An' he only after condemmin' the priest a little over a week ago," said Larkin. It had struck me already. "He was excommunicated you know," Larkin continued letting the one jam jar vibrate against the other on his bike.

"No he wasn't," I countered. "He was only refused the sacraments."

"He was so, I heard them talking last night. He killed fourteen men and put a notch on his revolver for each man."

I was eyeing him, narrowly. "Who said tha'?"

"Jackie Grennan an' he should know."

"D'you think he's in Hell?"

"Jackie Grennan?"

"No ya gobshite – Paxo!"

"For shootin'?"

"No ya gobshite – for bein' excommunicated?"

There were times Larkin riled me.

"Ya better ask the nuns," he answered.

Jackie Grennan had attracted a lot of respect on account of his son's tragic drowning. We met the postman, Jimmy Whitty. He stopped and handed me a blue airmail envelope. He teased me again about being an international Romeo. The letter, I knew, was from Mel. Larkin was dying for me to open it, but I told him to get lost. He tried to take it from me, but I gave him a few digs with my hurl and he knew better than to keep it up.

When we got to the forge, we were disappointed to see it was closed. We decided to go to visit him in his house. Hiawatha lived down a small laneway. The house was built beside a stream that fed into the Owenduff River. They called this place "The Glen" and Hiawatha had the word "Tigín" painted on a timber plate attached to the gate. The house was roofed with asbestos tiles and the walls were cement walls which were pebble dashed. A sheepdog came out barking. Larkin was used to them, but since I had been bitten once I was less than enthusiastic about the reception.

"Maybe we shouldn't have come," I said.

"It's only a dog," said Larkin.

"No, I mean, we never came here before. I mean, it's his private place."

"Hiya, Toby! Hello boy, atta good doggie, 'atta good doggie," said the professional shepherd.

I held out my hand stiffly and hesitantly. The dog suddenly licked it and I pulled it back, frightened. The dog growled and snapped with a sulky eye and slunk away. I had my hurley at the ready.

"Yer an awful gobshite," said Larkin, "the poor oul' dog an' he only lickin' ya."

The door opened and Hiawatha appeared. He whistled a type of sucked noise between his teeth and the dog, mercifully, bounded towards him. Larkin wasn't finished with me.

"Ya nearly set the dog on us." I was crimson.

"I can't help it," I said. Then I covered, "I thought he was going for me knee."

"You in yer arse," he muttered with scorn.

As we came closer, Hiawatha greeted, "Ho! Ho! – the two fishermen."

Larkin was in flow so he apologised for our presumption. "This door is always open," said Hiawatha. A naked electric light bulb hung from the boarded ceiling. There was a fan by the fire and a crane with a black kettle. There was a wet cell radio on the table and beside it a smaller electric one. The radio was on. The voice of Leo Maguire was proclaiming, "If you do feel like singing, do sing an Irish song" to the strains of "The Bold Fenian Men" march melody. There was an enamel basin with dirty water at one end of the oil tablecloth. A cup, saucer and a few plates were turned upside down on a washed breadboard. There was no picture of the Sacred Heart with its lamp, but there was a St. Bridget's Cross. On the high wooden mantel over the fire were a number of boxes. There was a long timber stool at the table which was called a form and was pronounced "furrem." There was a cloth-covered high-winged armchair and a smaller one opposite and a stuffed pheasant in the window, but what took my attention was the picture opposite the fire. It was an old print of a very large fish, apparently studied under water. The word "Catfish" was all that was visibly written. The fascinating thing was, the fish had tusklike whiskers.

"I think we have a fisherman here alright," he said. I retreated my inspection. His eyes were red but the fire had not been smoking. He started talking to us about fishing. We would have to learn the way of nature, if we did not, we would have no success. It was not the same as learning out of a book. We would have to understand through our own senses. We would need wisdom as well. That was where Finn MacCumhaill got his, from the Salmon of Knowledge. We knew from our school primers that Finn had pressed his thumb on the blister of the cooking fish. To soothe he burnt thumb, he sucked it and thereby became the first to taste it, so preempting his tutor's own design. By this accident, he was invested with knowledge.

Larkin brightened, "We're goin' fishing for salmon."

"No," said Hiawatha. "We're going fishing for trout."

He told us he had learned his skill from a Presbyterian Minister in the North of Ireland when he was a boy. "He taught me any religion I have," he said, "and I learned that from him while fishing. Aye, surely."

He taught us our first lesson in fishing that day. I did not know he had Irish.

"Éist leis an sruthán agus gheofar an bhreac." (Listen to the stream and you'll get the trout.) "It was a lesson for life," he said. He explained how a trout waits near currents for food. I found it surprising that a Presbyterian Minister from the Black North not alone could fish, but knew Irish into the bargain. Hiawatha amazed us. He told us the way nature waits until the fullness of time before things are allowed to happen. There is no point pushing matters before then. The river has to rise before the fish go to spawn. The temperature in the stream has to be right before the female will pick her spot and her spouse, quiver with him and lay her eggs for him to fertilise.

"Much like the bull an' the cow," Larkin said.

I laughed and looked at Larkin to see if he was well in the head.

Hiawatha smiled and said, "Something like that." I looked at Hiawatha to see if he was well in the head. "Each in it's own time," he said. "You can't force nature – it's much bigger than all of us. If you use the wrong bait, you're not fishing – you only fish when you sense."

"What about artificial wans," asked Larkin.

Hiawatha took down a box from over the fire and took out card after card of the most colourfully decorated fascinating wisps and whiskers deftly tied, concealing the treacherous barb of a small hook. There was every hue and colour.

"How do you know which ones to use?" asked Larkin.

"Experience I suppose – I'm not really sure, maybe it's instinct, trial and error – I miss a lot, more than I catch at any rate," he said.

On the way home I tried to do a bit of fishing of my own, about the bull and the cow, but Larkin began to make a skit of me saying I did not understand.

"I do too," I shouted at him.

"Well go an' tell us then; you just wants to find out."

I sulked the rest of the way home and told him forty times if I told him once to go and have a good shite for himself. That night on the landing I took out the airmail letter from the States. Mel was coming for three weeks holiday in July. I felt my heart skip a beat and almost immediately looked around self-consciously. I told myself I needed to cop myself on or I would be the laughing stock of the class.

⟡⟡

On Sunday afternoon, I told Larkin. He was delighted. This slightly unnerved me. I hobbled through the meadow down the moor getting used to moving without the hurley. It was a sunny Sunday afternoon in April. Maybe if we went to the bridge we could see the trout in the shadowed reflection. At the bridge a car passed. Thomas Whitney Junior and Agnes Maher were in it. They were being driven by Gerry Denn. Tommy was in the front and he waved at me. Gerry Denn was a Protestant I knew only to see. There had been a Protestant Bishop of Ferns one time who was called Bishop Denn.

The bridge over the little stream kept the community together without wet feet and connected the beach of Coleman to the countryside. On bright spring days the occasional family would come for a walk on the strand in the fresh air. Larkin and I were leaning down, looking over the bridge trying to see trout, when a boy of about five or six years of age came up to us with a hurl in his hand. It was an adult's hurl – far too big for him. He must have been there for a little while unknown to us. Larkin was showing me how far down he could bend over the side to almost look through the eye of the bridge at the far side, upside down. We had attracted the young lad's attention. His parents must have been coming from the beach because I immediately heard someone shout "Ignatius!" I looked up and saw the little fellow, he turned a sudden half circle away from me towards the voice. The handle of the too-long hurley poked Larkin in the arse. Larkin let a scream, released his grip and fell into the stream below with a ferocious splash. Just before the splash there was a very loud "Jee-ee-sus!" Massive waves disproportionate to the width of the stream circled outwards and back, splattering off the bridge and spraying back again. The fun of it died in my chest when I saw Larkin's outstretched form struggling well below the surface. It looked shallow, but it was deep. The memory of my uncle the night he nearly drowned went through my head.

"Larkin," I shouted. "Larkin," I roared again. I could not swim. I could not look. I tried to shout again, but no voice came. I dithered. I pointed and looked around. The man who was now holding the child was white in the face. He looked at me and handed the child to the woman behind him without taking his eyes from me. He ran to the bridge and took off his coat. He pulled the legs of his trousers over his knees and sitting on the bridge he swung both legs over. He held the bridge in two gripped downward palms. One of his knuckles was bleeding. Larkin did not look good. The man jumped in feet first but turned when he was falling and appeared to hit the water with his back. There was the sound of a flat, splat! Then a type of "harumph!" as the river accepted its second visitor. The woman on the bridge clutched the child away from the scene looking over her shoulder. A car came. It was Gerry Denn. He saw the commotion and stopped. The man in the water was wearing braces and had a fat stomach. He was not able to stand. He was too roundy to turn. He was trying to reach with his left hand while keeping his head up facing the bridge. Gerry ran to the end of the parapet. He squeezed between some strong buckthorn and the bridge. From there a buttress ran at a slope into the stream. He ran halfway down and jumped into the stream at the bank side of the support. He waded, chest high, around it towards the centre and reached down with his shoulders into the deep. There were bubbles and swell and splashing. There was a snort from him as he pulled his face back from the water retrieving a limp and dripping Larkin. The fat man was trying to stand and kept ducking himself, but he half staggered, tumbled and spluttered himself behind Gerry on to the grass bank. Gerry dumped Larkin on the grass. I ran to the end of the bridge to go down the parapet when Mary Byrne, the schoolteacher's daughter, who had not been noticed by me, stopped me.

"Stop there, do you want to be drowned as well."

"Lemme go," I cried as I wriggled past her. I shinnied down the buttress bank. There was green mossy weed on Larkin's jersey. He was coughing and spluttering and retching. The fat man was lying back on his elbows, soaked, with his knees up, panting and every so often he would laugh "Heh! Heh! Heh!" nervously and say, "Wasn't that a good wan?" Gerry was slapping Larkin on the back and saying "You'll be alright now. You'll be okay." Larkin got a fright all right. It was the first time I saw him crying, but he stopped himself and said "Shite!" instead and retched and belched. He started to shake and shiver.

"Jays, it's freezin' cowld," he said.

A Foxford rug was produced from the back of a car. Larkin's teeth started chattering just like my uncles.

"Whiskey!" I said.

Larkin shot me a look and continued to uncontrollably shake.

"The boys r – r – right," stuttered the fat man.

We were all taken over to Clarke's pub where there was a hot cinderey open fire in anticipation of a "hash Spring day."

"You look like a rat," I said to Larkin.

"Me hole!" he jerked.

"Maybe a weasel then," I teased.

A big tablespoon was produced, filled with whiskey and poured down his throat. He held his face expressionless and he was unable to stop a light snort through his nostrils.

"That's hardly enough," I said. He looked through me.

"Never took a shake out of him," said the fat man. "Give him another drop." The big silver tablespoon was produced once more and though he must have been whimpering within, all that the world could see was grit.

I think it was the first time I was in a pub with people drinking. Most of my relations were teetotallers and members of the Pioneers, the association of the Temperance Movement. At Confirmation we would be asked to take "the pledge" and not to drink until we were twenty-one.

"There you are now," I teased Larkin afterwards, "the first man ever to break his pledge before he took it." Not alone were we breaking the law by being in a pub under age, we were in Protestant company in a Protestant pub. The fat man was the manager of the Provincial Bank in New Ross. He knew Gerry Denn and Mary Byrne's father. He also knew my father and grandfather and Larkin's father, most especially he knew my uncle Peter. His name was Henry Ram.

The talk ebbed and flowed and inevitably the land and the fittin' of it came up. Gerry was a farmer's son who made a few extra pounds doing agricultural hire. Himself and Thomas Whitney Junior hung around together a lot. Both of them were "doing lines" with teachers. There was a fair sprinkling of people in the pub. A lot of them had come to pay their respects to Mrs. Sheehan although Paxo's corpse was in Dublin. The company I was in listened to the talk a lot. Mr. Clarke offered Mr. Ram a change of clothes and another spoon of whiskey to Larkin. He declined by saying he would go home and change. Larkin turned to Gerry and said awkwardly "Uh – thanks for pullin' me out." Gerry smiled and said,

"You're welcome." He left at the same time. As I walked home with Larkin I noticed my knee was all right. I was not hobbling anymore.

∽∽∞

The Easter holidays finished and the new recruits for primary school were there next morning with some relieved, some proud and some tearful mothers. There were no fathers. Larkin was out with the flu, "him havin' fell in the river" according to one of the telltale girls.

"Fallen," corrected Ignatius.

"Well he nearly drownded, a Shuir."

"Drowned!" she corrected.

"Yes, a Shuir, drownded."

The absence of Larkin put a little bit of distance between our last day of term mitching and the possibility of inquisition. Unusual for the start of term, Ignatius was quiet. She spent a lot of time at Catechism on the basis of our impending Confirmation.

The Bishop would be in Coleman tomorrow for the Patriot doctor's funeral. She told us how he had fought for Ireland and the way he was so kind to the poor. Ireland needed more men like him. His remains were brought to the church that same night, all the way from Dublin. Hiawatha was in a guard of honour at the gate. The old IRA men marched beside the hearse for the last hundred yards to the church. Peter was there. The place was thronged. There was a tricolour on the coffin. A lot of the women had fur coats. After the full rosary was said, people filed up to shake hands and offer sympathy to the relatives. Mostly people said, "Sorry for your trouble ma'am." I waited and waited for them all to leave. The sacristy door was open and I stayed discretely back out of view in the altar boys' room. Occasionally I would edge my left side out slightly to watch developments. A knock on the outside door made me jump. Someone with a Mass card for signing. When I opened the door, Sean Hanlon was there.

"Is the priest in?" he asked.

"He is," I answered.

"Is it okay to come in?" he enquired politely.

"He's in the house," I answered. "The hall door is over there," I pointed.

He thanked me and left with a flashlight in his hand lighting his way in front of him as was the fashion with people who rode bicycles on country roads in the dark.

On the Tuesday morning the school was full of it. Everybody was talking about it. Thorpey was the foremost authority, his father had been notified.

"She left yesterday," Larkin said.

"She left in the middle of the day on Saturday," Thorpey said.

"How the frig would you know?"

"Because Sean Hanlon told me Da, thass how, he got it from the horse's mouth Mr. Know All," said Thorpey.

Not to be outdone Larkin retorted,

"An' now we're gettin' it from the horse's hole." The picture began to fall into place. Elisha Hanlon, a Protestant, threatened with having to bring her children up as Catholics and send them to a Catholic school, had left home with them both. Her husband had spoken with the guards according to Thorpey, and this probably explained his visit to the priest the night before.

We were on our way from the school to the chapel to serve the funeral mass for the doctor when this latest row broke out between Larkin and Thorpey. In the sacristy they still argued about how she had left.

"She stole the car as well," said Thorpey.

"Hanlon's car is at home in their own place," said Larkin.

"I know," said Thorpey. "Me Da brought it back."

"Me Da – me Da – me friggin' Da – do you ever say anything else?" Larkin mimicked.

"Yer only jealous," Thorpey fired back.

"Go an' light the candles," I ordered him. He got the taper holder.

"Don't mind that eejit for frig's sake!" I said to Larkin.

The "priest" Doyle came in and got the long black soutane. He was focussed. He read the prayer for vesting from the wall as he robed. He went to the window, where he stood looking and waiting for the Bishop. The sacristy filled up with priests. There were people everywhere. I had never seen so many motor cars in Coleman.

The pulpit in our church was located in front of the altar at about the third row of seats. As the Bishop walked up its little stairs, it creaked. He wore purple. He had a lace surplice which was much longer than all of the priests'. In his homily he paid homage to the deceased doctor and how he had donated land in the Marian Year for the erection of a Marian Shrine. His attention to the Dispensary had been exemplary. His death had been tragic, but his life magnificent.

I wondered how the Bishop would deal with the excommunication. It was a big issue for me and my eager mind received and held it. "He had his differences with the church, but he resolved them in a way that committed people do." He praised his commitment and resolution as a hallmark of his life and a shining beacon for others. He was committed to his army and equally his church. Catholics should be as united as a disciplined army and make every effort to mould the public conscience in accordance with Catholic principles. He said there were lay organisations and societies available for people to join. These helped to foster religion. We should value and foster our religion, and defend it in public and private and repair any defects of our Christian way of life he said. Commitment and loyalty were the hallmarks of the doctor's life. He had involved himself in organisations to promote the welfare of the people for whom he cared. Others should follow his example. There were other organisations besides. These organisations to which he referred were well known. There was the Vincent De Paul Society, the Catholic Protection Societies, the Legion of Mary and a string of others culminating with what he referred to as "The

Commandoes of the church – The Knights of Saint Columbanus." (I knew Peter was a member and I felt great that he was in the elite squad.) God was Absolute and an Absolute Being demanded absolute faith and commitment. Faith was absolute certitude about what was true and this might well be defined as absolute knowledge.

When the bishop was finished, the "priest" Doyle attended him, leading him back into the sanctuary. The "priest" Doyle's face was glowing. I had forgotten that he was another one of "The Commandoes." Within myself I concluded that he must have been an infiltrator, much like the bad guys in the Westerns when they ambushed a member of the cavalry, stole his clothes and rode at the end of the cavalry platoon, awaiting opportunity to assassinate.

☙ ❧

It was a wet blustery day at the graveside. The sort of a day which cannot rightly make up its mind the season to which it belongs. The priests looked pale and windswept. The old IRA stood stiffly with no hats. Grey balding heads disturbed by the blowing revealed age and many wrinkles. Hiawatha looked the best. He saluted as the "last post" sounded just after the rifle shots blasted from the guns of the FCA, but if he looked the fittest his eyes were watery. I wondered if it was the wind.

Sergeant Thorpey and Garda Foran were directing traffic as the burial concluded. Larkin slagged Thorpey that his father was making a hames of it and causing all of the confusion. We got three pounds each and an introduction to the Bishop. Fr. Williams introduced me as Peter's nephew and I was rewarded with a smile after I had kissed his ring.

On the way back to school, we could see the Sergeant going in to the priest's house. He met the "priest" Doyle on the steps and they were chatting as we passed. I saw Peter going into the Priest's house as well. That night he called in at home and after I left for bed I could hear my father asking him the news. Peter said the children had been stolen, and the Unionists in the Six Counties were involved. One of them had been down to Sean Hanlon, the Sergeant had seen the car. He had been talking to the Bishop about it. Fr. Williams was hopping mad. Peter said Fr. Williams would have to be watched, as he could go off the deep end. My mother pitied poor Sean and said what a terrible thing it was to happen. Peter was less sympathetic and said that "If he was any friggin' use 'twould never've happened in the first place." I did not quite understand.

My father wanted to know what the Bishop thought, and Peter said he was going to involve the Knights of Columbanus in the North and wanted his assistance to do so. My father wanted to know why they were not making a statement. Peter said they were not sure of all of the facts "not alone must you be right, but you must be seen to be right" he said. This was excitement all right. As I dressed myself under the landing light, Fr. Williams came in. I stole down again.

"This is the worst ever," he said.

"She wants him to sell up and go off and become a Protestant as well as the children."

There was a stunned silence as everyone let the awful thing she was asking sink in.

"Is she cracked or what?" my father asked.

"Poor Sean," my mother said again.

"Oh to hell with that fella," said Fr. Williams.

"I have it up to here with him. Why couldn't he stand up to her and be a man like all the other lads around."

Peter agreed, so did my father; my mother stayed quiet.

"The most disappointing thing is we can say nothing," said my father. Fr. Williams said that two battalions of Protestants from Hell were not going to muzzle him.

There was a knock at the front door. I ran up the stairs. My mother answered and Sergeant Thorpey stepped into the hall, he was looking for Fr. Williams and had been directed here. My mother showed him into the parlour, brought the priest into him and left. Almost immediately the priest and Sergeant Thorpey came out. Fr. Williams stuck his head in the door of the kitchen and said, "I have to fly – there's been an accident." My father came out and spoke as they left. "It was just a friend – not a bad accident," the priest said.

In Coleman when storms arose they were usually preceded by a day of blustery wind. The next morning, a gale force eight had blown up and it was rattling every rafter, beam and slate on the church. Inevitably, a draughty church made a draughty priest's house – doors banged and rattled. The dark morning Masses were not a problem as opposed to the dark funeral nights.

After Mass I ran around to the priest's house to call into Mae to get the list of messages for the shop. Her hair was tossed as if she had ventured out but had retreated. It was cold in the kitchen. The aga had gone out. She was obviously under some pressure but was relieved to see me. "There's a great lad," she said with relief. "Run out and get me some anthracite from the coal shed. She was not yet wearing her wrap-around navy pinafore with the small floral motif which was typical of the day. This was almost akin to her being seen in her slip. Her relief at seeing me, however, outweighed her concern for her respectability, but, nevertheless, it was appropriate to address her composure now that assistance was at hand. As I left to get the anthracite, she moved to go to the hall where she would attire herself from the cupboard under the stairs.

When I arrived back with the anthracite she had not yet returned and the stiff draught from the southwesterly gale kept the kitchen door flung wide open. There as if in a state of undress I beheld the spectacle of the inner sanctum with the traces of impropriety and uncomfortable suggestion laid bare before me. Like a beacon flashing its signal of danger, the hall stand displayed the black fur coat. I felt like I was looking up under a girl's skirt, when suddenly Mae shuffled into the view, her visage drained. She had not expected I would be back so quickly that this could be witnessed. Her flaccid jowls stiffened and her demeanour changed. She immediately closed the door and said, "While I was getting my bib I noticed we need a box of red floor polish as well, the Cardinal red, if you have it." I took the list. I was going out my curiosity got the better of me and I went to the back of the outhouses. There, was Iníon Ní Breathnach's car. The left-hand front wing and lamp were dented and broken.

PART II

The Second Summer of Fifty-Six

∽ 8 ∼

Now Boys, We're in Business

After the doctor's burial, little enough was seen of Hiawatha. Larkin and myself thought he might have closed the forge as a mark of respect. We decided to call on him to see what progress was being made with the fishing rods. We called down to the little house but the door was closed and bolted and the curtains drawn.

We cycled back to Aughadreimne. Poll brought us in for tea and scones. In the course of this interview, Larkin had to relay the tale of his near drowning. It was early afternoon, and she asked me to bring a tommycan of tea to the Gort na Gheatai (Field of the Gates) where my uncle Martin was "fitting" the land. As we walked across, the haggard Ignatius came at us. I took to my heels, but Larkin grabbed a sprong and chased him off. I was at the far end of the haggard when I noticed he was not behind me. I looked back to see him facing and chasing the turkey cock back in a flurry of feathers and dust. The turkey's head was crimson and it walked jerkily in a hurt and humbled fashion. "That will teach that frigger," he said, dusting himself off like a rodeo rider who had broken a bucking bronco. I was amazed and chastened in one swoop. He had tackled one of my worst fears, defeated and made not the slightest issue of it. I looked at him, awestruck.

Up at the field Martin was working a horse making drills. Jim Eager was doing the headlands with a spade. He stopped the horse at the headland and we sat and talked. Martin had great yarns. He told the way Tommy Murphy came up home one night when Mrs. Doran from "The Black Knocks" was dying. She was a legend in her own dirtiness.

"How's Mrs. Doran?" my grandmother asked from the other side of the fire.

"Not too bad thanks ma'am," he said from the card table in the corner. Then he leaned in to the others, "She's down there now, with the tossils of shite hangin' out of her," we laughed again.

Jack Devereux nearly convulsed and the very next morning he burst out laughing while at Mass when he thought of it again. He damn nearly died. He higged at the desperate thought of it when he told it later.

"In Mass, ya' know, of all places."

"We have a big day on Sunday," the Protestant workman offered.

"We're gettin' a new clergyman."

"Is that so?" said Martin. He drank the dreggs of his tea and handed me his mug.

"We'd better get back to work I suppose," he said as he pulled himself up.

☙☙

On the way back Larkin wanted to go on the road because he had heard there were rabbits on Cummins' land and he wanted to see for himself. We walked down and peeped through the briars.

"I see's wan," he whispered, "in the drill over there."

There was one sure enough, sitting there.

"She's just sittin', he said. "We'll just frighten her with a stone to see where she goes," explained the hunter. The bushes in front of us were too high so we slowly edged down keeping on the grass margin but out of the drain. We kept our heads down. "Get a stone," he said. I looked around at my feet, but there was only a red rag. I looked on the road, but it was too well tarred. There was some broken glass at the far side. There was some chromium which glistened. I got it and Larkin said, "That's no friggin' use. That's a door handle."

"You don't want to kill her," I said. "Just frighten her."

He looked at me, took it and let fly. It bounced near the rabbit who never moved.

"She's dead," I said.

"Me arse, dead," said Larkin.

"We'll shout," he said.

"Hulla! Hulla! Hulla! Hulla!" we vamped our mouths like we saw the redskins in the "flicks." But the rabbit stayed put.

"Come on," he said.

He climbed on the ditch and a briar tore his leg.

"Fuck it!" he swore and looked at it. He rubbed it and spread the blood.

"Twill do," he said and offered his hand to me.

We went in to the field and over to the rabbit. It had a huge pair of bulging eyes. It's back rose and fell with each breath.

"The fuckin' myxomatosis," he said. I had heard Paxo speak of the rabbit disease in the shop. "It'll spread like wild fire," he had said. "Fuck it anyway, there won't be a rabbit left in the country," he stroked the dying animal. "Ya poor little fucker!" he said gently.

When we got back on the road, his leg was bleeding some more.

"Fuck it, 'twill ruin me socks," he said as we wiped it away with his hand. He had no handkerchief and neither did I.

"Give it a wash in the drain."

"Me hole!" he said.

"There's a rag there, I saw," I remembered. I got the cloth. "Jesus! 'Dass Hiawatha's," I said.

He wiped his leg with it.

"Be jays I think yer right," he said.

It was the red kerchief that he wore around his neck. We looked at the glass on the road and behind it was the skid mark of a car tyre. We came to the conclusion that Hiawatha must have been killed. We ran back to Poll and blurted out our tale.

"He's in hospital," she said simply. "He was knocked down last night by a car, he has a broken leg," she said.

We were speechless. She saw Larkin's leg bleeding and took a sponge with cold water to it. Then she dried it and got the iodine. He winced as she applied the dread potion, but he never uttered a squeak. Larkin was hard as nails, I felt. I would have loved to be as tough as him. I felt a 'Molly coddle' when I compared myself to him.

ᚙᚙ

We cycled back to the shop. *The Free Press* had just arrived. My father cut open the binding twine and on the inside page a headline proclaimed "Wexford Farmer Seeks to Recover Children."

"Yes, begog," said my father. There was also a big article on Dr. Paxo Sheehan. The "priest" Doyle came in to the shop. He took up the paper and read.

"Isn't that disgraceful," he said. My father acknowledged the reference.

"Sell up, go off to Canada and turn religion – did you ever hear the like in all your born days."

"I don't know what will be the end of it," my father said.

"This will have to be stopped one way or another," said Doyle.

"Faith and then, 'twill take stoppin'," my father said and to us,

"Get an ice-cream or somethin' for the two of yez and go on ahead." This conversation was not suitable for children. I got a chocice for Larkin and myself. The "priest" was going on about the Unionists in the North and their interference. As Larkin and myself were going out the door, I heard the word "boycott" used for the first time. The "priest" said that it had worked before and it was time for some Catholic action. Talk was all very fine he was saying, but now was the time for action. On the way home we dawdled. It struck me that Iníon Ní Breathnach's car was damaged. I had seen it when getting the coal for Mae. I connected the damage to Hiawatha in a flash of inspiration.

"Who?"

"She's the School Inspector wan you know, she stays with the priest."

"She wha'?"

"She stays with Fr. Williams off an' on."

"Is she related?"

"I s'pose she is. How do I know?"

We were approaching the church and as we came closer Larkin said he wanted to go and see the crashed car.

"Let on you came to get the coal for Mae," he urged.

"What do you want to see that bleddy oul' car for?" I asked.

"Ah come on," he said. "I just want to see it. I'm not going to take a lump out of it or an'thin'."

I was curious myself to see whether the handle of the car was on it or not. "Tell you what, s'posin' we leave our bikes at the field gate and go up through the two fields to the back of the yard, nobody will see us and none will be any the wiser."

He went with this. We walked up through a field of sheep and as we did it started to pelt hailstones. We ran like two devils escaped from hell into the hayshed. There was a good deal of hay in the shed, surprising for the time of year. The land was set to a local farmer who also availed of the hayshed. There was the best part of a span full. The hail rattled a deafening, drowning and engulfing noise on the corrugated iron roof which was painted with red lead. There was a ladder up which Larkin ran to the top of the rick and I scurried after him. Aloft and breathless we lay on the hay laughing.

"Jayus, we were nearly skint." The hailstones had stung. There was a musty smell from the hay. I pointed the car out to him in the yard below and indeed the handle of the left-hand side door was gone. The hail stopped as quickly as it had come. "'Twas a wonder she didn't kill him, look at the way the front is stove in."

The sun shone down with early summer shallowness, brightly but barely warming. The smell of the hay was deep and chesty.

"Let's go," I said as I went to get down.

"Hold on." he grabbed my arm. "Look!"

The hayshed towered over the small out-offices at the back of the priest's house. We could see into the little yard at the back. I could see Mae through the kitchen and scullery windows. Her two elbows were on the table reading the spread out paper. She was smoking a cigarette. He gave me a dig.

"What?"

"There!" he pointed.

The priest's bathroom was on the first storey at the back of the house. The window was completely open at one side. It was hinged on the sides and opened outwards from a centre sash. There was a woman standing at a wash hand basin. She was washing her hair. She was wearing a skirt and was naked from the waist up. It was the first time in my life I had seen a woman's breasts. They hung below her as she bent, and shimmered as she lathered her hair. We sniggered and tittered in a giddy fashion as she continued washing.

"Shaddup!" said Larkin. "She'll hear." After she rinsed her hair she took a white towel and started to dry like the dickens. Her full breasts, shook and dangled between energetic bursts of hand towel drying. We giggled and gawked. When she took the towel away and stood up her breasts sagged slightly. I had never thought nipples could be so big. She walked to the door behind her and retrieved another towel hanging there. When she walked back again she hung the first towel on a clothes horse. She turned her head suddenly behind her, back to the door and stopped drying. She went to it, the white towel protecting her breasts. She opened it and stepped back walking back over to the washbasin. Fr. Williams came into the bathroom and closed the door behind him. She continued drying her hair but almost immediately she closed the window giving us the last glimpse of her curvaceous figure. It was the first good look we got of her face.

"Iníon Ní Breathnach," I said.

"Yer wan," said Larkin.

For one split second we laughed and then stopped.

"We'd better get to fuck out of here," Larkin said.

We scarpered like two scalded rabbits. I was not really sure about what was going on, but neither of us were in any doubt about what we had seen – a pair of breasts. As Larkin said, "big boobies." In some strange way, seeing her exposed like that, I felt I had got my own back on her for nuzzling me at school the day she examined us in Irish grammar.

"Big muscley yokes," I jeered.

"Now ya know where babies come from," he said.

"Yeah!" I answered completely flummoxed.

I did not know what he meant and yet I felt informed, as if the experience had revealed something in me.

∞∞

On Sunday after Mass we decided to see if Hiawatha was home. On our way down we saw a big crowd of people at the Protestant church. There were quite a few motorcars. There were also ponies and traps. It was a bright fine day and had the promise of warmth. The ponies swished their tails at the flies, snorted and shook their heads and harnesses. A lot of the men who were going in had three-piece suits and hats. Most of the older men wore moustaches. There were a lot of pocket watches, revealed by their waistcoat chains, and the proud bellies of big men.

"Are ya goin' in?" I joked.

"Not with you anyway" he replied. "That last time ya went in ya thought hard of lavin'."

"Will ya stop!" I winced at the memory.

When we got to Hiawatha's, his door was open. He was inside sitting down reading the paper, his leg in plaster-of-Paris resting on a low three legged stool. He had a walking stick beside his chair. He beamed at us when we came in.

"Ah! My two pardners!" he grinned. "Aye, surely!"

He had a black eye and his left cheek carried scrape marks.

"We heard ya nearly killed yerself," said Larkin.

"I had help," he responded. He told us how he had been walking home when he was struck. The lady had called to him in hospital. He had been knocked unconscious but had come to in a short time.

We told him about the big crowd at the Protestant church. He said he had not met the new Protestant Minister.

"I heard you nearly drowned yourself," he said to Larkin who blushed.

"Ya couldn't kill a bad thing," I said.

"Which of us are ya talkin' about?" Larkin side-stepped.

Hiawatha laughed at the thrust and parry of his two junior disciples. He hobbled to the dresser. Sticking out over the top was his violin case and behind it were the tops of the bamboo canes. He called me to help him. He showed us where he had inserted copper ferrules, male and female, but he would have to bind them and glue them for support. We were thrilled. He certainly knew what he was doing.

"Do you need coal brought in?" I asked, trying in some measure to display my gratitude in a meaningful way.

"No harm at all," he accepted. "'Twill be a little before we need the fire."

"We could do the messages for ya," said Larkin taking up the cue, "until your leg gets better."

"That would be grand entirely," he smiled.

We left shortly after we had done the errands. The anticipation of an exciting summer lifted our spirits no end. As usual in such cases, Larkin could not contain himself.

"I'm goin' to fish for conger eeels," he announced. "And when I grow up, I'm goin' to fish for whales."

Moby Dick, the film, was on in the hall that afternoon. Typical of Larkin, one adventure complimented and became part of the next. The film was gripping. Gregory Peck played the part of the obsessed sea captain who hunted the waters attempting to rid his life of the monster that was devouring him.

"By feck!" said Larkin. "Did you see all them harpoons stuck in the whale? By jays he didn't half make shite of the ship. The size of the big frigger." Larkin's eyes were out on sticks.

⚮

It was nearly five o'clock when I got home. Peter was there. He was bringing my brother and sister back to school after the Easter holidays. I always felt sad when they were going away even though we knocked sparks off of one another when they were at home.

There was to be a meeting in the hall to see what was going to be done about the Hanlon affair. My father said he would not go on account of not wanting to leave my mother on her own yet with the three of us. She had come on a lot but still needed to go for a lie down during the day.

That night when Peter came back from the meeting, his face was flushed. My father wanted to know how the meeting had gone.

"God save us all from gobshites!" he replied. "Jackie Grennan proposed that we go and kidnap a Protestant child as a retaliation." My father laughed out; Peter shook his head, "Did you ever hear the bate of that?" My father laughed again. "Then the 'priest' Doyle wanted to boycott all of the non-Catholics and shun them completely, not even speak to them. I had an awful job trying to restrain the clergyman."

Peter had chaired the meeting. He had worked them around to a compromise with great difficulty. Someone had suggested a boycott. The Protestants were involved all right. Elisha Hanlon had been driven to the station in Wexford by someone. She got money somewhere.

"Her father had given her thirty pounds." Sean Hanlon had told the priest. Not all of the Protestants would be shunned, just the businesses. Not a boycott, but a protest.

"This could get very serious yet," said my father.

"Who're you telling?" said Peter.

At that point my presence was detected and I was sent off to bed. The implications were not immediately apparent to me. I was more preoccupied with Captain Ahab and *Moby Dick*. A funny thing, but it wasn't the big whale that kept me awake, but the thudding sound of Captain Ahab's wooden leg as he restlessly and relentlessly trod the boards of his nighttime deck, the ominous plod of the obsessed.

∽∾

The following day the priest came to school and told us all about the "Wren's Nest" in Dublin. It was a Protestant institution that had the declared purpose of taking in Catholic orphaned children and brain washing them to their beliefs, the priest said.

"In our own little parish," he told us, "Catholic children have been stolen from their Catholic father for the same evil purpose. This could not be tolerated and a protest has to be made. Some people around here have conspired in an evil way to bring this about."

We were all hushed. We were not to go to the Protestant shops and the easiest thing to do was just to stay away from them and work and play "with your own little Catholic friends."

At the lunchtime break, everyone was talking about it wide eyed. There were three Protestant businesses in the village, Barker's, Auld's and Clarke's pub. Barker's was a hardware shop and Auld's was a magazine and sweet shop. Nobody in school minded about Barker's, but Auld's was different. My father's shop was a grocery and though he sold sweets, even I could see he did not carry the variety nor quantity of Auld's.

"You may get yer ould fellow to get more sweets," Larkin said.

"Feck that!" I said. "What 're we goin' to do?"

"What do you mean 'what are we goin' to do?' " said Larkin.

"What about our partnership with Hiawatha?"

"What about it?" asked Larkin.

"Were you listening to the priest or wha'? Hiawatha is a Protestant you know!" I said impatiently.

It began to dawn on Larkin that the protest was designed to stop people from dealing with Protestants, and that included us and Hiawatha.

"Feck!" he said.

"What'll we do?" I repeated.

"Say nothin' for the moment," he said.

I thought this was good advice. It was the only advice. That same day we did nothing at school except prepare for Confirmation on Sunday week. We prayed for the souls of the stolen Catholic children.

The next morning before Mass, the priest told me not to go home until he had spoken with me. All during Mass I wondered whether it would be about Hiawatha and ourselves. As it happened, it had nothing to do with it. When he had his vestments off he called me. He was sitting in the sacristy chair

"A little bird told me something," he said.

"Where were you when Miley Cassidy broke into the Protestant church?"

I nearly passed peacefully away.

"Don't be alarmed now," he reassured. "I just want to get to the bottom of something."

I was afraid. I started to cry. I blurted the whole thing out through tears and sniffles occasionally getting caught with a cough.

"Well you're a great boy to tell me the truth," he rewarded. "Did you know that Miley Cassidy has been summonsed to court?"

"No, Father." I was shocked.

"Well we can't let him go to jail for something he didn't do, now can we?"

"No, Father."

"He is being charged next Thursday in Ballycullane court and I want yourself and Michael Larkin to come along and tell what really happened. I'll talk to your father in the meantime, but say nothing about this to anybody."

∞ ∞

The minute I got to school I told Larkin. Before I could say a word he told me the priest had been down in their place the previous night.

"Who told him?"

"Agnes Maher did," said Larkin.

"But why?"

Neither of us could figure that one out. However, the next day, the Protestant school where she taught was closed and a notice stuck on the door "Scoil Dúnta mar boycott sa Ceanntair" (School Closed because of boycott in the District).

So it was a boycott.

"Did the priest make her resign?" I asked Larkin, who was as confused as I was. .

"Do ya think she's thick?" he glared at me. Glaring worked. You did not have to explain.

⚯

It was midweek and we were going to see Hiawatha, who was still at the house. The forge was shut. We rationalised our position by saying he was a Presbyterian not a member of the Church of Ireland, and anyhow we were not doing business with him based on our being customers.

It was about five o'clock on a glorious May evening. We could hear the fiddle as we came down the little lane. He was playing a slow air and it sounded very sad. When he saw us he smiled and put the fiddle away. He told us the tune he had been playing was called "The Limerick Lamentation." He seemed heavyhearted.

"Aye, surely, 'The Limerick Lamentation'."

"How's the leg?" Larkin asked him.

"Comin' along, I suppose, comin' along."

We offered to bring in the coal. We both went out to the little whitewashed house with the black door. The door was tarred and had a latch and bolt. The house had two rooms, one had coal and sticks, the other tools, utensils and boxes. The side of one of the boxes had "USA" written on it and was covered in dust. When we came back in, he had a reel in his hand. It was shining brass. The transformation was incredible. We "oohed" and "aahed" over it for ages. The rod we would have at the end of the week.

For some time I had been thinking about making a "truck." Every boy wanted one and most had them. A truck consisted of a timber box with two wheels at the front and two protruding handles at the back. The handles were generally made from trimmed up broken hurleys. The truck looked in its functioning mode like a wheelbarrow, yet it was anything but. It was used like a prop for a stage, except it had a universal personality that altered with each changing situation – it was a covered wagon when we played cowboys, a racing car, a delivery lorry and a fire engine. It carried seaweed for the garden, weeds from the yard and sticks and logs for the fire. Owning a truck gave you status. The type of truck you had gave you personality. Larkin made one from a fish box. It was very wide but only six inches deep and it had the axle and wheels of a small pram. He said you could really motor with it.

Having seen the boxes in Hiawatha's coal shed I thought to ask him for the one with "USA." on the side of it.

"Do you know those oul' boxes that are thrun' out in the house, could I have one if they're no use to you?"

"Aye, surely," he replied.

I told him I would like the one with USA. on it if that was all right.

"Did you see what was on the other side?" he asked, and I had not.

Larkin and myself ran out to get the box. When we pulled it out, on the other side was written "Union Pacific TNT DANGER." There was a black skull and crossbones at either side. I was thrilled, Larkin was agog. We brought it in and he smiled at our excitement and reddened his pipe. We wanted to know if it really had been used for dynamite, and he said it had. He had used it. When he was coming home from the States he used it as a trunk. He looked wistful. We asked him to tell us about his time in the army. That faraway look came in to his eye and he drew on his pipe with heavy slow pulls looking into the fire. He dawdled a little, poking with the poker. He was a musician looking for the right note.

"I was a very young man then," he said. "The white man had forced his way across the prairies and the mountains. The red man let him at first and, when it was too late, he tried to stop him. I was in the infantry that time. I was barely gone twenty. They made me a Sergeant. I met Buffalo Bill you know."

Buffalo Bill – William F. Cody himself, who had fought the Indians and later set up a travelling Wild West show.

"Did you ever fight any Indians?" asked Larkin.

He smiled and said the Indian Wars were over by the time he had arrived.

"Did you ever meet any?" Larkin asked.

"I married one," he answered.

Larkin and I both knew he had. We wanted to know what they were like and if they really lived in wigwams and whether they danced around fires and if they called whisky "firewater." He sat that evening and talked until it got dark. He told us how the white man regarded himself as being chosen by destiny to rule all of America. They believed themselves to be the superior race and that they should be in charge of the Indians. They had a name for this, he said; they called it "Manifest Destiny." When he came to this part he looked in the fire for a time. " 'Manifest Destiny' – Aye, surely – 'Manifest Destiny'."

We left him with the promise of coming back soon. We never mentioned the word "boycott." I left there without speaking of my impending court appearance.

∞∞

Next morning after Mass, Fr. Williams told me to call up to him after my dinner. He would bring Larkin and myself over to the court. In the morning Ignatius explained what an oath was about twenty times, and she said we were to call the judge "Justice." On the way to Ballycullane the priest told us that all we would be required to say was that the door was open when we got there and that the window was broken when we were leaving, but not by Miley.

The courthouse was in fact "the Ploughing hall." The Ploughing Committee had organised themselves to build a hall for their meetings. They rented it to anyone, including the Minister for Justice. It had a small toilet and room to one side. The judge's desk was on a platform that covered the whole end wall. In front of this was another and to the side was the witness box. There was a long table with a long bench with a back. The platform was eighteen inches off the cement floor. The roof was of corrugated iron.

We sat enthralled and intimidated by our surroundings. The judge had not yet arrived. There were a lot of people in court. The priest went up to the bench and spoke to a man for a long time. The "priest" Doyle was there. I wondered why. The Reverend Hancock walked in and the place went quiet. He sat down at the end of the seat. Everyone was looking away from him. After a little while, the gravelly murmur of men's voices returned.

At the back of the hall there were bags of corn. They were being stored there by B.J. Doyle's, the local corn factor, undertaker and publican. Doyle's manager was Pat Shanks and after every court the judge would call into a snug at the back and Shanks would supply him with a deorum of whiskey, brandy or some of the other fine ales, wines, beers or stouts that was his privilege to purvey. The anointed in turn reciprocated in return, in this land of nods and winks and blind horses. When a case was called in court, there were certain defendants who had previously spoken to Shanks, and his manner and demeanour changed when their cases were called. He would stand up and without as much as a cough, the bench would become aware that this particular defendant had ameliorating qualities, the correct interpretation of which would not go unnoticed in the local hostelry or, by implication, with other acquaintances of the same Mr. Shanks without as much as a word spoken. It was part of the system of privilege, patronage and power that did not require an Act of Parliament, simply glickness. I was sitting at the back of the court, next to the wall with Larkin beside me. I was the farthest in from the passageway. The clerk came in and said, "All rise!" and the judge came behind him. Larkin fell when he went to stand. It caused a ripple of nervous sniggering around us. "Silence!" barked the District court clerk. Larkin blushed while he was getting up.

The court commenced its business in a brusque and busy manner. Initially it was interesting and new but it was difficult to hear and understand. Dull words such as "applications" and "licences" were used a lot. Our interest flagged and we looked about. There was no sign of Miley. The "priest" Doyle was called to the stand. We got interested. He said he was a clerk in the Shelburne Co-Op in charge of accounts and that George Ward had paid no money off of his account since the Co-Op had got judgment against him, in spite of being reminded of the consequences. Mr. George Ward was a farmer. The "priest" Doyle said the court had made an order that a sum of five pounds per month be paid, they had received nothing. Doyle's solicitor said they were applying to have him committed to jail for contempt. The judge agreed and with a few bangs of an indelible stamp which he held in his hand, he turned the page in the large book in front of him and said "Next Case!" The "priest" Doyle stayed where he was and started to give evidence in another case. I knew George Ward. He was a small farmer, and a Protestant.

The business of the court rambled on and on. The sun streamed through the fanlit door at the back and the new sashless windows. Every time Shanks stood up the reflection from his glasses bounced around the ceiling. He did not stand up very often but when he did, the judge looked at him. He did not appear to have a reason for being there other than he was just listening to what was going on and he nodded a lot.

Larkin started to yawn. The guards were giving evidence of dogs not being licensed. One case made the place laugh. It was against Tommy Murphy. Sergeant Thorpey gave evidence that on a night in August last he was coming out of Coleman when he heard the noise of a bike coming down the hill. The bicycle had no flash lamp. He called on the cyclist to halt, but he did not. He recognised the Defendant, Thomas Murphy, by his voice.

Justice: "Why had he no light?"

Sergeant: "I don't know Justice – he made a rude remark."

Justice: "What did he say?"

(Pause.)

Justice: "What did he say Sergeant?"

Sergeant: "He said it was up in his posterior."

There was a burst of sniggered laughter that quelled under the raised eyebrows of the clerk.

Justice: "Is he in court?"

Clerk: "Thomas Murphy, Rathhill, Shielbaggin."

Tommy blushed and stood.

Clerk: "Are you Thomas Murphy?"

Tommy: "I am."

Justice: "Why did you have no light?"

Tommy: "I forgot."

Justice: "You must have forgotten your manners as well. Why did you not stop for the Sergeant?"

Tommy: (No answer.)

Justice: "Lost our tongue as well, have we?"

Sergeant Thorpey was smug. I felt sorry for Tommy.

Justice: "Any previous conviction, Sergeant?"

Sergeant: "No, Justice."

The Justice looked back again at Tommy. "Did you not hear the Sergeant when he called at you?"

Tommy blurted out that the Sergeant had shouted at him that he hoped it would burn the backside out of him. (Mother of Christ!) Tommy had bungled into a warp where the tides of ignorance, pomp, innocence and power had met on the one strand. The effect was electrifying and paralysing simultaneously. The judge was struck dumb. Tommy looked stupid. The crowd sniggered. The clerk looked stone faced.

Pat Shanks sat down. Tommy was fined five shillings. The awkwardly smothered snorts revealed the presence of the oafs. The "priest" Doyle maintained his grim respectful reserve. Fr. Williams looked philosophical if a little pained. Tommy was either a smart-alec or a fool – he had nearly put himself in contempt of court.

Some papers were shuffled on the bench. Then the District court clerk called "Miley Cassidy of 'no fixed abode'." The Superintendent of the Guards stood up and said he was representing the State, but that the defendant was not present. The judge said it was a serious case and one which required the personal attendance of the Defendant. He said he would adjourn the case to the next court in June, and told the solicitor he would issue a warrant for his arrest to make sure of his attendance next time.

Although we were free to go, Fr. Williams stayed in his seat watching the other cases. The Reverend Hancock left immediately.

When the court was over, Fr. Williams spoke to the "priest" Doyle and Pat Shanks. Myself and Larkin stood there to one side waiting and listening. While they were talking, the judge came out from a side entrance.

"I'll have to go," said Shanks. "Himself will be wantin' a deorum."

As he walked away the "priest" Doyle regarded him. He smiled. A light curl barely grew at each end of the thin line of his mouth.

"There goes 'The Keeper of the Keys,' " he said as he turned to Fr. Williams. "Better than any solicitor," he winked, smiled and nodded at the priest. He noticed us and looked away. Fr. Williams turned and beckoned us "Come on boys."

∞∞

The next day, I was taken to the Co-Op where my father got my Confirmation suit. The only thing I did not like about it was the fact that it had knee length pants. The "priest" Doyle happened on my father and made a beeline for us. "They won't enforce the boycott here, you know." He said with evident displeasure. My father entertained him only briefly. On my way home in the car I asked him why there really was a boycott. He told me it was because the Protestants had helped Mrs. Hanlon break her word that she had given to bring up her two children as Catholics. I asked him if they were killed would they all go to Hell as well as their mother. He said he was not sure, but she had broken her word and that was a wrong thing to do. I thought about it for a little while and then he told me not to worry about it since it involved adults only. I took consolation from this because that meant it was okay for us to keep going down to Hiawatha, on my interpretation.

At Sunday morning Mass, the priest gave the sermon of his life. There was hardly a sound in the church. He told the congregation how only recently their Bishop had expressed the view that there was a need for Catholic action associations to promote the Faith of our Fathers. Little did he think of how prophetic his Lordship's words were and how imminent the test. "Catholic children have been stolen from this parish aided and abetted by Protestants from this parish," he said. He told how opportunity after opportunity had been given to have the children returned but they had been treated with derision and greeted with a list of demands including an additional requirement that their father damn his soul and self and become a Protestant.

He then outlined that there would be an exercise in Catholic action by the withholding of patronage and custom from Protestant people in business. This would be done in a dignified manner he said. There would be no heckling or jeering. No threats. No intimidation. We were free to favour whosoever we might with our custom – it was up to us to choose – and we would do so bearing in mind that he who caused injustice to my faith and my beliefs must answer to me. We would stand by our religion as stood our fathers before us "by dungeon, fire and sword." This would be a magnificent, dignified and loyal declaration of fealty to Our Faith, Our Pope and Our God – a dignified protest.

Some people said this was a B-O-Y-C-O-T-T and that was what was being organised. He had vowed never to use the word. There would be no deprivation of the necessities of life; human kindness and Christian charity would prevail. Some people might find reasons for not supporting this protest. They might remember the French proverb "He who excuses himself, accuses himself." All it would take for evil to succeed would be for good men to do nothing. They would be remembered for their loyalty to their faith by the next generation. They need have no doubt but that they would be attacked, but they need have no fear, their priests would never let them down or abandon them. They would be supported to the last.

The church was packed. Everyone knew what was coming, and they were not disappointed. After Mass, the "priest" Doyle was talking to Sergeant Thorpey outside the door. When I was going to get the collection box from the gallery, I heard him say that he was glad the priest had gone all the way with his suggestion. I told Larkin what my father had said coming home from the Co-op and we agreed that this was sufficient approval for maintaining our relations with Hiawatha.

"I wish to Jesus I was a Prod and maybe I wouldn't have to go to school."

"Yeah," I said. "But you'd have to be English to be one."

"What about Hiawatha?" he asked.

"That's different, he's Presbyterian – the Protestants are all the English," I assured him.

My father always cooked a fry after Sunday morning Mass because we fasted from Saturday midnight in order to receive Communion on Sunday morning. He made gravy by pouring some freshly wet tea on the hot dripping pan. It sizzled and threw up a cloud of smoke and was poured over the plates of rashers, sausages and puddings. It was a homely aroma. It tasted well, except he nearly always burned the sausages.

As we ate, my mother said she did not like the idea at all of the boycott. My father nodded his head up and down and that was the end of that. He said the Wexford team were going to America at the end of the month and that the Kellys would be coming back on the same flight. This sounded promising. My mother announced that her brother, my uncle, Fr. Michael, would also be home from the Missions in Nigeria before the end of June. He had gone there in 1949 as a newly ordained priest. That same year my grand uncle, who was a Monsignor in Johannesburg, in South Africa, died. My mother made us pray for him when we were going to bed, "May the Lord have mercy on uncle Fr. Willie's soul to heaven." He was the Dean of Johannesburg. We received photographs of his funeral cortege and it appeared he was very important.

∽∾

After breakfast Larkin called and we set off to see Hiawatha. When we got there, Pat Shanks was there and so was Miley Cassidy. They were sitting on the windowsill in the early morning sun. Shank's horn-rimmed glasses were like a Kaleidoscope reflecting the light.

We got off the bikes and stood waiting to be invited forward. Hiawatha bade us come in and told me to go upstairs to a table in his bedroom and bring down the reel. He told Larkin to get the rod from the top of the dresser. Miley was sitting on the stone trough of a yard pump located in the yard.

When we returned Hiawatha started to assemble the rod as the men spoke. I wondered whether Miley knew the guards were looking for him. He was sitting, hunched, his elbows on his knees, his hands playing with one another. He noticed Shank's yellow boots.

"Begog, Mr. Shank's, them's a mighty fine pair a' boots ya have on there," as he straightened one elbow.

Shank's removed the pipe he was smoking, raised the toe of his boot in acknowledgement and crossed it over the other, akimbo style.

"Mmmf!" he grunted. "We have them beyant in the shop for only seventeen an' six the pair. Ya could walk to Jerusalem and back in 'em and you'd never know."

Miley admired the boots and said, "Begog Mr. Shank's, sure yid only be goin' home."

Shank's grunted and Hiawatha laughed and looked at me, and laughed again. "You'll land yourself in jail yet Miley," Hiawatha said.

I winced at the accidental innocent declaration.

"Ah! Mr. Shank's is a friend of mine – he'll look after me," said Miley. Shank's ignored him like an indolent bulldog, basking in the Sunday sun, great jowls of flesh hanging down his cheeks.

"Mmmmf!" he grunted again.

Hiawatha assembled the rod in the presence of the audience. It looked tremendous to our eyes. It was ten feet long and had a terylene line. At the end there was a trace of "flies" attached and secured by invisible nylon or what we called "catgut."

"Now boys, we're in business," he said. "Let's take the flies for a swim."

Just as we were leaving the "priest" Doyle came down the lane. He told Hiawatha, it was alright, that he would call to see him again. We fished all the afternoon, and as the Gospels said, "but caught nothing."

⟨∘⟩

On the way home from Hiawatha's we saw the "priest" Doyle talking with Tommy Murphy. Mr. Doyle would seldom be seen talking to a workman unless it was in the line of work. Larkin shouted over at him,

"How a' ya Tommy, how is yer arse?"

Tommy would normally have shot back at him, but he only looked up and ignored him away again. The "priest" Doyle gave a long cold stare at us. Larkin knew he had put his foot in it. He had interrupted a serious conversation. "Be the fuck!" he said. "C'mon." When we were out of earshot he said, "That's some gobshite that fella."

That afternoon, the first round of the Junior Football Championships started. Coleman were down to play Gusserane in Gusserane Park. My father brought all of us and Larkin. The junior footballers were experienced adults who had not made it to elite senior status. They were the highest grade in our Club and for a good few of the clubs around. The Junior Football Championship at district level gave rise to great rivalry and, occasionally, animosity. My father parked the car at the sideline. Peter was there, so was Martin and Tommy Murphy was with him. Peter came over and spoke to my father through the open window

"The priest was fairly tough this morning," my father said.

Peter agreed. He would take handling, he said, and so would the "priest" Doyle. Larkin was listening, so was I.

"That gobshite!" my father remarked dismissively.

"He told Tommy he would have to stop getting his stuff in Auld's from now on."

He went on to say Tommy was in an awful quandary because he always got stuff on "tick." Could he be helped out? He would of course. He would come over in the morning. I was proud of my father. Larkin looked pleased as well.

The match was great, but it was useless. The lads beat them – which was great, but they trounced them – which made no match of it at all. We wandered over to the team as they were togging in, in the ditch behind the cars. They had beaten them by eighteen points. Tommy Murphy was in right form again.

"Nineteen points to a point." They had trounced them alright. Then in mock disgust threw the peak cap he was wearing on the ground and said, "God blast it lads, who let them get the feckin' point?"

They guffawed with laughter. Fr. Williams did not hear them, but was told what was said and he thought it was hilarious. The "priest" Doyle was not there. Someone said he left early to go off to referee another match.

∽∾

When we got back to Coleman, we went to Larkin's house first. There were two motorcars outside and one of them was the Canon's. I did not recognise the other. Larkin pricked up. A woman was coming out through the door. She saw our car pulling up and went back in. "There's somethin' up," Larkin said darkly. The Canon came out. My father got out of the car and said, "Stay with the lads there for a moment Michael." I looked at Larkin, he was quiet and his eyes were large and still. He was staring at the Canon. My father turned the Canon away from the car as they spoke. After a few moments he came back to the silent car. He called Michael out. He walked down the street with him, his arm on his shoulder. Larkin was walking very slowly. His hand went to his face, and then the other one. My father gave him a hanky. Hiawatha came out of the door of the house. His eyes were red. He looked at my father and Larkin across the street, turned away and pinched his nose between the eyes for a moment. He was crying. I was beginning to get alarmed. My two younger brothers started fighting and this distracted me momentarily. When I looked back Hiawatha was hugging Larkin. Larkin was crying. My father came back to the car.

"There's bad news," he said to me. "Michael's father is dead. He died suddenly when we were at the match." I could not believe it. My father touched his top lip with his tongue and his eyebrow quivered momentarily. " 'Twill be alright though," he said. "There's no need to cry."

I looked back at my friend as the car pulled away. I was welling up inside. He was standing beside Hiawatha looking pale and miserable, but he was not crying anymore. "He's an orphan now," I thought, and the notion of it frightened me. I turned to my father after a long while and asked, "What will he do now? He has no parents."

"I don't know," my father answered, absently and repeated, "I don't know." It was the first time I was aware that my father did not have the answer to a serious problem. He was always cool in a crisis.

"He has no relations," I said and this lingered with me. My concern for his future and his security took me over.

"God never shuts a door but he opens a window," my father replied.

That night, Larkin's father was waked. I was brought to keep Michael company. Everyone who came brought provisions. There was a shoal of women cooking and washing up and feeding. A school of men here were smoking, another sitting down to a meal, a mixture in the hall had glasses of porter in their hands. The corpse was upstairs. Larkin was in good form, which surprised me. I thought he would start crying when he saw me, because I nearly did.

"There's no use in crying," he said. "You have to get on with life." Larkin was trying to be very grown up. I thought he was fierce tough. I entered in to the spirit of it.

"You're a farmer now," I said.

He looked up at me and said, "I have a lot of responsibility now."

"Who will you stay with?" I asked.

"Hiawatha!" he replied. I was surprised.

"Me mother's brother was married to a sister of his," he told me.

He had said it one time before, but I had not believed him.

"That makes him your uncle," I enthused.

"Not really, but kinda" he said. "He's the only relative I have."

It was the closest to loneliness he ventured and it touched me.

"Where is he?" I asked.

"Upstairs," he said quickly. "Go on up."

I was sorry to the heart I had opened my mouth. The memory of Mrs. Jones' corpse was still fresh in my mind. I tentatively went up the stairs behind him. In the room was a crucifix between two candles and a table. Just in front was a sprig of palm in a bowl of holy water. He went up and shook the wet sprig on his father's corpse and put his hand on his forehead, as he must have seen people doing all the afternoon. There was a man and two women in the room, keeping watch. Larkin nodded to me, beckoning me do the same. I saw the brown habit, which I detested, and the wax-like fingers interlaced with the rosary beads resting on his breast. The nostrils looked dark, the breast was still. I took the sprig in my hand and dipped and blessed and put it back, and blessed myself. He nudged me and nodded at his dead father's forehead. I held my hand out and moved to the bed.

"He's in here," a deep voice on the stairs distracted me as two men came in to the room. I looked back at the forehead and the wisps of withered hair behind it. I touched it and it felt cold, so very cold. I felt the chill go through me as my heart got cold too. I moved back, my face was on fire. The corpse never moved. "Mind there young lad."

I was in the path of the newcomers. I moved to the back of the room where Larkin was sitting. I sat back a while, he leaned forward, elbows on knees, his hands together concealing the top of a beads just below the level of his knees. This was a pose I had seen many of the older men adopt in church. His father would have prayed like this. We stayed for what I thought was an awful long time. Occasionally, someone would come over and toss his hair and tell him he was "a great little man." A lot of the women looked drawn when they saw him. A few of them cried. They asked him if I was his friend, and he said my name and said yes.

I was sharing his grief with him and I did not know it. Sam Duffin came up and called the two of us out.

"You're in there long enough now. Come on and get some tea." I was glad to be out.

When we came down I saw the "priest" Doyle there. He was talking to my father. He was telling him a committee would have to be set out to enforce the protest against the Protestants. He called it a Vigilance Committee. My father was in one of his "passing him off" modes. I could tell by the way Doyle would say, "Isn't that right John?" everytime he caught his eye wandering.

Larkin's father was buried on Thursday; Larkin was not in school for the week. I called to him twice, but each time he was not there. On each occasion I came home and busied myself building and making my truck. The wheels were the problem. The wheels were always the problem and the main reason I had no truck up until now. We had very few carpenters' tools at home. There was, however, a hammer, a saw and some pliers. My father had a last for heeling our boots and shoes. I used to wear a pair of boots which were purchased at Halloween. They squeaked a lot. On All Soul's Night we used walk in and out of the church every few minutes making visits to the Blessed Sacrament which obtained a plenary indulgence for the particular member of the dearly departed we were praying for. I squeaked and squealed souls loose from purgatory "to beat the band." The boots had a steel heel to prevent wear. They made the sound of a man walking. I would wear them until the Confirmation on Sunday when my new shoes would replace them.

There was a type of unofficial dump at the Rockwell and though I traipsed through it all, I could find no wheels. I looked in the quay when the tide was out. I searched the caves and rocks on the shore. No wheels were to be found. I had the best truck in the business, but damned the bit of me could find one wheel, let alone two. The search would resume after the funeral.

Larkin's father was the fifty-fourth burial since the winter had started. The only non-Catholic at his funeral was Hiawatha.

"When the chips are down, they'll stick together like glue?" said the "priest" Doyle of the Protestants. "Didn't we see the crowd of them last Sunday week, the likes of which we never saw before – from all quarters, including Ross. Plotting and scheming to keep the children away. I'm tellin' ya – given half a chance they'd be priest hunting again."

This was said to Sergeant Thorpey as they came away from the priest's house after the first meeting of the Vigilance Committee. His Lordship, the Bishop would surely have something to say about it at the Confirmation on Sunday.

I met Larkin on Saturday. He was quiet and looked pained. He said he was "Grand, Grand!" but I knew he was not. Hiawatha was staying with him in the house. I could not believe it when he told me that Hiawatha was sleeping in his father's bed, the one he had been waked in.

"He's some man," I respectfully acknowledged.

"You're tellin' me," he said. "He gets up every morning at seven and sits like an Indian on the floor facing the sun for a half hour. "He says he's meditatin'." He never mentioned the funeral.

❧ 9 ❧

Transubstantiation and the Churching of Mrs Thorpey

The church choir was beautiful.

"Veni Creator Spiritus Mentes Tuorum Visita"
("Come O Spirit of the Creator, Take Your Rest in our Souls").

The invocation in sung Latin and the panaplea of gothic vestments, mitre and crosier combined to give an atmosphere of significant, distinguished and royal authority. "Confirmation is a sacrament which makes us strong and perfect Christians," the Catechism said. When he was preaching his sermon the Bishop quoted it. He emphasised the words "strong" and "perfect."

He spoke of the persecutions of Christians in Russia, Eastern Europe and China where, daily, "thousands faced martyrdom." But it was not enough to merely preserve our Faith he said. He had spoken recently in this very church on the need for soldiers for Christ. That was on the occasion of the death of a well-known soldier patriot and doctor. It seemed as if God had planned it that he should have given the sermon then that he had, in the light of events that had unfolded since.

"Here in this Catholic country, in this very parish, attacks are being made on the church and its Ministers. The response of the church and its people to attacks and misrepresentations must be to arm ourselves with the truth and in that way, fight error.

There seems to be a concerted campaign to entice or kidnap Catholic children and in that way deprive them of their faith. In the current dispute, it is quite clear from the evidence produced so far that help was sought and procured in the commission of this grave offence.

The people of God must express their resentment and justified indignation. This is the responsibility we have as Soldiers of Christ. It is a time to stand up and be counted and, within the bounds of what is just and charitable, a solid and dignified protest of loyalty must be made.

This dispute was not started by any action of any Catholic person, and it can only be finished by those who started it. It is right and fitting that their errors be pointed out to them so that they must not be deprived of the opportunity to correct them. This is the sacred responsibility of your Bishop and your clergy and it is your sacred responsibility as confirmed Christians – the Faithful – to loyally follow that leadership.

These young men and women here today will follow in your footsteps. Make sure those steps follow the right path – the path that your church has pointed out under pain of sin, the awful sin of disobedience. We are members of the One True Church established by Christ when he handed Peter the keys and said 'Upon this rock I will build my church and the gates of Hell will not prevail against it.' This promise is made to those within and is the threat to those outside. 'For eye has not seen, nor ear heard what things God has prepared for those who love him.'

With the authority vested in me and given freely from the hand of Peter's Successor I commend you for your loyalty and steadfastness in the Faith and I bless you, in the name of the Father, and the Son, and the Holy Ghost, Amen."

After the ceremony we all had our photograph taken. Hiawatha was there with Larkin. They were both the subject of pity and admiration. The Bishop walked like a shepherd amongst his flock afterwards. There was a group photograph taken with the Bishop. It appeared in *The New Ross Standard* the following week. Wherever the Bishop went he was followed by Fr. Williams, who was followed by the "priest" Doyle. He spent some time talking to my uncle Peter, who went into the priest's house after he had given me a fiver. Larkin was beating all records with the money he was getting. He told me twice how much he had and what it had increased to.

Hiawatha kept standing in the one spot and, like an errant foal, Larkin would canter off, darting in and out among the adults, but ultimately finding his way back home to deposit holy pictures, medals and money. Mostly, he got money. Mostly, I got holy pictures.

Fr. Williams introduced the Bishop to Larkin and in turn to Hiawatha. The Bishop received the Presbyterian courteously, who reciprocated graciously. They moved on and Hiawatha let them. He put on his terylene coat which he had carried on his forearm whilst holding the lapel of his three-piece suit. He looked distinguished, even with the plaster-of-Paris sticking out under the ripped seam of his navy blue trousers. My father spoke to him for a while and they both laughed a good deal. They got on well together.

The nuns fussed, especially over the girls and their stupid veils that kept blowing up in the mid-May wind. Some of them kept getting them tangled in something or other. If it was not the bolt of the church door, they got caught in someone else's hair slide or new watch. They were as giddy as chickens at a fox's funeral. Helen Martin kept coming over to me telling me I "looked grand entirely" and then she would run back tittering to some of her silly friends who would snigger and gather in to a corner, all facing in to the middle like fowl at a feeding trough, chucking and gaggling.

"Ninny-hammers," I said to Larkin, nodding at them.

"I'd say the Martin wan fancies ya alright."

"Would ya ever shag off!" I told him. "That wan is as stupid as a blind cow."

"Ho! Ho!" he said and then jeeringly repeated, "Ho! Ho!"

I was glad to get out of the churchyard. That afternoon my father took us all to see his mother and afterwards to my mother's parents. They were looking forward to Michael coming home. I remembered before he left some seven years previously there had been a big gathering of the family. Fr. Michael was great craic and got on well with all the kids. I was looking forward to his homecoming, not only from the belief that my new spiritual status would not pass unrecognised and unrewarded, but I liked him because he was jolly.

The next day at school we got notice that the inter-parish school sports would be held on the third Sunday in June. We also got notice that the Feis would take place on the last Sunday of June. The nuns would be most interested in this. This meant the next month would be taken up in school learning and practising poetry, singing and story telling and dancing. Other schools would take part and the competition would be lively.

Larkin was back in school again. At first I thought he had gone quiet in himself. In the 4 x 100 relay race he was third leg and I was fourth. As he handed the baton to me in practice, he dropped it and blamed me. I protested loudly and while remonstrating with him I noticed my voice had broken. It put me off my stride a little, so I conceded to him more or less on the basis of the hard time he was having. Afterwards I told him I was making a truck. We decided we would give it attention after school.

After I had observed the rule of the house at home, namely, "no play until all homework and housework are finished," I went down to Larkin. Gerry was there talking to Hiawatha. Since Hiawatha was handicapped from his injury, he had to get someone to help. We searched around Larkin's outoffices and up in the lofts to see if there was a redundant wheel anywhere. We came across an assortment of pulley wheels and cogwheels from a horse drawn binder, but they were not suitable. Hiawatha sent us to bring in the cows. Gerry Denn shook out the hay for the weary animals and put turnips in their stalls from a barrow. He milked them by hand, whenever Larkin or myself would be close by he would skurt the cow's teat, with a white jetlike stream, into the puss. Larkin could milk, that was how he got his warts.

"Maybe Hiawatha has a wheel in the forge," I urged Larkin. There was nothin' to be lost in asking.

"Maybe there is," Hiawatha responded and then to my disappointment added, "but I doubt it." On seeing this, he asked us if we had considered making one.

"Makin' a wheel?" I asked disbelievingly.

"And did you think they grew?" he asked. Larkin laughed at his question.

"I thought they were made in factories and places."

"And so they are. So why not – let's try," he invited.

"God gave you a brain and a pair of hands."

We were off on another adventure. It was agreed the making of the wheel would be deferred until all of the spring farm work was finished. In the meantime, we could start planning its manufacture.

Initially as we went around the farm we would come across some unfinished item of work. A door half-painted because of a shower of rain or some such, a shed half-tidied with the intention of completion later. But they were never finished by their originator, and each time we would happen on this, or a coat that had been hung up and not brought in, Larkin would fall silent. He would not speak about it. Tactlessly, I asked him once whether he missed his father, and he told me not to be "such a shaggin' eejit." I could have bitten off my tongue. He got annoyed with the hay he was piking at the time and pulled a much bigger shkeal off of the rick than he had intended. He staggered under it to the cow house out of temper.

The nuns seldom asked him questions in school now. He was doing his Primary Cert with me at the end of June and then he would go to work on the land as his father had always intended he would. When he talked it was always about Hiawatha. He could not believe the amount of books he had upstairs, he told me. He played the fiddle every night and read the Bible every night. He told him stories about Arabs and Marco Polo. He showed him shipping charts and maps of the United States. They were "Engineer's maps," he told Larkin. I was envious of all of the attention he was getting, but yet I was glad for him.

One evening just before the end of May, an incident occurred. We had brought in the cows for Gerry Denn to milk when we met Mary Byrne coming out. She was wearing a scarf and her head was bowed down. She almost walked into the first cow. It had a horn that was turned down and had succeeded in practically gouging out its eye. Mary took a start and when she saw the cow and uttered "God!" Mary's face was red, she had been crying. "I'm sorry," she apologised as she passed us going out. We both looked after her as she mounted her bicycle with attached front wicker basket.

Gerry was preoccupied and silent. It seemed as if that was the prevailing mood everywhere in Coleman. My father was preoccupied and so was my mother. Hiawatha was not as cheerful as previously and now here were Gerry and Mary Byrne in the same mood. A gloom had descended. Mary McIntosh, who always got her milk from the Whitneys, no longer went for it. James Mooney, who helped out in Clarke's pub on Saturday nights and Sunday nights, no longer helped out. Mary Molloy crossed the street rather than meet Rebecca Auld coming down on the same pavement. The Morans stopped going to the Coopers where they used to play cards every Saturday night. Only the innocent were not affected so far.

When the cows were milked Larkin and myself got our tea. Hiawatha had cooked for the four of us. Immediately we finished, we ran out to play hurling in the yard with a rubber ball. There was a porch to the rear of the old farmhouse and a surface water shore ran beneath it. It was a nuisance from our viewpoint because inevitably the ball would find its way into it and get stuck there. On this occasion, we tried reaching with hurls to no avail. Larkin went for a long handled pike. The adjacent kitchen window was down and I could hear Gerry tell Hiawatha that it was off between himself and Mary because the priest had made her. It was off between Tommy Whitney Junior and Agnes Maher as well for the same reason. Gerry appeared to be very subdued. Hiawatha was very quiet. When Larkin came back I told him what had been said. "The boycott," was all he said. We retrieved the ball and hurled away. Boyfriends and girlfriends would always be a bother whether there was a boycott or not. At least you could be sure life was worth living as long as there was hurling.

Hiawatha had not opened the forge since before the boycott began when he broke his leg. One day when he was checking it out, the "priest" Doyle called and told him he was glad to see the forge was re-opened. Larkin had been with him. The blacksmith told him he would not be re-opening it until he had the plaster off. Doyle responded by saying that everyone was looking forward to him re-opening, including Fr. Williams. It seemed he was not to be boycotted, Larkin concluded.

Clarke's pub was deserted. Auld's shop was empty. My father worked away in his shop serving Protestant and Catholic alike. The "priest" Doyle spent a lot of time around the place. Every evening, he sat in his car in the street, occasionally lowering his newspaper to see who was coming and going and more to the point, from where and to where they were coming and going.

Hiawatha never mentioned it to us. One evening he asked us to go to Auld's for a plug of tobacco and gave us sixpence for sweets for ourselves. Larkin took the money and went out the door. When we were outside I looked at him. The "priest" Doyle was sitting in his car in the street. I stopped.

"Well are ya comin' or not?" he said to me. I was in a dilemma. The news would be home before me if I went. I had to serve Mass in the morning. Was I going to refuse Hiawatha, who was going to make my truck and its wheels, who had taught us to fish, who had been our advisor, counsellor and storytelling companion for so long. "I'll go down with ya as far as the shop and wait for ya outside," I compromised.

As I waited outside for Larkin I felt like the lookout at a bank robbery. I knew I had made a big mistake. Larkin was inside out of view and here was my presence outside, naked and exposed to the world at large, declaring to all and sundry who cared to look that I was ignoring the protest. I could feel all the eyes on me. The "priest" Doyle's paper was down. Larkin was taking ages. Would he ever come out? I was dying a slow agonising and lingering death. When the door opened behind him the bell rattled loudly and I almost jumped.

"What kept ya?" I darted.

"What's wrong?" he said. "I couldn't have been faster, 'cept'n I was to stale the stuff." He handed me a chocolate drumstick. "Stick that in your gob, it might help to stop you bullshitting."

He seemed totally unaware of what we had done. As we walked back up the street the "priest" was reading his paper again. When we passed his car Larkin gave me a big wink and said, "I think the G-men are in town." I winced. Doyle had eyes that would pierce you, a nose that twitched unerringly and pathetically at deviation and a pair of ears that had a multifunction aspect. Not alone could he hear the grass grow, but he could almost smell with them when he had a cold and his nose was dysfunctional. They promised to be pointed, the crevices all sloped upwards to a point, but the rim disappointingly flattened depriving the complete caricature.

When we got back to the house, Hiawatha lit his pipe and started talking to us about making the wheel. We were not long there talking when a knock came to the door. Larkin answered. "Could I speak to Mr.

Watchorn please?" the "priest" Doyle asked. Larkin showed him in to the front room. I nearly died. What would he say to him, what would he say to Hiawatha? Larkin appeared unperturbed. When the door opened after their discussions were over my heart stopped. The blacksmith showed his visitor out. When he came back he said to me that I ought to be going home now. I was glad to leave. But my anxiety came with me.

⚭

Back at home the radio had announced that the Hanlon case had been left open by the judges in the Belfast High Court. The reason for this was that Mrs. Hanlon was not there and she had apparently fled from the country. There was no one to make an order against. My father said it was a conspiracy. They were all in on it, "judges, barristers, solicitors the whole bloody lot of them."

Peter arrived later and said the Bishop had been on to him. He was furious at the result of the High Court case. He had asked him to assist in organising the Knights of Columbanus to become the eyes and ears of the Catholic Party in the search for the children. He was going to Dublin tomorrow at the Bishop's request to see what could be done. Things were beginning to hot up.

Elsewhere, Wexford had beaten Cork in the Polo Grounds in New York, seven goals and fifteen points to five goals and five points. We were all thrilled. When Fr. Williams arrived later, he took this good news in his stride. I was ordered to bed, but tonight of all nights, I needed to eavesdrop. Fr. Williams had been unable to look at me when he came in. I knew this was trouble.

He waited for a while and then the subject with the Belfast court case came up. "I think we might have some more trouble," he said. "William Doyle called down to Larkin's this evening to collect the Easter Dues that had not been paid. He was told there was little or no money in it at the moment."

My father thought there would be no trouble with the blacksmith.

"I know he's a Protestant and all," he said, "but he's not a bigot."

The priest said he had believed the same himself, but now he was not so sure.

"It's a Catholic farm," he said, "and Catholic dues should be paid from it. I am a bit concerned about the way he's going on," he said soberly. There was a silence of anticipation. And then he said it.

"He made young Larkin and Jack break the boycott this evening."

They were not using the word "protest" anymore. My father went quiet. The curate explained.

"I'm sure it was harmless, Father," my mother volunteered. "Jack would never do anything deliberately wrong and I am sure Mr. Watchorn wouldn't deliberately make him do anything wrong either."

The priest said he was sure she must be right, but the matter had to be addressed. "You just don't know," he said. "He's a Protestant and you just don't know what lengths they will go to with children. I think it would be better for young Larkin if he was packed off to St. Peter's College in September."

I nearly froze on the stairs. I knew I was going to that secondary school for a long time. If I wanted to make a life for myself, I needed to be educated. But Larkin had a farm and hated school. He had his heart set on farming and the prospect that he might be sent to a boarding school would appeal to him like a prison, given the free spirit he was. I scarpered up the stairs, leaped into bed and covered my head.

∞ ∞

Fr. Williams now appeared to be preoccupied as well. In the morning he barely acknowledged my presence which in some sense was a relief. However, when I got home my mother satisfied herself about the previous night's happenings.

"I know these are difficult times for everyone, particularly since they are your friends, but we have to stand by our Faith, difficult and all as it might seem. We have to do the right thing."

In school I was entered for the dancing competitions in the Feis, the storytelling (scealaíocht), recitation (filíocht) and the flageolet or tin whistle (feadóg stáin). We had a marching band of flageolets with percussion accompaniment. It sounded terrible. When they all played together it sounded shrill and doleful like a whining wind through a raftered roof. When they did not play together it jarred on the nerves and was only mildly more embarrassing. The only instrument that sounded any way right was the drum. It was a snared side drum. Larkin was the drummer. He had a natural gait and could rattle a snappy march beat. Hiawatha had shown him. I did not know how I was going to tell him about what the priest had said. I decided to put it off until that evening.

When Sr. Ignatius was in form she would promote argument and debate. Eagerly and easily I would always respond. Larkin did not enter into things of this nature quite so easily. Doctrinal interpretations of religion were always a source of debate. She would explain the background to some ecclesiastical, historical dispute which either resulted in a schism or an encyclical or a decree excommunicating the heretic. Around this time she spent a lot of time dealing with the Real Presence in the Eucharist and other matters which "Martin Luther, suffering from the sin of pride, was unable to accept."

We asked whether the Lutherans had Mass and she told us they had Service and *The Book of Common Prayer*. They believed that the Eucharist was a representation of the Last Supper and therefore only symbolic, whereas we believed that Christ was actually present in the Host.

Larkin put up his hand. "You mean Sister, that it's like magic – that the priest is like a magician – like."

Her eyes narrowed. "There is quite a difference, young man, between magic and a miracle." It was the first time that Larkin had volunteered anything in school for ages. We were all taken aback.

Steadily, Ignatius went on to further elucidate how King Henry VIII, having first supported the Pope against Luther, turned against him when he would not dissolve his marriage and he martyred his very own Chancellor, St. Thomas Moore, in the process.

Larkin listened to her as his smouldering black pupils defied her.

"You still have a problem, Master Larkin."

"I do sister."

"Out with it!"

He paused, reluctant to commit himself. He was beginning to push it again. (Jesus but she would kill him.) I looked down.

"I thought – er – I thought it was to do with turning our hearts an' stuff."

"What was?"

"I thought taking part in the Eucharist was to – sort of like – change us, not the – er – Host."

She was momentarily disarmed. This was not just a challenge to Ignatius, but to the church itself. Yet what Larkin said appeared to have a certain ring of sense to it.

"Some men's hearts will never change," she said. "Which is why we submit to the teaching authority of the church."

Larkin resumed his seat. Ignatius kept her gaze on him steadily. A look of triumph was beginning to appear in her eyes.

"Happy?" she asked.

I prayed that he would say that he was.

"If you say so, sister," he replied politely.

"Oh it's not what I say – it's your question." She was not letting him away so lightly. There was a pained silence as everyone waited.

"I just don't see how bread can turn into flesh if it's not magic" he blurted.

There was a deadly silence. Once more she was stunned by his candour. She could see that anger was not going to work here. Deviously she said she would refer the matter to Fr. Williams for explanation. Almost immediately one of the other nuns, Sr. Berchmans arrived in and announced that Thorpey's mother had given birth to a baby boy. There was an enormous sigh of relief hidden in the gushing reception which the class gave to the news of the birth. Sr. Ignatius' stiffness did not go easily, even when she was told the baby would be called "Ignatius." Larkin and myself looked at one another revealing a mutual desire to get sick. Thorpey beamed at the girls who were doing their usual fussy stuff about babies. Ignatius's voice became jerky and her movements exaggerated, as happened whenever she became selfconscious.

Larkin had sailed very close to the wind. When I called down to him after my homework he was still talking about her. They were having their tea. "On the one hand she says she wants you to speak your mind, and then if you do, you run the risk of bein' bloody slaughtered." Hiawatha said we should never be afraid to speak our mind. It was a free country now, he told us, in spite of what was going on around us. I remembered what the priest had said about Larkin going to St. Peter's College and I said it out. It stopped the conversation dead. I felt like a traitor. They both stared at me. "Well that's what he said." I was fully conscious of the bad news I had brought. Larkin was white as a sheet. Hiawatha turned to the cooker and got the kettle to heat for washing up. He hobbled to the bucket and filled cups of water from it in to the kettle. When he placed it back on the hob, it sizzled. It was the only noise in the kitchen. Larkin said he needed to change his hanky and went upstairs. I sat down by the fire, both of my hands in my pockets feeling very sorry for everyone, especially myself.

"I'm sorry," I said.

"It's not your fault," Hiawatha said.

"Will he have to go?" I asked.

Hiawatha never answered.

The following day there was a hullabaloo in Coleman. Sean Hanlon had come home from Belfast where his application to the court had not been successful. The word was out that himself and Fr. Williams had nearly come to blows over the boycott. Sean Hanlon was completely against it. "Oats for the Protestants," the "priest" Doyle condemned him to Fr. Williams after Mass "and the Protestant Bishop coming today as well." The new Protestant Rector, the Reverend Deacon and the Reverend Hancock were there to greet him. All of the Protestants for miles around were there.

It was a wet summer's day, clammy and dead. The rain fell slowly for a long time. The birds all sat, brooding and dour. Larkin and myself wanted to see if the Bishop wore breeches and purple stockings, but he was wearing a soutane and we never found out. We were given a half day from school to prepare for the sports. On our way to the sport's field, we saw the complete show. It was like the meeting they had after Elisha Hanlon left which they said was to greet the new Rector. Fr. Williams said it was to organise the conspiracy. We saw our fill and moved on.

I told Larkin that Mel would be home the following week and that my uncle, Fr. Michael, was coming on Sunday all the way from Nigeria. He appeared to be preoccupied with something else. He was that way a lot of the time now. Larkin had spoken very little for a long time. He seemed to be holding a lot in. He never spoke of his father. He never spoke about the college. I felt uncomfortable with him now and then when these moods came.

When we arrived back from the sports field, there was a large crowd in Clarke's pub. Thorpey was playing with a wheel and a stick outside. He was wearing an elastic belt and had a homemade sword stuck in it. It was an ash plant and he had the lid of a floor polish tin, pierced through to act as a hand protection. It was supposed to be a rapier. The tin lid read "Cardinal Polish" and had a picture or drawing of a Cardinal with his red hat. The tin had contained red floor polish. In every house where there was a cement floor there was a box of Cardinal Polish.

We got off our bikes and went over to him. We admired the sword he said his father had made. He had found the stick in a grove behind Clarke's pub at the side of the road.

"Jays there's a right bend in it," said Larkin testing it. "They'd make right bows an' arra's."

We set off to explore. We passed three men sitting in front of the pub. One of them was Gerry Denn; he was wearing his hat on the Kildare side. The others looked sober enough. A girl was taking a photograph. He put his arm around the man beside him and said, "Sure if I can't have a girlfriend, maybe I'll get a boyfriend Ha! Ha! Ha! Ha!" he laughed.

"I suppose that's why they calls it a boycott – cause they won't lets you catch the girls – d' ya get it?" he nudged his companion. "D'ya get it?" and he laughed stupidly and merrily.

We passed him but he did not notice us. The others appeared embarrassed. Larkin laughed and so did Thorpey.

"He's langers," said Larkin. They brought him back into the pub as he started singing "My Mary of the Curling Hair."

"He has a bad dose of it," said Thorpey.

"His heart is broke," said Larkin.

I laughed at Larkin who seemed concerned at the threatened romantic breakup.

"You got a problem?" he eyed me, challenging me.

"No," I stuttered. "No – no – no I was just ..."

"Well don't just – he saved my life – remember!" No wonder he was so defensive. "I'm sorry," I apologised. Larkin was deep alright.

When we got to the grove we cut down a couple of sticks with Larkin's penknife. We had only started to cut off the shoots when James Clegg came out to us. He was the manager in Clarke's. He was a young man who was recently married. He took his responsibilities so seriously that he seldom smiled.

"What are you young fellows doin' here" he growled.

"It's a free country," said Larkin.

"For some people maybe," he snarled. "This is Mr. Clarke's property you're on."

Thorpey blushed when we both looked at him. He had landed us in it again. "Leave those sticks there and be off with ya" he said.

"Go an' have a shite!" Larkin defied.

"You leave those down at once or I'll tell your father on you," he threatened.

Larkin went white in the face at the mention of his deceased parent. He dropped all of the sticks except one. He raised it slowly and threateningly at the manager

"Put that down," Clegg said. "Put that down or you'll be sorry."

Larkin struck him full on the side of the head knocking off his horn rimmed glasses. He was not cut. Larkin let a roar. His face was redder than Ignatius in full flight – either Ignatius. The manager fled as Larkin flailed him from behind. I was terrified at the level of anger in Larkin. He was fifteen, but he was big for his age. However, it was the level of his anger not his size that frightened.

When he came back to us, his breath was coming in gasps that doubled on themselves. It was as if he had been crying, but there were no tears. Thorpey's mouth was open. At least mine was closed.

"Fuckin' oul' bastard!" said Larkin at last. "Leave his ould sticks," he commanded.

They were instantly dropped.

"Gobshite!" I concurred with a dedicated frown.

We rounded the corner. There was no one outside the pub. Thorpey went to the door and opened it. He stuck his head in and shouted,

"Proddy – woddy – woddy!"

Suffering Jesus! We nearly died. The gobshite. We ran up the street like the clappers. It was the best bit of training for the sports we did all day. I was out in front, head down and booting it. I ran smack bang into my father. "Shite!" I was flummoxed and winded. Larkin kept going, so did Thorpey. Mr. Clegg had come out through the door followed by Mr. Clarke and they saw I had been stopped. He called to my father. He gave me the condemned man's look.

"Go on home," he said. "I'll deal with you later."

He walked down the street to the manager of the licensed premises. I trudged home with a heavier spirit than a convict to the gallows.

When my father returned I was sent to bed. There was no discussion. He looked very cross. I felt sick myself. Next morning when I came in from Mass he told me he would deal with me that night. I felt the world had conspired against me once more. What had I done? I was only a witness. Larkin had used the stick, Thorpey had called the names, the gobshite, all I did was run. There was nothing wrong with running was there? Were we not told running was good for us? And to run often? And here when you go and do something that's good for you, you end up in trouble. There was no point in explaining it. No one would listen. Not my father, nor my mother. Grown ups were all the same. They could have their boycotts when they did not get their own way. It was different for kids. They got stolen and sent to bed and beaten by the nuns or bossed around. Just because Larkin beat up one of them you would think there was going to be a revolution of children and they were going to have to put down the ringleaders.

That night I got my sentence. I was to go down and apologise to Mr. Clegg and Mr. Clarke, bed every night at 8 o'clock for a week and no "down the street." What was I going to do – sleep and read and bore myself out of existence?

I took my punishment. Next day I went down to apologise. I rehearsed and rehearsed every single word I was going to say. It would be short and to the point. "I'm sorry for takin' your sticks and callin' you names. I'm sorry for takin' your sticks and callin' you names." When I walked into the pub both Mr. Clarke and Mr. Clegg were there. It was four o'clock. Gerry Denn was there as well. He was reading the paper and when I walked in he looked up.

"Well," says he. "I'm glad to see there's at least one not afraid to break the boycott. Mind the priest doesn't turn you into a frog when you go back."

"Stay quiet Gerry can't ya," said the manager. Mr. Clegg looked at me very seriously and said, "Yes?"

I was very nervous.

"I'm sorry for stealin' yer nicks ..."

Gerry snorted and guffawed and slapped the counter.

"Gerry, be quiet," commanded Mr. Clarke. "Yes?" the proprietor intoned once more. I got it right the second time and blushed.

"Let it not happen again," Mr. Clarke said stiffly. "Run along!"

Clegg had a black eye where the ash plant had caught him. He was not wearing his spectacles. He looked comical. Although I was in no mood for laughing I nearly did so.

⚭

The Corpus Christi procession always took place at two o'clock in the afternoon. The parade of the Blessed Sacrament took an hour and a half culminating with Benediction. This year it was to start at twelve noon. The priest announced this at Mass two Sundays before the day. I wondered at the time if it was on account of a match, but none of the big matches were played on feast days or holy days. Initially, it looked as if the priest wanted a big show of Catholic strength and was getting the word in early on.

After Mass, Larkin told me of the lecture he had received from Hiawatha, who had his plaster removed at last. He had brought him to the pub to apologise as well.

"Was Gerry there?" I asked.

"For a wonder he wasn't, but oul' Whitney Senior was, and it a Fair day an' all. Hiawatha says he's finished as a cattle dealer on account of the boycott."

"What did Clegg say to ya?" I was eager to see how this resolved.

"He said he was sorry for sayin' what he said."

The unfairness of life was monstrous. Here was Larkin havin' caused the whole business – well mostly – and he was getting an apology.

"For what?" I asked.

"What do ya mean for what? For saying what he said."

"What did he say?" I persisted.

"I told ya he said he was sorry," Larkin was getting hostile.

"No, I mean what did he say that he said he was sorry for saying?"

"You're reading too many riddles in the *Ireland's Own*," snapped Larkin.

Then I remembered about his father.

"Gobshite!" Larkin said as he took off his soutane.

Larkin was not in good form. It was his father's month's mind and he had been prayed for at Mass. On the way home, I told him I had two more days of my sentence to serve before I could go down. He told me he would not be in school during the week as he was thinning beet and they had to go to the livestock mart in New Ross on Tuesday which was only recently opened. I was looking forward to Fr. Michael coming home. Mel would be home as well before the end of the week. He brightened when he heard Mel's name mentioned.

Fr. Williams had been ordained with Fr. Michael in 1949. He was invited to the homecoming celebration. When I met Fr. Michael, he started playing with me, saying how big I had grown. He would let on to box and could easily get past my defences when he would tip me on the cheek with his fingertips. He had a lot of clichés. "Set like a jelly" was one he repeated regularly.

My cousins from Cork were there. We played hurling in the yard, Cork versus Wexford. Five of my cousins had the same name as me. One of them was a good hurler and could do a good solo run with the ball. I tried to stop him doing this by jamming him against a drainpipe, but I fell in the washroom drain. My father laughed and said it would crown me. His father laughed and said it was a typical Coleman tactic. My father checked me as well and told me to "take it aisey," and when the rest were not looking I caught him winking at another uncle.

In the middle of the afternoon there was a feast just like we had when Fr. Michael was going away. The kids were in one room and at the other end of the house were the adults. The women carried hot dishes to and fro. We stuffed ourselves crooked. There must have been thirty children present, there were certainly more than on the last occasion.

After the dinner Fr. Williams and Fr. Michael strolled on the front lawn. My grandmother sat in with the women and small children. My mother helped my aunts clean up. My grandfather sat in the sitting room with Canon Harpur who had just arrived, as had Peter. My brother and myself lost the tennis ball we had been using as a hurling ball in a bramble of briars and bushes. We used our hurleys to poke and peer.

"Couldn't you mind what you were doing?" he grumbled.

"Couldn't you keep your eyes on it?" I growled back.

"That's the second ball today," he complained.

"Well I didn't loose the first one," I clarified. "I'll get in to the field and see if it went through," I volunteered.

I went to the road, walked to where the gate was and climbed over it. I walked by the ditch that bounded the lawn and the yard. As I rooted down the drain in search of the ball, three men could be seen seated on a Victorian white garden seat in the shade of a monkey puzzle tree in front of the house.

"It's getting very serious," my father was saying.

"Thomas Whitney's business is gone. There was little or no stock for sale at the last Fair and the children are beginning to get in on it."

Fr. Williams said he knew it was not easy and it would probably get worse before it got better. Bishop Staunton, he said, wanted it spread nationally.

"Mother of Christ," my father said. "He's wantin' another shaggin' Civil War."

"Take it easy Fr. John," said Fr. Michael.

"Michael is right John, all the Bishop is trying to do is get the children back," said Fr. Williams.

At that stage I could see through the briars that Peter was joining them. I had lost interest in looking for the ball. He shook hands with Fr. Michael and said how delighted he was that he was home. Fr. Williams had to go. The three remaining sat down. They stayed with the news.

"The Protestant's Bishops visit stirred up a thing or two," said Peter. The Protestant's Bishops visit was covered in the Sunday papers saying that he deplored the whole business. The paper reported that, according to the Bishop, there had always been good relations between Protestants and Catholics and now the innocent were being victimised. Peter was annoyed. He said if the Protestants really wanted, they could get the children back alright. The Protestant Bishop apparently also said he would get a new teacher for the school. My father asked Peter whether it was true that Bishop Staunton wanted the matter spread nationally. Peter said the Bishop, who was a Knight of Columbanus, was raising the matter with them.

"This thing will turn ugly yet," my father said.

Fr. Michael concurred.

"We can only hope and pray," said Peter resignedly.

∞·∞

Next morning after Mass, the priest again asked me to wait. He asked me to leave on my surplice and soutane. I saw the Sergeant's car parked outside and a shiver went up my spine. When the priest came out he was divested of his vestments and was now wearing a surplice and a white stole. He looked at me and said,

"Mrs. Thorpey is to be churched this morning."

I had heard of "churchings" before but I had never served one. This was a function reserved for the "priest" Doyle, who, apparently, was away today.

"Just do as I say," said the priest. "Get the holy water."

I got the small brass bucket with the sprinkler. The inside of the bucket was green where it was dry. I went out on the altar, but there was no one in the church. I stood at the foot of the altar facing the tabernacle. The priest genuflected, I followed suit. He turned towards the absent congregation and indicated to me with his hand to walk down the church. I had no idea where to go, except to keep going. When we got to the back of the church, he stopped and opened his prayer book.

"Open the door," he said to me. I stepped forward and there at the other side holding a candle was the timid shape of an embarrassed and frightened Mrs. Thorpey.

"Adjutorium nostrum in Nomine Domine," the priest invoked as he sprinkled and splashed the holy water.

"Qui fecit coelum et terram," I responded.

The priest presented me with the extremity of his stole that hung around his neck down over his left shoulder to give to her. His back was turned to her. She took it in her right hand while rising up from her knees and walked into the church behind the priest holding the candle in her right. I led the small procession to the altar as the priest muttered away in Latin. She was brought to the statue of the Blessed Virgin, just behind the altar rails. The priest closed his book. He recited in Greek

"Kyrie Eleison," he intoned.

"Kyrie Eleison," I replied.

"Kyrie Eleison.
Christe Eleison.
Christe Eleison.

Christe Eleison.
Kyrie Eleison.
Kyrie Eleison.
Kyrie Eleison."

And presuming Christ who was Lord had forgiven her her defilement, he took the water sprinkler and blessed her in Latin. She gave the priest the candle and he extinguished it and handed it to me. The priest indicated and I led him off the altar leaving behind the Catholic mother whose head was scarved and bent. When we went back in, I went to the priest's sacristy to bow to the priest.

There was a knock on the outside door. It was the Sergeant. He was using the occasion of his wife's churching to visit the priest. He had money for him. He asked me to tell the nuns that the Plain Chant would be on in New Ross on Friday week. This meant an increase in work in the school. On top of the preparation for the Feis, there was the Plain Chant to be prepared for, not to mention the Primary Cert. Each school in the district would enter a choir in the competition, which sang in very monotonous highpitched tones. The hymns were all in Latin. The only good thing about it was that it was a day off from school. Every year we would go in to a shop in New Ross and buy water-squirting pistols known as "squirting guns." We would then attack the townies who would call us "culchies."

The priest called to school that same morning and told us that we would have an excellent opportunity of rehearsing our chant at the Corpus Christi procession. Mostly we sang hymns to Our Lady and the odd Latin hymn. This year it would be all in Latin. "We will chant going up and down the main street of Coleman without apology to anyone," the priest said. The only deviation from the Latin would be "Faith of Our Fathers," which would be sung in the square.

We had been standing in choir formation in front of the blackboard. Ignatius bade us sit down. The priest told us there was a possibility, mind now, he was not saying for sure, but there was a possibility that we might be asked to sing for the Cardinal when he came to Wexford at the end of the month. He was coming for the annual general meeting of the Catholic Truth Society. The nuns' expression was excitement. The stupid girls began to giggle. "Ciúnas," Ignatius demanded.

They fell quiet. The priest was delighted with the response. He complimented us all on how good we were at the Confirmation. He said how important it was for us to hold on to our traditions, how grateful we should be to our families, to our parents for all the sacrifices they had made. If any of us ever had a problem, no matter how big, no matter how small, the holy nuns were there to help, so were our parents and he was there to guide all of them as best he could. Just as he was about to start the Catechism class Ignatius stepped forward and said,

"I think we have either a budding heretic or theologian in our midst – where is Master Larkin?"

I answered and said he was thinning beet.

"Maybe you could tell Father the nature of his question?"

Once more I was being lobbed in it.

"Well Jack?" the priest enquired.

"It was to do with Transubstantiation, Father."

"Yes?" he enquired.

"I think he wanted to know if it was magic."

"You mean a miracle?" he asked, and then answered himself.

"Yes, it is a miracle. It is called the miracle of Transubstantiation. The Bread and Wine are turned into the Body and Blood of Christ. The Protestants say this is not so – they say it is merely symbolic, a representation. But ours is the only church that has the Real Presence as a doctrine. We are asked to believe that Christ is really present under the form of Bread and Wine. Does that answer you?"

"Well, sort of," I answered trying my best to be both honest to Larkin's enquiry and at the same time doing my best to wriggle out of it. The priest looked disappointed.

"I think he meant about Him coming into our hearts."

"And so He does, at Communion," he answered. "When we receive Christ into our bodies, we take Him into our hearts and minds. Does that answer it for you?"

To have gone further than that would have been pushing it. I would have to fight with the priest to get him to listen more carefully. I lied and I said, "Yes, Father."

"There you are now," he said, "how do you think them up, Jack?" The class laughed. "Where do you get them at all?" They laughed more.

"Oh it was Michael Larkin's question," intervened Ignatius. She was disclaiming the credit from me and for Larkin with a smile. The smile withered on her face as a furrow on the brow of the priest appeared.

"You did say right enough it was Michael Larkin's question, didn't you Jack?" and without waiting for my answer, he frowned more deeply and said, "Dear Oh dear! Oh Dear! Oh Dear!" The laughing stopped as the priest got up and ushered the nun from the room.

∞ ∞

After school, I asked my mother to let me see whether the priest's housekeeper needed to have sticks brought in. I was secretly hoping she might need messages from down the street and in this way allow me off limits to see what was happening in the outside world. When I got there, the door was open, but she was not there. There was a cigarette in the ashtray which was streaming smoke. The door to the hallway was closed but since she seldom ventured outside, it was the most likely avenue of her absence.

However, because the area was off limits, I could not be sure that she was the only person present. My initial thought was to see whether I could observe her and if so to then hail her. Gingerly, I opened the door to the hallway and as I did I heard the toilet flushing and a sharp loud click of the retracted bolt. I left the door ajar, as if to imply that she had not correctly secured the same on her way to the toilet and thereby justify hearing her presence. Instead in one fell swoop, I lost all of my innocence. The next step was not the side shuffle of Mae and her stick, but the heavy groan of the staircase under the stomp of a greater weight going up the stairs from the mezzanine-floored lavatory. Mesmerised, I stood in the opened doorway gaping at the balcony with its balustrade banisters which came in decorative circular fashion from the priest's room down the stairs to the mezzanine and in spiral fashion to the hall. As I stood gawking at the unbelievable, the unspeakable happened. The stairs had linoleum but reported no shoe. At the top of the stairs, Fr. Williams walked nakedly into my view. He could not see me without looking down and at an acute angle. I immediately looked away. I had seen his penis. It had to be a mortal sin to see a priest's penis. I had looked on his nakedness. Abraham's sons had walked backwards when they clothed their naked father least they should see him naked. I was stuck in the door wanting to unsee what I had seen. I heard him open the door upstairs; a voice, which was female, said something and laughed and he laughed too. It was Iníon Ní Breathnach's voice. I let the door close silently and looked quickly around, Mae was not back. I had just witnessed a crime worse than murder. The blood drained from my body without a wound to justify its exit, it had turned to ice.

I left the kitchen – the door still open. I heard the scrape of a coal shovel on the ground of the coalhouse. She was filling a quarter bucket of coal. I tiptoed past, holding my breath, and ran as fast as my two legs could carry me until I got home. I felt what I had seen was awful. I believed what I had done was wrong, but I had not intended to do anything wrong. I felt disgusted everytime I remembered seeing his hairy penis. I felt sick. I could not retch. I could not remember his face. I remembered his big arse, white and flabby, and his boney legs. I had never seen another boy naked when we togged off for football. We were all very modest. Sometimes in the boys toilets we would spray piss over the divided wall on the girls and they would run out screaming. Occasionally, an odd girl, would make a run at the "modesty wall," try to catch the top and pull herself up to have a peek and run off squealing and sniggering, but I had never seen anybody naked. Edward Foley pulled down Thorpey's elastic-waisted khaki shorts when we were playing football one day. None of us ever wore underpants. He was exposed to the girls who called him "Mickey Mouse" for a long time afterwards. Larkin belted Foley because it was a lousy thing to do on anyone. I knew I had committed a sacrilege and its features were indelibly printed on my brain to torture my life until the end of my days. I could not cry. I could not talk to anybody about it. I just continued to feel sick.

That night I told my mother I wanted to stop serving mass.

"Why Jack?" she asked. "I thought you liked serving mass."

"I did. I do," I answered. "It's just I'll be leaving school shortly and others should be doing it."

"I'm sure they'll see to that in plenty of time. Is there anything else?" she sniffed. I left her with a denial.

Next morning I could not see the vestments on the priest. Everytime I looked at him I could see nothing but his arse and his "mickey." I knew this must be scandalous and it worked and wormed its twistedness into my torment. I told myself I had to pull myself together, but I had a hard time doing it.

After school that evening, my suspension was up. When I finished my homework I cycled off to Coleman. The newspaper had it there would be racing cars on the strand on Sunday week in Coleman. I could hardly wait to tell Larkin, but when I got to the house there was no one there.

I decided to try the forge and when I got there Larkin came out. He beckoned me away. "Gerry is in there," he said. "He says he's goin' away, and Hiawatha is talking to him."

"What's wrong?" I asked.

He told me he had gone on an awful batter on the drink over the weekend and his father had told him to "Shape up, or ship out." After a short while the two men came out.

"Think it over, Gerry," said Hiawatha.

"I've done enough thinking," said Gerry. "I think it's time for action."

"When it's time for action, Gerry, you won't have to think about it," said the wise blacksmith.

Gerry went down the road in his shirtsleeves, wheeling his bike, a haversack on his back.

"Maybe just this once," he said. He wheeled the bike away.

When we went into the forge, Hiawatha showed me the two wheels he had made. They were brilliant. They were timber-spoked cart wheels – a miniature version of what the covered wagons used in the Old West. He showed me the truck – he had an axle fixed. The handles were not hurley handles, they were like the shafts of a horse's cart. It looked absolutely brilliant. He then produced a yoke. It would attach to the carrier and rear wheel of my bicycle. This was pure genius and no mistake. Larkin told me he had helped him during the evenings, but he could not tell me on Sunday because it was to be a surprise. It was one of the best presents I had received in my life. The excitement took me over. He grinned at my excitement. The wheels were fitted and were perfect. They were banded with an iron hoop and sounded just like a cart going over stones. "This could do serious work," Hiawatha explained. "You could bring sticks for the fire, heavy messages – no tellin' what you could do."

Next moment, in walked Fr. Williams to the forge. My heart sank to my boots. The blacksmith told us to run out and try it. Larkin showed me the hangnails he had from thinning beet. He was not doing any today because there had been fresh showers all day and the drills would be all muddy and clammy. I sat in the cart as he pulled me up the hill. I let him in on the way back, but he was too heavy for me and at the bottom it twisted in my hands and he fell out on the lawn at the back of the forge. Both of us were breaking our hearts laughing.

"Where's the rod?" I asked.

"'Twould be a right day for fishing."

"'Tis probably back in his own place," he answered.

We were both sweating. "Let's get a mug of water," I said.

There was always a bucket of fresh drinking water in the forge drawn from the nearby well. As we walked towards it we heard a shout; "We'll see about that!" Fr. Williams stormed out of the forge to his car and slammed the door shut. As the wheels spun before they gained purchase on the road and he sped off. We both walked in to Hiawatha who had taken the kerchief from around his neck and was wiping his shining bald pate.

"Come in boys," he said.

"We came to get some water," Larkin said.

"Aye, surely," he said. "Get some there, get some. I think I'll even have a drop meself," he said brightening. When I had finished, he looked at me and said, "Was there a little somethin' in school today?" he asked.

I blushed – I thought about seeing the priest naked, and thought Hiawatha was referring to that because it was so much to the forefront of my mind.

"No!" I answered, trying to conceal my discomfort.

"Somethin' about Communion'?" he prompted.

I was relieved. "Oh that!" I said. So I told them both what happened with Ignatius and the Real Presence and the priest and Transubstantiation. "Did I do wrong?" I asked.

"Not at all, son," Hiawatha answered. "You did perfectly right."

I pedalled home with the new truck fixed to the back of my bike. I pedalled steadily home. No charioteer entered Rome more proudly than I entered Coleman that night. My younger brothers thought it was the greatest invention since fried bread. I was my own hero for once. It felt good.

∞ 10 ∞

"CúChulainn has Webbed Feet"

Mel arrived the day before Corpus Christi. She would stay for five weeks. A lot of the news I had written to her. She told Larkin she was sorry about his father. I told her, on her own, that he never spoke about it.

"But he has gotta talk about it, he's jus' gotta."

When Mel got things into her head, there was just no getting them out again until they were dealt with.

At the Corpus Christi Procession, I did not feel very well. The District court in Ballycullane was on the next day at 3 o'clock. That morning the priest told us he would bring us. I told him my father said he would come since the shop was shut for the Holy Day of Obligation. He told Larkin, in that case he would bring him. I wanted Larkin to come with us, and so did he, but we thought it wiser not to cross the priest.

The bags of corn were still at the back of the ploughing hall. Pat Shanks was in his usual position beside the door. Miley was sitting between two guards. It was a quarter past three before we got there. The court was already underway. Larkin was up near the front with the priest. We stopped just inside the back door, so as not to make a fuss. A guard was giving evidence in a case involving cruelty to a dog. He said he had found the dog chained to a tree out in the open weather with no shelter.

"What type of tree was it guard?" asked the solicitor.

"A wooden tree," replied the flat faced guard. The courtroom laughed. The guard looked blank. The court clerk called for silence. The solicitor cross-examined him again, but the judge convicted his client. My father winked an acknowledgement at Shanks, who shook his head in a knowledgeable response to the case's outcome.

"The people at the suit of the Attorney General versus Miles Cassidy of no fixed abode," proclaimed the clerk. The two guards stood up, Miley stood up, Shanks looked up. Sergeant Thorpey said he had arrested him that day. The charges were read out and words such as "breaking and entering" and "trespass" and "burglary" were used a lot. The word "sacrilege" was used and both churches Catholic and Protestant were mentioned. A solicitor stood up and said he was representing the accused. The judge seemed surprised. Miley turned around and said "God Bless ya, Father." The clerk told him to be quiet. The solicitor told, the judge no evidence was being given in the Catholic church case. The judge told the superintendent of the guards he would strike out those cases. Shanks was standing up now. The superintendent acknowledged. The judge asked the solicitor if his client knew what was happening. Miley was looking at the roof. The solicitor went over to him and whispered to him. Miley said "Heh?" real loud and the crowd sniggered again. "Silence," said the clerk once more. The judge looked ponderous, prepared to ensure that explanations were seen to be given, however comical or undignified. The solicitor moved away having explained. Miley smiled at the priest and said "God Bless ya, Father," and again the crowd laughed. The priest put his head in his hands, blushed and killed a laugh with a headshake.

The judge then said they would proceed with the case involving the Protestant church. The judge made the clerk ask Miley if he pleaded "guilty, or not guilty." "As innocent as the Lamb of God," said Miley. The crowd laughed once more. The clerk called for "Silence" once again. The Reverend Hancock went to the stand and swore the Oath. When he was seated he asked very politely if he could say something. He said the case involving his church had only been brought at the request of the Civil Authorities and neither he nor his church had any wish to bring any further misfortune on the accused. You could hear a pin drop. The judge looked at the superintendent as he stood up.

The superintendent looked at his papers, shuffled them uncomfortably and asked bluntly, "Do you not wish to give evidence, then?" The Reverend Hancock shifted uncomfortably, paused and said, "No," he added, "but I do not wish to be unfair." The judge asked him how he thought he was being unfair.

The Reverend Hancock replied there appeared to have been a change of climate.

"Indeed," said the judge. "I've noticed the change in the weather myself." There was great laughter and the judge received the applause. "My job, Reverend, is to decide whether and what is fair, that is not a job for you! Do you want to proceed superintendent?" asked the judge.

"I do," said the superintendent.

In answer to his questions, the clergyman told how he was the Rector of the church and he had sole responsibility for it on behalf of his congregation. The caretaker, Mr. Boland, also had a key to the church. No one other than the caretaker and himself had authority to go in. He had locked the church after Service on the Sunday and nobody had opened it by authority when the accused had been found in it.

Miley's solicitor cross-examined him about whether the church might have been left open by mistake. He said he thought it hardly possible. The solicitor suggested somebody else might have broken in before his client. The clergyman said that was a possibility, perhaps.

The caretaker added little to what the clergyman had said, only to say he had seen the broken window and tidied it up and mended it at a cost of five shillings. "Ya were robbed," said Miley "Ya were robbed." There was more laughter. The judge looked disdainfully. The clerk called for silence. The crowd nearly reacted.

The solicitor said there was no evidence to suggest Miley had committed the offence.

"Was he not found on the premises?" asked the judge.

The solicitor said the complaint was not about his being there, but how he got to be there.

"There is no evidence that he did anything illegal."

"What about the broken window?"

"There is no evidence that he did that."

The judge asked the superintendent if he had anything to say and he said he was relying on the case that was presented to him and then, before we knew it, the case was over.

"Case dismissed for lack of evidence," the judge said.

"You're free to go Mr. Cassidy," said the judge. "I won't fine you anything this time."

"Begobs," said Miley, "sure I'll try to find a few bob meself."

The guffaws could be contained no longer. It was the end of the court for the day. The judge smiled as he departed

"All rise!" said the Clerk. Everyone stood. The Reverend Hancock looked perplexed. Fr. Williams was already smoking and was now beaming. Shanks laughed with my father about what a "quare fellow" Miley was. Nobody laughed or spoke to the Protestant clergyman as he excused his way through the crowd. Shanks departed. My father acknowledged Thorpey, who was filing past. The priest was talking to the solicitor and the superintendent. My father decided to leave. As we passed up by the pub, we both saw the judge and Shanks go in through the back entrance. My father said nothing until we were nearly home. "court rooms are places to try and stay out of," he said. My mother was glad I did not have to give evidence; so was I and so was Larkin.

We had decided not to tell Mel until the matter was over. When we did tell her the next day, we got more than we bargained for. It was on Friday after school. Larkin had not met her since she arrived. I could see he was entranced. She looked very pretty and was a lot more developed. Larkin told her that Miley had been charged with breaking into the Protestant church. I told her he had been charged with breaking into the Catholic church as well and that I was a witness to both charges and that the priest had seen to it that these charges had been dropped. Larkin said that he was a witness for the charge in connection with the Protestant church and that the case had been dismissed and no witnesses were needed.

"You mean he could have gone to jail?" she asked.

This was not the first time either of us had considered this prospect.

"I suppose so," I mused.

"Whadda ya mean ya suppose – ya mean ya don't know?"

"We're not lawyers," I answered.

"Do you have a tongue? Can you ask a simple question like – 'What happens if he is found guilty?'"

"Come on," said Larkin, "that's grown up stuff."

"You sicken me," she said, "the pair of you."

"You both knew he was innocent of any crime – and you nearly let him go to jail."

"We went to the court to say he didn't do it," I protested.

"You went because you were made to go," she accused.

"We went to tell the truth," said Larkin.

"You went to tell half the truth."

"That's a lie," I protested again.

"So when were you going to tell them I was there?" she asked.

"We were protecting you," I shouted back at her.

"And what were you protecting me from?" she asked coldly.

I felt she was so ungrateful. She had no idea what Larkin had been through with the death of his father and this on top of it. She had no idea what I had been through worrying about her being dragged in to it. She did not understand what was happening in school or at home or in the village. It was alright for her, she did not live here. She could go back to the States and forget all about it, but we had to live here and do as we were told. If we were older, that might be a different matter, but we were not. We had no choice. It was just so unfair. I thought she would have understood and so did Larkin. She cycled off in a huff.

"Girls," Larkin said. "They're all the same. Once they get a notion, that's it, God man nor the devil wouldn't change their minds."

<hr />

By the time we got to Larkin's house we had sorted out a lot of stuff. You could not depend on grown ups. You could not depend on girls. You could not depend on anything, really. Life was such a muddle. If you did one thing it was wrong with someone; if you did the other it was wrong with someone else. You just had to be tough and put up with it, we both agreed.

When we arrived, Hiawatha was in the kitchen with his coat on. He had apparently arrived in just before us. He was reading a letter. Larkin was now calling him "uncle." This unsettled me the first few times I heard it, but I got used to it. I almost called him "uncle" myself once or twice, but I caught myself just in time.

"We're going to the cattle sales in Ross tomorrow," he said to me, "would you like to come?" They were going to sell some store cattle. Larkin told me they were getting £65.00 a head, or so, in Wexford and it was a good time to sell. It was easy for me to believe him, as I knew very little about farming.

Hiawatha took us down to the river to fish. We spoke about Mel and both Larkin and I were disappointed she was not with us so that we could show off our newly acquired skill. On our way to the stream we continued to give out about her. We were expecting Hiawatha's approval, but again we were disappointed.

"Seems to me you both think she might have a point," he said

"No we don't, we think she's wrong," said Larkin.

"If she is wrong – she is wrong, so why give out about her. In my experience people only give out about other people when they think they might be right and can't accept it."

We were flummoxed at his insight.

There was a stiff breeze on stretches of the river convenient to allow a decent opportunity with the wetfly. As we edged down along, flocks of starlings and other birds swooped and flocked the sky above. Coming on to 9 o'clock, the sky got very red. We had fished well and landed four trout.

"We'll shortly have to use the worm," said Hiawatha.

He let us cast for a while as he sat and smoked his pipe facing the setting sun.

"Is there anything as piercingly sad as the end of a summer's day?" he mused, revealing a hint of his own loneliness.

The red rays of the crimson light spectacularly trimmed the soft puffy clouds. There was a smell of new mown hay which the dew was invading. There was a fishy smell from our hands. The odd tractor could be heard in the distance. Larkin reeled in the last fish. Hiawatha let him without interference, watching and smiling. He stood up and banged his pipe on his heel and said,

"Five o'clock said the cock."

He stood over Larkin removing the hook.

"Time to go said the crow."

He put the pipe in his pocket.

"Away, away, said the jay.

After dark said the lark,

Wait a bit, said the little tomtit."

That night, I sat on the stairs while my uncle Peter, Fr. Williams and my father discussed the week's events. Sean Hanlon had an unmerciful row all right with the priest over the boycott when he had returned home. My father hoped the children would soon be returned. "A stubborn woman, that lady," the priest said in reference to Mrs. Hanlon.

They spoke about people who were no longer speaking to one another. Different events were recounted where people had crossed over from one side of the street to the other rather than meet their neighbours.

There was a mixed response to this. The priest kept referring to so-and-so as being "sound" in that he could be relied upon to observe the boycott. My mother thought it was sad and though my father agreed, he felt it had to be for the moment. Mary Morrissey, who was an old age pensioner, defied them all and kept going down to the Whitneys for buttermilk to bake bread. When challenged by the "priest" Doyle she told him that she wasn't getting the milk from the Whitney's, she was getting the milk from the cow, and the cow had no religion. As disapproving as Fr. Williams was of her action, he nevertheless could see the humour. My father thought it was hilarious.

They spoke about the forthcoming Feis and the sports. They were amused at the notion of the racing cars coming to race on the strand on Sunday. The bell rang and Mr. Byrne was admitted. Everyone was surprised to see him. I hid at the top of the stairs until he was safely ensconced.

"I have some bad news," he said. "Bobby Rackard is gone to hospital with a damaged leg – he'll never hurl for Wexford again."

A chill went through me. They were shocked downstairs. Suddenly, Wexford's hurling heroes were seriously depleted. How was it that just when things seemed to be at their brightest, the gloom always came along. My father said it was always the case – when things are going well for you that's the time to look out, because when you turn the next corner "there will be some hoor waiting to give you an all merciful root up the arse." They all laughed.

∞ ∞

The cattle Sales were different from the Fairs. There were pens and corrals for the animals. There was a big shed where the animals were auctioned by the auctioneer. But most of all, there was commission. The cattledealers did not like the Sales. There had been a big debate about it in Waterford. Most of the cattle dealers had said they would boycott the Sales, but then some of the bigger ones broke ranks and slowly but surely the Sales got bigger and the Fairs started to get smaller. Some of the dealers tried to resuscitate the Fairs by purchasing large numbers of cattle and then putting them for sale on the fairs. It did not work. The Fair dealers dealt privately with farmers from place to place and some of them never went near the Sales mart after that. Thomas Whitney Senior was a Fair dealer and when the Protestant boycott was called he was the hardest hit. Everyone acknowledged he was "the most decent man in the whole of Ireland." For all that, a lot of people did not deal with him on account of the boycott. They were afraid. He was also a keen angler. He was the agent for a Waterford Exporter, who was a Catholic, but this made no difference. One man actually took a cheque from him for cattle, but handed it back before delivery could be taken of the stock. "We'll all be killed, we'll all be killed," said the man handing back the cheque, and although everyone knew Thomas Whitney could have taken him to law and won, that would have made no difference to the rest of his business. People were embarrassed. He had plenty of land and had no difficulty in making a livelihood. But when he was shunned by the people he had helped and dealt with all his life, it hurt him very deeply. He stopped dealing. He stopped fishing and he stopped going out.

Hiawatha brought us to the Sales. These were dull compared to the Fairs and a bit boring. There was a lot of cement and sameness and the only life apparent was from the monotone drone of the microphoned auctioneer. Bids were given and received by nods, winks, the odd grimace and an occasional flick of the hand. Still, we sold, and that was what we came to do. Mel had come with us and she stroked every beast's nose in the mart. She made a holy show of us and kept saying, "Aint they priddy?" We were afraid she would be overheard or, worse still, that we would be recognised. We were mortified.

The cattle had been brought to New Ross in a tractor and trailer with creels and Gerry Denn drove us to New Ross in his car. Gerry bought us ice cream as we waited for Hiawatha to come back from transacting some business. We were fairly fed up by the time he returned. He had an envelope under his arm which was bulky from the papers within.

෨෨

On the way home, himself and Gerry spoke as we sprawled out on the big leather seat and Foxford rug behind. Mel did not like it. It tickled her bare legs, preferring instead to sit on the warm leather with the rug turned back. Though the windows were down, we felt sleepy. As we lolled along, the drone of the engine was hypnotic. Larkin suddenly came to life as he spotted a car in front of us towing a racing car on a trailer. "Look," he shouted. We came back to life. Gerry overtook it and, as he did, the excitement of the prospect of the next day's gymkhana overtook us. The summer of '56 had been great, but the summer of '57 would be better. As we turned to look out the back window we jostled for position, straining the sprung leather seat sufficient to draw chastisement from both adults in the front.

When we arrived home, it was early afternoon. Sandwiches were made "to fill the gap" and we raced to the beach to see all that was happening. We sat on the grassy bank.

"Jays, the silver lad's flying," said Larkin.

A silver car sped up and down the beach as we watched it in awe, witnessing the fastest men alive in Ireland.

"Someone said an aeroplane is goin' to land on the strand and give rides," Larkin said.

Mel said she had often been in an aeroplane. We asked what they were like and she gave us details. The noise had stopped for some time before we realised it. When we did look, we saw the silver racing car had overturned. There was a crowd gathering.

"Crikey," I said.

"Don't go over there," said Mel nervously.

We watched and watched as people ran to and fro. After a while, the new doctor's car drove on to the beach. We waited some more. Fr. Williams arrived. Still more time passed. We looked a lot more than we spoke. Mel held my arm briefly, but when I looked she let go again without looking at me.

"He must be dead," Larkin said.

It left a raw feeling.

"There were two in it," I said, inviting the anxious.

"I'm goin' over," he said.

"Don't," said Mel.

"C'mon" he invited.

"No!" she said.

He climbed down the small rocky slope and ran off to the crowd.

"Don't go!" she said to me pleadingly. It was no trouble for me to oblige. I had seen all the dead people I ever wanted to see in my life and if

I never saw another corpse, I would live very happily with the deprivation, thank you very much.

One of the men, the driver, was dead. He was taken to the public house and, later that evening, to the chapel. Larkin and I served the priest. A lot of people, some of whom were the recently arrived, bathers for holidays and the like, attended the church. It threw a gloom over the place. The gymkhana for the following day was cancelled.

This was the first funeral Larkin had been at since his father had been buried. He looked sombre, but inquisitive. The priest recited the Rosary on a most brilliant June evening. The setting sun streaked a long red finger through the half-opened double door in the western wing and reflected off the shining marble altar enveloping the sanctuary. I thought of Hiawatha's words so recently uttered about summer sunsets. It was indeed, very sad.

Afterwards in the sacristy, as we took off our soutanes, Larkin said, "That's number fifty-six since we started counting."

"He doesn't count," I said, "he's a stranger."

We had an argument then about whether he did or did not.

"We didn't count the Box Whitney," I said, "because he was a Protestant."

"We didn't count him because we didn't serve him," he said.

"What does that matter?" I said.

He said it was like keeping a score until we finished serving altogether to see what our record was. Rather than exaggerate our score we decided to keep it pure. Larkin agreed the next one would be fifty-six.

The next day there was nothing to do. The car racing had been cancelled and the tide was out. Wexford were not defending their Leinster crown until the following Sunday so there was no point in listening to the radio. Larkin decided we should start collecting car numbers because of the amount of cars the good summer was bringing. We started with the strange hearse that brought the deceased sportscar driver away.

We broke up for dinner and in the afternoon the pickings were good. Half of those that arrived thought the races were going ahead. Others came to see where the crash had taken place with the car. By half past three we had over forty-five numbers each. The second number I had was my father's Morris Minor KI-5334. The last one was IP-4279. We saw it driving out of Coleman at three-thirty. It was Iníon Ní Breathnach's car. She drove to the small nine-holed golf links with Fr. Williams. The golf links ran along the edge of the strand divided only by the sand dunes where courting couples spent many a happy Sunday afternoon out of sight of public and clergy.

We had been standing at the junction at the bottom of the main street and we decided we ought to check out the strand for more numbers in case some of the cars got down there unknown to us. Mel got the hang of it early on. On the beach she ran ahead of us darting here and there scribbling. She was wearing shorts again this year. It was a beautiful afternoon and though the tide was far out the bathers still came to paddle and dip.

We were almost at the little stream which ran through the golf course when a golf ball landed "Thop!" right in front of us. We heard a shout and looked around. There on a slight hill with a golf club in his hand was Fr. Williams. The others who were with him could be seen intermittently through the waving reeds and rushes of the intervening sand dunes.

"It's the priest," said Larkin.

"I'll bring it up to him," I offered.

"Lick-arse!" he said.

"Michael!" Mel reproached.

I lifted the ball and ran towards the dunes. The priest came to the boundary fence of the golf course. I climbed up the steep warm sand, my sandals filling as I went. I pulled myself up by grabbing at clumps and clusters of grass weed and rush. As I ran through the narrow strip of dune, I tripped and fell into a hollow. There was a shriek as I fell in on top of Agnes Maher and Thomas Whitney Junior. They were in their swim wear and had been courting. She jumped up in an embarrassed flush. Thomas sat up sheepishly, rubbing his head. I had dropped the golf ball. In a flustered fashion I looked around for it. "I'm sorry," I said reddening. There was a picnic cloth and a basket. I looked behind and under them. Agnes saw the priest when she stood and blushed some more and knelt, looking away from him. He was a little more than ten yards away.

"Christ!" she said as she knelt. She put her hand under her knee. "Is this what you're looking for?" She handed me the golf ball and I ran with it to the clergyman who was standing holding the paling stake of the fence with one hand, and the golf club with the other. He was looking down at the grass.

"Who's there?" he asked.

"Mel and Michael" I answered.

"I mean in the rushes?"

I blushed and told him.

As I stumbled back cursing my luck for having betrayed my friends, Agnes called me. She looked pale. Thomas looked pained.

"What did he ask you?" she enquired. I hung my head.

"He wanted to know who was here." I tried to stop from crying, but I revealed myself.

"It's okay, it's okay," she said and she moved to put her arm around me. I moved back when she came forward. She paused. Tommy got up.

"It's okay, Agnes, leave him alone. It's okay Jack, go on ahead – don't worry about it – there's a good man."

I came away feeling like Judas on the way to the "Potters" field only to find someone had stolen the halter.

"But they were only neckin'," Mel said. She clearly did not have the slightest notion about company-keeping, let alone the boycott. Larkin looked at her and laughed. She was getting mad. "Well it's only natural," she protested. "What is it with everybody around here?"

We tried to explain as best we could about company-keeping and how it was frowned on, unless a couple intended getting married.

"But how do people get to know one another?"

"They meet at dances and places," I said.

"You mean rock n' roll and stuff?"

We told her rock n' roll was frowned upon as well. This was too much for her.

Our notebooks for the car numbers had long since been put away. We were carrying our sandals. I had the thong of one fastened on the buckle of the other and they hung around my neck Robinson Crusoe style. We were walking back along the strand towards Coleman. Mel was finding it hard to understand why rock n' roll was not allowed in the local dance hall and we were finding it even more difficult to explain.

"It's just that it's different here," said Larkin.

"I s'pose," she said.

"People are different everywhere," I added wisely.

"Yeah," said Larkin "everywhere."

"I s'pose so," she said.

ᙣ ᙢ

This year Mel was staying in Rathroe with her mother. We cycled back with her and between slow bicycle races, which Larkin always won, and nattering, it took us the rest of the late afternoon to get there. The smells from the meadows were sweet. If it stayed fine, they would cut the hay next week. We passed the Protestant church and the Protestant school. As we passed the school, I noticed Sammy Duffin's maroon coloured Rudge bicycle. We stopped to look at it. "That's some bike," said Larkin.

It was new, the most remarkable aspect of anything in our lives. Everything we had was either old, used or in some way second hand. I had tried to ride it when the men were working in the fields, but it was too big and cumbersome. The saddle was too high but we used to be well able to ride the lighter versions of the men's bikes, by leaning the bicycle to one side and placing the right leg under the crossbar and pedalling in a bent leg fashion.

"Jesus – but it has tyres on it like a tractor," said Larkin as he lay his chest lazily across the handlebars of his own, his long legs traipsing the ground behind.

"D' ya think we'd get a bite if we went fishin' later on?"

"Maybe," he said and he perked up at the mention.

When we arrived home with Mel, Poll was out in the yard. Ignatius had broken out and was in the orchard. She needed us to chase him out. I felt my heart reduce itself almost to extinction. I was sure there was no pulse in it. The pendulum of life was just lying there within, hanging. I looked at Larkin and there was not as much as a shake out of him. I looked at Mel and, as the man said, "there she was – gone!" She had retreated to the end of the lane, about thirty yards away when she heard mention of the turkey cock. She stopped there. Poll laughed. Larkin laughed and I let on to laugh. Poll acknowledged the situation by shaking her head and smiling. "He jumped at her yesterday," she said. Mel had never said a word. I wished I had the bravery to be as cowardly as she was and retreat.

"I'll block the lane," the spirit moved me to say. It was a half commitment to the task – it meant someone else had to go in among the leafy apple trees and long grass to hoosh him out.

"I'll get him, Poll," the hero volunteered. I envied him his nerve. He took nothing with him except a fist full of stones from the gravel lane. I stood there like a sentry. I could not see over the lane ditch in to the orchard, but as Larkin disappeared to the gate I could hear the kneeweakening "gobble gobble" of the turkey cock. Patiently and easily I perspired. I could sense the dewlike glisten of my skin under my earnest nostrils. The bicycle had one handle bar grip of rubber, which was getting softer by the minute. Suddenly there was a great commotion of flapping of wings and Larkin shouted, "He's gone through – there's a hole in the ditch where the galvanise fell."

The turkey might not have had much of a brain, I decided, but it was able to remember the skutching Larkin had given to it. He strolled manfully out as I shouted to Mel, equally manfully, that the coast was clear. She asked me if I was sure and waited for confirmation, before venturing forward.

"Thanks, Michael," said Poll

"Not at all," he grandly responded.

Mel looked all aroused and her acute focus, though relaxed now, was taking Larkin in.

"Are you alright?" I asked.

"I am now," she admitted and looked back at him.

"C'mon," I said, "we'll catch nothin' if we don't move."

"See ya," said Larkin back to Mel.

"Come on," I said again. I had to nearly pull him.

We raced back to Coleman meeting all the traffic from the beach. It was the first time I saw Larkin stop at the cross below the Protestant church. The traffic was emptying out of the village, motor cars, ponies and traps. As we were stopped, Sammy Duffin came from the Catholic Church direction on our left. He was able to cycle with both hands in his pockets. He shouted hello from his big Rudge as he cheerily sped on. Larkin made to go after him, but a car came and he had to stop. It was Iníon Ní Breathnach and Fr. Williams returning to the curate's house after the golf. Larkin had to check his enthusiastic start and stop, with both hands. Iníon

Ní Breathnach's eyes narrowed briefly and then relaxed. The priest waved and I saluted in reverent, if military style, as we had been trained to do when meeting the priest. This was because at any time the priest might be coming to or going from a sick call carrying the silver pyx that enchambered the Blessed Sacrament in gold lining.

As we moved on down the hill, Larkin freewheeled with both hands off. I could nearly do that, but pedalling with both hands off was a different matter. Larkin could both freewheel and pedal with his hands stuck in his pockets. As we freewheeled down he pedalled backwards, tentatively and focused as if to get used to leg movement, hands free of the bike. He was in great form.

"Who told you I couldn't ride without me hands?"

"The rubber gennet!" I roared with gusto. "And who told you?"

"The monkey on the shed," he answered.

This was one of those odd language fashions that appear in conversation, from where no one knows, and just as unnoticed they disappear again.

"Yippeeiaay – yippeeiooh!" his well-cracked voice yodled.

When we arrived at Larkin's, the "priest" Doyle's car was outside. The brake lights were just going off as we passed in under the arch of the farmyard. Hiawatha opened the front door and the back door to the hall slammed from the draught. We were about to go through, but Larkin stopped. He put his index finger to his lips and winked me quiet. I halted, surprised. They were talking about the mart. However, Hiawatha had not invited his caller in.

"A bit of a chill in the evening all the same," idled the "priest".

"Was there something you wished to talk about?" the blacksmith asked him directly.

It was about the Dues. Now that the cattle were sold it would be time to pay, not to mention that the Pius list would be for reading next Sunday.

"You expect a fourteen-year-old boy to pay like an adult?"

"The farm is a Catholic farm," said Doyle.

"I'm not a Catholic," said Hiawatha.

"You're not the owner."

"I'm in charge."

"By what authority?"

"Get out of here before I lose my temper."

"You got off lightly so far," Doyle darted. "That can change too – you know. This is a Catholic country, this is a Catholic farm and those are Catholic cattle." Hiawatha banged the front door firmly and growled into the kitchen. Larkin looked at me. We were delighted that "the priest" got his belly full. Hiawatha was angry.

The back door suddenly opened and we were surprised. "I thought so," he said. "Snooping on people's private conversations."

"We were just comin' in," said Larkin.

"Get in the pair of ye, I'll deal with you in a minute," he continued as he passed us out on his way to the privy.

Gerry Denn was milking the cows. He was continuing to give a hand, particularly since the boycott had started. When Hiawatha came back in, he lectured both of us. Gerry would be going away shortly and Michael would have to be giving most of his attention to the farm. His foot was still sore, even though the plaster had since gone. He would have to open the forge again. All hands would have to pull together. He was the best I ever heard to turn a lecture into an exhortation of encouragement and enthusiasm. His anger had gone. He had expressed it to the right man, in the right place in the right way – without calculation but honestly and surely. We noticed it and consequently his exhortations were received all the more sincerely. These were difficult times. Bad things were happening, but if they were, everybody would need to keep balance. He would not refer to his disagreement with another adult to us – least of all with the "priest" Doyle. At least not overtly. But he knew we needed some reassurance. It was difficult with his being a Presbyterian. He was equal to it. He told us a story – it was definitely a parable. We all knew it, and it was thinly enough disguised at the end.

There was a tribe of Indians he had heard about one time who were starving. They lived in bad circumstances. There was no buffalo to hunt and the winter was hard. One evening a stranger came into their camp. He was dirty and torn and weary. They fed him some soup and washed him and bathed his wounds. He rested with them for a long while and, as his strength returned, he discovered their plight. He felt sorry for them. One day he sent word to their chiefs that he had something to say. "I can call the buffalo," he said, "and I will help you."

The stranger left camp that night, but was back before the first red man was up. He walked to where the women were washing in the stream and handed one of them a small bit of buffalo meat with fat and lean and said "When you have had enough, save what is left and give it to someone else." He did this for a number of weeks and gradually the people began to realise this indeed was an unusual man. One morning he came and said, "Tomorrow the buffalo will come. Make four surrounds and take what you will, then let them go."

The next morning, a great bull buffalo came over the ridge and down to the valley, followed by a great herd. The Indians surrounded them and took every scrap from the plains. On the third surround, one of the younger warriors frightened them into a stampede. As they were getting away, the stranger rode to the pass and waving his spear in front of them, they turned back, trampling and killing the marauders behind. On the fourth surround they did as the stranger had bid and the rest of the herd moved on as the villagers harvested the buffalo plains behind.

"Did the tribe survive?" asked Larkin.

"It did," said Hiawatha. "They reaped the reward of what they were sent."

This, no doubt, was why we had to work, I surmised.

But he surpassed me.

"The gift of God to the world is freedom, true freedom. It allows choice and it breeds love. The gift of the devil is ownership. It requires control and it breeds greed. You can own nothing, not even your body – but you will really only care for anything if you love."

What he said burned in me and it has never left me. There were two benefactors – God and the Devil – and you could, in your heart, decide what gifts you would receive from each benefactor. He reminded us we could choose to own and control everything and thereby move against the providence of God or we could decide to belong and accept what was offered and work with that, and in that way counteract the Devil. Personally, I didn't want any gifts from the Devil; belonging sounded good to me.

We got the tea, but there would be no fishing tonight – it was too late to prepare. Maybe during the week if we got the hay saved. Maybe when the weather broke. Maybe another time.

∞∞

As we finished the supper he got up and went to a drawer in the dresser. He took out an envelope. I recognised it as the one he had taken from New Ross on the day before. He asked me to ask my father to sign the papers in them. Michael would get them from me in school tomorrow.

When I got home it was nearly half past eight. I gave my father the papers and went outside to play ball with my younger brother. The youngest was in bed and my sister would be home during the week for her summer holidays. My older brother was doing his Intermediate Cert and would not be home for almost a fortnight. My class were doing the Primary Cert the week after next. In spite of that, preparations for the Feis and Plain Chant would proceed regardless.

My father was a Peace Commissioner, a reward for political loyalty. It was a position respected in the community and bestowed a status on the office holder and the privilege of signing summonses for court at the request of prosecutors and police, and also formalising legal documents of various kinds. He was signing them all when Fr. Williams came in. I went to bed. Though the sky was a summer pale navy, the absence of daylight still conjured up the demons we had been presented with day in and day out. My anxiety was automatic in the dark.

I dressed myself for bed and recited my night prayers silently
"Live, Jesus, live,
So live in me,
That all I do,
Be done by Thee,
And grant that all,
I think or say,
May be Thy thought,
And Word today."

Silently I stole down the stairs. The clergyman was talking about Hiawatha not paying the dues. He was concerned about his influence on young Larkin.

"He could be a bad influence on young Jack."

"I'll see that he's not," said my father.

"I'll talk to him as well," said my mother.

"It may not be enough," said the clergyman.

"Sure then we'll see as we go," said my father.

"We'll see by and by," said my mother.

The priest hummed and hawed a bit. My mother made the tea. As usual on a Sunday night, Peter arrived. The priest wanted him to come to the Vigilance Committee during the week. They spoke of the boycott and the effect it was having on securing the return of the children.

"Too early to say," said Peter.

"It will have to be stepped up," said the clergyman.

"The Cardinal is going to preach on it," said Peter, "at the Catholic Truth Society General Meeting in Wexford on Sunday week – or at the Mass."

"The day of the match?" said my father.

"The very day," said my uncle.

"Blast it!" said my uncle again. "I had forgotten about the match."

"Oh they'll trounce Kilkenny," said Fr. Williams.

"I don't know about that," said my father.

∞ ∞

The County Council were giving a civic reception for the Cardinal, and Peter had to make a speech in the parish church in Wexford. It would be another big day. It was also the date for the Leinster Final, unless Wexford failed to beat Laois on Sunday next. This would be a big surprise since Laois were a football county.

The Bishop wanted to spread the boycott. Peter had told how the Bishop had gone to Dublin and had requested the Knights of Columbanus to use their influence in other regions to force the Protestants to bring the Catholic children back. But the Knights were reluctant to do anything for the moment.

The next day, the dispute took a bitter swing. A new Protestant teacher had been announced on Sunday for the Protestant school to substitute the Catholic teacher, Agnes Maher, who had resigned. Although we had known it would happen, we did not expect as bad a reaction. When the teacher went to the school in the morning there was a note stuck up on the door "Scabs beware of the lead," and someone had rolled a rock up in a tricolour and thrown it through the window of the school.

The nuns disapproved. This would bring disgrace, they said. The name of Ireland and Nationalism would be besmirched. The Protestants would use this as propaganda. This dishonoured Catholicism, the Pope and Religion.

In the course of the morning Fr. Williams came in. He spoke to us about the teaching authority of the church. Normally, this would have put us half to sleep but, because of all that was going on, we were very much awake. The Bishops were the successors to the Apostles of Christ. It was for them not only to teach us what was true but to show us also what men must observe in their conduct. Actions spoke louder than words. We act what we believe. We were told to look at our own actions and if they were not true we must examine our belief. "When we believe the truth we act the truth," he said. He never said "stone," "tricolour," "threat note" or "Protestant school," yet we knew.

He then started talking about hurling and we reacted with enthusiastic predictions about Sunday's clash and an equally optimistic anticipation of the outcome of the Championship. He teased that really Kilkenny were the better team, then he would argue that the girls were better than the boys in class, or those from the country were better than those from the village. He always got involved and he gave everybody the opportunity to express themselves in an atmosphere of relaxed authority.

While he was speaking, Fr. Michael, my uncle, arrived. Fr. Williams introduced him and said he was on the Missions in Nigeria, far away, saving souls for God. I was very proud of him. Ignatius took a back seat while the male clerics held centre stage. He had been her pupil as well.

Fr. Michael started to tell us about the Missions and how his parish was as big as the whole of County Wexford. Why, he might as well be a Bishop, I thought to myself. His uncle, my granduncle, had been the Dean of Johannesburg. I had seen photographs of his funeral. They looked very impressive and very important. He wanted to know if we had any questions. Some of the stupid girls wanted to know about the black babies but Larkin was far more interested in the motorbike he used in the bush.

Thorpey wanted to know if he had converted many pagans and what was it like. Larkin lost interest again. He had lapsed into his preoccupation mood again and was quiet. I wanted to think up a question, a good question – the best question. He was my uncle, after all. He told Thorpey there were many religions out there and many people who had none at all and, yes, many had been converted to Catholicism but there was a lot to be done to bring Christ to the foreigners.

Padraig Byrne asked if he was ever lonely and he said he missed Ireland and home a lot, particularly at night. Then I thought of my question. I put up my hand and he smiled "Well Jack?" I was the only one he really knew. "Did you ever have to exorcise anyone?" There was a hush amongst the children. Fr. Williams smiled knowingly. Ignatius was intrigued. He told us he had not personally exorcised but he knew priests who had. He told us the way they had aged almost overnight whilst in the process. People who had become possessed were people who had not maintained their religious practices and had fallen away from the sacraments. Then he summed it up by saying? "I often heard people, priests included, say they often doubted the existence of God, but I never heard one of them say, they doubted the existence of the Devil." This got enormous attention in the class. The nun looked at our reaction and smiled at Fr. Williams. He smiled and looked at Fr. Michael.

"Anymore questions?" he asked.

Larkin put up his hand. "What do you think of the boycott, Father?"

I put my head in my hands and could feel my embarrassment. (God's truth – how could you put up with this for a friend?) There was a stunned silence. Fr. Williams recovered first.

"Father is here to answer questions on the Mission, Michael."

Larkin was slouched in his seat and had not bothered to sit up straight when he asked the question. Both of his hands held a pencil which he twirled. His hands were resting on the polished desktop.

"Straighten up!" barked Ignatius.

He eyed her, daring her. She straightened, he stiffened – but he did not move.

"Straighten up!" she reddened.

"Leave him be!" Fr. Michael said.

He then dismissed the class by saying he wanted a photograph taken with us all outside.

They trooped out and Larkin sulkily got out of his desk, he put his hands deep down in his pockets, shoulders hunched, head down. The priest tried to arrange us for the photograph while Fr. Michael looked on, standing near the doorway, both hands in his pocket. Ignatius came out, saw him and flew at him. "I will thank you not to undermine my authority in front of the class, in future." He was earnestly surprised, she said more, but I could not hear. He looked at her for a little longer and then shook his head and walked sadly away. She disturbed the gravel as she turned on her heel and stormed in. Larkin saw it and brightened a little. "Oul' hoor!" he said.

♋♋

Mel came down on her bicycle most evenings after school. This particular week she helped bring in the hay. Every hand was needed. Larkin did not have a tractor so the work was slow. Sam Duffin was there to give a hand. There was also Hiawatha, Larkin, myself and Mel. Hiawatha worked the horse-drawn mowing bar in the field beside us and, as in everything he did, his skill with a horse was second to none. Gerry Denn was not there. Early in the week he had left. Hiawatha said he was going away for a little while. But what nobody knew was that Mary Byrne was gone as well.

Mel thought this was so romantic. Larkin thought it was just more of the ould stuff from the boycott. I was just surprised that Mr. Byrne had let her go. Larkin said she had gone without permission. This looked bad right enough. Mel thought it was even more romantic. Larkin had some of his information from Hiawatha, more of it from Sam Duffin and the rest of it from listening to Sam talking to people coming to and from the farmyard for milk, or meeting them on the road or the street.

"Sam says the priest helped them," said Larkin as the three of us tried to make a cock of hay in the field.

I could not imagine the priest helping a Protestant boy elope with a Catholic girl. Mel asked why they needed help. I explained to her that what Larkin was referring to was financial assistance – money.

"Not just that," he added mysteriously.

"What are you on about?" I asked.

"I cannot say," he said.

It always annoyed me when Larkin went on like this. It was always to give him some power, like he knew what I did not.

"Stick it up your arse so!" I vulgared.

Mel asked Larkin about his experience of being almost drowned. I had written and told her about it. He described Gerry as a type of CúChulainn with webbed feet. She listened awestruck as I busily worked away on the cock of hay.

"You must have been scared?" she minded.

"Yeah!" said Larkin. "Only for him, I'd be dead."

She was wearing jeans. She was really more a hindrance than a help at the hay. She was wearing a boy's shirt. It was a red tartan design. Larkin went on talking about how Gerry went on the drink and how sorry he was about it. Mel wanted to know if he had always been a drinker and we told her it was only since the boycott started.

Sam Duffin joined in to help us with the cock and in a few minutes we had it finished and were starting a fresh one. The mowing bar stopped. Sam went to see what the matter was. A stone maybe had broken a "tooth." Larkin went with him. If some part was required for the machine Larkin would go on the bike to the yard or the shop.

Mel became more relevant to the work because of the reduction in numbers. She tried to wind a small shkeal around the pitchfork to bring it from the sward to the round. She tried to lift it in to the circle, but was unable to get it to her shoulder. She carried the load on her pike like a flag bearer on parade, up, but not to the perpendicular. The sward had been cut earlier in the week. The withering grass fell from the pike top around her. She dropped her load off awkwardly and brushed her face and shirt with delicate long fingers. She was blowing and phewing hay dust away from her nostrils. A finger struck open her cleavage button. She did not appear to notice, but I did. When she stood erect it was unnoticed, but when she stooped her soft alluring breasts dangled tantalisingly gently. Whilst most of them were on view, the eye did not reach what it sought.

I was afraid she might see me and I was embarrassed by my desire and how it might be noticed. I could not remember having had trouble like this before. I was torn between wanting to look at her and failing to stop myself doing so.

"Michael is taking a long time," she said after a while. I busied myself more with the hay. The sweat streamed into my eyes. I wiped them with my shoulder while holding the fork. The chaff from my shirt entered my eye. "Shite!" I said. I took out my handkerchief to blow my nose and hold my eyelid in the generally agreed manner that would extract it through internal ducts through the palate.

"Here let me," she said. "Open your eyes!" she commanded.

"I can't," I said. "There's stuff in it."

"Open your eye and look over there" she said.

She took my handkerchief and with the corner proceeded towards the cornea. I pulled back.

"Hold still!" she said.

She placed her left hand on my forehead and with her right hand proceeded to draw up the inside rim of my lower eyelid. I flickered.

"Hold against me, I see it," she said.

I could feel her form against my chest. I could feel the fork of my trousers against my leg. I wanted to stay there forever and at the same time I wanted to race away from the Devil.

"There now," she said suddenly and smiled.

I blinked and blew my nose and generally tried to refocus from my "injury." She stopped to pick up her pitchfork only to confirm for me that her shirt was still open. I was more confident now that the confusion of the grit was concealing my urge. A noise made me look away. Larkin was coming back.

"Your blouse is open," I said.

She simply fastened it.

"He only stopped to oil it," he said.

We continued with our work.

Occasionally we broke off from this adult mode to snigger or giggle. For a finish, Mel just stood and looked, as each of us piked and out-piked the other. "Boys are stronger than girls," she flattered. I could not help but feel there was something doubly wicked in what she said. I wondered a lot more about her. I wondered if she remembered the kiss she had given me last year in the Protestant church. I wondered if she would do it again this year and if she did not, I wondered if she would let me or whether I would have the courage to try. I felt she preferred Larkin. I was jealous. I did not like the feeling.

Little by little it began to dawn on me that I was falling in love for the first time. I always regarded Mel as my friend and Larkin as my best friend. Larkin was my best friend – but Mel was – well, different. She was my different friend. With Larkin you could fish and play football, shout and roar. With Mel it was different. She was delicate – no, not so much delicate, as precious. Not that she held herself holy or fragile, but she was just naturally vulnerable and soft and gentle. I noticed how soft her eyes were, so gentle, so utterly pure. I longed for her to look at me. I wanted to let her see into me. I wanted to see into her. It was useless to resist, I was smitten and no mistake. A big problem arose for me. How was I going to hide it and how was I going to show it? If I did not show it, it was only a matter of time before Larkin did. If I did show it, what could I do about it anyhow? Mel was going home to the States in a few weeks. Life was confusing and problematic.

Later that week Sean Hanlon called down to the field. His scuffle had broken while he was working and he needed Hiawatha to braize it. It was the first time in weeks that work was done in the forge. It was in the evening at about half-six. Larkin had gone for the cows and Mel, Hiawatha and myself stayed on to finish the last cock. He told Sean to leave the scuffle down at the forge and he would call down later in the night to fix it. He spoke of why he had fallen behind in the farm on account of the commotion over Elisha and the kids. Hiawatha asked him if there was any news. Sean Hanlon sighed. He had been told of a sighting in Bray and after he had spent two days there, the children who had been sighted were strangers. Hiawatha said it was hard lines. Sean agreed that it was but now he had to resign himself that there was nothing more he could do. Hiawatha thought he must be going out of his mind with anxiety. Sean replied that when he was in Bray after they discovered they were the wrong children he had gone in to the church and he had handed the whole matter over to God. "It is in His hands now – there is nothing I can do," he said. Hiawatha told him he had great faith.

Mel asked me to tell her what Elisha was like, and the children. She wanted to know about the house they lived in. When I told her it was a castle, she could scarcely believe it. She kept saying "You mean a castle, like a real castle with battlements and stuff?" When I told her this was so she said "Wow!" I looked at her. She had a fairytale look in her eyes. The story was so bizarre it must have looked larger than life to an outsider. Prince Charming separated from Cinderella by the wickedness of life while the Prince pined away in his castle. I told her there was no drawbridge, but this was a detail, which mattered little to her. I felt the absence of a moat and drawbridge took from the whole thing. "Oh it is so sad," she said. I did not like the way she said it. She was beginning to sound like some of those stupid girls in school who used to swoon over film stars and the boys going to the Vocational School.

Mel and I went home for the tea. Afterwards we joined up with Larkin again. We cycled to the forge. Hiawatha was there fixing Sean Hanlon's scuffle. The fire was only barely lit. He was smoking his pipe studying his task. He told us not to bother him. We were about to depart when in walked Miley Cassidy.

"God save yiz all."

Hiawatha looked up and smiled. "If it isn't the Count of Monte Cristo in person. Aye, surely," he said. Miley looked his usual bleary self.

"I suppose a cup a' tay 'id be out a' the question."

"You'll have to bide your hour," the blacksmith answered.

Almost on his tail, a dark shadow arrived. Larkin and myself froze as the voice of Sr. Ignatius said, "Good evening." Another nun waited behind.

"God save you ma'am," said Miley.

The blacksmith looked up, "Can I help you Sister?" asked Hiawatha.

She looked as uncomfortable as we felt. "I must apologise for the intrusion – but we were wondering whether you might assist with the music at the Feis?"

"That's Sunday week, I think?" he said.

"If it is convenient of course?" she did not like asking for favours.

"I don't see why not," he answered.

"Diddle-di-diddle-di-diddle-di-di-di," said Miley.

The nun looked at Miley.

"Mr. Cassidy!" said she sarcastically.

He answered "A grand even'."

We had a snigger. She noticed. She smiled at the tramp sardonically.

"A lovely evening for a stroll." She was displaying her unflappability.

"If ye had somewan to stroll with itself," reflected Miley dolefully.

"You should have got married," she said to him.

"Sure isn't it a wonder you never got married yourself, Sister," he parried.

"Oh but Miley," she countered, "I did get married – I married the Lord."

"Be God Sister," he said, "you couldn't have married in to a more dacent family."

We turned away. Hiawatha laughed and looked at her.

"I think you will have to concede."

She was blushing and making as good as cover as she could. Lamely she said, in mock good humour, "Oh little apples will grow – won't they Mr. Cassidy?"

She turned to go and as she did, Miley said, "Be God they will Sister – and so will big wans."

She was going and she kept going. Miley looked after her

"Doesn't poor ould Jaysus have a lot to put up with married to that wan." He spat on the floor as our guffaws burned the ears of our oppressor, swishing along the dusty road back to the convent.

II

Extreme Uunction, the Happy Death Cross and "Don't Pull the Knickers off Her Altogether"

O n the 23rd of June 1957, Wexford beat Laois in the Leinster Senior Hurling Championship Semi Final. Laois were not a test and nobody was fool enough to read anything into the result. The old foe, Kilkenny, were the ones to watch for. Wexford had won three Leinster Finals in a row, but four in a row was unheard of – by anybody. The trip to the US had not dulled their enthusiasm and the match against Laois went down as a mere pipe opener. The Kilkenny match was fixed for Croke Park on the 7th of July.

⊂⊃⊂⊃

A lot was happening in my life just then. We were preparing for the Primary Cert, which would be held the following week. I had to be sure that I would pass it, otherwise I would not be eligible to go to second level education and the career of my choice. Although preparations were continuing apace for this exam, lots of time was still devoted to religion. We were told stories about the black babies in Africa whose little pagan souls were being saved by the heroic missionaries like Fr. Michael. The manner of treatment by the Communists of the church and our Clergy in Russia and China had an affect on me. Whether it was Cardinal Wyzinski, a prisoner in his own palace, Ivor McGrath, a Columban missionary in a 6 by 3 feet cell in a Chinese Communist prison, it mattered not, they were all heroes. They did not have the fancy ways of high society but they had really "recognisable big hearts." I felt for them all and regularly I would make a little sacrifice from what errand money I could and put it in the mite box for the black babies. This did not escape the quick eye of Ignatius. She cornered me one day after I had been despatched to fill the big cocoa kettle from the water can, which was kept in the nun's room. She asked me whether I was looking forward to leaving primary school, whether I had spent much time with uncle Fr. Michael, since he had come home, when he was going back and how he was getting on in Nigeria – as if I really would have known It was all leading up to something. She asked me about a new weekday missal I had and whether I would like my name scrolled on the inside and I told her I would. She asked me when was the Entrance examination for St. Peter's. She then asked me what I would like to be when I grew up. I paused. I felt for a while I would like to be a priest on the Foreign Missions. "I think I would like to be a priest," I said. "Then let it be our secret, and tell no one yet." I felt a door had been closed behind me. I left the room with a sense of newly accepted obligation. I knew she would ask me about it again and I realised I had let her in to a private room out of which she would not easily go.

That same week Larkin got in to more trouble. During Catechism class Sr. Ignatius was teaching us all about the Sacrament of the Dying, or Extreme Unction as we were taught it. At the mention of death, Larkin went quiet. She explained it could be given to those who are seriously ill and in danger of death and often times it made them better. It took away all trace of sin and, better still, all trace of the remains of sin, guaranteeing immediate and straight passage to Heaven without any necessity of even a courtesy call to Purgatory on the way. Its tradition went back as far as Constantine, the Roman Emperor, who was baptised on his death bed – even to my then young mind this appeared to be too cute by half – I never believed God was a gobshite and you would nearly have to be if you were going to fall for a stunt like that.

Padraig Byrne asked whether it would not give an awful fright to someone who was very sick to discover everybody else thought that he was dying. She said it had the opposite affect, that it calmed the mind because it healed the soul and gave confidence in Divine Mercy and helped the sick person resign themselves to the will of God. Mary Molloy asked what happened to the souls of the dying who did not receive it. She said that it depended on the state that such a person was in at the time. If they were in a State of Grace, they would go straight to Heaven, such as the saints and martyrs, but if they died like the rest of us poor sinners, then they would have to experience the flames of purgatory before they could advance, if not worse. This was also another reason to say such prayers and do such good works as obtain plenary indulgences in order to avoid a total dependence on the Sacrament of Extreme Unction. She said there was a very strict obligation, under pain of grievous sin, on those in the company of sick persons to send for the priest on time. Thorpey asked, "Supposing the person who is with them does not know that." "Then," she said, "there would be very serious consequences for them both." Larkin just kept looking at his inkwell. "That's nonsense!" he stated very quietly. He might as well have shouted it because everyone was stunned into immediate silence. She looked at him and instantly realised what was wrong. Hiawatha and his father had been for a few drinks on that Sunday afternoon when his father had died. Hiawatha had gone for the doctor. The doctor's wife phoned for the priest because Hiawatha, had not done so. To compound matters the curate was at the match and the Parish Priest was living more than two miles away. The doctor had kept a pulse going for a little while, but the life left the poor man's body as the priest was pulling up outside. The Canon administered the Sacrament "on the off chance." It was the first question everyone asked when they heard of a sudden death. Most were compassionate: "Still, you never know – only God knows when life leaves." But that was not what they believed. The doctor dealing with a sudden death was almost always able to say when the person died, and the new doctor in Coleman always did. In the case of Larkin's father, it was a pity, but it was too late. It was a pity that Hiawatha had been with him when a thousand others would have called the priest first and not the doctor. It was just too bad, but there it was.

Ignatius thought it better not to confront him and diverted by ignoring the remark saying, "The church, however, has Masses said for the happy repose of those souls and these are said almost immediately." Everyone heard her say "almost." That stupid eejit of a Thorpey had to ask the bloody question, why could he not keep his big "duck house" shut. He always had to bladder and all he was doing was licking up to Ignatius. Larkin was very subdued.

Almost immediately she got us out in choral form to sing "Cibavit," one of the hymns she had selected for the Plain Chant competition. The prize was a silver school cup and a chance for the first three choirs to sing in the High Mass for the Cardinal on Sunday. The fact that the Feis was on the same day bothered her none. High Mass was on at eleven o'clock and everyone would be back home in Coleman in plenty of time for the Feis in the afternoon.

While we were singing the door opened and in walked Fr. Williams. He said he thought it was a choir of angels as he walked up the path to the school. Ignatius was chuffed but, in typical fashion, was unable to receive the compliment. "There is a lot of work to be done yet," she jerked.

She showed the priest from the room and told us to sit down and start memorising our Irish poetry. When they were both gone and the door shut I was just about to speak to Larkin when it reopened. She stood at it and threatened if she heard a sound there would be "wigs on the green."

After a short period of great boredom she came back and asked Larkin to come out. He blushed, but did as bid. Her tone was not severe. When she had shown him out she came back in to the room. He was outside, most likely with the priest. She asked us to recite the poem.

"A dhroimeann donn dílis,
(My beautiful offspring)
A shíoda na mbó.
(Pride of the land.)
Cá ngábhann tú san óiche?
(Where do you go at night?)
'S cá mbíonn tú sa ló?"
(Where in the daylight?)

When I had finished she explained the poem was not about a little one that had lost its guardian – but it had a more patriotic meaning. She explained the poet was using the situation of pain that a little one experiences when abandoned by its minder as being the same as his feelings about the desertion of his country. She said it required great sensitivity to express these things and to feel them.

When Larkin came back he had a look of pain on his face. His eyebrows were furrowed and the inner corner of his eyelid betrayed a dark shadow revealing the upturned line of a piercing pain. Every so often he would drag his jaw in a determined way as if by doing so it would pull the pain away from his eyes. Ignatius asked him if the priest was still there and he said that he was. She threatened silence once more as she left the room.

Thorpey turned around and looked at Larkin's face and asked what everyone was wondering, "What did he say to you?"

Larkin looked at him and said, "Fuck off!"

The girls gasped.

"What are yiz all gawkin' at?" he rattled. He took his school satchel from underneath the desk, pucked me on the shoulder and said, "Give us a hand." I looked at him as he went to the window. "Come on, give us a hand," he said.

He wanted me to help him lift open the bottom pane of the eight feet high school window. It was very heavy, but we managed. When it was opened he threw out his school satchel on the lawn. I thought he was going to leap out but he told me to pull it back down again. I tried to hurry. The rest of the schoolrooms' eyes followed Larkin who was flushed now from his exertions.

Ignatius came back and thanked everyone for being so quiet. She looked pleased.

"Right," she commanded, "back out in to the choir once more."

Everybody got out and stood in their place which had been regimented by the General herself. The space beside me was empty. It was Larkin's place. He was still sitting in his desk. She was foostering with the sheet music and had not noticed him. She had her back to him. We were facing them both. He stood and as he did, the iron hinged seat of his desk clanged in to its upright gravity position.

"I won't be singing," he said.

She looked up from the music to the now silent choir and was obvious in her surprise that the speaker was behind her. She turned round.

"I beg your pardon?" she challenged.

"I won't be singing – I am leaving school." He was steady and deliberate.

"Just who do you think you are that you can speak to me like that?"

She reached for the stick and walked menacingly towards him. She raised it to hit him and as she drew it towards him, he caught it.

"Give it to me this instance," she said with as much ice and subdued bitterness as she could invoke.

He was standing in the passageway between the desks at one side, but he quickly moved through the desk and up the other passage to the front where the choir was. Instinctively they recoiled, lest that in any way they should become part of the scene. She stood between him and the door.

"Give me that stick!" she growled. She was white in the face, her female snarl was gathering.

"Get out of my way," he shouted fiercely. He looked like a frightened criminal. "I am going out." He was pointing the stick at her, panting.

"Give me that stick, I said" she repeated.

He fired it to the neutral corner in the room, like a gun slinger tossing his six gun aside for the bare knuckles.

"Get out of my way," he said his breath slowing down.

"Bring me that stick Michael Thorpey."

"If you move Thorpey, I'll break your puss," he countered.

Thorpey started to cry. Larkin made a burst for the door. She had the knob in her hand but his strength and impulse was the stronger and she had to let it go. She caught him by the hair but he stepped back in to her and drew back with his elbow in to her stomach, a feat I had seen him perform many times on the football field with very effective results, then and now. She fell to the floor holding herself. He opened it and walked over the threshold. He looked back at the crumpled mass of upturned black cloth, slip and stocking. Next moment he was gone. Thorpey went to help the struggling nun up the rest of the way. "Oh leave me alone!" she revulsed. He drew back. She was tough. She saw Larkin collect his satchel from the lawn and he ran off down the path out of sight, out of the school, out of her life forever. Once more I envied him his courage and his strength and ability. He tore the arse in it once more, and once more got away with it.

She bade us sit down and then she left the room. We could hear the other nuns join her. Everyone spoke in huddled whispers, except me. My friend was gone. I sat quietly for a while, thinking about him and his confidence in spite of all the disadvantages in his life. I wished I could emulate him. I found myself at the forbidden cupboard. It had banged open when Ignatius had fallen against it. I could see the little aeroplane she had confiscated from me the previous year. I put my hand in and took it back. As I did the door opened and she surprised me.

"Put that back this instance," she ordered.

"It's mine," I said.

"Hand it over, this instance."

I bowed my head, shame facedly and handed it over. I could feel the tears coming.

"Sit down out of my sight," she growled. She had had enough for one day. She would not dignify me with a beating. I felt very humiliated. I never saw the little plane again.

I thought school would never end that day. There was no more singing "Cabavit." That afternoon we were put writing essays and the title of the essay was, "Why I Must Always Do As I Am Told." Usually there were pointers and guides on the blackboard – short precise phrases that indicated what was required in an essay. No such aids or prompts were given today. It was the worst essay I ever wrote. Every time I tried to write, the words just would not come. Finally, I settled for writing the Fourth Commandment and tried to remember what I had been taught in Catechism class about it. I was upset but my feelings required to be sat upon, if trouble and pain were to be avoided.

∞·∞

That same evening I went down to Larkin straight after school but he was not there. I cycled out to Mel and told her what had happened. Nobody knew what the priest had said to him that triggered the whole affair in school. Peter was away and only Mel and her mother were about. The day was dull and when it started to rain we went indoors. It was one of those times in between. We felt restless until Mel's mother suggested we play "checkers" – the Yanks, name for draughts. We searched the sittingroom but could find none. To begin with, I felt there was little likelihood of finding anything remotely approaching a toy in Peter's. We tried in Peter's office and Mel found a pack of cards. In the course of the search, I came across a typed document which was headed,

"ADDRESS." I tapped Mel on the arm for her to see. The document read:

—253—

"ADDRESS FROM THE MEMBERS OF WEXFORD COUNTY COUNCIL TO HIS EMINENCE, JOHN CARDINAL DALTON D.D., ARCHBISHOP OF ARMAGH AND PRIMATE OF ALL IRELAND ON THE OCCASION OF HIS VISIT TO THE COUNTY

ON THE 29TH/30TH OF JUNE 1957. MAY IT PLEASE YOUR EMINENCE; YOUR MOST HUMBLE AND OBEDIENT SERVANTS, THE MEMBERS OF THE WEXFORD COUNTY COUNCIL, WELCOME YOU AND REJOICE WITH THE PEOPLE OF THE DIOCESE OF FERNS THAT YOU HAVE HONOURED US BY THIS VISIT. WE ARE UNANIMOUS THAT ADVANTAGE BE TAKEN OF THIS MOMENTOUS OCCASION AND CONVEY TO YOUR EMINENCE AN EXPRESSION OF LOYALTY AND AFFECTION FOR YOUR DISTINGUISHED PERSON; FOR THE HIERARCHY OF IRELAND, AND THE SUPREME SOVEREIGN PONTIFF, HIS HOLINESS, POPE PIUS THE XII.

YOUR EMINENCE COMES TO US AS THE DISTINGUISHED AND SCHOLARLY SUCCESSOR OF PRELATES REACHING BACK TO THE DAYS OF OUR GLORIOUS PATRON, ST. PATRICK AND IT IS THE SINCERE PRAYER OF THE COUNCIL THAT DIVINE PROVIDENCE WILL SPARE YOU LONG TO PRESIDE OVER THE DESTINIES OF THE HOLY CHURCH IN IRELAND.

IN THIS PERIOD OF DANGER FOR CATHOLIC TRUTH, FAITH AND MORALS, WE BELIEVE THAT YOU HAVE PROVED AND WILL CONTINUE TO PROVE A TOWER OF STRENGTH IN MAINTAINING THE EFFICACY OF THE CATHOLIC WAY OF LIFE IN IRELAND IN THE FACE OF THE MATERIALISTIC AND PAGAN TENDENCIES SO MARKED THROUGHOUT THE WORLD TODAY.

ONCE AGAIN, ASSURING YOUR EMINENCE OF THE SINCERE DEVOTION AND FIDELITY OF THE WEXFORD COUNTY COUNCIL HUMBLY ASKING THE BLESSING OF YOUR EMINENCE ON THEIR WORK AS A LOCAL AUTHORITY."

Some of the words were big words, but we understood them all. I was very proud of Peter. He was a very important person now. Mel said she was chuffed. Peter would make this speech in front of all of the other important people in Wexford and the Cardinal and Bishop on Sunday. Fr.

Michael would be there as well. The Catholic Truth Society Annual General Conference would be bound to discuss the boycott and Peter's reference to "period of danger" was "giving the nod" to the clergy as to whose side the Council of the County of Wexford and Peter were on. I stayed for the tea and I played cards until Peter came home. The rain kept at it all evening and it was miserable.

When Peter arrived he brought me back to my own home. He asked me to relate what had happened in school and I told him. News certainly travelled fast. When he drove past Larkin's, there was a light on in the house.

"Keep away from young Larkin for the moment," he said.

I was shocked. This was not the Peter I knew.

"But he is my friend," I persisted.

"I know that," he said, "just until the holidays. We don't want you getting caught up in this stuff."

"I'll talk to my mother," I pouted.

When I got in home I went into the back kitchen. My mother was there washing up after my father's supper. I told her what Peter had said. I asked her to talk to my father to please, please beg him to say that it was all right for us to meet. All the fun would go out of life if there were no Larkin to do anything with, which also meant no Hiawatha. This had all in some way to do with the boycott. There was only one way to find out. I got a cup of milk and a currant bun, which I ate in the back kitchen. I got my schoolbag and left it in the kitchen for the morning. I said goodnight to them all and went to bed. I silently stole back to the bottom step. I was only just in time. Peter was relating how the priest had spoken to Hiawatha about sending Larkin to St. Peter's and had spoken to Larkin that day. The priest was convinced it was the only hope for him. He was disappointed that Isaac Watchorn had not been more co-operative. The priest was taking legal advice on what should be done. There might be ugly scenes down there yet and it would be as well if "the young fellow" – a reference to me – "be kept out of it for the while."

My mother disagreed. Peter argued it was to spare me any hurt. My mother said it would be a greater hurt entirely to separate two friends like we were. The outside door opened suddenly and Fr. Williams walked in and surprised me.

"Eavesdroppers never hear anything good about themselves," he said to a reddening culprit.

"I think we had better let everyone know what's happening!" He opened the kitchen door and ushered me in. I came sheepishly. "This young man would like to hear a little more of what everyone is talking about," he said.

I hated him for it. My mother blushed and Peter looked exposed.

"I'll bring him up!" she said.

My father got the coal bucket to stoke the cooker. My mother lectured me, but I knew her anger was not for me. I dressed myself for bed and felt my innocence shedding with each item of apparel. They were all determined they were right and wanted to make it be so.

In school next day, Thorpey had it that Larkin was going to be arrested. The priest had called to his father and he heard his father tell his mother. I had to get word to him someway. My parents had not forbidden me to go near the place, but I knew if peace was to be kept this would have to be carried out with a fair degree of secrecy and alibi. I hit on a plan. During the dinner break we would practice the relay race for the sports. I volunteered to tell Larkin that we would practice in the sports field that evening.

Thorpey protested, "if he is not going to school, he can't be on the team."

"He was entered from school," I answered.

Thorpey would not buy it, but the others did, and so I was volunteered. I went down, but he was gone away and so was Hiawatha. I went home and did my lessons.

☙❧

When I was finished I volunteered to go to the priest's housekeeper to see if she needed messages from the shop. This was again in the vain hope that he might be in when passing. When I called at the priest's house, I walked straight into Iníon Ní Breathnach. "My genius!" she said. I blushed. She asked me some questions in Irish, which I answered. We were in the back yard. While we were talking Sergeant Thorpey came in.

"Iníon Ní Breathnach, I have to speak to you for a moment."

He had some papers in his hand. I left them and went in to Mae. I was telling her who was outside when Iníon Ní Breathnach came in with the papers the Sergeant had given her.

"Where's Fr. Bill?" she asked. Her makeup was streaking.

"I think he's in the garage," said a shocked Mae. "What was that all about?" she asked, as the schools' inspector rustled back outside.

I was surprised as well. I took the grocery note and went down the street. Larkin was still not home. When I came back Mae told me Iníon Ní Breathnach had been given a Summons on account of the road accident involving Hiawatha. No wonder she was upset.

In the sports field that evening there was still no sign of Larkin. Padraig Byrne said they had gone off for good. Thorpey said that was not the case. I told them I had seen a light in the house. One of the Doyles said that he heard Larkin had been stolen by the Protestants with the help of Hiawatha and that they were going to come back looking for more children. He was an awful gobshite.

For the rest of the week I did not see Larkin. Gerry Denn was back and was doing the cows. He was in great form. He was living in Hiawatha's house with Mary Byrne. They had run off to Gretna Green and had married. The whole place was stunned when they returned with the rings. Gerry's father would not accept it but, in fairness to Mr. Byrne, he helped them with the furniture. Hiawatha told them before they went away that, they could have his place for a while. What surprised me most was that Fr. Williams had helped them as well. Gerry told me that both Hiawatha and Larkin had spent most of the week going in and out to New Ross.

On the Friday the choir were taken to New Ross to sing in the Plain Chant competition. When it was over we followed the usual ritual of buying water pistols and ran around the town skurtin' at the townies. They called us "culchies" and we called them "town hawks."

As we were running through the town, I saw Larkin and Hiawatha coming out of a solicitor's office. They were both nearly as delighted to see me as I was to see them. They had come in to New Ross on the bus each day and had gone home on it as well. Hiawatha insisted on buying tea and buns for us. When he went to the toilet Larkin told me that Fr. Williams had been trying to put pressure on him to enrol as a student in St. Peter's college. He was convinced Sr. Ignatius was involved. Himself and Hiawatha had been involved in signing a lot of papers and doing a lot of legal stuff, getting matters sorted out. Larkin's father had died without making a Will and although he was entitled to everything his father owned, a guardian had to be appointed.

I told him how pressure was being put on me to stay away from him. He told me he would never go back to school or the nuns as long as he lived. We saw Thorpey pass the window of the café. He was running, skurtin' his water pistol at someone. A few minutes later he came running back, obviously retreating from returned fire. He ran in to the café to hide. He closed the door behind him quickly. His hair was drenched, and he was panting. The others who were following ran past. He had escaped for the moment. He saw us and came over.

"You're in big trouble," he said solemnly.

"And you have your shite," said Larkin.

Hiawatha returned just in time to hear Thorpey say,

"The priest says you're to be summonsed."

When he saw Hiawatha, he blushed and, sticking out his tongue at Larkin, he ran out the door straight into the arms of his pursuers. They held him and doused him.

"Serves him right – him and his big mouth," I said.

When we heard him crying, however, we knew the townies were beating him up. We both ran out and chased the others away. His nose was bleeding and his clothes were sogging. An empty sweet-can was rolling down the street having been abandoned by the water marauders. Thorpey carried the contents of it on his clothes.

Thorpey was still snivelling. "Me mother'll kill me," he said. "I need it again for Sunday, an' the new tie as well."

The shirt looked wet, but the tie looked to be in severe trouble. Some of the red die from it had run in to his shirt.

One of the townies stuck his head around the corner and shouted,

"Janey mac, me shirt is black!

What'll I do for Sunday?

Got to bed and cover me head

And don't get up 'til Monday."

We ran at them and they chased off.

"Can't you wear your shirt open?" I said.

"Not for the singing," he sobbed.

"What singing?" I asked.

"We came second in the competition and now we definitely have to sing for the Cardinal on Sunday."

I had left before the results were announced. We tried to dry Thorpey. He acted the eejit a lot but, when it came down to it, he was one of our own, and we could not abandon him to the townies.

"Who told you I was going to be summonsed?" asked Larkin.

"The priest called down to see me father," he admitted.

"He wha'?" said Larkin.

"He called down to see me father about summonsing you."

Thorpey started to cry. We just stood lookin' at him. The realisation of all of Larkin's misfortunes, and his own, had taken Thorpey over. I felt a lump in my own throat. It really was an awful lot to carry. I looked at Larkin. He was looking away at nothin', which he had seen at the end of the street. After a few moments he said, "Fuck 'im," defiantly, and added with conviction, "Fuck 'em all." Thorpey stopped higging. I took back my handkerchief. "I'd better go back," said Larkin, and he disappeared back in to the little café.

∞∞

A complication arose on Saturday night. Because we were singing in Wexford on Sunday morning it meant an early start. Whereas I could serve first Mass, I could not serve second. Fr. Williams could drive quickly to Wexford after second Mass, and just about make it, but the choir had to be arranged well in advance. All of this meant that Larkin was needed to serve second Mass. Only Larkin and myself knew the Latin. Since he had left school it was now an issue as to whether he would serve or not. On Saturday night I went to Confession. When they were finished, I told the priest that I would not be able to serve second Mass. He was in the sanctuary when I spoke to him. The "priest" Doyle was putting flowers into vases. Fr. Williams paused for a moment and then said,

"I'm sure Mr. Doyle could help out." He turned and addressed him. "William, could you serve second Mass tomorrow perhaps, and accompany me to see the Cardinal afterwards?"

He thought all his birthdays had come together. His face lit up like a harvest moon. "Why certainly father, I'd be delighted."

A part of me was disappointed they had got off the hook and another part glad that Larkin had not been cornered.

When we arrived in Wexford, it was a beautiful summer's morning. The place was covered in bunting and brass bands. We arrived at a quarter to ten, an hour and a quarter before Mass. The place was crowded. There were bands and boy scouts in the church grounds. Sodalities of the Sacred Heart of the Precious Blood, Children of Mary, Knights of the Blessed Sacrament and, of course, the Knights of Columbanus.

There were six choirs in the church, the biggest organ I had ever seen and another brass band – the Confraternity band. We were herded into a corner of the gallery and Sr. Ignatius said "Ciúnas!" There was a lot of hugger-mugger with the adults as they excitedly checked hymnals, veils and hats in a flurry of muddled anticipation.

We were to sing "Cibavit" at the Offertory. There would be only one hymn in English – "Faith of Our fathers" – the rest would all be in Latin. This had a recent resonance – the same policy obtained for the procession at home. Whatever we had, or didn't have, we had Latin – the common tongue of the Universal church a sure sign – if not one of the four marks. The church was thronged with clergymen in surplices and soutanes. When the hour of eleven struck, a hush descended. The main choir intoned "Ecce Sacerdos Magnus – Behold the Great Priest." There were five Bishops, an Archbishop and the Cardinal himself. It was very impressive. It was also very stuffy. I thought of our Palm Sunday procession and it compared like a bad recitation to the Hollywood production of *Ben Hur*. I saw four thuribles and there were so many crozier carriers and mitre minders, the only things missing were a few Spartan slaves.

When they got to the altar there was virtually a fog of incense and the smell was so acute, it hurt. The choir sang the "Te Deum." The Cardinal imparted his blessing on the congregation and the Archbishop announced there was a three hundred days' indulgence for all those present. I wondered whether that included the crowd who were listening outside in the churchyard and, if it did, why not those who were listening to it being broadcast on Radio Athlone. And if it did not, did it only include the main body of the congregation and not us, who were suspended in mid-air, a limbo between the seven choirs of angels and the throne of the red-hatted

Cardinal. It was semantic nonsense of a type that smart-alecs challenged authority with. I hated when my head played games like that.

When the Mass came to the Gospel, it was half past eleven. At that rate of going, we would be there until teatime. The ceremony got boring and monotonous. I was in the front row looking down on the congregation. Thorpey was beside me. He placed both of his hands on the rail in front of him. He knelt forward leaning his chest on the backs of his hands. He was bored as well. His jaw dropped open in a sort of a loll. He yawned. As he opened his urging palate, a dollop of saliva flowed out and went splat on the seat in the church below. I looked down and he pulled back. A nun looked up and saw me. I reddened and pulled back. That gobshite of a Thorpey. I closed my fist and looked to see if Ignatius was looking. She was engrossed in the liturgy. I darted at his leg with my clenched knuckles, but he moved and I got him in the balls. "Yeouch!" he cried out. "That was me balls." Ignatius looked over and then down at the congregation and back again. I could see heads below looking up. She came over and stared darkly, "I will deal with you tomorrow," she said quietly slicing me in two with her eyes, her words chiselled through clenched teeth. I hung my head. How did it always happen to me? If I had been in the friggin' Garden of Eden, I would have been blamed for giving the "Granny Smith" to Eve.

I lost total interest in what was going on and it was only when I heard Bishop Brown who was giving the sermon say "boycott" that I awoke. He was talking about home and the children of Sean Hanlon.

There are some men who claim to be religious but who regard the truth as of secondary importance or less important than sanctity or morality. But Christ said He who believes not will be condemned. Would they have us deprive our children of the opportunity to believe? Pilate asked Christ 'Truth, what is that?' The acceptance of the truth is the first step to true religion and spiritual progress. Truth is the conformity of mind with reality. Truth comes from God alone, and only from Divine Revelation can clear and certain knowledge come. For this reason He gave His Church, His Apostles and their successors, your Bishops, His teaching authority. We will not let you down now as we have not let you down in the past. When Catholic action is called for, Catholic leadership is given. It is called for now and now we give it our stamp of approval, like the hallmark that is made on gold."

There was not a murmur in the church. The Cardinal was sitting on his throne and the Bishops had variously their heads bent forward or back, their mitres resembling the open beaks of a bird's nest awaiting the morsels from mother. The rest of the clergy were riveted. Ignatius looked as if she had just been anointed, and it was working for her. When the Bishop finished, it was nearly surprising no one clapped. The atmosphere was dripping out of the drenched ears of the Faithful. Ignatius leaped into action. She made us stand. As the Arch priest directed the altar servers to the cruet alcove, Ignatius hummed the note "Hmmmm". The choir leader took it and sang "Cibavit eo portante ramos olivarum." At that point the choir joined. It sounded haunting and in stark contrast to the rest of the ceremony because it was plain and had no accompaniment, just the barenaked country voices of simple young children. Ignatius was pleased when it was completed. She inhaled the smell of anticipated success. When Mass was concluded the Hierarchy and his Eminence came out to the platform to the strains of "God bless our Pope, the Great, the Good." A second concession to the English language, which could drive home the prestige of the people whose language, the driven could only marvel at.

All of the Municipal and Local Government Councillors and Officials were there. Peter was on the platform. Bishop Staunton was over with the Knights of Columbanus. The "priest" Doyle was there. Lots of people were smoking now.

The freedom of the Borough of Wexford was given to the Cardinal. Then Peter spoke. His voice carried loud, clear and high over the houses of Wexford town through the loud speakers resting securely on the buttresses and battlements of Bride Street church. The Cardinal spoke. He said there was a certain magic about the name of Wexford. When we started to learn Irish history first, we soon realised that Wexford played a striking part in the story of our country and had been foremost in the struggle of Faith and fatherland. It was not surprising that it had to suffer for the Irish and Catholic cause. The town suffered massacre at the hands of Cromwell and his ruthless fanatics. The story of Wexford's achievements in '98 would always be a source of inspiration to Irish youth. The men of Wexford then showed they were cast in an heroic mould. They continued to fight when others had given up.

In this day and age, Ireland was being sold off once more. It reminded him of the poem from "The Boree Log:"

We'll all be ruined said Hanrahan before the year is out." There was polite laughter from the crowd. "It was necessary for us to eliminate pessimism and restore confidence in our future and our Country with its own character of sturdy independence. Wexford was the model county. It was a splendid example of establishing flourishing industries on its own initiative – it was probably the best tillage area in the country. The Wexford Hurlers had won many laurels and seemed destined to win many more. Commodore John Barry, an illustrious son, had recently been honoured as had the leader of the Irish Party, John Redmond. The Wexford Festival had acquired an International reputation second to none. "My earnest prayer is for Wexford to maintain its fine tradition, and continue to set an example of enlightenment, courage and self-reliance."

The crowd clapped and clapped. The Mayor of Wexford presented an illuminated parchment certificate of the Freedom of Wexford Town. It was placed in a handsome casket bearing the gold plaques of the Arms of Wexford and the See of Armagh.

The Cardinal received the generosity of the people graciously. He spoke with the Mayor and the other dignitaries, but he left the grounds of Bride Street church in earnest conversation with my uncle Peter.

Thorpey had disappeared in the crowd when we came out from the church at first. I saw him across the churchyard and went after him. By the time I got there he had vanished again. Still, I knew he could not avoid me at the Feis because we were dancing a three-hand-reel together. I would be like Larkin – I'd kick the shite out of him for getting me into trouble.

The Feis raised funds for the parish, in addition to providing an outlet of national culture. It was held in the Fort in Duncannon, a village five miles away. The Fort had been a military installation since the sixteenth century at least, and probably for a long time before. During the War, soldiers were billeted here. They came every summer from the Curragh Camp. The various messes and quarters were sufficiently close together to allow easy access from one competition to the next and sufficiently far apart at the same time to not have the singing interfere with the recitations, or other music. My father collected the entrance fees on the gate. The school band marched through the small village leading the various competitors. There was no drum, however, because Larkin did not show.

The Fort had a ravined moat thirty feet or so deep. Mostly it was kept locked when the Army was not there. A caretaker kept an eye. Parts of it were spooky, in particular the Croppy Boy's cell. This was located down some twenty steps and had very little light or ventilation. The Fort was besieged in 1645 during the Great Rebellion and various attempts had been made to starve the inhabitants. In more recent times, when a contingent arrived from the Curragh once, without fresh meat, one of the cooks phoned the quarter-masters' store at HQ to ensure that the convoy coming next day would bring it. When the lorries arrived they were provisionless and blamed the quarter-master's staff for not relaying the message. Greatly annoyed the cook phoned again and immediately he was answered, he released a tirade of abuse and bad language. When he had finished, a rather cold voice at the other end said,

"Do you know to whom you are speaking?"

"I don't," replied the cook.

"This is Lieutenant Colonel Karl O'Sullivan," said the voice.

The cook paused and then asked grandly, "And do you know to whom you are speaking?"

"No," replied the voice.

"Thanks be to Jaysus," said the cook and replaced the receiver.

The Department of Defence always made the premises available to the parish. After I had made my recitation I went looking for Thorpey for the three-hand-reel. Padraig Byrne, who made up the trio, searched high and low for him, but he was nowhere to be found.

Mel was there. She thought we looked lovely in our orange kilts. Some of the crowd from other schools kept saying we were wearing skirts. I kept looking among the large crowd in the square for Thorpey. I was in trouble enough with the nuns on account of him, without compounding it by his not showing up for the dancing. Mel barely knew him, but she looked as well. He had been in the parade so he had to be someplace about.

"I guess you should tell them you can't find him," Mel said. That would be snitching. There were times I despaired of Mel, and this was such a time. Maybe he was in the Croppy's Cell. The thoughts of going down that dark damp passage held little appeal. He might be down at the Sallyports, which opened to the moat. We went down the winding steps. I told her to watch out for nettles. Nobody was supposed to leave the main square of the fort. There was nobody in the Sallyport. We walked through out in to the moat. We could hear the accordions playing for the dancers on the farmer's trailers up above us in the square. There was nothing in the moat that we could see, except what appeared to be a well, at the corner. It had a sign which read "Danger."

The sun was beating down on the wild skutch grass of the moat. Maybe he was around the corner, I ventured. Stalkily, we picked our steps, avoiding thistles and prickles on both pairs of untrousered legs. Careful as we were, Mel caught a nettle on her inside leg.

"Ouch!" she said.

I turned around.

"I've been bitten," she cried. She was rubbing her inside thigh. "I've been stung," she said again with the fear of a white man in a foreign jungle. Was it nettles, was it wasps?

"Show me!" I said. She lifted her skirt high enough for me to see the little white blobs of nettle sting.

"It's okay," I said. "A dockleaf will fix it."

"It really stings," she said.

"I know," I said. "I'll fix it with a dock." I saw a cluster and picked a fist full. "Here," I said.

"What do I do?" she said. "Ooh – ooh – they really hurt – what do you do?" she cried.

Her pain outstripped her modesty and she was now holding her skirt revealing the bottom portion of her knickers. The sting was located halfway up her leg from her knee. My eyes were reluctantly dragged back to the sting where I knew they must remain under pain of mortal sin. But she was really in pain. The dock leaves needed to be rubbed on the sting to break the leaf down and release the sap that would salve. She was just holding them on it.

"That won't do," I said. "You'll have to rub it."

In the innate gentle way that she was, she simply touched them with it. I was torn between putting my hand near a place that was forbidden and the desire to relieve her obvious and very upsetting distress. Her tears were coming. She had been stung in a very tender spot.

"It's not working," she sobbed.

"You're not doing it right," I said, utterly frustrated by her inability and my own capability which was forbidden. She dusted them once more to my utter exasperation.

"No," I said again. "Not like that – like this."

"I can't," she cried. "I don't get it."

It was too much to watch. Something snapped inside me. The barrier had breached.

"Let me do it," I said. She handed me the leaves. I held the back of her leg with my left hand and took the bunch of leaves in my right. "This might hurt a little," I said.

I rubbed furiously up and down on her thigh initially very nervously and, on that account probably more robustly than was necessary. I needed more leaves after the first batch had virtually disintegrated on to her legs. She had stopped sobbing, though the trace of her tears were fresh and the remains were falling. I came back with the docks, and as I did she lifted her dress once more. I eyed my target again, but removed my gaze back to the stings. I held the docks on them in a pressed conscientious refocused, medical and helpful way.

"Thanks," she said as I sat on my hunkers with my hand up under her skirt.

A voice behind me said, "Hey lads, Leacy's havin' a feel of his cousin."

I nearly died. Mel ducked down in the long grass and knocked me off my hunkers and fell on top of me. There was another shout.

"Ah Jaysus, don't pull the knickers off her altogether."

"Oh God!" said Mel.

I got up. It was Thorpey. He was behind the cover of the well. He was smoking a cigarette. Jamesie Scanlon from fifth class was with him. They were both laughing. The hallmark of the cur, jeering.

"I hope we didn't disturb ya then," they laughed again.

I was raging. I tore over through the long stumbling grass which was almost chest high in clusters. Scanlon had a fag in his hand and the other one behind his back. Thorpey had a fag in his hand which he threw in the well. He backed away a little and put up his fists. I was going to burst him. As I passed Scanlon, he swung the stick he had concealed behind him in his right hand and struck me full on the face. It was a well-aimed full belt. Everything went black. I was dazed. As the black dissipated and things were spinning I tried to get up and failed. I tried again when Thorpey came forward and kicked me straight between the legs. The pain was excruciating. I remembered feeling sick in my stomach and throat. Then the lights went out. When I came around there was a man holding me whom I did not know.

"You're alright son – you'll be okay – you're alright – you'll be okay."

I was gone again. The next time I came around I was in the tearoom. I was lying on a trestle. Sr. Agatha, one of the other nuns at our school, was cleaning my face with water and cotton wool. My father came in. I went to get up.

"Lie still!" the nun commanded. My father came over.

"What happened?" he asked.

"Leave him for the moment John," said Sr. Agatha. "I think he might be concussed."

"Where's Mel?" I asked.

"I'm here," she said. She was drinking tea and had a coat over her shoulders. She was still crying.

"Are you alright?" I asked.

"Yes," she said, "I'm fine." She cried some more. "How are you?" she asked.

"I'm alright," I answered. The nun came back with a sponge.

"Sit down there now Miss and drink your tea. I'll look after this young man."

When my mother came in she was shaking. The nun made her have some tea. Before the Feis was over I was better. Not alone was I better, I was much better. The word had gone around that myself and my cousin had been attacked by two thugs and God between us and all harm but what were things coming to if you could not be safe at the Feis in Duncannon.

The President of the GAA was at the Feis and he had to give a speech that night at the concert. He was a Wexford man. He even referred to the incident at the presentation of the awards.

"The way of the thug and vagabond has never been our way," he said, "that is why there has been such universal condemnation of that dastardly attack on a young boy and girl and an attempt to mar and damage the name of our ancient festival. A festival founded on an ancient culture based on Christianity and sanctified by centuries of sacrifice and suffering, where our people faced eviction, transportation, the gruesome hardships of the coffin ship, the mental and physical torture of the prison cell, the hangman's rope and the firing squad who, 'walked the blood stained ways to meet their death with glowing eyes."

I had told nobody that it was Thorpey and Scanlon and I told Mel to say we did not know who they were. In any event, she did not know them herself. This had the unintended effect that mystery adds to trauma. Someone suggested after the GAA President spoke that it might have been another attempt by the Protestants to carry off two more Catholic children, but much as imagination required an explanation, no one seriously believed this. And although they did not believe it, it was surprising how many repeated the story.

At the concert I received first prize for my recitation of "Droimeann Donn Dilis" and I got the loudest clap of the night. Mel said afterwards she never had drunk so much "pop" nor eaten so much "candy."

When we got home, Mrs. Kelly was there with my mother. They had tea ready for everyone. The GAA President came in with Peter. I had never seen so many important people in one day. He told me I was the best little man he had ever met and he was not in the least bit surprised that I had won first prize. Mel and I ate our tea in the back kitchen. My older brother and sister joined the adults. Mrs. Kelly wanted my father to tell more of the yarns she had remembered from last year. Fr. Williams came in. Another cup and saucer were produced. Talk changed to the Cardinal's visit. Fr. Williams said he had spoken to the Bishop before he came away and, as a result, he had missed the Feis. Mr. Kehoe, the GAA. President, went on to say how outstanding the Feis had been.

However, it was plain to see that the priest had something on his mind and did not wish to discuss the Feis. He said it had been a great day for the church and the culture, which after all were the same anyway. He turned to Peter and said,

"The Bishop asked me to hand deliver this to you, it's from the Cardinal. You made a very big impression there."

This was a moment of some importance and the hushed quietness reflected it. Mel and I came silently in to the kitchen as the priest handed a brown bulky envelope to Peter. It was opened. The priest regarded the proceedings and Peter, with the smile of a man who knows he is the carrier of good news. Peter opened the envelope and took out a crucifix. "A happy death cross!" he said. The priest smiled and said,

"There's a letter in there as well in the Cardinal's own handwriting to the Bishop – Dr. Staunton asked me to give it to you."

Peter took it and read it. The priest watched him as he read, smiling all the while. When he had read it Peter simply said,

"God bless us."

He then handed it to my father who in turn handed it to my mother, to Mrs. Kelly and on to Mr. Kehoe, who handed it to me to give back to Peter, but I read it while the distracted conversations allowed me the opportunity. The letter read:

"My dear Lord Bishop,

Before I leave this noble place I must put pen to paper. I wish to thank you most sincerely for your great kindness to me during my visit. It was altogether an inspiring experience and in particular in the present circumstances it should do a lot of good.

I see from the papers the Protestant Bishop of Ossory is on another tack this morning. I think the first thing that should be done on our side is to insist on the return of the children. Protestants are certainly adept at propaganda.

Will you kindly give the enclosed to Mr. Leacy, a little momento from me. Say I am deeply grateful to him and send him my blessing.

With renewed thanks and all good wishes.

Your sincerely,

+ John Cardinal Dalton."

The reference to the Protestant Bishop referred to a request to meet the President of Ireland. The matter had spread nationally and a report of it had been carried in *Time* magazine, and here was my uncle Peter right in the middle of it. I wondered whether I would ever be as good a man as he was. He used to give out to us now and again, but that was to be expected. He had very high standards and it would be very hard to live up to them. They used say he was a devil after the women – but he used say they were all cracked about him and they were always fighting over him. This would be said to my mother and any others who teased him. He had great energy and determination and when on odd occasions he would go to count the cattle, I used to have to run to keep up with him. He had a pressing agenda, always and relentlessly he followed it. "Not alone must you be right – but you must be seen to be right," was one of his regular mottos. My father used say, "He never takes it easy, he never takes a rest." Whenever he did, such as after his supper or before going to a meeting, he would be great fun.

"The Devil finds work for idle hands," he used to tell me. At that early age I began to wonder about God and the Devil, and it appeared to me that somehow the Devil had got the better end of the bargain. It seemed as if the Devil was going around having all the fun without a care in the world whereas God was sending around a host of pale-faced, black-clothed preachers, whose remedies for dealing with life always knocked the fun out of it. We were expected to be cissy-like, white-faced angels with gold curls who would wince and turn away everytime someone said "shite" or "fuck."

❧ 12 ❧

A Bad Confession

The Cardinal's visit was widely reported in the papers, both national and local. Bishop Brown's support of the boycott hit the headlines. The nuns arrived in school with a newspaper. This was the first time I had ever seen this happen. Ignatius started the day by complimenting everyone on the wonderful weekend, starting with their success in New Ross on the previous Friday. She remarked how well the choir had sung and that the Cardinal himself had paid special tribute to the choir that had sung "Cibavit." I wondered whether she would remember the incident with Thorpey and myself in the gallery.

She spoke of the Feis and how well the school had done. She then referred to the assault and asked me to stand. Thorpey was not in school. She asked me to tell what happened. I told her it was all kind of a blur. She accepted it. I felt she did not want to alter her view of all that had been achieved. It seemed as if the incident with Thorpey and myself in the church would be overlooked on account of my injury.

The Primary Cert Examination was being held on Friday, but if it was, there were more pressing matters to attend to. She read all of the Bishop's sermon and told us that last weekend would be more important to us for the rest of our lives than next Friday. This would be almost the last time that she would be able to talk to us about these things. A heavy responsibility was laid on her shoulders that she should properly instruct us, she said.

"For those of you that will enter into marriage, you should do so only after great care and advice has been taken. We are all only too well aware of the problems that mixed marriages can cause. It would be far better if they were not allowed at all. They are allowed, I know, but I tell you if you want to enter into a happy marriage, do not enter into a mixed marriage.

Only yesterday, even the Protestant Bishop himself said that he carried no responsibility for Mrs. Hanlon and his church would have nothing to do with her."

As she was speaking she had a glowing look in her eyes. It was that look which the GAA President had referred to on the previous day. She suddenly turned a tack which almost unnerved me.

"There are plenty of good Catholic boys and girls to keep company with and get to know well enough before marriage is embarked upon. You have all heard before about company-keeping and what is allowed and prohibited, and if in that course there are any acts or touches or looks which are impure and improper it can be rectified and must be dealt with in Confession under pain of mortal sin. The Protestant boys and Protestant girls do not have the same restraints as we do, consequently keeping company with them is a source of great danger."

She went on some more about other advantages and disadvantages of going out with Catholics and Protestants. The only words that kept ringing in my ears were "any acts or touches or looks" had to be reported in Confession. I was back to feeling miserable. I remembered last year and the sin of kissing I had not confessed and how this year the same thing again, only worse.

Marie Doyle interrupted Ignatius. "Is it a sin to kiss a Protestant?"

Ignatius replied kissing in itself was not sinful, but it depended what was meant by the kiss. If it was done for pleasure then it did not matter whether it was a Catholic or a Protestant, it was simply wrong (de-daa!). My mind nearly snapped. There it was – old bean, old sport. Kissing for pleasure was wrong – full friggin' stop. No let offs this time me ould flower – no hook slippin' this time. Sin is sin and guilt is guilt, and boy was I guilty. In it, was I, up to my knees, up past Mel's knees as a matter of fact. How was I going to get out of this one?

"Bless me Father for I have sinned. I told lies twice, I cursed three times, I rubbed dock leaves on me cousin's fanny and had a little gawk as well."

I could see the priest coming through the confessional grill, biretta and stole and surplice roarin', "You little friggin' pervert, sin is one thing, but perverts need to be put down."

Excommunication? I could hear the priest respond.

"Excommunication? Excommunication me arse, castration perhaps but nothing as mild as excommunication for this little weed. An altar boy if you don't mind. Serves mass every single day, including Sunday and then the minute the priest and congregation turn their backs he rubs dock leaves on his cousin's fanny."

Slowly down the shadowy shore I could see my life slink away. Ebbing like blood, blob-blobbing in unstemmed haemorrhage leaving behind a weak and worthless thing. Unwanted, useless, a limp and flaccid lump of flesh with softened bone. I felt ill. I asked for permission to go out which was given. While I was outside, I sat on a warm grassy bank out of view and thought to myself how I would like to go for a swim. Confessions were on Saturday, the sports on Sunday.

At dinner time my mother told me that Peter had been unanimously reelected Chairman of the County Council. I consoled myself that at least one member of the family could keep up the good name, but I was very obviously a hard case. Maybe in time I would improve, but I had serious reason to doubt it. I tried to tell myself that what I did was wrong but I was unable to bring myself to confess it. I tried to tell myself that I was sorry – and in a way I was – but I knew well enough given half a chance I would be rubbing her leg again and this time, if I could manage it, without the aid or assistance of any dock leaves. That afternoon Fr. Michael and two nuns came to the school. Sr. Ignatius had told the class of the necessity of making a good Confession always, and that each Confession after a bad Confession made every subsequent one bad as well until the bad had been atoned.

The nuns that Fr. Michael had with him were from the Foreign Missions. Usually these events required songs, poems and a display of dancing, but their mission was otherwise today. The nuns were enlisting vocations and Fr. Michael was acting as chauffeur. They handed out holy pictures and spoke about the black babies and their pagan parents. They spoke of the need for young boys and girls to go on to be priests and nuns. They asked us to pray that Russia might be brought back home again, to pray for the priests and nuns sacrificing their lives amongst the heathens and savages to bring them the Kingdom of God.

As they were speaking Fr. Michael took out his surplice and purple stole and put them on. He took a prayer book and started looking for a page. Ignatius went out and brought in two candles. She got a linen cloth from her desk and, with the crucifix that decorated it and the two vases of posies, she made a little altar.

All offerings for the Missions were very helpful and all the gold milk bottle tops we had collected would go to good use to keep up the good work for the Blessed Lord and his Holy Mother. They asked us to stand and sing a hymn with them. As we stood, Fr. Michael looked down at me and beckoned me to come up. I left my desk just as the classroom started to sing.

"Mother of Christ, Mother of Christ
What shall I ask of thee?
I do not sigh for the wealth of earth
For the joys that fade and flee;
But, Mother of Christ, Mother of Christ, this do I long to see
Bliss untold which thine arms unfold
The treasure upon thy knee."

Ignatius told them to sit down. She had handed me a little bowl containing Holy Water with a sprig. Fr. Michael addressed the class.

"Hands up the boys and girls leaving school this year."

I raised my hand as did my five other classmates, Thorpey and Larkin were absent.

"As you know the Cardinal visited the diocese yesterday. I was honoured to be present at that celebration. I spoke with the Bishop afterwards and to mark the occasion in every parish, each class that is leaving school this year will be given a General Absolution for their sins."

It was only in a case where a Bishop was satisfied that there was serious reason that this could be done and he had deemed that in the times that were in it, children who left school to go into the world were at grave risk so the law was satisfied to enable a General Absolution be given. I had never served at General Absolution in my life and consequently I was a bit apprehensive.

"I want all of the boys and girls of sixth class to now fully understand they are now entering in to Confession," he paused. "Close your eyes," he said. They did and so did I.

"I want you to understand that every sin you have ever committed will be forgiven today, any sin you have forgotten or omitted to tell in Confession previously, will be remitted, providing you enter in to this Sacrament purely and with a humble heart."

The penny dropped with me. Here was my chance. All of my guilt to be washed away forever without a mention to anyone. I could not believe my luck.

"Pause and remember the sins you want forgiven."

I did not have to pause.

1. – I kissed Mel last year

2. – I rubbed her, eh – leg and uh – touched sort of nearly her – uh – fanny

3. – I had a look as well

4. – I cursed (oh fuck the curses, I don't mind telling them) – was there anything else?

5. – Yeah – lies – I hated confessing to lies – just lies in general – I can't think of them all just now.

"Adjutorium Nostrum in Nomine Domini."

6. – I just can't think – how the hell is it when you want to you just can't

"Jack!"

"JACK!"

"Uh, (Jesus! Fr. Michael was speaking to me.) He looked at me and said, "Adjutorium nostrum in nomini domini."

"Uh – Qui Fecit Coelum Et Terram."

"Confiteor Deo Omnipotenti ..." he commenced.

When he finished and I had responded we all said the Confiteor in English. He then told us we should now just refer back to the sins we had found and remembered. I smiled to myself and internally said, "All of the above." He paused for a moment and said some Latin prayers silently and then more loudly he said, "Dominum Noster Jesus Christum Te Absolvat ..." He mumbled on to the spot, which we all used to look forward to in Confession – the safe spot – "Deinde ego te absolvo a peccatis tuis, in nomine Patris, et Filii, et Spiritus Sancti. Amen."

He finished – we were free – out, home, clear, free, fresh as newly baptised babies and not even a penance. I smiled and swore to Christ I would never sin again as long as I lived and all girls and their stuff could go and shite. It was hurling and football from here out and with the help of God I might get a vocation for the priesthood, if I did not already have one, and enter the seminary after my Leaving Cert and save my soul and, as Larkin used to say, "Fuck the lot of 'em."

CO CO

When we got out from school, I headed for Larkin's. Peter would be away and I knew if I had gone home my mother would want me to do my homework on account of the Primary Cert Examinations on Friday. When I got there he was in the haggard, piking hay. He came down from the rick and asked if I could loan a hand. I asked him why he had not been at the Feis and he said that himself and Hiawatha had gone fishing. I felt distance had grown between us and I felt sad and ashamed. I was not sure whether I had let them down or they had let me down. He shuffled and said,

"They are quare times."

"They are," I said.

"They are trying to make me go to college," he said.

"You told me," I replied.

"They tried to say Hiawatha wasn't related to me and he couldn't look after me."

I was stunned.

"That's why we were away all the time, he had to get out papers to say he was my guardian." (He had told me some of this.)

"You mean like your father," I wanted to enter into it.

"No you gobshite, my father's dead – like, instead of."

"Oh yeah, yeah," I backed away.

"And that oul' fucker of an Ignatius tried to say me father was in Hell – well fuck that for a yarn," he threw a stone at a weather vane, but it missed and struck the corrugated iron roof with an empty, bitter, hard bang. "I am not going to Mass anymore 'aither," he said.

I was shocked.

"Hiawatha says I have to, but I'm not goin' to. Why should I? He doesn't have to."

"Yeah, but he's not our religion," I said.

"Yeah, well nayther am I," he said bitterly. "They can all go shite."

He was very angry and he seemed to have built up more resentment since he had left school.

"What about the sports?" I asked.

"Fuck the sports!" he said.

"I'm never havin' an'thin' to do with that school, or them nuns, ever again."

I felt I was making a hash of everything. My timing was wrong. I had been out of touch for too long. This was a different Larkin, a hardened Larkin, a bitter, hurt and angry Larkin.

"I suppose I had better go," I said. "Mel might be above."

At the mention of her name he brightened.

"How is she?"

"Grand, she's grand," I replied.

"Was she askin' for me?"

I saw an opening "She was," I lied.

"Tell her I was askin' after her," he winked.

I said I would, as he left to go back to the rick. It was the first bit of good humour I had seen in him in a long while. Larkin would be fifteen on the 5th of November but that meant he had to go to school until then. We all knew that. Mostly a blind eye was turned, particularly where a family needed someone else to earn a wage. But the law, was the law, nevertheless and if they decided to enforce it, to school he would have to go.

That evening Mel came down and most of the time we spent weeding the vegetables in my father's garden. My mother was great at flowers and kept a number of beds and a rockery. I preferred vegetables, ever since I had read the book *Jo's Boys*. The romantic presentation of boyhood and nature appealed greatly to me and inspired my gardening enterprise. From late spring, after Hiawatha had made the truck, I had dragged seaweed from the beach and dug it into the garden on Hiawatha's advice. This seemed a rather strange thing to do and I asked him for the reason. As usual, he was philosophical.

"There has to be death before there is growth," he said. "It's a rule of nature, the seaweed will rot and in doing so new life will come from it."

It was something like saying if you want to get to the west you have to keep going eastwards. It was a paradox, not a contradiction, once more.

I had sown lettuce and parsnips and carrots and potatoes. It was funny to hear Mel calling them spuds. We were weeding them with a hoe. She was wearing my mother's gardening gloves which were only a little too big for her. It was a warm evening. She was wearing a cotton dress with light blue and violet pansies on a yellow background.

Mostly I hoed down the side of the potato drills chopping and tearing the weeds away from the plants. She came behind with a rake and dragged, hauled and pulled the fallen weeds into an aluminium bucket which served as a water can in its youth and was serving out its battered retirement as a weed bucket for the garden. The truck was kept at the end of the drill and was filled from the bucket as we went. As we walked, we talked. I told her about Larkin and that he had been enquiring after her. She seemed chuffed. I told her he had been in such bad form since his father had died and since the boycott commenced. I told her how tough he was and how he had flattened Sr. Ignatius the day he left school.

"He won't run in the sports on Friday night," I said.

"That's such a pity," she said.

"I know," I said. "We have no chance without him."

"And would you win if he did?"

"We would have a better chance."

"Does he know that?"

"Oh, he knows it right enough, but he's terribly stubborn, nobody would be able to change his mind." (Clever enough, me ould sagotia.)

She kept on doing her weeding quietly. I looked to see her response and instead saw most of two voluptuous breasts. They were so alluring and gentle. She was lifting weeds with her hand to the teeth of the rake to the bucket. When she bent, the flat top of her dress leaned towards the ground revealing the warm relaxed curves. A gentle smile was forming itself in a relaxed manner in my mind. It turned in to ice and shattered to a million frosted particles as the memory of my newly obtained guilt-free absolution returned. I turned away immediately back to my task.

"Can you give me a hand?" she asked. I turned around struggling with my resolve to resist temptation while facing back into it. She was holding the handle of the bucket, which was full, and facing away from me towards the truck. I caught the handle and we walked to the end of the drill where we spilled the debris into the improvised wheelbarrow, my truck.

When we came back, I asked her what she thought of Larkin and she said she liked him. I really wanted to know how much she liked him and whether she preferred him to me and I also wanted her to ask him to run with us on Friday night.

"Will you come to the sports?" I asked.

"Would you like me to?" she manoeuvred.

"Yeah. Sure I would, 'course I would." I mean what else was I going to say put on the spot like that. I continued on with the hoe. "Course if Larkin was comin', there would be great craic entirely."

She took the bait.

"Do you think I should ask him?"

Steady boy, steady.

"Yeah, well, I think if he wouldn't go for you, he wouldn't go for anybody."

She beamed. "Do you? Really?" (Girls were all the same.)

"Well I wouldn't say it, if I didn't." (Seems boys could be the same as well.)

There were times girls just did not know their own minds. It was times like that they really got on my nerves.

We were progressing steadily and I knew that shortly she would start gathering the weeds with the rake and start pulling them into the bucket. Would I position myself so that I could see what nature had offered her and was displaying to me? "Jesus Mary and Joseph," I prayed the Aspiration to myself hoping the notion would pass, hoping the opportunity would not arise. I only thought of it (them!) all the more. This was so unfair. I remembered someone had told a yarn that a naked lady had walked in to the back of the church when a crowded mission was in progress. The preacher roared at the tempted male population that whoever looked around would be struck blind. One ould fella said to the lad beside him placing his hand over one eye, "I think I'll risk one of them all the same."

The more I thought about it, the worse it got. The perspiration was on my palms now and I was not sure was it on account of the sun, the work or Mel. If it was Mel, it would not be long until my almost moustache got dewey. Larkin used call them "Buzzooms" and "Diddies."

"Jack, where is the fork?"

I never used the word "Diddies" myself because I thought it was a swear word.

"Jack!" I was not sure where I got that notion because neither the nuns nor my parents had ever heard it, I was sure.

"JACK!" roared Mel.

I leaped out from my daydream.

"There is no need to yell!" I said.

"I called you three times – you were miles away," she little knew how close I was.

"Whasswrong?" I asked.

"Where is the fork? It is easier to lift the weeds with a fork."

"In the diddy-house," I answered.

"The wha'?" she looked at me in a strained way.

"I mean the outhouse – the ould outhouse" I flustered.

"Oh," she responded. "Which one is that?"

I had got away with it – but only barely.

"Jack!"

"What now?"

"Really, there are times when I wonder about you guys, which one is that?" she asked.

She had me, she was just playing with me, I just knew it.

"Which one is wha'?" I blushed.

"Which one is the old outhouse?"

Off the hook again.

"Oh – that one," I pointed.

She left me shaking her head. As she did, I uttered a solemn promise that if St. Michael the Archangel himself descended from Heaven and presented a pair of them to me on a platter, I would not have the slightest compunction in telling him to shag off for himself – nothing a three-hundred days indulgence could not cure. The other stuff was more serious than telling angels to shag off.

As per usual, it started to rain towards evening and when Peter arrived towards nightfall to collect Mel and her mother, Fr. Williams was with them. They spoke with my father in the kitchen. They had been with the Bishop most of the day making phone calls. They had been getting calls from all over the country as well. Everyone was in support they said. The Bishop had again asked the Knights of Columbanus to convene a meeting of the Supreme Council for the purpose of getting their backing to extend the boycott all over the country. We were in the national eye. Already, Sean Hanlon's photograph had appeared in *Time* magazine. Peter looked worried but the clergyman was flying high. He believed himself to be "the man."

It was still bright when they all left. The priest walked out to Peter's car still talking about who needed to be phoned or contacted. When the priest had gone, Peter and my father stayed talking at the car. Mel was inside waiting. I had come out with them and stood looking down over the harbour in the fading light. The moon was up and the evening star had appeared. I heard Peter say that the Cabinet were split on the issue. He had been talking to Dr. Ryan.

"Feck the clergy!" said my father, "Didn't they excommunicate half of them during the Troubles."

This was a reference to the Cabinet of the Old IRA Veterans. Peter said he knew and nobody better, but some way would have to be found to placate everybody before matters got entirely out of hand. I kept looking at the evening star and remembered the chorus of a song my father sang for us when we were much younger.

"Star of the evening,
Beautiful evening star,
Star of the evening,
Shining on the cookhouse door."

The rain which had started earlier had passed off, leaving a clear blue twilight. Miley Cassidy came up the road singing "Hail Glorious Saint Patrick" off key and at the top of his voice.

"We'll go in," said my father.

"Bad 'cess to the lot of 'em."

"You had better go," said Peter. "It's getting early," he remarked sarcastically. "I can hear the dawn chorus," he nodded at Miley. He drove off in his black Volkswagen.

"Goodnight Mel!" I shouted.

"Goodnight Mel!" imitated Miley. My father laughed a sort of snort.

"Daddy!" I chastised, feeling a fool.

He only laughed all the more and when I was going to bed and saying goodnight to both himself and my mother, he waited until I was at the door and teased, "Goodnight Mel" again in high pitched tone, in mock imitation of the little tramp.

⁐

Thursday the 4th of July 1957 was my last official day at school. On the 5th of July the Primary Certificate Examination would be held and no teacher would be present. This was my last day under the smacht of the nuns and I sat in my desk savouring it. What would freedom be like? Would I have anyone to make me do what was right? What if I went astray? Mostly, we had been kept in line by "the stick" – occasionally we were sent to stand behind the front door. When I was at school I thought the idea of being put in this spot was to keep children who were being punished out of the draught of open doors. Behind this door, however, was a print in colour of a painting of Dante's Inferno (after some of the Florentine Artists). It was a fascinating picture and showed a lot of drunkenness and debauchery as nonchalantly they wound their way down the winding slippery slope into Hell and the eternal inferno. It never occurred to me we were put there to contemplate the consequence of what and where our evil ways could and do lead.

Some visiting nuns arrived and an impromptu concert was put on. Being American Independence Day, a command performance of "Barbara Frietzche" by me was required. The priest called to the school with a sweet-can of hard boiled sweets, compliments of the Shelbourne CoOperative. The nuns were delighted at this acknowledgement of their labours. While they were there, Fr. Williams came in and the party broke up so we were all let out to play. Ignatius called me and asked me to go to the shop for a bottle of milk. Since the annual account at the shop had been discharged during the week, she bade me wait for money. The adults were all in the senior room and I waited in the hallway for Ignatius to return from the nuns' room. The doors were open.

"Dev has come out against the boycott," said Fr. Williams.

The other nuns' response was surprise

"God bless us. God between us and all harm."

"It is a dreadful blow," said the clergyman.

The "priest" Doyle stood up. "The vagabond – he has pitched capped our clergy, I would have expected nothin' less." The "priest" Doyle was Fine Gael.

Ignatius came back with the money. "Don't be long," she said.

Down the street I met Larkin. He was in good form. He had met Mel on the way to the strand with her mother.

"Are you goin' to the sports tomorrow night?" he asked.

"Of course I am," said I. "Will you come?"

"Of course I will."

"Will you run?"

"D'yiz want me to?"

"Of course we do."

"Give us a shout so, with whoever is givin' ya a lift."

We had a chance of winning the relay race now. On the way back to the school I went in buck jumps. I gave the nun the milk and she asked me to see her before we broke up. I got that sickening feeling.

Shortly afterwards, the adults came out, but not before we were all corralled in the playground for the last group photograph and, to my absolute consternation and embarrassment, Sr. Ignatius wanted an individual one of myself. Thorpey who had been out "sick" with an eye infection started sucking his thumb while she was taking it. I bit a smile in order to avoid a rebuke. My mother would be given a copy, she told me.

"I want you to give me a hand washing up," she asided to me. " 'As go bráth' with the rest of ye."

School was dismissed, the term was ended and I was still trapped. The other nuns made themselves scarce as she asked me again about our little secret. I tried to "yes" my way out of it, only to find myself drawn more deeply in. She would like me to call to the convent during the holidays. She would like to call in home to see me. She would like to call to the college to see me. She would like me to call up during the Christmas holidays to see her. She had her teeth in. She would get her credit for this vocation.

When eventually I did get out, I felt as if I had no space left. Everyone was entitled to some bit of me, except myself. Maybe, I promised myself, maybe when I do get away, maybe I really will get to be free.

⋄⋄

On Thursday night we all had to stay quiet for the radio news. The boycott was the headline. The Taoiseach said he deplored the situation in Coleman. He was reported as saying that he hoped it would end and still believed it could be ended. He said the boycott was ill-considered and futile and would not achieve its purpose. He urged all to use their influence "to bring this deplorable matter to an end."

My father and mother had listened very earnestly.

"If that feckin' Hanlon had been any use, it would never have happened," said my father.

My mother got up and asked me if I had everything ready for the morning. I asked my father if he would bring us to the sports the following night.

"I will bring you over," he said, "but there is a Fianna Fáil meeting tomorrow night so I will have to ask Mr. Doyle to bring you back."

"Can Michael Larkin and Mel come too?"

There was no problem. The next morning after Mass, I set off to do the exam that would obtain the Certificate which would pronounce I had obtained the requisite skills that the Primary National Education System demanded in English, Irish and Arithmetic. It was the first examination I had ever sat and my first experience of the nervous tension and anxiety that attended academic matters. It was the start of a very long road and at each mile post along the way the same symptoms would manifest themselves. While the examination results might vary, the sense of relief and "cold-turkey" that followed never changed. There was always that tired, used feeling from the overconcentration of focus, by comparison with the sharpness that had been present earlier in the anticipation of the test. The adrenalin source would leave when the purpose seemed reached. It was as if the effort never produced the sustained elation promised.

In the case of my Primary Cert Examination, there was a double dose of charge. I was very excited by the prospects of my first exam but I was equally anticipating the sports which were also a qualifying round for the county sports.

The inspector was there when we got to the school. When I saw her, I almost died from shock. It was Iníon Ní Breathnach. She started to blather "As Gaeilge." She kept her distance from me, or maybe she read me. My body language must have been hostile because she asked almost everybody to do something apart from myself. There was no eye contact.

We had two exams in the forenoon and by the time lunch came we were ravenous and anxious to let the tension out which came in mad bursts of tittering and gawking. We swapped answers and looks of despondency were exchanged with delight as comparisons revealed the sometimes awful truth and the sometimes terrific achievement.

We returned to our desks in the afternoon, unable to believe that our lives had so quickly passed on before our very young eyes to the place and point where we would complete our last appropriate act, the signal of the end of this time in our lives. We could neither stop it nor start it, but we still had to do it.

As I wrote the last lines of my English essay, I paused and slowly smelled the inkwell. I felt the blotting paper and tried to remember what the grain was like in my highly polished desk. I looked at the pictures on the wall, soaking them in, as if in smuggling their memory it would sustain me in the future. It was an unexpected feeling. I had believed I wanted to get away from the bad memories of beatings so badly that wild horses would not have dragged me back. Yet, here I was, reluctant to leave the place of my first formal learning experience, and early torture, and yet it passed quietly away in the afternoon sunshine of early July in 1957. When the exam was finished we gathered up our equipment, pens, pencils and rubbers – no schoolbags. Everything was neat and tidy, but yet it had the feeling of being grotty, tired, used and spent. I left the school for the last time with a feeling of sadness and relief.

I was hardly home when Larkin was in. He wanted to see the exam paper. He looked at all the questions. When we had discussed them fully, he swore he was glad he had not done it. It was wiser to agree with him when he swore and we were on our own. "No fuckin' way!" he repeated. "No fuckin' way."

Mel arrived and because of the day that was in it, my mother served tea to us. She sat down and we all talked. Mel called her "Aunty Statia" and Larkin "Mrs. Leacy." When I spoke to her, I always called her "mam," but when I chided with her she was "mother!" When I spoke about her she was "me mother." I was always concerned she would say the wrong thing in front of my friends and let me down, but in fact it was quite the opposite. Larkin was cracked about her and Mel adored her. I think it was because she was always interested in what was being said. You never felt tolerated. We sat there like two wise old men reminiscing. It was the first time we told her about the day we mitched from school. Mel thought it was hilarious and my mother thought we were "two right little devils." She pitied Thorpey, but she was on her own in that. "Fool, that fella!" said Larkin with passion. "Gobshite!" was the ultimate title of disparagement but not pronounced in adult company. We were relaxed, but not reckless.

✣✣

The sports were to start at six o'clock in Gusserane. My father arrived at half five and brought all of us. My mother came and brought my two younger brothers. My father had arranged that the "priest" Doyle would bring us back to Rathroe where he would collect us after the Fianna Fáil meeting that night.

Maybe it was the smell of freshly cut grass or maybe it was simply the level of excitement, but, that evening, this atmosphere ingrained itself on my memory in the manner of a photographic explosion. It was an evening I can recall with all my senses. With great intensity I ran and won my heat and the final of the one hundred yards under fourteen. I won the two-twenty yards. Larkin came third in the pole vault. Mel cheered and jumped and clapped and waved. Team points were awarded; three points for first place, two for second and one for third. For the first time in our lives we were level with Gusserane for the school prize. It all came down to the relay race. There were four one-hundred yard legs where each athlete would pass the baton to the next. Larkin would run the first leg and I would run the last one. When he handed the baton to Thorpey, he was second. When Thorpey handed it to Byrne, he was first, but Byrne slipped and when I got it we were in second spot again. My rival was two to three yards ahead of me with fifty to go. I drew on every inch and ounce of determination I could muster and willed myself forward to breast the tape in front of him. I was the hero of the hour. It was the proudest moment of my life. The crowd were screeching their excited praise. Larkin and the others ran over and we hugged and jumped in the frenzied excitement of the unbelieved, but the greatly desired, realisation of ambition. Mel joined us and in that moment of unconscious celebration, I hugged and kissed her and so did Larkin. When later I thought of what I had done in public, I nearly passed peacefully away.

The "priest" Doyle had been recording the winners all evening and it fell to him to present the medals. There was a loudspeaker which operated from the roof of a Volkswagen. Each time I went to receive a medal, I was given a great cheer and when it came to receiving the school trophy and the relay race medals, I was deputised there and then as captain. Receiving the laurels of victory was a moment of great satisfaction. But if it was, it was almost the most bitter. When I received the cup, the "priest" Doyle gave me the medals but he only gave me three. He said quietly to me and aside from the crowd, that there was a question mark over Michael Larkin's. It was a most cruel and devastating moment for me, but I rose to it. I looked him back in the eye and said,

"In that case, he's getting mine."

"Don't you dare," he threatened.

"Just you watch," I back answered, imbued in my new-found freedom as an ex-primary school pupil.

In the excitement, neither the conversation nor the number of medals had been noticed. It was only later when they were comparing their medals was it seen. It was Mel, of course, who noticed it.

"But you have only three medals," she said. "You won four."

"Where is the other one?" said Larkin.

I thought initially to say I had lost it, but when the question was put I reddened and jittered. It was no good to lie; I told them. Larkin paled when he realised what happened.

"Take it back," he said.

"No, you keep it."

"Take it fuckin' back!"

"Look, fuck ye, he'll get away with it with you, but me father will make him give it to me."

"Me father, me father, always me fuckin' father – I'm sick to the teeth of listening to 'Me father."

He threw the medal on the ground and stormed off. Mel was shocked. I was shocked. I was also very angry. I was angry at Larkin, but I was more angry at Doyle. I looked down at the medal which Mel picked up and gave to me. She touched my arm.

"Leave me alone!" I snapped.

She drew back. I thought for a moment and said, "I'm sorry" I meant it.

She knew it and said, "That's okay, I understand."

The "priest" Doyle brought us back to Rathroe, everyone except Larkin, that is, who got a lift with somebody else. I felt like a stone. Here I was under the compliment of a lift from that hard-hearted manipulative monster. I sat in the back of the car. Everything about him I hated. The smell of his car, the back of his head, the way he drove, even the way he sat. It was only five miles from Gusserane to Rathroe, but it seemed the longest journey of my life. I hated sitting on his seat. I wished I could suspend myself off of the seat but that meant pressing down with my hands and I did not want my hands to touch his seat either. I wanted no part of him.

He spoke to my mother all the way home and carried the deception off. Nobody in the car, apart from Mel, was aware of the situation. I noticed her glaring at him and inwardly I smiled at her loyalty. But I would not let the hate go. Some fine day, I promised myself, some fine day. I was not specific about what was going to happen to him but I was clear that it was not going to be good and equally clear that I was going to be the cause of it. Revenge would be mine. I daydreamed darkly about all the lovely horrible things that could happen to him. When I had finished dreaming we were at Rathroe.

"What do you say to Mr. Doyle?" said my mother.

We all said "Thanks" except me. It did not pass her though.

"Jack?" she raised her voice in a queried lilt.

"Where's your manners?"

"Thanks," I said to the ground.

"Don't mention it I'm sure," replied the ould bollocks, sweetly.

There was still light in the evening.

"I am staying out for a bit," I told my mother who was bringing in the two younger ones.

"Don't stay out for too long," she said. "When it gets dark, it gets chilly."

Mel went in with her. I wandered out to the haggard. All the fowl had been put in for the night. There was the sound of a railway train in the distance. Ponto came to me, but I was in no humour for him. A dog barked in a farmyard a half a mile away or more. My anger left me and I was left with a feeling of sadness. Something was ending inside of me. I had always expected that life would be happy, but I was now realising that happiness in life was not guaranteed.

∞∞

I picked up the hurley at the cowhouse door that Hiawatha had banded for me. The tin had cut through most of the insulating tape as the blacksmith had predicted. It was sharp right enough. There was a noise in the cowshed. I looked in. There were two late calvers in the stall. The tail of one was up and the animal appeared to be ready to calve. I had never seen a cow calving before, but I knew I was right.

I ran to the house to tell my uncle. On my way I saw the lights of a car coming up the lane followed by another. When I got in, I found that my uncle had gone to the meeting also but the cars signalled their return. Peter was with him. My father was in the second car. They all came to the cowshed and when they got there the second cow had started to calve. "Run down to the Nook and get Tommy Murphy for me as quick as you can," Peter told me.

I ran down the lane as fast as my legs would carry me. Here I had two options – I could go the road and put a half mile on myself, or I could cross the fields in quarter of the time. The fields it would be. I crossed the little stream at the end of the first field by jumping. I landed in the "Pairc Uafasach"(The Awful Field). It was called this because it was here the dead soldiers had been buried in a mass grave after the Battle of Rathroe in 1645 during the Great Rebellion. I was not long in it when I remembered both it and "The Chapels" field beside had the reputation of being haunted. It had been a church with a graveyard. All evidence of the church had disappeared except for a water font. There was no evidence of the graveyard whatever. The moon was up but the sky was cloudy. I kept my mind to my task. When I got to the Nook, which was a settlement of six houses, I saw Tommy sitting at the window. He was reading the paper. I hesitated in knocking at the window lest I might frighten him and make him jump. Yet when I did, he simply turned his head and said, "Yes?" as if, as regular as clockwork, he received raps at the window in the dead of night. I was breathless.

"Peter sez the cows are calving and yer to come up."

"I'll be up on the bike in a minute," he answered.

I tore back over the fields and just as I came to the brook, the moon went behind a cloud. It darkened. I jumped the brook and landed on the far side. I put my hands in front of me peering in to the darkness trying to see with my palms and eyes where the narrow path was. My hands came down on the chest of a man with an overcoat.

"Goodnight," said the voice.

I nearly collapsed in a weakness. It was Miley Cassidy. He was crossing the field to spend the night in Cummins' barn. I felt like kicking him for giving me such a fright and at the same time I was entirely relieved it was him.

"Miley you damn near frightened the shite out of me."

"Begor'n I'd say ya did a bit better than that yerself. I thinks I feels somethin' in me trousers."

I laughed. He obviously had been surprised as well. I left him and ran home, the relief in me occasionally allowing me to laugh.

Up in the yard, there was great activity. It was heading for eleven o'clock and my father had to bring my younger brothers and my mother home. The first cow had calved, a beautiful Friesian bull calf. It was a half breed. The second cow which was a pedigree Friesian heifer had been in calf to a pedigree Friesian bull. She appeared to be having more difficulty. The vet had been called. Rolled up sleeves were on display as coats had been discarded long ago. Tommy Murphy arrived. The feet of the calf were visible under the cow's tail. A noose was made and secured. The men heaved and pulled, but to no avail. After twenty minutes or so, they debated if the calf could still be alive. Some had seen worse and the calf had lived, others where the cow had died. My father told me I could stay the night in Rathroe. I was becoming useful, or maybe I was getting a timely instruction.

"Keep an eye out for the vet," Peter told me.

He arrived about ten minutes later. He was too late to save the calf but in time to maybe save the cow. He came to the back of the cow and his hand disappeared under her tail up to his armpit. He commenced preparations for his operation. He wanted water, hot and cold. Most of the rest of the night I spent ferrying can after kettle to the cowshed.

When the vet left, Tommy Murphy and Peter took the unborn calf to the field at the back of the cowshed and with the aid of a torch they buried it in a corner.

"An' the other little calf, a grand wan entirely," said Tommy.

"Did you ever see the bate?" said Peter.

"'Twould never happen th'other way."

"Whad ye mean?" said Murphy.

"Ah – it would be surely the pedigree would die," said Peter.

For a small while there was only the sound of the spade on the clay and Tommy panting. He stopped and stood the spade. He looked in the hole and spat. "Sure who's to say it did" he looked up with a dulled glint in his eye.

Peter looked at the carcass. Replacing the live calf for the dead pedigree would be fraud.

"Well Tommy," he said, "if you were going to do a job like that, only one person would want to know."

As much as he trusted him, you could trust nobody on a mission of that nature.

"You're too shrewd to be born," said Tommy and he left it at that.

It was midnight when we came in to the kitchen for the tea. "What a day!" Peter remarked. He was exhausted and looked it. Poll served up the tea. He had been in Dublin all day and had rushed back for the Fianna Fáil meeting. Poll had not seen him and was bursting to know everything.

"Dev's statement put the kibosh on it," said Peter. 'The Knights' felt there were enough involved without getting involved themselves, exactly what they had indicated previously."

"They're useless," said Poll.

"When the Cumann was split, some of them wanted it stepped up and others wanted it finished."

"What do you think?" said Poll.

"I don't know what to think anymore," he finished wearily. "There is no pleasing any of them."

"Politics is a dirty game," said my uncle James.

"And none dirtier than church Politics," said Peter.

I went to bed with a mixture of all of the day's experiences. It had been a very long day. Mel had fallen asleep in Poll's double bed. My brother would sleep in the single, in James' room. I got the low bed in the spare room beside the bathroom. I almost fell asleep immediately, but I slept badly. I awoken at seven and heard my brother go off to fetch the cows. Tired though I was, I could not sleep. It was the first day of the holidays and should have been full of freedom. A dark cloud hung over me on account of Larkin. How could I go near him. I blamed the "priest" Doyle. I got up and washed and headed out into the bright July morning. It would be a scorcher again today. The fowl had been fed and already Martin was feeding the pigs with buckets filled from a sour smelling cauldron of scraps, skins and meal located in "The Ould' Kitchen." Previously this row of out-offices had been the low thatched dwelling before the new two-storey residence had been erected in 1933 at a cost of three hundred pounds.

I let Ponto out and fed him. He leaped up at me in his usual frisky way, but I told him to "go down ou' a' tha'" in the way I had seen others deal with him. The cows were not yet back and I took the hurl from beside the cowhouse door and ambled off to see if there were any rabbits about. I went to the moor. This was the marshy ground by the side of the front lane and opposite the field called "The Chapels." There was a light thin fog, like drifting smoke about two feet or so off of the ground. It meandered like the rivulets of a stream. The field looked enchanted, and though it was a beautiful summer's morning, there was an eerie almost weird atmosphere about the place. The wonder of it took me. I paused and sat on a rotten stump. The trickle of the boggy field into the gutter could barely be heard. The good weather was drying everything up. A blackbird was bursting its breast singing and occasionally a woodquest would call out "ruckoo! ruckoo!"

A light tap-tapping could be heard. Initially I disregarded it, but it was so persistent my thoughts came back to it. I let my eyes follow my ears through the lacy fog and there, in the corner of the field, I could see a scrunched up figure facing into the corner in the way we were told the fairy people and leprechauns did. My eyes watered in disbelief and I swallowed, the more to hear the magic hammered tap. I had heard stories from the ancients about the Ceo Draoicht and the Poll Light. I never expected to find myself witness to it. The figure stood and stooped again. My disbelief evaporated for I could not deny the evidence of my own eyes. I realised I was in the middle of some magical enchantment. I panicked. My fear rose and I quickly gathered as much energy as fright would permit and burst through briars and skeaghs out of this wicked spellbinding place towards the orchard. My sandals wedged in a boggy part of the orchard. My eyes were stinging from the want of a good night's rest and the harder I tried to make progress over the boggy spot, the more tired, bothered and fearful I became. I looked over my shoulder convinced the fog was steadily creeping towards me. I dislodged the sandal with a squelch and soggily and sloppily plodded the grass, my breath coming in gasps, I jumped the little stream towards the haggard. Gingerly, I held down the wire fence with the hurl as I negotiated the barbed wire on tippey toes. In the relative safety of the farmyard, I examined my wet sandals.

A voice called "Jack" and I looked up to see Mel coming across the haggard with a cup of tea and a plate of bread in her hand. "Here's your breakfast." This was peculiar. She was in her pyjamas which were typically American, with pink hearts. As she walked towards me she could not see Ignatius fanning out his feathers to full tension power behind her. "Mel!" I screeched. She just smiled and kept walking. She would be savaged by the enormous fowl. The ferocity of his nature was bursting his red head through his evil eye. There was terror in my heart. I lifted my hurley with both hands. The turkey uncoiled. Mel was only feet from me. The cowardly monster attacked. I stepped past her and with a left-handed puck of the hurl, belted the bas in to the turkey cock's puss my dead level best. That blow was the culmination of months of ambition and deprived desire. I unleashed my fears in a moment of unsurpassed passionate anger on the living presence of my worst nightmares.

I struck my target mid-throat and almost immediately a fountain of blood gushed up in to the heavens from where the severed head had been moments before. There was a flurry of feathers and scraping and writhing. The ferocity of his attack carried his headless body past me and Mel, covering us with blood as it crashed into the chickenwire fence. The carcass fell back heaving and retching, weaving and waving its open neck like a fireman's water hose spurting blood in spurts and gushes. Mel was screaming and screeching and ran in an hysterical fashion across the dung hill stumbling and falling, covering herself with manure and soiling her night clothes. I started to hyperventilate and nauseate simultaneously. The open throat of the dying cock snorted a clotty guttural gurgle as if it would heave and gather itself together from spite and evil and have its last revenge yet. It arched its back and slackened. In a daze, I jumped the fence and sobbing from confusion and exhilaration I ran back to the orchard towards the moor. I ran through a clump of stinging nettles and was stung. I ran on to the moor and remembered the fog and turned for the lane when who should be driving up towards the house except Fr. Williams, Sister Ignatius and the "priest" Doyle. I turned back to the moor, moaning pathetically with each exasperated stride of my uncoordinated trot. I was heading towards the corner where last I had seen the figure of the leprechaun. He was gone. When I came to the ditch, I fell in to the white skutch sobbing my heart out in helpless gulps.

"What's wrong there young fella?" I leaped with the fright. It was Miley Cassidy. He had a toothy grin and was holding the school cup we had won at the school sports. He must have stolen it, I concluded.

"How's da young wan den? Yer fond of her aren't ye? Well she makes her shite the same as the rest of us."

"Give me that!" I said reaching out. "You stole it, you're always stealing."

"Hold on dere me boy," he said pulling back, "not so fast me boy."

I leaped at him and we struggled.

"Jack! Jack!" said Poll.

"You're dreaming Jack. Wake up, you're dreaming."

It took me a little while. She was in her dressing gown. James was behind her. I was in the spare room in the bed.

"What's up? Is he alright?"

"He's okay" she said "go back to bed."

My brother came next. "What's up with the lad?"

"Go back to bed," said Poll "he was just having a nightmare."

He looked at my uncle and started to grin a patronising smirk. James laughed quietly. I was raging. Feck them for nightmares. Mel never awoke. I looked at Poll's watch. It was four o'clock. I was very embarrassed.

Only the Messenger

The priest was not backing down. Neither he nor the Bishops nor any priest would ever ask the people of Coleman parish to back down one inch or apologise. He said he had the utmost confidence "that my people will persevere unflinchingly and will not allow anything to happen to mar or besmirch this grand, dignified, noble, loyal, legal profession of their Faith." He repeated it again because people were trying to misinterpret and make capital.

"We must make no mistake by letting ourselves down and we must make no mistake by not standing up for ourselves and our Faith and Religion. We will be and are being condemned from all quarters but our God comes first above all. Remember the words I used here some time ago he who excuses himself accuses himself."

He then quoted Cardinal Newman who at one stage apparently stated "Truth in combating error never grows angry. Error is never calm in combating truth." He urged everyone to read what the Bishop and the Cardinal had said on the previous Sunday. The Protestants had a saying in the North of Ireland "No surrender – not an inch!" Well I tell you now, here is a new saying from the Catholics in the South of Ireland: "we will never be sundered – not even half an inch." He left the pulpit to the imagined tumultuous applause he believed the electricity of his invective inspired.

It was the first day in two years I had not served mass. Thorpey and Byrne were making a mess of it.

There had not been a sound in the church when he was preaching and occasionally people stopped breathing simultaneously, the better to make sure they heard what they believed they had heard. As the collectors were on their way to the Communion rails for the collection box, a man stood up four pews from the front of the church. He passed out of his seat, past two people who had to stand to let him out and in doing so someone hit their heel on a kneeler. It reverberated. The man genuflected to the Tabernacle in the aisle, turned and walked resolutely and sedately against the stares of the seated staring congregation. It was Sean Hanlon and he was making a sacrilegious protest.

"Feck that fellow, he's always looking for attention," my father said over the fried breakfast later. "And then he gave an interview to the papers when he got outside. He's making a holy show of the lot of us. He's not worth a shite that fella!"

They talked about it all over breakfast. Whose lead was going to be followed? Dev or the church, Black or White. My parents both agreed something should be done to end it, but the Catholic children would have to be got back, and yet they knew they would never come back as long as the boycott was on.

∞∞

I listened openly. There was no whispering and no hugger-mugger. It was a beautiful Sunday and as soon as breakfast was over I slipped off down the road to see Larkin. When I got there the panes of glass in Hiawatha's bedroom were covered in cardboard. The windows had all been smashed. They were visible from halfway up the street. One piece of cardboard said "Shelburne Co-Op Creamery Butter" and the other one said "Chivers Jelly." One pane had a colourful yellow hen with chicks on a navy blue and white squared boxes background which proclaimed "Birds Custard." It looked like someone had thrown a bomb. I had been at hay all the previous day in Rathroe, only driving home late in time for bed so I had heard nothing. Hiawatha called me in when I knocked. Larkin was gone with the cows and would be back. I had a few comics under my arm as a type of excuse.

"You heard what happened?" he asked.

I feared the worst.

"No," I answered.

He was washing cups and saucers in the aluminium basin which he rinsed and left upturned on the table oil cloth. "Michael is a very angry young man at the moment."

"You mean with me?"

"I mean with myself – with everybody."

"About the medals?" I asked.

"Yes and no – but not really," I was confused.

"Michael was very attached to his father and when he died he got very angry."

"I thought people got sad," I offered.

"They do too – but they can get angry as well. Michael is only getting his anger out now and it will take him a while before he comes fully back to himself. He does not realise this yet, but he is still looking for his father and he hasn't really accepted that he won't be coming back. He is vexed with him – and he is annoyed with me – as if I was stopping him one minute and helping him the next. That's what happened to the windows."

"What?" I asked.

"On Friday night he came in to my room, he became hysterical and cut loose with a hurley."

"What time was that?" I asked.

"About three or four in the morning," he answered.

There was a lot of it about on Friday night I mused to myself. Larkin on the rampage would be difficult to contain.

"But why?" I asked again.

"The only pure love, unconditional love, you get in your life is from your parent, everybody else puts conditions on it but it does not matter how you are, your Daddy knows and loves you like nobody else ever will."

"I know that," I said.

"We spend the rest of our lives looking for it in other people, places and things but we never find it again because it's gone." I thought this was very sad. "Except when you die and go home to Heaven," Hiawatha smiled. "That's what the Good Lord said anyway. I come from the Father and I go to the Father," he sighed. I remembered it from the Gospels.

"He was talking about God though," I said.

"So was I," said Hiawatha. "So was I."

⋘⋙

The whirr of the bike and the clatter of the chain guard denoted the return of the drover. I went out to him. He was red in the face and looked flustered.

"That fuckin' "priest" Doyle's at the door again," he said. "I don't want to have anything to do with that hoor ever again." I stood there like a fool, my peace offering ignored. "What do you want?" he said gruffly to me. "Come in or are ya goin' to stay there in the cowld?"

It was quite warm actually, but I was disadvantaged and allowed myself to be compromised by following him in.

Hiawatha was at the front door with the "priest" Doyle.

"Maybe this is not the best time?" Doyle said.

"It's as good a time as any," the blacksmith answered.

He showed him in to the kitchen. Myself and Larkin went to leave. "Stay, Michael," said Hiawatha. "This probably concerns you more than anybody."

"I'll go," I said taking the hint.

"It concerns you too," said Doyle. I was surprised and nervous.

"Last things first," said Doyle. "I have a medal here in my pocket which belongs to Michael, but only if he is attending school."

"Keep your ould medal," said Larkin.

"He won it fair and square," I protested.

"Quiet boys!" said Hiawatha sharply. "Let the man finish."

"If he does not return to school, you know he will be prosecuted."

"Prostitute yourself," Larkin, said incongruously

"Michael!" said Hiawatha sternly and looked away.

"There is also the whole question of his secondary education not to mention that the Dues for Easter and the Pius List have yet to be paid."

"I see," said Hiawatha. "Anything else?"

"Yes," said Doyle. "I would like you to make it plain to people around here that nobody marched to this house and threw stones at the window with all the cardboard in it."

"I see," said Hiawatha once more. "Anything else?"

"Finally, if nothing is done, the whole question of the guardianship will be raised."

Hiawatha bristled, but bit on it. "I see," he said. "Anything else?"

"That's it," said Doyle.

"Do you have the medal?" said the blacksmith.

"I do," he said.

"May I see it?" Doyle foostered in his pocket and took out a little cream coloured box. He opened it and there resting on the cotton wool was a gold medal and a runner, and the letters BLE in the Irish mode inscribed in a quarter crescent surround, denoting Bord Luath Cleas Éireann (Irish Athletic Board). He handed the box to Hiawatha. He inspected it. He put the cardboard cover back on, he eyed Doyle evenly and put the medal in his trouser's pocket.

"Now you have no medal," he said quietly.

Doyle was shocked. This was not playing by the book.

"You can't do that," said Doyle limply.

"I've just done it," said Hiawatha. This was brilliant.

"If that is the way you want it, then that's the way you'll get it," said Doyle as he fled the floor.

"Take your time," growled Hiawatha. He froze the sexton with his primeval growl. He took out a blue twenty pound note.

"That's for the Dues," he said. Doyle was stunned.

"It's not from me," he said. "It's from Michael, providing he's no longer a schoolboy."

"I'll have to see the priest."

"So will I," said Hiawatha. "But this is the second time you have come for this. Now take it. I don't want you coming around a third time."

Doyle took it, a look of sick weakness on his miserable face. "It's up to the priest though, I want to make it plain – I am only the messenger."

He was pathetic, I felt. As he was going out the front door, Larkin came to life and shouted after him just as Hiawatha closed the door behind him.

"And stick it up your arse!" he said.

I laughed. Hiawatha shot him dead with a glare.

"Save that for the corner boys," he said. He took the medal out of his pocket.

"Don't lose it," he said.

"Thanks," he said.

When we got outside we laughed and laughed.

"He's not a patch on a man's arse," said Larkin. "If the 'priest' Doyle doesn't have rules, he's bollixed."

"Be Jaysus you'll head the Pius List," I said.

"Holy Shite!" said Larkin. "I'd love to see their faces."

∞∞

In the afternoon it got very warm. Mel arrived with her mother. My father wanted to listen to some of the matches on the radio. He sat out in the yard with the window open, a white hankie knotted at two corners and the other two tied together acted as a sun hat. Mary Kelly and my mother were going for a walk and Larkin called for me to go for a dip. Mel had her bathing togs, but there was the matter of my two younger brothers and who would mind them. When they were younger, they were less of a handful, but as they grew they became more and more of a nuisance. My mother brought one in a pushchair but either my sister or myself would have to mind the other. He was a tearaway and required every inch of concentration. Negotiations were resolved with my being required to take over duties at five o'clock.

Mel took a lift on Larkin's crossbar because I had my sister's bike, which was a lady's bike with no bar, and anyway I doubted whether I had confidence enough. Larkin had loads for both of us. I could feel the envy sweeping me as I sped down the rest of the hill on towards the beach. "Yahoo!" roared Larkin in full throat with an air of devil-may-care about him. Mel tittered and giggled nervously and excitedly. "Yahoo!" I roared, with as much conviction as I could muster but not fully convinced.

We headed for the rushes. Decency required that Mel retire to an adjacent bower to undress. When she emerged, she looked stunning. The depth of her increased figure was now obvious. She ran past us as we struggled with our towels and trousers.

"Last one in is a rotten egg," she gurgled with giggling mischief.

Larkin looked at me and uttered one word, "Wow!"

"Feck off!" I said, "she's my cousin."

I am not sure whether the emphasis was on "my" or "cousin." Larkin had his togs on first and I struggled to correctly get my foot in to the leg of mine, he pushed me when I was off balance and I fell in the sand head first exposing my rear end to the sky and Larkin's raucous gaze.

"Ah God," he roared. "I thinks I'm struck blind."

I heard Mel shout, "What's wrong?"

"Leacy's lost his head," he laughed, "and all I can see is his open throat."

I struggled with the togs and got them on awkwardly and embarrassedly and then I straightened them.

"Ya hoor!" I roared and I chased him down the strand in to the sea. I splashed him but he dived on his flat belly covering me with a salty spray that sent me panting and snorting and then he ducked me and half-near drowned me and collapsed me all in the one go.

Mel stood in the shallows waiting for the horseplay to stop. I could not swim nor could Larkin but Mel could and boy, could she move in the water. Backstroke, dog paddle, butterfly, sidestroke, left or right. We lolled in the warm shallow water soaking in the sun and drenching ourselves with the holiday atmosphere of relaxed freedom, I could feel myself fatten and lay there, resting on elbows, lazy and lusty in the afternoon balmy warmth.

After a while we walked to see where the racing car had turned over. We told and retold the awful story to ourselves. When Larkin asked the time, he had to rush to get the cows so that they would be in by five.

He headed off while Mel and I wandered over to look at the Caves at Carrigastira. Stones, seagulls' feathers, salt-worn timber and the odd tyre were the seashore debris. Sand combing could be interesting and there was always a most unusual shell or a stone was green just like a jewel or a diamond. And as we walked, we talked. Gingerly we toed our way over craggy outcrops of cliff which disappeared into the warm-hard sand.

"I'm goin' on Saturday ya know," she said. I knew. We were looking in a pool where the little cherry pumps which lurked near pools of water on the underside of rockpools hid. When you pressed them they spurted out their spray. "I know," I said. There was a dead crab turned upside down in the pool. It was white underneath and at least two of its legs were gone. She touched my arm as I reached to turn over the crab. "Will you miss me?" she asked. It was the question I wanted to hear and the one I wanted to ask more than anything. I looked at her beautiful eyes; they looked sad, earnest and sincere. I was frightened. I reached in to the pool and took out the dead crab and examined it carefully. I said nothing. I could sense her disappointment. I started taking off the dead crab's legs one by one, "she loves me, she loves me not." The crab had five legs. When they were gone, I turned it over. It had a hard shell which was a type of russet and brown, very like the rockweed about. She stood up. "It is getting late," she said. She lied. It was no more than half past four.

Here I was madly in love and unable to utter a single coherent sentence. If Larkin was here, he would have something to say – he would have done something! My anger against myself rose. What was wrong with me. Why did I always have to be so good. What was wrong with God for making me so bad.

"You coming?" Mel asked four paces in front of me.

"Mel wait," I said.

She stopped and eyed me. No revelation there now, just a tense sentry who feared being caught smoking on duty and was going to downface her accuser's perception. I started to talk with my hands hoping my voice would decide to follow before too long.

"Look," I said. I wanted to explain how I felt about her and how I would miss her and how I would love to run off with her, there was nobody like her but, we were too young. "We're too young," I blurted.

"Too young – too young – I only asked you if you would miss me."

She stomped her foot in the sand and stormed off across the rippled strand splattering wet-muddy sand on her elegant legs as she went. That stupid voice of mine. I would have to get something done about it. It always came out at the wrong time. Maybe if I tried to give a reason. It did not occur to me then nor for many years to come what an utter recipe for disaster that was.

She went to a spot in the rushes to dress. I was dressed long before she was and sat beside my folded towel looking down on the rippling blue and white summer waves trippling on to the beach, gently. I was reflecting. She was the nicest girl I had ever met. So why was I unable to say she would be missed by me. Why was I so confused. Of course, I would miss her. What was I going to do for the whole summer without her. Larkin would be working and I would be roped in to fill a working gap somewhere, half noticed and yet completely ignored at the same time. She noticed me. Why did she have to ask the obvious. Suddenly she was standing beside me.

"Okay then?" she asked, matter of fact.

"Will you sit for a minute?"

"It's time we were getting back!" she said, testing.

"Will you sit for a shaggin' minute?" She sat. "I am no good at this stuff!" I apologised. "I get all awkward – and – well – I don't know what to say at times. I will miss you – of course I'll miss you – sure all the fun will be gone," I said throwing a stone I found on to the sand, picking and throwing and picking as I spoke, looking at it buried in the soft, dry, loose sand.

I turned to look, but before I knew it, she had moved in over me with a pair of melting eyes that sparked their romantic notion of lost love and she fulsomely kissed me on the mouth. She caught me a little "on the hop" and I missed my breath. I sucked through my nose afraid to let go and torn by not doing so. I heard a voice. Jesus if we were seen. I pulled away quickly.

"Someone might see," I said. She got up and took her towel.

"Boys!" she said, "ugh!"

What the hell was wrong with her now? I told her I would miss her. She'd kissed me – and now she wanted me to perform in public as well? There were, clearly, a few things that Miss Mel did not understand about Ireland and, equally clearly, there were a few things I could not understand about girls. Still, her kiss was soft and gentle, as if it really fitted. I could have sworn I nearly felt her tongue, but I doubted it. It must have been her lip, or something. I was intrigued.

◦◦

We walked back through the rushes and as we did, we met Agnes Maher with Patrick Parle walking arm in link towards the Strand. Agnes blushed and smiled when she saw me. I was sure she was recalling our last encounter on the banks. Her new beau simply saw two children going home from a swim.

I walked behind Mel sneaking a glance over my shoulder at the courting couple. The arm linked turned in to arms around backs. Females – I would never understand them. There she was a week or so ago bringing the odium of God and the church down on her head for being with a Protestant boyfriend and now here she was with a grip on her new man like a half-Nelson. He had as much chance of getting away from her as a worm on a hook. It was unlikely that he would try. I began to perceive the first traces of the female fang. I felt like a gummy myself.

Going home through the village, we noticed a large crowd at Jamesie

Clarke's pub. It must have been the first since the Protestants gathered at the start of the boycott. It seemed the sun and the bathers from out of our village had no respect for the way things were and thirsts would be slaked with Protestant stout whether retailed by a Catholic or Protestant publican.

Mel maintained her stiff poise and when she went home later in the evening, I was left to stew in my own juice. I took a hurl and a ball at the gable end of our house, excoriated all memory of her and replaced Nicky Rackard on his proper and lawful pedestal. To hell with them all I said and repeated Larkin's regular put down, "they're all the same with a bag over their heads." I belted the sponge ball until the beads of sweat ran down my neck.

ᴄ◌·◌ᴅ

That night the question arose with my parents about what I would do for the holidays. After considerable deliberation between my staying at home "to mind the two young lads" – a fate worse than death, not to mention the severe risk of being called "The Governess" or worse still – "The Nanny" – or going to help in the shop for the summer. By the narrowest of margins – my mother's intuition – I was defined as grocer's assistant to my father – the merchant.

On the Monday morning I was put sweeping the floor of the shop, a menial task I had performed previously. I would be shown a new task each day and then expected to perform. "Once is enough to be shown anything," my father used to say. "The second time should be boring unless you were asleep the first time." I was allowed to tot up accounts – but they had to be checked by himself before being submitted to the customer for payment.

When the papers arrived, I was handed a list and delegated to write the name of the regulars on them and "Spare" on the balance. Tom Hanton arrived in the shop at about eleven and sat on the form to smoke his pipe, dawdle and give a courtesy inspection of the news and deaths as usual. He crossed his legs revealing black, high-laced ankle boots and brown stockings.

Business was slow. I was put weighing the flour and wheaten meal in to half-stone and one-stone brown paper bags. Bag after bag was weighed on the scales until there was a sufficient supply – two dozen or so of each.

The bag was tilted and flip-flapped in to a neat compressed tidy sealed top. It took practise and a sharp eye.

"Holy Jaysus," said Hanton. "Hanlon has a letter in the paper."

My father came out from behind the small privacy screen which separated the accounts desk from the public. It was here accounts were made up and private correspondence attempted whilst allowing an eye be kept on the business on the shop floor.

"You're jokin'," he said.

"I'm not be Jaysus," he earnestly replied. "Listen to this." He read it aloud without fault, grandly and eloquently!

"Dear Sir,

Judging from past experience, I know that whatever I say will be very strongly criticised and as to whether I should say anything at all or not it may be questioned to an even greater extent by many of my neighbours.

As readers of Irish Newspapers are now aware, a difficult situation exists in Coleman, a situation which may deteriorate still further, to the detriment ..."

As he was reading aloud a car pulled up. It was Peter.

"Hold on," said my father. "Wait for the councillor."

When he came in, the letter was started again. The letter went on to say how both churches had now become embroiled and no member wanted to see their own church lose face.

"My personal views on this boycott," the letter went on, "or whatever name you wish to call it, have already appeared in the Press. I leave the ethics of the matter to Moralists and Philosophers, but should there be a post-mortem on this sorry business let every investigator entering this District beware of propagandists without scruple and gossips without decency or honour."

He went on to say what his obligations as a father were to mend a broken home. "Can the events in Coleman since early May be shown to have assisted me to obtain my goal, and what of the future? Can it hence be expected to follow a different pattern? I believe all sides made mistakes – the rash word, the accusing finger.

"Now to my fellow Catholics everywhere, may I say this: why not make use of our church's greatest weapon, prayer? If, as we are told, it could solve the problem of Russian Communism, could it not also solve a much smaller problem here? I therefore ask your prayers for all of us fellow Christians who all worship God, even if at different altars.

"Yours faithfully,

Sean Hanlon."

"It will take more than prayers!" said Peter.

"T'aint a bad letter all the same," said Hanton.

"Well bad cess to him," said my father. "I said it before and I'll say it again, if he was worth a feck 'twould never 'a' happened."

"Ah John, you're too hot entirely."

"Ah hot me arse, a bit of spunk never went astray on anyone, feck him to hell."

∞∞

Peter said nothing much. He had come for pigmeal and he called me to give him a hand. While we were in the big store, Mel came up the road on her bike. Peter saw her. I prayed she would not come into the store. Peter must have read my mind for he looked at me and said,

"I suppose you will be going back to the States on Saturday?"

Mel rode her bike into the store, considerably increasing my embarrassment.

"Hi," she said.

"Hello Mel," said Peter cheerfully.

"Looking for the boyfriend?"

"I guess!" she said naively. I could have strangled her for even implying an admission.

"This sounds serious," he grinned. "I'd better leave you to it."

He got back in to his Volkswagen and reversed it out of the shed implying that the coincidence of his having finished his work had nothing to do with his evacuation.

As he was about to drive off my father came out of the shop and called him shouting "The Bishop's Secretary is on the phone!" When he got out of the car, he looked back in to the shed as I maintained a pose which said, "I am waiting for you to leave." He looked wickedly at my father and said, "Do you think those two are alright in there on their own?"

My father suppressed a chesty chortle which came out as repressed snigger and melodramatically looked away in a manner which only accentuated exposure.

"What does he mean?" asked Mel.

"Oh nothing," I said resignedly with a slight hint of sulk.

I made to look busy. There was a platform in the store where the bags of animal meal had been placed on the floor. This was about thirty feet long and six feet wide and was nailed securely to timber mineral boxes which kept it a foot or so from the ground. This avoided the inflow of surplus rainwater and paraffin spillages which would otherwise pollute and toxify the meal. There was a five-hundred gallon paraffin oil tank near the door and about five tons of loose coal and a combine harvester, which belonged to "the company." The meal was stacked six bags high or so, down the length of the platform.

"I would like to talk to you," she said.

"I am listening," I said unhelpfully, as I looked for the scrub.

"Can you be still?" she asked.

Girls always had to have your attention. I stopped. I thought I heard a trickle and looked at the tap on the oil tank.

"Are you going to listen? "I am sorry for getting annoyed," she said.

"That's alright. I get annoyed when people get distracted when I am wanting to say somethin' too."

She looked at me impatiently. "Jack! Would you just shaddup and listen." She meant it. I listened. I am sorry for getting annoyed at you yesterday. I was disappointed and I behaved badly."

"Oh, that's alright" I shrugged.

"No, it's not alright," she countered. "The reason for my disappointment is another matter," she coaxed. "But there was no excusing my behaviour."

"Uh. I see," I lied.

"I suppose true lovers are disappointed all the time."

"Huh?"

"You know, like Bing Crosby and Grace Kelly in 'High Society' –

If I give to you,

As you give to me,

True love, True love, she sang and her eyes sparked.

"Some people search the whole world over and never find it," she said.

"Begor, that's the truth, young wan," came the voice of Miley Cassidy from behind the bags of meal. Mel jumped an embarrassed startle.

"I searched the whole a' Battlestown Bog wan time for a week for Gerry Connors' ass an' devil a bit could we find of him from dat day to diss. Iss awful hard to find what yer lookin' for when you can't find it," he said as he waddled out the door.

I looked behind the bags and there was the telltale trace of puddle and pool which the unconcerned tramp had urinated.

"Oof!" said Mel.

"Less' getoutta here."

I went to the stream and got a bucket of water and with a sprinkle of Jeyes fluid re-hygiened the meal store with a scrub.

Miley Devereux from Curraghmore pulled up with a horse and cart for meal. He secured the piebald to a ring in the outside wall. "Two bags of bran and a bag of Componus." The bags of bran were half-hundred weight but bigger outside than the hundred weight bags of pigmeal compound. I lifted the first bran bag from the platform and carried it easily to the cart. In the shed, the sixty-five year old was struggling to pull out the heavier but smaller sack of pig meal Componus.

"I'll give you a hand in a moment," I said as I got the second bran bag and deposited it on the straw strewn floor of the cart, beside the other bag.

"Well shit!" the voice from the store said. He had pulled the loosened bag and though he had held its ears, the bottom was too heavy when it came and its thud burst the sack open.

"Hold it there – don't budge," I said as I moved to save most of it. I lifted the bottom and stood it on its top. "Hold that for a moment." He balanced it. I got some twine and I ravelled the split seam in to a throaty neck and secured it, cutting the twine with "the knack."

"I'll put the rest in a bag," I offered and we took the casualty carefully to be laid length-wise cross-shaft in the cart.

"You're a tarlint man, alannah," he said.

None of it had passed Mel by who was holding her bike in the morning sun – and none of it was intended to pass her by.

Fr. Williams arrived and was talking to the "priest" Doyle. Agnes Maher arrived up on her scooter but parked away from them. Fr. Williams said to Doyle,

"Dublin, you know – of all teams, Dublin."

"The replay will crown them," said Doyle.

They walked towards the shop and the ball passed from one to the other at the doorway. Devereux went to the shop.

"I'd better lend a hand," I apologised to Mel, "there's a crowd."

"When will I see you?" she surprised me.

"Uh – I don't know – whenever I can," I blurted, which seemed to satisfy her. She smiled and mounted her bike. Girls like boys at the strangest times. The minute you thought you were landed, you were drowning. The minute you were drowned – you were saved.

When Peter came out, Fr. Williams followed him to the car. The pressure was beginning to tell on Peter. The strain had begun to cut and etch a permanent piercing furrow between his brows. He held his forehead a lot with the forefingers of his right hand while his thumb pulsed on his side temple. His elbow rested on the steering wheel as he faced the priest who was sitting sideways in the passenger seat beside him. The priest was speaking animatedly. The windows were closed on this warm morning and the only concession to comfort was the open fly window when they started smoking. As I passed in, the priest just repeated, "The children! The children! The children!"

Inside, the phone rang again. "Get that," said my father. When I answered a woman said "Mr. Peter Leacy, please." When I called Peter he asked me to get her number and he would ring her back in a few moments.

"This is Dr. Ryan's Personal Secretary," she said.

"Can he please ring Dr. Ryan in the Dáil immediately?"

I went back to the car and told Peter who it was and as I did he winced.

"Good man," he said. "I'll be in, in a moment."

My father tended the "priest" Doyle who had moved away from the subject of the Kilkenny draw against Dublin and was talking in an authoritative fashion about Munster Hurling and Cork's defeat of Tipperary.

"They have a saying in Tipperary," he said. "Happiness is 'the hay made and Cork beat'."

"I'm sure," said my father.

I got the groceries for Devereux as Agnes Maher rambled around the counters collecting items as she went. Few were allowed this privilege, but my father had a "soft spot" for her and she was allowed. My uncle James came in and instantly she fell in to conversation.

"I've heard you started college," he said.

She looked puzzled.

"I heard Tommy and the Collegians were giving free education last night in the hall." She blushed. This was a reference to a showband. Devereux came alive to the craic.

"Is this little girl going to school?" he asked with mock sincerity. She blushed and sniggered, knowing she was caught at the butt of their humour. "And what class are you in now?" he asked.

My father copped the fun and added, "Patrick Parle says she's in a class of her own."

The word was out. She blushed still more. Hanton laughed.

"A fine dacent fellow," he offered. Peter came in, very intent on his mission.

"I'm going to use the phone," he said to my father.

"Work away!" he replied.

Devereux wanted rashers. I went to the meat room and while there I heard Peter say

"The Judicial Inquiry won't work – I'm telling you now – they won't wear it. Tell them to keep quiet up there for Christ's sake – they're driving everyone wild down here."

When he came out, he spoke to my father who turned and said to me, "You go with Peter. He needs a hand for a few days. I'll drop down your pyjamas and collect you at the end of the week."

This was unexpected. Now I would be spending a lot of time with Mel and her mother.

When we got there, I was surprised to see Larkin's horse and cart there also. Hiawatha was there and so was Larkin. The horse was secured to the iron rings of the meat shop, away from the slaughterhouse. Hiawatha was smoking his pipe and Larkin was talking to Mel who had not yet put her bike away. Peter's brow lightened and furrowed and smiled. He waved in acknowledgement and parked the car. He opened the door opposite Hiawatha and swung his feet out on the ground while remaining seated.

"Well for some," he joked.

"So they say," said Hiawatha.

"Will we get aera supa' rain?"

"We'll get our fill of it, never you fear."

I left them talking and went over to the pair. "What has ya in this neck o' the woods?" I asked.

"I could ask the same question."

"I'm here to work," I said spitting on my hand.

"God help us," said Larkin. Mel brightened.

"I have to do the chores and Peter wants me to clip a few hedges and do some painting."

"I'm goin' to jail!" he said.

"Not before time."

"I'm not coddin'."

I could see he was serious.

"They're threatening to send him to reform school if he doesn't go back to school after the holidays," said Mel.

"Well they can fuck off," he said.

This was serious all right. Larkin was serious. Mel was shocked at his language. I became serious. I volunteered this was on account of the episode of the Dues between Hiawatha and the "priest" Doyle on the previous day.

"I don't think so," said Larkin.

"Guard O'Sullivan came down with a summons this morning for Ballycullane next week – that feckin' Thorpey was afraid to come," he said.

I looked over at Hiawatha and he had handed a paper to Peter who was reading it in the car, one foot now on the ground, the other on the running board. Hiawatha had one hand on the jamb of the door and the other on the lip of the door itself, his pipe having been safely put away by now.

"Peter'll fix 'em," I said proudly and defiantly.

"I hope to fuck he does. I hope I don't have to spend a cowld winter in a reform school."

I looked at him. Some people just kept on getting kicked. Poor oul' Larkin, I felt. Why could they just not leave him alone? He had no father and mother – he looked vulnerable. But he did have Hiawatha.

Mrs. Kelly came out and called Peter. He was wanted on the phone again. Hiawatha and himself had finished talking. Having called Larkin and waved to both Mel and myself, they leaped on the side lace of the car, reins in hand, brought the horse round with a "hey up" galloped up the lane crunching and chomping the gravel with the steel hooped cart wheels as they sped off.

◌◌ ◌◌

Eiley was Peter's housekeeper. She was a big swarthy woman of about thirteen stone and five feet eight. She was mid-fiftyish with big rubber lips and a rosy pair of cheeks. Tommy Murphy said "she was the closest thing to a white nigger" he had ever seen. She served up dinner for us in the diningroom where Peter announced he had to go to Dublin. He was not sure whether or not he would be home that night. I was to put one of the spare beds in his room and sleep in it.

Most of the afternoon was given over to this task, mainly because we could not find the proper bolts for the iron-framed bed. Eventually it was assembled and was placed at the other side of the door from the bedroom to the bathroom. The bathroom had two doors, one led from the main bedroom, the other to the landing.

As it came towards evening I fed the fowl with Mel's assistance. There were a few ducks and one of them had hatched some chicks. They were getting hardy and needed to be fed but the mother duck was not anxious to let go of her weaning process. My experience with "Ignatius" had made me suspicious of beaks so rather than risk the wrath of this flat-billed protectress, I used a beet sprong, a six-pronged fork with muffled tags, to scoop her gently and lift her from the nest. She gave the odd twang at the sprong handle and I complimented myself on my ingenuity for negotiating my way around a very difficult personal issue without having to actually deal with it. This was all done in the fowl house out of view of Mel, who preferred to avoid these types of issues in a more obvious manner.

The stopcock on the cattle trough in the "leanto" of the hayshed was checked and the hay was forked into the overhead manger, which we called "the stalls." There the cattle would wander towards nightfall during summer, whether being fattened or simply waiting the butcher's knife in the morning. Later that evening after our supper, we walked the short half mile to the sports field where preparations had commenced for the Under Fourteen Hurling Championship. The evening was sultry and would have been good for fishing. The midgets nearly ate us alive on our way home. I was sticky with sweat from hurling. I needed to wash. As we walked home I knew in my heart there would never be times like this again and the thought of it made me very sad.

"Isn't it just so beautiful?" I could feel we were about to set sail on the sea that had ebbed with Miley Cassidy's flow in the store that morning.

"I'm just going to miss it so much."

"So am I," I said quickly. (There was no friggin' way was I getting caught out on that one a second time.)

"Wouldn't it be great to own a cottage down by the river?" she said.

I thought about this carefully for a little.

"I suppose," I said. She smiled beautifully. I thought some more and realised my ambition extended beyond this. "I'd prefer a castle though." Her eyes narrowed. I defended. "You know – like Sean Hanlon's," I reminded her. Her eyes were still narrow. "Though, then again, a cottage does have charm." She smiled once more.

"It's so sad to be leaving," she said. I looked down. I hated sad things. There were too many sad things. "I feel a pain," she said. I looked up quickly.

"Where?" I asked. "Here!" she indicated and cradled her two hands underneath her right breast near her ribs.

"Do you think it might be your appendix?" I asked.

She looked disgusted.

"You really are useless," she glared at me. "Have you no feelings?"

I was utterly bewildered. I was the height of compassion; I was the breadth of understanding; I was the depth of feeling; I was also exasperated, frustrated and confused – and now she was very slowly beginning to make me feel constipated.

"What the heck is wrong with you?" I demanded.

"It ain't me it's wrong with, buster," she snarled and stormed off down the avenue to Peter.

I stood there, amazed, surprised and deflated. What was she doing to me? The minute things were going well, she was unhappy, the minute I agreed, she disagreed and the minute things were wrong – she was right again. It was just so unfair again, the same thing all over.

A hare flashed across the avenue from one field to another. I looked over the hedge as he flashed down the valley. What was he running from? Where was he going? The smell of woodbine drew me to the hedge and my task tomorrow. I heaved a philosophical sigh. I hung my football boots around my neck, stuck my hands deep in my pockets and kicked the living shite out of every ragweed, buchallan and weed that stuck its head out under a briar or skeagh.

When I got in, Mrs. Kelly had a glass of milk ready and a scone. Mel had gone to bed.

"Were you fighting?" she asked.

"No," I answered, honestly bewildered, "honest – well not really," I admitted.

"Pay no heed – Mel's just in one of her moods."

Now there was an understanding woman. Somewhat relieved of the guilt I knew not from where, I trudged up to wash and bed. I knelt by my bed and recited the litany of indulgence aspirations and prayers which I had been taught lest the Devil might yet find a chink in my spiritual armour and get through and take possession of my soul.

Later when I was in bed I heard Mel going to the toilet. I heard bolts slam on the door. I heard the initial drill of urine, quickly corrected to the toilet bowl. I wondered about her.

That night at two o'clock the phone rang. I leaped in the bed. It continued to ring as I ran down the winding stairs to the tiled hall and answered, "Coleman 11 – hello?"

"Could I speak to Peter, please?" the voice said.

"He's not home," I answered. "May I take a message?"

"Who's this I'm speaking to?"

"This is Jack," I said, "I'm his nephew."

"Well Jack, tell yer uncle Peter the boys are all behind him."

I was glad of that.

"Who will I say called?"

"Tell him – tell him the Boys from Garryowen."

Before I could ask where Garryowen was, the receiver was replaced. When I looked up Mrs. Kelly was coming down the stairs in her dressing gown. She asked me who was on the phone and she wrote the message on the pad.

"Did Eiley not waken?" she yawned.

Eiley did not waken from the time she got up. She certainly would not waken when she went to bed. I went back to bed and dreamt about Mel.

The alarm went off at seven in the morning. Peter was not there. I got up early, eager to assume the responsibilities that would mark me with the indelible seal of indispensability. Corn had to be ground from the loft through a "Hopper" through the chute into a bin below. The fowl had to be fed and the pigs and cattle watered. During the summer the cattle and sheep in the seventy-acre-out-farm at Ballyedock needed to be at least counted and the aluminium ballcock in the cattle trough needed to be checked. There was also a small vegetable garden and I had received a general instruction to trim the hedge and clean it from the gate to the house at the end of the avenue. If this was complete the garden rail was to be painted. In case of an unforeseen break in the weather, the wainscoting in the toilet needed to be painted. Eiley said if this was done she would herself paper it. As long as it was fine, nature was providing plenty of outdoor herbage to subdue and maintain.

The morning was fresh and warm. The smells of dry corn, creosoted loft floors and fowl dung intermingled in a sour-smelling togetherness which was barely tolerable, although not unpleasing to my young nostrils and palate.

Eiley was going away for a few days holiday to her sister and when I arrived back from the morning chores at five minutes to eight there were four cuts of bread with farmers' butter waiting for me, and a leather case bound with a string for security which she told me she wanted carried to the head of the lane where she would catch the half past eight bus.

The radio was playing some dreary-type classical music as I sat down to sup. The pips came for eight o'clock and the news announcer commenced "Here are the News headlines. There has been a call on the Minister for Justice to set up a Judicial Tribunal to inquire into the Coleman Boycott Affair."

It took about two seconds for it to sink in.

"D'you hear?"

"Whisht! Whisht!" said Eiley.

The announcer went on, "Cardinal Minzenti – the Catholic Prelate – has been released."

"Praise be to God."

"Good morning everyone!" said Mary Kelly.

"Whisht – phisht," we urged in response to Eiley's gathered intensity.

"Oh dear!" said Mary feigning put out.

"We're on the radio," I apologised.

"The boycott!" said Eiley.

"Oh!" said Mary surprised and then she said "Oh!" again, but this time in a much lower pitch.

The announcer stated that Thomas Whitney wanted a Tribunal set up to inquire into the boycott because it was a matter of such importance. No one was to be spared. He wanted the enquiry to investigate what caused his daughter to leave, who encouraged her, who helped her in any way, who told lies about it and added to it, why there was a boycott and who was responsible for it?

No wonder Peter had not come home. When the news was over I walked Eiley up the lane to the bus carrying her bag.

"I don't like the sound of this," she said." I don't like the sound of this at all."

"But maybe it will finish it," I said.

"It won't finish as easy as that I'm afraid – it's very hard to put sand back the way you found it," she said philosophically. "Never mind – those things don't affect you. Make sure you get all your jobs done before I get back."

When I got back to the house, Mel was not yet up. Mrs. Kelly asked me who were "The Boys from Garryowen" that had rung during the night. I explained I did not know nor for that matter did I know where Garryowen was.

"Will you miss Mel?" she smiled.

"Yeah," I said. "I'd better get started on the hedge."

I brought a stool, a rake, a clippers and wheelbarrow and headed up the lane. The hedge had grown in clumps, leaving great gaps for weeds to flourish. Interlaced through it was a wide fence with rusting iron stays. Each clump had to be cut to its own dimensions because every second one was a runt, each had to have its integrity preserved independently. The result would be a non-uniform collection of hedges trimmed with box-like edges, each cube different and out of proportion to its neighbour.

At half nine, my father arrived with an assortment of teeshirts, a spare trousers and a few books from home. He had heard Coleman mentioned on the news. When Mrs. Kelly called me for the ten o'clock tea, Mel sauntered into the kitchen in her pyjamas and dressing-gown.

It was after eleven o'clock before Mel came up the lane and when she did, she appeared to be ensconced in her previous mood. She looked at me clipping the hedge.

"You're perspiring," she volunteered by way of hello and semi-criticism.

"It's warm," I apologised.

"You goin' to be doin' this for long?"

"As long as it takes."

"Guess I'll see what's happenin' in the village."

The freedom of the idle rich. I stoomed inside of me.

"See you later, hoh?"

"I guess," I responded – (Fuck it!).

I had not meant to involve myself and here I was giving myself away. She walked back to the house to get her bike – my bike! She had not asked me for it directly. She had not asked me for it at all. Yet how could I possibly not know that she would need it. I had to choose to either confront her or not. I clipped and pruned, occasionally taking a skelp here like a man with a mechanical mouth a bite here, a munch there – dribbling the overflow down on to the ground below. My feet were covered in dead sprigs and clippings from the hedge. I busied myself in an adult "Let's get on with the job" fashion. I felt hurt. Why did I feel hurt? What the hell was wrong with me?

She had cycled past me without stopping, simply saying, "See ya'!" I watched after her and when she disappeared from view I stopped clipping and kicked the barrow in temper.

∞∞

Mel had gone about half an hour when the "priest" Doyle drove down the avenue. He stopped the car and turned off the engine and rolled down the window.

"That's for your uncle Peter," he said. "Will you see that he gets it?"

He handed a letter to me.

"He's not home at the moment," I said.

"I know," he replied. "I phoned."

I stuck the letter in my rear pocket and buttoned it to keep it safe until dinnertime, which was little less than an hour away. The "priest" looked down the lane at the house. He stared at it. He had restarted his car.

"Do you know the history of that house?" he asked me. I was surprised by his conversation.

"No," I answered.

He told me it had belonged to the Parish Priest of Coleman during the 1798 Rebellion and recounted the song which gave the graphic story of the "Croppy Boy," who confessed his sins and his part in the Rebellion to his confessor. He little realised that the man in priestly garb was a disguised Red Coat Captain. This incident had taken place in Peter's house he said. I had never heard this before. "It's true," he said. The real priest had been himself praying when the Red Coats had arrived. They took him down into the valley at the back of the yard and suspended him over the bridge with his ankles dipping his head in and out of the stream below, leaving him almost drowned, until they would again pull him out and start once more with their cruel torture. Then they fired at him for target practice and his life's blood dripped down on to the stones in the brook and they remain stained and crimson to this day. "They have an awful lot to answer for," he said as he restarted his engine.

I worked away strongly for the rest of the morning and when I was called for lunch, Mel had still not come home. It started to rain and Mrs. Kelly gave out about her being so late. When she did return she was soaked and I had already abandoned the outside chores and was painting the door in the bathroom. The door to the landing was closed because it was easier to paint it that way. I had heard her ride in to the courtyard through the open bathroom window and her mother remonstrated with her. She was ordered to change her clothes. I knew she did not know where I was. I was still hurting from the morning.

I heard her go in the room opposite. I wondered was she still sulking. I peeked through the large keyhole in the bathroom door across the landing. She had her back to me. She removed her shirt and jeans. She had left the door open. I felt myself throb. I knew I should not look. This was a sin and no mistake. But it happened by accident, but then that made no difference. I had not thought this would happen when I looked first. I had only looked to see what was happening and anyhow she should have closed the door. I thought again of the man at the mission under threat of being struck blind. I had an idea now how he must have felt. She stood with her back to me, the bed to her right hand side and the full length wardrobe mirror in front of her.

She stood looking at herself. She turned sideways revealing her sprouting profile emerging in to her brassiere. She turned to her left, still admiring herself and when she turned back, she put both hands around her back to uncouple her breathtaking harness. I swallowed, blinked and tried to slowly exhale through my nostrils. She removed her brassiere and walked to the wardrobe opening the mirror door. She removed some clothes and stooping, she opened a small drawer and took out what appeared to be underclothes. I felt fully erect. This was not new to me, but it was never so much that I was so utterly conscious and alive that something was going to happen. She stood facing the clothes in the wardrobe, breasts exposed as she denuded, exposing them to the unappreciative array of limp cardigans and skirts. Suddenly, she turned around. I stared incredulously and simultaneously felt the release of pent up energy whimpering its unstoppable journey from my core.

"Oh Christ!" I croaked. I was screwed up into pinch-nosed agonising pleasure which was forbidden but fortunately expending itself in spurts and jumps that staggered and startled me. The next moment the door opened and hit my head, knocked the paint tin over and Mel screeched back to the refuge of her bedroom. The paint spilled all over the lino. The paintbrush fell from my hand which I had tried to use to protect myself spontaneously. It messed my face and clothes on its downward journey. My groin felt warm. I was blushing like a rose.

"Who's that there?" Mel bawled. I could not answer. Mrs. Kelly heard the commotion and came running.

"What's the problem? What's the matter?" She went in to Mel and then opened the bathroom door to confront the mess.

"Oh dear me!" she said, as I struggled.

"Jack!" exclaimed Mel.

I was struggling with the embarrassment of everything when Mrs. Kelly looked at me and said, "There's a stain on your trousers." (Oh God no – spare me that embarrassment at least.) "Look!" she pointed, calling on the whole world at large to witness my lustful debris. "White spirit is the only thing," she said. "Take your trousers off immediately."

(Not on your nanny, granny.) I backed off defensively, crouching to conceal shape and stain.

"Come on Jack," she said. "If I don't get that paint off now, it will be too difficult later. You have another pants to wear?"

(Paint? Did someone say paint?) I looked down and there sure enough was a blob of white paint. This meant other matters had gone unnoticed. "Jack, you gave me an awful scare!" said Mel.

I was coming around slowly. "Ugh, sorry. I didn't know you were there."

" 'Course, how could you?" said Mrs. Kelly. Unbelievably, for once, I had blurted out the right thing. "Go in to your room and give me those trousers out straight away."

"I think we had better clean up the floor first," I volunteered.

"Very well," she said.

Silently and busily, I helped, focussing to a degree of my concentration I had not believed myself capable. Oh, sweet object of desire, but the timing was terrible, enjoyment engulfed by the enemy, destroyed by disaster. As we tidied, I got uneasier. If pleasure had had its way, could guilt be far behind. This was clearly one of the biggest sins I had ever committed.

∽14∾

No Dust on the Catafalque

My misery was the worse for knowing I was hardly likely to receive general absolution from Fr. Michael or from any other Father either.

This time we were talking about face-to-face combat, the confession box. I would be sent to Confession on Saturday night now that school was out. If I failed to make a good Confession on this occasion then I was off down on the slippery slope once more and would I ever get off again.

I needed to get away from Mel for a little, so the following evening I told Mrs. Kelly I needed to go home to get some things, but I would be back before it got too late. As I pedalled off down the road it was not yet seven o'clock in the evening. The sky was filled with white, fleecy summer clouds, transparent and light. They looked warm and relaxed as they lazed off to the southeast. I thought once more of Hiawatha and his observations on the sky. I needed to talk to someone, it occurred to me, someone who could tell me what to do. It was a pity, I felt, he was not a Catholic, I could have asked advice from him if he was. As I digested these dilemmas spinning along I discovered I was almost at his home where Gerry Denn was now living with his wife and recently born baby. Mary must have had a tough time with Confession, I decided. Gerry waved at me as I passed and I answered his salute. I remembered the day he was going to go off on his bike. He spoke of it afterwards and about how upset he had been. He had fought with his father. His mother was so sure she would never see him again, she ran after him and snapped him with her brownie box camera as he turned and answered her call. People had so many problems I thought. Hiawatha negotiated that one for him, for Mary.

When I got to Larkin's, Hiawatha was playing his fiddle. It was another beautiful melody and it hung in the evening air, slowly falling off. He greeted me in his usual cheery way. He told me it was an ancient love tune entitled "Not for Ireland would I tell you her name."

"The slow airs have great feeling," he said. "They are the only real survivors over the centuries, the others have been fiddled with to suit the times. It's funny the way the love tunes were never changed at all. I suppose love hasn't changed that much over the centuries. Aye, surely." There was a bottle of stout on the table. He lit his pipe.

"Where's himself?" I asked.

"He is gone to get the evening paper for me," he answered.

The evening papers came on the half-six bus from Waterford where they had already arrived on the evening train from Dublin. They arrived in Coleman at half-seven. Larkin had gone early, probably so that he could meet and gab to the lads in the village.

"Mel was here yesterday," he said.

"Oh?" I revealed my ignorance.

"Did she not say?" he said, surprised.

"Well, I was only talking to her briefly," he detected the whiteness of my lie.

"Ho! Ho! me boy," he said with a twinkle. "Is she giving you the treatment?" and laughed.

I blushed and asked if I could have a cup of water.

"I'll tell you about women," he said. "They're God's gift to men." I sniggered. "It's true," he said. "The trouble is though, you don't always necessarily get what you're looking for in a gift."

"Yer about shouting it," I said and I blushed at my give away response.

He kindly did not take advantage. He smoked and looked thoughtful. "I'll tell you somethin' now," he said. He paused. I put the cup down on the table. I was not able to look at him. "Love is the real gift and we've been given an abundance of it, all sorts of it, but some are afraid of it. And because of this, they call love sin." I knew I had heard something important because I felt myself unconsciously alert and focused. "Sin is when we deny love – and do you know – that is the only sin."

"The only sin?" I asked.

"The one and only."

"But what about stealing and murder and the commandments and all that?"

"Simply people who do not know how to love or maybe not able to let themselves be loved."

He seemed to be wrapped in his belief. I wondered if this was what all Protestants believed or simply Presbyterians or was it just Hiawatha. I was tempted to ask. It was a pity that we Catholics did not believe that I felt. I got another cup of water.

As if he could read my thoughts he said, "All the christian churches believe that, including your own. We need to forgive ourselves first before we can start forgiving others. Some people are just afraid of it – that's all." I looked at him in disbelief once more. It was very difficult to believe. "You'll see in time," he said. I wondered if this generosity applied to bad thoughts and desires but I doubted it.

∞∙∞

Larkin came in with the newspaper and handed it to Hiawatha. He went straight upstairs and came back down with some comics. "I've read these," he said, "you can have them." This was a straight gift – no swap or anything. I was delighted. There were three in it – two classics and a 64-pager. The 64-pager was a story about *Buck Jones*. The other two were *A Tale of Two Cities* and *The Prince and the Pauper*.

"Those two aren't bad," he said. "But that wan is great," pointing to the Buck Jones book. I could see from the cover.

"Thanks," I said overcome by his display of kindness.

"No problem," he answered.

We walked out to the yard.

"He's funny," I said.

Larkin looked at me enquiringly.

"Hiawatha," I explained.

"What about?" he asked.

"He was talking about love," I answered and realised I had gaffed.

"Love?" he laughed. "Do ya think yer in love," he jeered.

"Thass not it at all," I growled.

What had started out as a promising evening and a good idea, was quickly beginning to fade.

"Bejaysus I thinks I'm right," he laughed.

"Ah feck off with yerself."

"Why didya cum down eh?" he asked.

"More fool I was," I sulked.

"Were you afraid the fairies were after gettin' me?" he jeered again.

I hated him when he was like this.

"They'd leave ya back quick enough," I said as I headed for my bike.

"Are ya goin' off already?" he asked.

"I have to," I lied. "I'm stayin' at Peter's."

I left him wondering.

I was not in a good humour when I got back. I had brooded most of the way on my bike. I consoled myself by looking forward to reading the comics I had secured to the handlebars. It was still bright and Mel came out when the sound of the bike in the yard alerted her.

"Where were you?" she asked, eyeing the comics.

"Larkin's," I answered.

"Are these for me?" she asked.

I looked at her curiously.

"They're mine," I answered. "But you can look at them if you like."

"Did – uh – Michael mention me?" she asked.

"No," I said in matter-of-fact form.

I brought the comics up to my room and left Mel looking at *The Prince and the Pauper*. The smell of the fresh paint from the bathroom invited me to inspect my work. I bent to touch the paint to check if it had dried. The floor board creaked under the lino. The paint was dry. There was a mousehole. It was difficult to know if it was new or old. I was surprised I had not adverted to it when I was painting. I bent to examine it. The bathroom shadowed as Mel gave me a start by her unexpected presence.

"Jesus you frightened me," I said as I looked up.

She was wearing a short dress and it was possible to see up her soft thighs to within a few inches of teasing desire.

"What're you doing?" she asked.

"I think this might be a mousehole."

She shrank back.

"Then again, it might not, it's a very old house, you know."

She was interested and I told her what the "priest" Doyle had informed me of its history. The gory details of the unfortunate priest's blood dripping and miraculously staining the stones numbed. It frightened.

"Let's go see the stones with the blood," she pleaded.

There was still plenty of light as we went to the valley at the back of the farmyard. The track led down to the little bridge which allowed access across the small ravine to an old lane at the far side. It was a Mass path I explained, where people passed across fields going to worship. We looked under the bridge and there sure enough jutting from the stream was a dark red stone fully illuminated by the descending crimson sun.

"Gee whizz!" she responded.

I was impressed myself. The bridge looked picturesque nestled in the valley, garlands of ivy hanging out of it. The pointing of the sandstone was revealed behind the see-through veil. The birds warbled and the thyme oozed its magical scent. I took a deep breath and sighed. She placed her hand in the stream letting the flowing water coolly soothe. A waterhen startled and excitedly skipped over the stream chuck-chucking in a high pitched excited squawk. Slightly startled she withdrew her hand and stood nervously up. "It's only a waterhen," I said.

The evening dew had started to fall and the grass was wet. The light fog down the valley turned colour in the setting sun. It all hung together in an atmospheric experience of pure beauty. In the distance we could hear the clackety-clack of the railway train from Waterford to Rosslare bringing emigrants to the lonely boat and their belief of foreign fortune. They were leaving all this behind.

"You look sad", she said when we got back up on the bridge. I decided to keep my thoughts to myself by dropping stones in the stream. A cow lowed. "Is there a reason? she prodded.

"For what?" I had forgotten.

"For looking sad," she said impatiently.

"Just things now and again," I offered.

"What things?"

"Things about people leavin' an' stuff," I owned up.

"You mean people leaving the country?"

"Yeah," I said dropping in another stone in a semi-distracted way. "Ya know what I mean," I lazily insisted.

"I'll write to you," she said as she touched my hand.

"Hoh?" I enquired.

"Don't be sad," she said. "I'll write to you every week – honest I will."

The common mistake between us was immediately noticed by me for once.

"I will miss you," I advantaged.

"I know you will," she responded.

She moved to me quickly. She held my hand and drew me to her.

I felt awkward, a little embarrassed and shy.

"You're sweet," she said.

Hiawatha's words of love came flooding back.

"Love is a real gift."

Oh I loved her all right.

She kissed me as I stood there mesmerised, torn between desire, fear of exposure and uncertainty as to whether Hiawatha or the Catholic Church was right.

"Oh God," I pleaded internally.

However, it seemed He was busy elsewhere. She looked at me and said, "I kissed Michael yesterday."

I looked at her in disbelief. I was stunned. How could she? Why was she saying this? I could not accuse, I had no cause. But, yet I felt I had. "Well maybe he kissed me."

The bastard! No wonder he gave me the comics free. Conscience money!

"Are you jealous?" she provoked.

"No, not at all." I offhandedly replied.

"You don't mind then?" she said.

"Not at all." I lied.

"I told him so," she said.

"You told him what?"

"I told him you wouldn't mind," she answered.

On that mortal spot I resolved his execution. I wanted to say that I loved her, but that would lead to sin. I wanted her to go away and be for someone else and I remembered Hiawatha once again. But nobody said it was all right to love and everybody said it was wrong to be so close unless there was a sacred intention. I knew – I served Masses where it was told, over and over again. She had awoken me in a way I had not known.

I threshed around inside me. I was angry at her and yet there was no way I was going to let her see how I felt. I wanted to let the love in my heart out so that she could see how I really felt. I wanted to run away so that I would not say anymore. More than anything I wanted to go to her and feel her breasts. But more than anything I really wanted to break Larkin's neck. She sat on the low wall of the bridge facing the sun. I sat beside her. "This is just so Irish," she said. I looked at her. "You know," she said, "Sitting On the Bridge Below the Town." I think I wanted to throw up. (Toor-a-bloody-ooril!) She took my hand again, and my stomach settled again.

I looked at her inviting eyes. I looked at her inviting legs and swallowed. She inclined her face to me as her lips parted. I kissed her, my right hand resting on her shoulder. Before I realised what was happening my hand wandered off on its own accord up the nape of her soft neck and glided down the front of her buttoned shirt lightly caressing with the back of my hand. I opened my hand gently to receive the full softness of her pinnacled mould. Her tongue entered my mouth.

"Jack!" A voice shouted from the gate not fifteen yards away. I nearly swallowed her tongue with the fright. We both jumped apart in a fluster. It was Peter. He had obviously returned. Even more obvious was our state of consternation at being caught in "flagrante delicto."

"What were you doin'?" he smirked.

"We were looking at the red stones under the bridge – you know the ones with the priest's blood."

"A history lesson," he codded.

"Ya know the story – the 'priest' Doyle told me and Mel wanted to see it."

"C'mon in," he concluded. "I'm told you have some messages for me."

It was the last opportunity I got to be with Mel in an intimate way before she went back home. It set a pattern which was to maintain itself in my life for many years. Almost always when events seemed to be presenting me with what I believed I wanted some circumstance occurred to remove it right from before my very eyes.

That evening I was brought home and although I felt not in the least like sleeping I knew the adults wanted to talk to Peter in my absence. On the stairs that night I discovered that although the Knights of Columbanus would not entirely promote the boycott nationally, the influence of Bishop

Staunton locally meant there was an undercover operation afoot in the diocese. Dev had issued an ultimatum to his cabinet that they would have to choose between membership of the Knights and membership of the Cabinet. The day the article appeared in the paper about the Inquiry for a Judicial Tribunal, shots were fired in the dead of night at Thomas Whitney's house. That was the same night I had taken the phone call from "the boys from Garryowen," a euphemism for the IRA I now understood. Things were taking a turn for the worse, Peter had said.

Peter had made a statement backing the Bishop after all the Orangemen had denounced the boycott on the 12th of July in Northern Ireland. He had received letters from cranks threatening him. It was a rewarding eavesdropping. There was talk of more trouble along the border. "That feckin Treaty," my father said. "I knew well 'twould settle nothin'. There's only one language the British understand. They'll never come to their milk until they see trainloads of coffins pullin' up in Waterloo Station."

I could feel the blood of my convictions rising within. The great conquering British bulldog was causing it all again. Why could they not leave us to our own country. How would they like it if we moved in on part of theirs and turned it Catholic.

But that was not all.

"There's this business with young Larkin."

I pricked my ears.

"It's due in court next Thursday."

They discussed what the outcome would be and the consequences. This would not be good for the resolution of the boycott.

"Did you speak to the priest?" my father asked.

"Like talking to a stonewall," said Peter. "He feels he owes it to everybody."

I strained to hear more.

"It'll come to blows yet," my father volunteered.

"Or worse," said Peter.

They spoke about court again. There was a silent pause as everybody waited for the inside track. He lowered his voice. Blast it, I missed it. I was off the steps of the stairs and my face pressed to the keyhole.

"No coddin'," said my father.

"This was to do with his being knocked down."

"He told me to tell his Reverence he'd drop the case against her if the case against young Michael was dropped."

"Well?" said my father.

"These things are not as easily stopped as they're started."

"Did ya have a word with Sergeant Thorpey?" asked my mother.

"Are you out of your stone latitude mind? he asked. Her silence revealed her puzzlement. "Subverting the course of justice is a crime," he said.

Whether my mother felt put down or not I do not know but shortly after this she put the kettle on and set the table for the tea. When she was gone, both men spoke about the Leinster Final on Sunday which pitted the old firm of Wexford versus Kilkenny. They smoked and talked and laughed and when eventually Peter got up to leave my father walked out to the yard with him in the balmy night.

"Where to now?" my father asked.

"The boycott?" he queried. "What else? I have a delicate mission ahead," he said.

I listened through the open window. The curtain lightly waved in the moonlight. Peter opened his coat to reveal a document protruding from his inside pocket.

"If this doesn't work," he said, "I don't know what will."

"Don't tell me anymore," my father said as he left the politician to his business.

It was the envelope the "priest" Doyle had given me in the lane. When they were gone I sat at the window and opened the curtains letting the moonlight stream in and flood the room. My brother was fast asleep. I rested my forearms on the sash and lay my chin on top. I looked down on the rippling twinkling silvery lines that suggested a becalmed night. As I lay there musing from some deep recess in my mind words came: "Night is darkest before the dawn, the sea is calmest before the storm."

The night was the brightest I had ever seen and the sea was the calmest. The metaphor was twisted. There was an atmosphere of paradox or contradiction maybe. Would there be a dark morning because there was a bright night or did it work in reverse. Would there actually be a great storm because the sea was so calm. I lay in the bed a long time thinking about the boycott and the six counties and Larkin and the "priest" Doyle and Mel. When the moon went behind a cloud, I covered my head with the clothes and fell asleep.

On the Friday night before Mel left, myself and Larkin cycled up to her to say goodbye. Everything I wanted to say to Larkin was left unsaid. I could say nothing without revealing my own hand, a hand I had never declared in any event to either Mel or Larkin. I had not a foot to stand on. Maybe it would be better to say nothing – least said easiest mended, Poll used to say. Still, I could not deny to myself that I was smitten.

When we got to Peter's, Mel ran out to meet us. Peter was inside with Mrs. Kelly and Eiley, who had returned from her sisters. We decided there were too many adults within, so we strolled to the orchard. It had been a good summer and the apple tree branches were beginning to bend with their slowly ripening fruit. I walked in front down the winding steps to the orchard that overlooked the valley with its little bridge and stream. The evening was getting a little chilly. Mel was wearing her sleeveless cotton frock. She shivered and rubbed her arms.

"Oh my," she said, "it's gone chilly."

Sensitive to her needs and anxious to improve my standing I volunteered to get her cardigan. She was chuffed at the attention and beamed my reward to me. I lightly took the steps three at a time in the manner champions do. I remembered where her cardigans were. I remembered her breasts. My God, I had been so close to touching them. I paused, at least I had not sinned that way. But then I remembered caressing her left one with the back of my fingers and that was touching. Typical of me – the misfortune of being caught for the crime without the benefit of enjoying the booty. I decided if I got my chance again, I would take it since I was going to be hung for it anyhow.

Inside Eiley was finished papering the bathroom. When I went to Mel's room she called me.

"The very man I want to see," she said.

She handed me the enamel bucket she had used for the wallpaper paste.

"Take that down to the stream and rinse it out for me. I don't want the paste clogging up the drains."

Eiley always found something for me to do. I left the cardigan and made my way to the valley. I got down at the back of the bridge from where there was easiest access because of the presence of two big stones at the edge of the stream. I rinsed and scoured the bucket methodically. I could not see the blood stones from this side because I was looking through the eye of the bridge to the bright sky. I thought again of the evening before and where we had been sitting when Peter called. I looked at the spot as I climbed up and winced as I paused to reflect on the moment and its incongruous conclusion.

As I turned to go I heard a laugh. Shielding my eyes from the brightness I looked towards the orchard. At first I could only see the trees but as my eyes got used to the light I could see the figure of Mel through a hedge-gap. I was about to shout when Larkin's figure came between me and her. He was much bigger and his rangy shoulders revealed the cliché of his regular farmwork. He stooped towards her and my blood froze. No, this could not be. I was transfixed. They were hugging and kissing. Larkin stopped and looked towards the house. He looked back at her and they kissed again. (How could she do this to me? How could he do this to me? How could they do this to me?) My head was in a spin. It stopped when I saw Larkin put his hand on her front. (The bastard. The dirty little bastard.) The anger rose in me. I would never talk to them again as long as I lived. I would become a priest of God and if I ever got the chance I would deny both of them absolution.

I turned and ran back to the farmyard tears streaming from my face. I left the enamel bucket at the back door and went to the corn loft. A few pigeons flew out when I opened the door to go in and for a moment I was unsteadied in my pursuit of selfpity as I shielded myself from their awkward panicked fluttering wings. I sat on an upturned bucket staring at the floor. I was only a fool. A big frigging eejit. She had never promised me anything so what was the big problem. And then I thought of Larkin kissing and fondling her and a great wave of anxiety came over me again as I felt her being used by him, and me by her. I felt my tears scalding my face as I realised I had not meant to her what I believed I had. Soon my tears stopped and I fell quiet, periodically higging, as my feelings tumbled, settling back into place.

A little time afterwards I heard them come into the yard and go inside, only to come out again in a few moments. When they started calling my name, I felt my anger return and I sulked. They could all go shite. I never wanted to see them again. When I heard them shouting down in the valley I stole from the loft and taking my bike, I rode home from Peter's. As soon as I had negotiated the noisy gravelled front yard, I hoped they thought I had hurt myself and that they would be worried about me. I imagined them running to and fro' shouting, "Try the well" and breathing sighs of relief fro' because I was not in it and then, "Check the fall at the back of the bridge." Well they might worry, now they would appreciate me a little more. And then I thought of them together again and the wave of pain swept over me once more. Feck them anyhow, feck them again.

When I got home my mother asked me if anything was wrong but I denied it and went to bed. Mel would be gone to Shannon first thing in the morning and I would never see her again. Larkin was supposed to come to the match with us on Sunday but as far as I was concerned our friendship was ancient, destroyed. He had been too clever for me. I sat there wallowing in my fully justified selfpity, resolving ways and means of avoiding delusions of this sort in the future. I discovered a neat answer. From now on, anyone who wanted to be a friend of mine would have to prove it. I would ignore people who were mostly friendly, those who were friendly would be observed with a caustic eye, those who were very friendly would be treated with contempt and if they survived this by not withdrawing their friendship, then they could be trusted. I was not going to allow hurt like that anymore.

I had a terrible dream. I was present at the trial of Christ and John the Baptist. People came up to me saying, "Are you the one that denied him three times." I kept saying I was not and they said, "Who is he then?" and I answered, "He is the King of the Jezzamells," and everytime they laughed at me and everytime I tried to correct the word, it just come out Jezzamels.

In the morning I believed I was so far gone I was now dreaming sacrilege. The outlook was bleak.

◌◌◌

Mel was going. It was a busy day in the shop. There were Confessions that night. The Leinster Final was next day. At breakfast my mother asked me what had happened at Peter's. Apparently he called much later because Mel was afraid something had happened because I went home without saying "Goodbye."

"I'm sorry," I said.

"They were very worried."

"I'm sorry," I said again.

"What happened?" she asked again.

"Please mother!" I pleaded.

"Oh very well then if you don't wish to tell."

All women were the same I vowed. I felt like taking an oath of celibacy and a vow of misogyny on the spot. I went off to work with my father shaking my head. He looked at me with a mischievous brow.

"Domestic problems?"

I looked at him and simply said "Daddy!" a rebuke to his teasing. He laughed.

"Don't worry," he said, "It will all be over before you're twice married and wance widowed."

I worked hard that Saturday ferrying groceries from shelf to counter, and counter to car, cart and carriage. In the middle of the late evening surge, John FitzJohn came in with a long list.

"Feck that fella anyway!" said my father. "At home sittin' on his arse all day and nothin' to do, and then lob in at the last minute and expect hands under feet."

But it was only a groan. When they were all boxed I brought them to the car and there I saw Louise. She had the brightest eyes and they flashed a surprise beacon of welcome as I opened the door of what I believed was an empty car.

"Hi," she said. I blushed and excused myself as I put the groceries on the back seat.

"I don't see you at the tennis much," she said. I told her we had been busy with one thing and another. She added, "I heard Mel has gone back." News certainly travelled fast. "Would you mind bringing me out a bar of chocolate?" she asked and handed me sixpence.

As I was going out of the shop with the bar my father winked at her father and said, "Yes, begob!"

It was only when I was handing it to her and receiving her bemusing smile I realised how things must have seemed. She hardly did it on purpose, I promised myself as I came back to the shop. It was extremely harmless, how was she to know that I would go to the car with the

groceries. If she had wanted to see me, she would have come into the shop and seen me. It was harmless I knew. I knew she would have had to speak to me in front of everyone if she had come in. I stopped myself. What was I doing? She asked me to bring her out a bar of chocolate for Christ's sake. Still, she could have asked her father to get it I was becoming exhausted. Girls, they were too much effort. Just let me go to Confessions and get all of them out of my life forever more. Amen!

The thoughts of Confession were driving me cracked. I had to tell these sins or I was in over my head. I started rehearsing on my way home from the shop in the car. Silently and internally. "Bless me Father for I have sinned. It's been a fortnight since my last Confession. I cursed three times, I told lies four times, I had impure thoughts and desires ..." How would I take it from there? Maybe if I made a sort of run at it and mumbled "actions" next I'd get away with it. No. You had to have a pure heart so it would have to be said so that it could be heard by the naked ear. Maybe if I changed the words a bit by saying, "I got involved in impure thoughts, desires and actions." Everyone knew what "involved" meant, didn't they? And if they didn't, they could always ask, couldn't they? Shit! Supposing he did ask, what was I going to say? Supposing he asked me with whom? Oh Jesus, I hated girls. Fr. Williams would never ask with whom, right enough. But supposing it was the Canon. But the Canon would never hear Confessions in Coleman except on rare occasions. Unless there was an emergency.

After my supper I was sent with the groceries to the priest's house and Confessions and my impending execution. "High upon the scaffold tree ... and they went like foes undaunted to their doom." I took a deep breath and resolved to seek inspiration during my examination of conscience, pre-Confession.

When I got to the priest's house there was no sign of his car and when I checked the rear, Iníon Ní Breathnach's was there. I asked Mae where the priest was and she said he was gone to Dublin and would not be home until Monday. I asked who was hearing Confession but she did not know. I got that sinking feeling.

I walked to the church unsteadily. Maybe I should give it a miss, but that would involve more excuses and more lies. I walked to the pews in the middle of the church. I knelt opposite the men's confessional. The priest was in there, but who was it? I was kneeling next to the "priest" Doyle. He was reading prayers from *The Sodality Manual* and his rosary was acting as an interleaved bookmark. He was flicking from the marked page to other pages in the manner of ease of an orchestra leader with sheet music. His demeanour forbade interruption. Thorpey got in before me.

"Who's hearin'?" he asked.

"Dunno'," I answered, cutting off his unwelcome intrusion.

I tried to plan my formula based on the assumption it was the Canon. If he asked me who I was with, I would say she was a visitor. If he asked me what I had done, I would say we had kissed, and if he asked me had we touched, I would say ... I would say ... shite ... what would I say ... not really ... that sounded hedgey ... maybe if I said, "only barely," then would he ask me to explain. I panicked a little as the "priest" Doyle left me for the confessional.

"Are ya going to the match tomorrow?" Thorpey whispered.

"Shag off!" I snapped.

Jesus, here I was trying to restore my salvation and God sends me this gobshite to topple me into the hands of Satan.

"Jays!" said Thorpey, "You musta murdered someone."

The lady came out of the female box signalling the commencement of the male confessional. The "priest" Doyle would not be long. What would I say if he asked me how we touched – I got it – I would say I touched her tops – that was it – any gobshite would know what that meant including the Canon – not that the Canon was a gobshite, Lord, but you know what I mean.

The door opened and shut releasing the "priest" Doyle into the light. I got up and opened the door and allowed myself be swallowed by the penitential darkness. It was like the start of the hundred metres, waiting there for the starting pistol, not sure whether you wanted the starter to fire in the air to start the contest or just end the misery of the terror. How was I starting again? I heard the slide go back on the other box. My stomach tightened. There was an agonising pause, the hangman's step from the convict to the lever. Phisht! It slid back. We were off.

"Bless me father for I have sinned, it's been a fortnight since my last Confession."

"Yes, my child."

Shit! It was Uncle Fr. Michael! This was family. I was going to have to expose my dark secrets virtually to my mother, the next best thing.

"Ugh!" I grunted.

"Do you need help?" he asked quietly.

"Ugh! Well no, Father."

"Very well" he said.

"Bless me Father for I have sinned ..."

Oh Jesus, I realised I had already said that.

"Tell you what," he said. "Did you curse and tell lies?" (I did.)

"I did, Father."

"Did you kill or steal." (What?)

"What? – I mean – ugh – no Father."

"What about impure thoughts, desires and actions?" (Shit!)

"Ugh – yes Father."

"How often?" (Did he say "how awful!")

"Ugh – yes Father."

"Was there someone with you?"

The shame of it – oh God – the big admission of really serious guilt.

"Yes, Father."

"Well sure you'll do your best not to do it again."

"Yes, Father."

"Ten Our Fathers and Ten Hail Marys for your penance. There's a good man ... 'O my God'..." He started me off on the act of contrition and then commenced his Latin absolution. Home at last.

"O my God I am heartily sorry for having offended Thee and I detest my sins above every other evil because they displease Thee my God who art so deserving of all my love and I resolve with all my heart never to offend Thee again. Amen."

"Deinde ego me te absolvo. In Nomine Patris et filiis et spiritus sancto. Amen."

Phew! Not so bad after all. Could have been much worse.

"Jack, tell your mother I will be down for the tea after Confessions." (Oh Shit!)

"Uh – oh – sure thing."

Well bollix! How could I look him straight in the eyes ever again. Still, he did not look for too much details. All the same it was a bit much to say that to me. It was not as if my mother was never there. He could have let me think he did not know who was confessing. I had momentarily considered disguising my voice when I realised who was hearing. Still, at least it was over.

∞∞

When he called down later I felt a bit coy, but he appeared to take the awareness of his debauched nephew in his stride. I was in the middle of cursing Mel to myself when Larkin rode into the yard.

"Where did you go after?" he asked.

"Home," I answered perfunctorily.

"Why d'ja do tha'?"

" 'Cos," I answered.

" 'Cos why?" he asked.

" 'Cos, just 'cos, okay?" I leaned.

"Is somethin' up?" he asked.

"Wha'd you think?" I elbowed him.

"Sure seems like it."

"Sure seems like it to me too."

"Well spit it out."

"You spit it out."

"Spit what out?"

"Whatever you have to spit."

"I've nothin' to spit."

"Well then don't bother your arse spittin!"

Silence ensued as I ignored him by looking down on the evening harbour as the Rockabill spumed its funnel of thick black smoke, its curved aft laying a snail's trace in the swelling billows behind.

"Jeez, I don't know whass got in to you lately."

"Vice versa."

"Wha'?"

"The same as tha'!"

More silence. "You goin' to the match?"

"I might."

Fr. Michael came out with my mother. He came to us and handed us a ten shilling note apiece. It knocked the stuffing out of the two of us. It was, he told us, for serving Mass for him and he was bringing both of us and my father and sister to the match. We were thrilled. "Set like a jelly," he said and threw a boxer's feint at both of us. Larkin entered into it. My, how his humour had come around over the last day or so, I annoyed myself. Fr. Michael went off. Larkin was off the hook for the minute. "See ya in the morning," he said. Larkin was beginning to give me a pain in the arse again. Not content with the near rape of my female American cousin, he was now taking undeserved advantage of the generosity of my missionary clerical uncle as well. He needed to be taught a lesson, I felt. The unfairness of life tortured me and my anger grew.

∞ ∞

I slept fitfully and it was not until I got my mind from Larkin and Mel and their "carry on" that I finally started to rest. I focused on the hurling. My own heroes – no one would treat any of them like that. Once more I resolved that the focus of my energies from here out would be to represent Wexford at hurling and this task involved total dedication. This time I would stick to it. I fell asleep determined the next day would be the start of the rest of my life.

When Fr. Michael called to the house at 8 o'clock he had already said Mass. We would get half-eleven or twelve in Inchicore. We had a half-sized biscuit tin filled with sandwiches, a basket full of mugs and spoons, a bag of buttered homemade buns, six bottles of orange and two flasks of tea. Larkin came independently prepared and full of excitement. My previous night's bad humour had evaporated with the expectation of the day's promise. My sister hung out of my father who responded to command.

The journey was tiring in spots, but it livened up as we passed through Graiguenamanagh, the enemy heartland. The flag of war was hanging out all right. We had the flag with 1955–1956 emblazoned in silver and gold across purple and gold colours of the model county. It looked a bit tired from the previous year. The Kilkenny Cats would have their fill of us before the day was out.

"Four in a row," my father said. "Never been done before." Well we have the men to do it.

"The Assyrian came down like a wolf to the fold," the poem in our primer read, "And painted their arses in purple and gold," we finished.

Fr. Michael concentrated on his driving and got intimate details of each of the Wexford players from my passionate father.

"The Referee?" said my father. "I wonder who's doin' it? It could be the saving or the losing of it." Fr. Michael agreed.

When we got there eventually there was a tremendous bustle of activity. Hawkers were crying out, "Apples, oranges now or chocolate."

"Ice-cream! Ice-cream! Lucan Dairy Ice-cream!" in rounded, sweaty Dublin accents.

"How much are d'apples missus?" shot Larkin.

"A tanner a pair sunshyen."

"I don't want pears," he back-answered her.

"I'm sure you don't want turnips either Son, but look a' da head a' ya." Larkin had met his match. It served him right. I sniggered and pointedly looked away.

"Whass wrong with you?" he blustered at me.

"Cat got your tongue?" I jeered.

"No," he said. "But Mel did."

I was paralysed. That was Larkin. He just went too far always. I was badly stung. I sat beside him in the long stand. This decision was not of my making. My sister sat beside my father and he sat beside Fr. Michael. I brooded.

We stood for "Faith of Our Fathers." We stood for the national anthem. The ball was thrown in and there was a schimozzle in the middle of the field as the striped black and amber devils weaved and darted against the courage and open strength of the descendants of the rebels of 1798.

"Up the Yella Bellies!"

"C'mon the Cats!"

"Sit down be goddammed' til we see the match."

A point for Wexford. We jumped and cheered. The ball was pucked out and driven back in. The pace was terrific. The great Ned Wheeler doubled on an overhead pull, and the ball increased its pace and direction to the forwards. A roar from the crowd, the ball was still in play, the referee blew his whistle.

"There was no free there."

"Wheeler is down."

We looked back up the field and there sure enough was the level form of our champion centre fielder.

"The dirty bastards" shouted Larkin.

"Wha' happened?" I asked.

"Don't you see what happened – they were out to get him."

Some of the crowd started to boo.

"Give them their belly full of it," roared my father. "We're takin' it long enough."

A Kilkenny fan turned around, "'Twas an accident," he said. "I seen it."

"Me arse!" said my father.

"It was an accident," the Kilkenny fella shouted back. He was standing four rows down shouting red faced back at us.

"Put some manners on that fella beside ya Father," the Kilkenny fella shouted at Fr. Michael. Fr. Michael bristled.

"He's badly injured," a reference to Wheeler pronounced Fr. Michael.

" 'Twas a goddamn accident!" shouted the Kilkenny fella again.

"Here now, here now," some voices rebuked the profanity.

"Maybe he struck himself," my father scored.

The crowd laughed. The red-headed red-faced Kilkenny man turned back to his support. Wheeler was carried off to the defiant applause of the restrained Wexford supporters and the excusing, explaining and headshaking of the Kilkenny followers.

The game went nip and tuck until halfway through the first half. The match moved to a blistering pace again. Then disaster struck. Sean Clohessy scored the first goal for Kilkenny, Dick Rockett scored the next, then Billy Dwyer and Clohessy made it number five before half time. A numbness had descended. All trace of humour had departed. The Kilkenny crowd were cock-a-hoop. There was nothing to be said. When Clohessy made another daring run, one of the Wexford backs upended him and he was carried off with a hip injury. It was the turn of the Kilkenny crowd to protest. Every last vestige of pride was disappearing with the match.

But Wexford had risen from defeat before. Had they not been fifteen points down against Tipperary at half time in the League Final last year and turned around for a finish and beaten them? But, in the second half, the rain came and a grey drizzle emphasised the dreariness felt in every Wexford heart. My champions were dying in front of my very eyes. The days, we were told, that were the justification of righteousness, clean living and a National Catholic life style, were draining down into the sod of Croke Park, a weak, limp and soggy memory. Kilkenny scored six goals and nine points and poor Wexford only scored two points in the second half to record a final tally of one goal and five points. Nicky Rackard retired after the match.

We left Dublin on that wet July Sunday evening dejected and disappointed. We had been humiliated by the old foe. The thoughts of taunts in Graiguenamanagh occasioned a reappraisal of the return journey home. We went home the coast road, a route that though it was ten miles longer had the advantage of not passing through any part of Kilkenny. The Wexford flags hung lifeless and drenched. There seemed now to be nothing to look forward to except the autumn. My perception of life was beginning to slowly alter and illusions were beginning to tarnish and blur. It was very difficult to believe it had happened, but it was impossible to deny. Conversation in the car was subdued. Occasionally it would rise, but it would fall again.

"That damned referee, he should have put off half a dozen of the hoors," my father said.

"Too many of them played too badly," Fr. Michael said more reasonably.

After a while my father said, "The rain didn't help either."

"Nor the trip to the States," said Fr. Michael.

"Making heroes out of them," my father, said. "Sure, they're only human."

"They made gods out of them."

"They did indeed," said my father and then reflectively said, "Poor ould Wheeler."

I felt sorry for them all, especially Wheeler.

∞·∞

My sister and Larkin talked a bit on the way home. I researched my life to see what I had to look forward to and the next big event that was looming before me was secondary school – St. Peter's College – SPC – my brother said the initials stood for State Prison Camp! When I said I was looking forward to going, it seemed I had confirmed his worst suspicions about me.

"Are you on a vow of silence?" Larkin said to me. He took me unawares.

"I was just thinking," I said.

"Wha' about?"

"Goin' to college and things."

"Are you still mad at me?"

The last thing I wanted was a discussion on Mel in the presence of my sister, father and my uncle Confessor.

"No!" I lied.

"Good," he said. "There was nothin' to it anyway – I was only blackguardin'."

I felt the relief of acknowledgement and looked at him, but I was still bruised.

"Alright," was as good a bland response as any and right then it was the only one I could manage.

"She's all right you know."

"Wid ya shaddup?" I gritted.

"Dey can't hear with the noise of the engine."

"We'll talk about it again – okay?"

"Okay! okay! God's truth, but yid break a Saint's heart."

We were sort of back on sort of terms, sort of, maybe.

"No sign of Peter?" said Fr. Michael.

"Oh he was there," said father. "He's staying over tonight. He's doin' something about the boycott tomorrow," and they were off discussing the pros' and cons' as they let time commence its healing way on the scars that had been cut deep in Croke Park that day. It appeared, however, whenever one set of champions were put down the next invincible heroes were searched out. The discussion moved rapidly to the Orange Protests of the 12th of July.

"Nothin' only a shower of bigots"

Fr. Michael agreed.

"What about this Inquiry?" he asked.

"Shot down," my father whispered.

"I thought the Protestants wanted it?"

"They wanted it to embarrass us – Dev was up to them. The Minister had no power to set one up."

Fr. Michael looked surprised, but as my father explained it was a matter that could be done only if both houses of the Oireachtas decided it. There was talk of a Conference as well, and this apparently was where the whole notion of the Inquiry came from.

"Why don't they just sit down and talk?" said Fr. Michael.

This seemed an eminently sensible suggestion to me.

"I think that's what Peter is about," responded my father.

The whole business of the boycott was becoming very complex and I found it difficult to follow all the issues. There were those who wanted it demonstrated loud and clear what Mrs. Hanlon had done was wrong and nothing short of putting that right was acceptable. Everyone agreed that she was wrong her father, her Rector, her Bishop and her lawyers even. The only one to demur I had heard was from my mother.

"When I thought I was dying," she said to my father, "I could think of nothing but the children."

"And only for the priest you would've been gone," he argued.

"A mother thinks of her children first," she answered.

"And a father, his family," my father countered and added, "and where would we be if stuff like this was allowed?"

"They would probably all be living together quite happily," she said.

It was a difference between them that they never fully resolved. There were different perspectives and different points of view. It seemed the only way to settle matters was either to win outright or run away from it. In the case between my parents, they let it be. "We'll agree to differ," my father said resignedly.

The atmosphere had changed though. Clarke's pub and Auld's shop had suffered dreadfully. The initial excitement of determination had softened. The boycott was yielding nothing except a lot of bad publicity and bitterness nationally. Fr. Williams would not back down, however, and he was encouraged and supported fully by the "priest" Doyle and his fellow commandoes from the Knights of Columbanus. Peter's position was very strongly supportive of the Catholic Church. However he knew the boycott would not win. He had a foot in all the doors. More than most, he was very aware of how lethal and delicate the position was. The pressure was telling on him, but he was a determined, fit, emerging politician and had a tenacious disposition.

The Protestant Bishop of Ossory, Ferns and Loughlin had been to see the President, Sean T. O'Kelly himself. Senator M.F. O'Hanlon, who lived in Dublin and was from the area, went to see Dev. The National Council for Civil Liberties went to see Dr. Ryan. All of the papers had been carrying letters. The pressure had been building up producing the proposals for a Conference and subsequently the Inquriy, but all of the politicians were afraid of what such a confrontation might yield.

On the Monday after the match, I was in Peter's. He had not returned from Dublin. It was not the same there without Mel. I was on the last of the hedge when I noticed two nuns coming towards me with capes on. The capes stopped about nine inches from the ground and from the distance they appeared to have no feet. They looked like big penguins. One of them taught in Ballyhack; I did not know the other.

"Are you Jack?" the Ballyhack one asked.

"I am, Sister."

"Sister Ignatius would like to see you at five o'clock this evening in the Chapel in Coleman. She wants you to show her where the Altar of Repose is."

"Yes Sister," I answered.

Nuns were nosy. Not content with delivering their message, they had to know all about my brothers and sister and, after that, they had to go in to see Eiley. When they were leaving the strange nun complimented me on what a great job I was doing. I took her compliment uneasily trying to hold back from being drawn. They glided up the lane. My day was ruined. The prospect of being cornered by Ignatius anywhere unnerved me. I planned that I would go early and have the altar ready for her as if I had to go someplace else.

It was a quarter to five when I walked in the back door of the church. There was an aluminium bucket half-filled with water containing flower stems and cuttings. The chopped greenery gave a salad smell of freshness and preparation. The sanctuary lamp was down and the red oil glass was removed. As I walked towards the sanctuary the "priest" Doyle came out with the refilled red glass. A voice behind him called and he went back without having seen me. I stood there in the nave. It was like walking into a ladies bedroom while she was absent in the bathroom. Everything was strewn and dishevelled. The strict propriety of presentation was replaced with the disorder necessary for preparation. Old flowers now discarded were thrown on newspapers, buckets ready to receive them, a scissors, a dustpan, a brush and a vacuum cleaner made up an atmosphere of industry and reformation. Effort, energy and diligence would recreate a disciplined theatre with its essential refurbishments conducive to appropriate liturgical demeanour.

When the "priest" came back to the altar the sanctuary lamp was now lighting in his hand, although the tabernacle door was opened and the Blessed Sacrament was obviously absent. He saw me and refocused the lamp.

"Well?"

"The nun was looking for me."

"She's inside." (She was there already!)

He placed the lamp in the ornate silver container which was suspended from an invisible pivot in the apex of the gothic roof. She was in the priest's sacristy wearing white gloves. There was a tin of Brasso and Silvo. The Sacred Vessels were on a table. The gloves were not protective of the hands, but of the vessels. It was prohibited to handle them with the naked flesh. Padraig Byrne caught the Communion Paten by the surface and had to confess it. He got ten Hail Marys for his penance, seven more than the usual. Some said the "priest" Doyle was allowed to touch them, because he had been ordained a Deacon, but others said that did not count after he had left the seminary. I never saw him touch them.

"You're early," she said, and before I could explain, "All the more you can help me with," she added. "Bring those clippings in the church to the fire in the garden," she commanded.

Fr. Williams came in with a stepladder as I was going back to the church. It annoyed me that I had not been let explain. It was typical of Ignatius – no room for anyone's agenda except her own.

I took the bucket and papers to the garden. The smouldering compost heap gave off a burnt musky smell. It stung my eyes slightly. The washing snapped in the breeze. It was odd to see a pair of lady's knickers in the middle of the priest's shirts. Iníon Ní Breathnach's presence had established itself on the clothesline. As I passed in by the hall door I saw her coming out of the house.

"Did you see Father?" she asked me. She was wearing a tweed jacket and shirt. She had her handbag.

"He's in the chapel." She seemed flushed. "He's fixing something with Sister Ignatius and Mr. Doyle."

She turned away from the sacristy where she appeared to have intended her direction.

"Oh," she said. "Just tell him the boycott is over. It's just been announced on the radio."

She disappeared around the corner of the house.

I went straight to the priest. He was fixing the sanctuary lamp and Doyle was holding the stepladder. The nun was polishing the door of the tabernacle.

"The boycott is over," I told him.

He stopped. He got down.

"What?" he asked. I repeated. "Who told you?"

"It's just been announced on the radio."

"Who said?" asked Doyle.

"Iníon Ní Breathnach."

There was a strange pause.

"Thank God!" said Ignatius.

Fr. Williams looked puzzled. The "priest" Doyle looked anxious.

"Are the children coming back?" he asked the clergyman.

"We'll have to find out – we'll have to hear more," the clergyman said.

"We certainly will," said Doyle as he followed the urgently departing priest into the house.

"Well thank God!" said Ignatius again.

I left the can down and went into the sacristy and pulled out the tabernacle of Repose behind the catafalque in the large press. There was no dust on the catafalque. But then why would there be. Larkin and I had served fifty-five funerals through the winter into the summer, and it had been used for most of them.

The tabernacle was dusty and I busied myself cleaning it.

"Where will I leave it?" I asked her. "I have to do some messages before six for my father."

"Maybe you will call up to the convent next week, I would like to sit down and talk to you," she said.

Out of the frying pan into the shaggin' fire. I should have dealt with her in the church. Now there was going to be a whole goddamn ceremony, afternoon tea and buns and every shaggin' nosy parker of a decrepit nun coming in to see "the County Council Chairman's nephew" or worse still – "the boy who is going to be a priest."

꘎ 15 ꘎

Principally a Man

The announcement of the end of the boycott arrived in the village with the same suddenness as the proclamation of its commencement. People were not ready for it at the start and some were not ready for it to end. It seemed like change could not be accepted without great difficulty and, when it was, it could not be abandoned lightly. Strength and security were the great implicit ambitions after a history of turmoil and poverty which had been the lot of "the mere Irish." Now that there was stability and relative prosperity, great astuteness was still required in discerning the true direction of survival. The announcement of the end of the boycott was welcomed, but for the moment that's all it appeared to be – an announcement.

Everyone had questions. Did the church authorise it? What about the children? Would they go to school now? Where was Mrs Hanlon? Was she coming back? Supposing she never came back? Supposing it happened again? What were the Protestants saying really? Would people go back to Clarke's and Auld's shop? How would the people who had shunned each other face each other again?

Fr. Williams came into my father's shop on Tuesday morning. He was looking for Peter, who still was not home. He wanted the full "low down" and in his absence felt my father might have had contact with him. They were not to be disappointed because shortly after the Angelus bell had sounded noon, the black Volkswagen of the Chairman of Wexford County Council pulled up at the shop.

Tuesday was my father's half day and the shop closed at half-twelve. It was quarter-past-twelve and my father told me to close the double doors that day and if anybody knocked, I was to tend them. If somebody was looking for him, I was to take a message and inform them that he would contact them later. I was mildly disappointed that he did not see I could handle the shop on my own and that he had felt the need for the doors to be shut. However, it had its compensations – I could hear the whole story without even an interruption.

I was consigned to make the tea. When I eventually brought in the tray the smoke swirled in the little office. This, in spite of the fact that the four windows along the narrow sided room were open. Peter looked tired, but his face revealed the benign resignation of the marathon runner who had finished the course. The clergyman's intense gaze revealed anxious consideration, contrasted with my father's relief and supportive admiration for his younger brother's achievement. Household names were being dropped to impress nobody. "Dev" and "Ryan" and "McQuaid" were regular, but new names came into it like "Hederman" and "Bell," the lawyers for the Whitneys.

It appeared that Dr. Ryan arranged to meet Peter and the vigilance committee representatives at home in Delgany. Unknown to them, he also invited Tony Hederman, who was the Barrister for the Kellys and a member of the National Executive of Fianna Fáil. He was a great rally organiser in the Party and was regarded as being two-sided, as opposed to two-faced. He had the charm and finesse of a diplomat and the passionate conviction of a rebel. He had the ability to slice and cuddle, depending on how he viewed his quarry. They had seen him speak at the Ard-Fheis. When the delegation heard he was in the house, they almost left. Dr. Ryan's house was located in the shade of the Sugar Loaf. It was a beautiful mansion with more than a hint of Victorian splendour. It was incongruous to imagine that the architectural lavishness intended for the gentry had ended with one of the rebels. The other question was – had the rebels taken on the manners of their masters?

The Minister for Finance received them in his drawing room but when they understood Mr. Hederman was in the study, they felt they had been betrayed and words were exchanged. Peter was brought into the kitchen, so was Hederman. Instantly they recognised each other from the National Executive of Fianna Fáil, as Ryan knew they would.

"Sure he was one of our own," said Peter to the priest and my father.

"What did he say when he saw you?" my father said.

"He started talking about cattle."

"About what?" said the priest.

A herd of heifers were grazing the lush pasture outside the kitchen window which framed the bald mountain. Deftly, the lawyer had moved to comfortable familiar ground, the better to ease their rapport. He wanted to be informed about the cattle, their worth, whether for export, breeding or slaughter, the relative merits of the breed over others and slowly they drifted into politics and the times and ever more slowly to the boycott.

They both agreed there should be an effort to end it, but it was difficult for the Catholics to accept there had been no plot by the Protestants. Apart from which it could not be countenanced that the salvation of the souls of both children could be bartered or bargained out of expediency. It was a difficult situation, but not one where the Catholics felt negotiations were open. The children had to be brought back to the family and the fold.

The lawyer accepted that. Everyone accepted that. Nobody was saying any different. The Whitneys did not know where Elisha was and they would sign whatever was necessary to say that. They believed once she had given her word she was bound by it. They would sign to say that as well, he was sure. What was more, her father would condemn her actions in unequivocal fashion. How could any future Protestant rely on her actions to support a similar strike.

Hederman then revealed that as a Catholic himself he felt bound to reveal he had received the appropriate Episcopal approval from Archbishop McQuaid to institute Civil Proceedings in court against the local church, clergy and the members of the Vigilance Committee. (A threat?)

"For what?" asked the horrified priest.

"He had a lot of legal stuff," said Peter. "But mostly it was to do with conspiracy and victimisation of people not involved."

"They were all involved alright," said the priest.

A man's word was his bond. The Gospel said "In the beginning was the Word and the Word was with God and there was nothing of the World that was not of the Word and was not of God"

Peter ignored it. "What shocked me was the Archbishop gave permission to sue."

"Never trust a lawyer," said the priest.

"I had it checked out," said Peter.

He went on to say that he felt there was nothing to be lost by getting him to put his proposals in writing. Peter took the proposal to the Bishop, who amended them slightly after consultation, and it was then only a matter of getting the Whitneys to sign. Hederman had undertaken to get them to agree to sign it. For his part, Peter got the approval of the Hierarchy and the Knights of Columbanus who returned the draft through the "priest" Doyle to Peter through me in the lane when I was cutting the hedge that day. Did I know the importance of the documents I had in my hand? A most unlikely Moses with a most unlikely Tablet. That was how it was all worked out. The Whitneys went to Dublin and signed.

"I still have my reservations," said the priest.

"We have to try to make it work," said Peter.

"How would it look if they said they would abide by the word she gave when she married and they trying their best to get the young lads back, but we wouldn't agree. Sure we'd be the laughing stock of the whole world. We'd have to insist all Protestants were liars."

"There's grounds for maintaining that," said the priest defiantly, "going right back to Martin Luther and Henry VIII."

"Wouldn't we look sweet in court trying to back it up?" asked Peter rhetorically.

"Oh, I take your point," said the priest.

"I think we're bound by the Bishop and his Eminence," said Peter.

"His Eminence?" The priest looked up.

"Don't you know right well?" said Peter.

It appeared he did not know right well because that more or less ended the discussion. When they emerged at a quarter past one they were talking about Wexford's defeat. There was an air of resigned depression.

"Our day will come again," said the priest.

"I think we might have seen the best of them," said Peter.

The priest turned to me and said, "Here's a tenner – run down to Clarke's and get a bottle of brandy and a bottle of Irish whiskey and say I sent ya."

"Here goes in the name of God," he acknowledged to Peter.

When I got to the pub, I handed in the tenner. Mr. Clarke was behind the counter. Very stiffly he handed the ten pound note back and said, "Whilst I would very much like to oblige the Reverend Father, I am prohibited by law from serving drink to minors. Please tell him I would be happy to serve himself if he calls, or any adult on his behalf."

On my return to the shop the priest was flabbergasted.

"Of all the downright cheek," he said, "and we doin' our best to end matters"

Peter said to the priest, "Show them what you're made of."

The priest looked at him, paused and with the revelation of mystical insight said, "Upon my soul, but you're right, we never had reason to hide or apologise and we have none yet."

He walked down the street like Wyatt Earp on his way to the OK Corrall. The "priest" Doyle was reading the paper in the car. When Fr. Williams emerged from the pub with two brown paper bags, Doyle got out of the car. They spoke for a while. Doyle seemed agitated and when the priest came back to the shop he said to Peter and my father that it was not going to be so easy.

"Give it time," said Peter.

"Did they say anything?" said my father.

"A stony silence," he said and paused. "Mr. Doyle isn't going to be convinced easily – he told me he was disillusioned."

"That fella me arse," my father said with passion.

The priest laughed and shook his head. Peter got into the car with Fr. Williams. It seemed more talking needed to be done. My father drove home for his half-day. On the short journey home, I asked him if the boycott was really over. He said it was. I asked if everyone would go back to the Protestant shops. He thought some would and others would not.

"Some people can't live without boycotting," he said strangely.

"You mean the "priest" Doyle" I asked brazenly.

He looked at me quickly as if I was becoming too cute by half. "I mean 'some people'," he said deliberately.

∞·∞

And he was right. That evening I went down to Larkin's with the intention of hurling or fishing. We went fishing. The priest had called to Hiawatha and told him he was going to Sergeant Thorpey to drop the truancy charges against Michael. In turn, Hiawatha would go tomorrow and indicate that he would not give evidence in the traffic accident case against Iníon Ní Breathnach. It seemed as if common sense would prevail after all. When myself and Larkin got to the river bank, Thomas Whitney Senior was there threading a fishing gut. He surprised us.

"Hello boys – going to do a spot of fishing?"

"Yes Sir," I answered.

"There's great fishing to be done here you know," he said. I thought it was an odd remark. "Yes indeed," he continued "Even when there's none of them biting."

That was even more strange. He looked a sad man. I knew him as a bigger person, generous, deliberate, staunch. Now he looked tired and disappointed. The boycott had broken him. He had no part in it, but was its biggest victim. He cast a fly. We were fishing with worms. He moved on downstream casting and hauling as he slowly fished.

"I think he's gone in the head," said Larkin. I looked at him. "Did ya ever hear the like 'There's great fishin' even when they're not biting'?"

Maybe the fish were taking the fly, or maybe they were not. They certainly were not looking for worms. Maybe it was a great evening's fishing for old Thomas Whitney, but it was a bad evening's fishing for us. We traipsed home at half past nine grudgingly nudging our pedestrianised cycles up the hill. As we passed Clarke's, Miley Cassidy came out and stood on the sidewalk. He pulled back the lapels of his jacket and gripped his gallasses with both hands.

"I am a man of principle," he announced grandly, "because I am principally a man."

We both sniggered. He slightly staggered. Pat Shanks came out behind him slightly flushed. He regarded him unkindly.

"Go home you fool," he bade Miley and departed up the darkening street.

Miley caught him with his squadron leader's eye at two o'clock and pulled his left shoulder out of his way for a better view.

"Ya fool, yerself," he spluttered. "I have no home to which to go."

He rubbed his balding, curly, dirty head. The "priest" Doyle was walking down the street. Miley saw him coming.

"Mr. Doyle Sir, could ya spare us da' price of a cup a' tay fer me breakfast?"

"Clear off home out of my way you," he cut at him.

"The blessings a' God on ya and yer dearly departed wife and mother. I'll say a prayer for yiz all," Miley said waddling after him.

"Jus' for a cup a' tay." Doyle was heading towards the barracks and the

Sergeant's house. Miley kept tagging. "For the sake a' God an' His Holy Mother," he entreated.

"Oh here, dammit!" said the sexton and dug deep in his pocket.

"Be off with ya and don't annoy me 'til Christmas, and don't spend it all on drink," he chastised. He disappeared in through the garden gate of the barrack's house. Miley praised his patron and then opened his hand to reveal the tanner.

"Bejaysus," he paused. "Bejaysus, I'll buy a motor car."

Larkin burst out laughing.

Hiawatha came down the street. He brought us into the pub and bought us a mineral each. Larkin had a bottle of red lemonade and I had a bottle of lemon soda. Miley came in. He stood at the counter and ordered a bottle of stout. Mr. Clarke poured it into a tall glass. "One and a penny," said the publican. Miley put a tanner on the counter and his left hand rummaged in his pocket, while his right hand tilted a gulp down his throat. He took out a length of binder twine and placed it in front of the po-faced licensee. A washer, two big brown pennies, three half-pennies and a penknife with no sides on it followed. Larkin was engrossed. Hiawatha had his pipe steaming.

"You're four-pence halfpenny short Miley,'" said the publican testily.

"Begobs I thinks you're the wan thass short," said Miley.

Larkin laughed out again. Hiawatha smiled and shook his head.

"Take that up to him," said Hiawatha as he handed Larkin a six-pence.

"The blessins o' God on ya young fella – there's the makin's of a priest-in ya – isn't there Mr. Clarke?"

"No more o' your guff or I'll have to ask you to leave," said the publican.

"I was thrown out of finer places than this ya know," he answered him back.

Clarke eyed him unable to respond to the unseating wit of the little tramp. Mikey turned fully around and faced us. He raised his glass and said, "Here's to the health of all of d'Indians," he smiled his mixed-up over-familiarity to Hiawatha who laughed out. He tried to draw him.

"And are ye not goin' to toast the cowboys Miley?"

He looked down the counter at Mr. Clarke who was busy washing glasses. "There's too many a' dem about," he nodded and went back to his drink.

Shortly afterwards Larkin walked home with me in the dark. As we idled up the hill to the gentle clicking of the purring bicycles we could see cars parked outside of our house in the balmy moonlit night. There was the Sergeant's car and the "priest" Doyle's and Peter's. The light was on in the room my father called "the front room," and my mother "the parlour." I went into the kitchen and my mother was there with my sister. The two boys were in bed.

"You're not to go into the front room," my sister bossed when I came in. "There's a meeting on in there."

I ignored her and followed Mammy into the back kitchen. She was preparing tea and scones for the men.

"What's the meeting about?" I asked. "Is it the boycott?"

"I think so," she whispered. "There's some trouble about the court on Thursday."

This concerned Larkin. The door into the front was in the hall which suddenly opened and my father roared at the top of his voice

"Get the hell outta here the pair of yiz – a pair of friggin' Blueshirts is all yiz are."

"There'll be more about this," said the "priest" Doyle.

"Not in this house there won't," he replied. Thorpey was saying little. "You can take moochey-arse with ye," he disparaged the uncomfortable fearful Sergeant.

"Your tongue will get you into trouble one of these days," Thorpey managed to retort.

"There's no great fear that'll happen to you. I suppose scaldy arse sez enough for the two of yiz."

"I'm not taking that from you," said the "priest" Doyle.

"Get out of here before I drive your arse out through the roof of yer mouth, ya little ould bollix."

Peter came into the kitchen shaking his head. When my father came in they remonstrated with each other.

"Feck 'em to hell," said my father. "Who the hell does he think he is? Little ould consequence and he not as big as a fairy's fart."

We were packed off to bed. It seems that Doyle and the Sergeant came together to confront Peter about the case against Larkin and Iníon Ní Breathnach not going ahead. The sergeant was put out that he was going to have a lot of explaining to do to the superintendent of the guards and maybe even to the District Justice. Peter was accused of fixing it.

"Conspiracy to pervert the course of justice," Doyle called it. Peter replied it could hardly be his fault if Fr. Williams as school manager did not wish to give evidence against "young Larkin."

"We all know why he won't," said Doyle. "The blacksmith won't testify against the priest's girlfriend if the priest doesn't testify against the young fella."

The gloves were off and no mistake. Doyle had crossed the boundary against the priest. That was when my father blew up. My mother was shocked at Doyle's bitterness and how could he say such an awful thing. She was sure it was just the fraying of tempers on account of the tensions caused by the boycott. She kept shaking her head in disbelief at what Doyle had said. It was much later I realised the only person telling the truth was the "priest" Doyle. It also struck me that my mother was the only one who tried to entertain it, but each time her loyalties to the church overtook and submerged her feelings.

But the cases were dropped and neither the superintendent nor the judge passed the slightest remark, to the huge disappointment of the "priest" Doyle. His resentment went deep. Perniciously, he spread his story in a subtle way.

"So far as I am concerned, the boycott is still on. The children are not returned. I am a man of principle," he would say and leave it at that, begging the question about others, chiefly Fr. Williams.

I told Larkin and Hiawatha what had happened and what Doyle was now saying.

"I am a man of principle," mimicked Larkin. "Principally because I am a man," he finished imitating Miley. We both laughed.

Hiawatha smiled and said, "You can't beat the tinker."

Then another rumour started. People said the Knights of Columbanus were on Doyle's side. Some said Doyle had bought a camera and was going to maintain surveillance on the priest's house. I did not see Iníon Ní Breathnach for a long time. Some people said they used to meet some place and he would smuggle her into Coleman under the rug in the back seat of his car. There was one last mention of her after which I never wanted to hear her name again. On the Saturday night after the boycott finished I brought the Saturday night groceries up to Mae. The priest had just finished hearing Confessions and I met him driving his car just as I was going into his house. Larkin had arranged with me to go fishing after he had "put the cows up in the Protestant field," their field beside the Protestant church. He hated it when the cows were being pastured there because it was the furthest of their fields from Coleman and it was a series of slow and steep meandering hills the whole mile up. He more than made up for lost time on the way back down, however, as usual.

It was always the way with Mae when you were in a hurry, she had a job for you to do. When I went in she was on the phone in the hall.

"You've just missed him," she said into the phone."He's gone to play golf," she paused."The bus at seven-thirty in Campile. Very well Miss. I'll do my best."

She was a little time in the hall before she came back and when she did she had a note in her hand. The door once more was open. She got a start when she came in and saw me.

"An angel sent you," she said. "I want you to take this note to the priest in the golf links like a good fella."

He was to collect Iníon Ní Breathnach from the train. I went like the hammers of hell and caught him just as he was about to tee off. He read the note and looked at his watch.

"I have to rush off to a sick call," he lied to his golfing companions.

I cycled back to Coleman in the wake of the petrol fumes from the over-revved engine of the priest's car. That might have been when I started to wonder about him, but I cannot be sure. I had to cycle home before going fishing to see how long I could stay out. Larkin's bike was not in place as I passed so I knew I was all right for a time. The front door was open. As I looked up the street I saw Thorpey coming down on his bike. He looked as if he had seen a ghost. Even his knees were pale. He braked hard and skidded. His face was soft and loose.

"Michael!" he stuttered. "Michael!" he stuttered again.

I looked at him, aware of his fright.

"The priest!" he said. "Fr. Williams is after knockin' Larkin off his bike."

"Is he hurt? – Where is he?" I asked.

"Up there" he said pointing up the hill.

I felt my breath get shallow. I kept walking with my bike. I could not let it go. I saw the crowd. There was my father, Hiawatha, Gerry Denn and some women. Mrs. Clarke was there. I wheeled my bike around the edge of the crowd slowly. No one noticed me. And then I saw him. His legs were like a puppets, lifeless and loose. His face was the whitest I had ever seen. He was wearing the old FCA jacket. There was not even a mark on his face. I could see no blood. Mrs. Clarke had been a nurse. She was kneeling behind his head. She had a handkerchief in her hand. I thought she was using it for his brow. When I saw her drying her tears I looked back at him. I knew then he was dead. I saw where his nose had bled down on his green jacket. It made the same colour as it did on his football jersey the night he got the clatter in the mouth in Tom coole. I kept looking at him waiting for his eyes to flicker and burst open and laugh that he had codded all of us, but he just lay there. I strained to see him breathe, but there was no motion. Then I heard my bike rattle. It shook and shook. I heard my father say, "Jesus, it's Jack!" When I looked up at him, his eyes welled and just said, "Oh Jack – Jack." He turned me away and handed my bike to Gerry Denn. Fr. Williams was sitting in the passenger seat of his car with his feet on the road and his head in his handkerchief covered hands. Hiawatha was standing beside him, his back was to me. The red kerchief was in his hands.

As we walked up the hill all my father could say was, "It will be alright – everything will be alright." I was not able to cry. I wanted to go back, but he wouldn't let me. I just knew he would get up if they let me talk to him. I just knew it, but they did not let me go back and he never did get up.

My mother burst into tears when she saw me but I just hung my head as she hugged me. I went up to my room and lay on the bed with my clothes on. I knew how it happened. He was always tearing the arse in it. That was what got him in the end. I told him it would. Often and often. If he had only listened to me, just once, he would still be alive and we would be down there now fishing. Why the hell could he not listen? I must have been there a long time. When I woke up it was dark. I forgot he was dead. When I looked at my clothes on me it all came back and I wondered for a little if it could have been a dream, but I knew he was dead alright. I was starting to play little games in my head again. I hated that.

I went to eight o'clock Mass in the morning. A strange priest was saying it. He read out the Dues. Larkin's name was at the head of the list.

For all the priest knew it could have been his father or his grandfather, but everyone else knew. There was nearly a double gasp in the church – one for his being head of the list and the other for his being dead. He was still tearing the arse in it – even when he was dead. I smiled as I remembered Hiawatha giving the money to the "priest" Doyle. The ould bollix' I thought. I blamed him for Larkin's death. If he had not put the priest under pressure then he would never have had to rush off after Iníon Ní Breathnach's bus. What was the point? I was playing the little games again.

At breakfast my father felt I ought go to my aunt in Ballycogley for a few days – until things passed off. But I would not go. My mother said she would go to the wake in the afternoon, as she was washing up. I said I wanted to go as well and I started a row between the two of them.

I sat inside my father's garden looking down on Waterford harbour. There was a slight fog on the horizon. A fog gun boomed a muffled echo. I thought about all the comics we had swapped, all the masses we had served and all the funerals. Now here was his funeral this very summer – number fifty-six. This was the summer we would never forget – the second summer of fifty-six, but it was the summer of 1957. My father would not let me go to the wake, but we compromised on the aunt's. I would go there after the funeral, and it was some funeral. A funny thing happened at the church. When the coffin was taken out of the hearse, Gerry Denn stepped forward to carry it. He had saved him from drowning. Mr. Clarke with his po-face stepped forward from the other side. Everyone looked as he gripped the funeral linen to carry the coffin. Eager stepped out, then Mr. Auld and two other Protestants I did not know. It happened so awkwardly it revealed its spontaneity. The "priest" Doyle was there at the fringe of the crowd. He looked smaller than usual. The Protestants were helping by responding emotionally.

They buried him on the Monday. He had a High Mass. Thorpey made a balls of the thurible as usual. I could nearly hear Larkin say "gobshite." Sean Hanlon was there. When he came out of the church he carried the coffin for a spell on the way to the graveyard. He carried his black beret in his hand. The beret was his signature mark, his token of individuality. It was resented by some. "Who does he think he is with his great notions and his black beret? He thinks he's different." But he did know who he was so he wore his beret, some might say, to spite them. Coming out of the graveyard he turned around to Fr. Williams and said, "Now father, the boycott is over!" Fr. Williams looked drawn and grey. The turmoil of the parish and his own anguish was etched on his face. All of the contradictions, expectations and condemnations had savaged his countenance. He was getting a very hard time from himself.

My father was a teetotaller. On that day, however, he brought me down to Clarke's pub. It was the first time in my life I had been in there with him. He bought two lemon sodas and a drink for Hiawatha who had not spoken with me since the accident. He was shaking hands with a lot of people and was engaged in a lot of small talk. Miley was there. He came over. Hiawatha was touched. Miley was not yet drunk, but he was working on it.

"Well Miley it's waiting for us all."

"I hopes it don't run out of patience," he said.

Hiawatha laughed a little.

"It doesn't respect anybody or anything" he mused. "There's young Michael now – the whole farm there waiting for him, all left behind."

"I had a brother the same," said Miley.

Hiawatha looked at him. "Go to heck," said the blacksmith.

"Aye indeed," said Miley. "He died and left the whole world behind." Hiawatha shook his head laughing. "The best day is a funeral," he said, "No suit to be paid for – no wedding in tow and a hoor of a great drinking session."

And so the sad story came funnily to an end or maybe it was the funny story came sadly to an end. Or was it a true story after all or maybe it was just a lie. And if it was a lie, who was deceived and if it was the truth, what did it reveal?

I did go to my aunt's on holiday and forgot about most everything while I was away in that honest, selfish way of adolescents. When I came back there was a letter from Mel. She had written the letter before he died. She asked for him and would I ask him to write. I took my time about writing back to her.

The time was approaching for me to go to St. Peter's. It distracted me. My mother was putting pressure on me to go to see Sr. Ignatius, but I resisted. I worked for Peter for the rest of my holidays. He got great praise for ending the boycott. I was very proud of him. We never spoke about the accident. I felt he did not wish to make me cry – and I did not for a long time.

Little by little, my life moved on. Very slowly at first, as if to linger was to prolong his presence. For a long time I believed I would never be happy again and for a long time that was the case. Then one morning I heard that the fox got the turkey cock in Aughadreimre. The news appealed to my perverse nature, and I began to feel a little bit human again.

The following January, 1958, Elisha Hanlon returned home. Initially the papers descended on the family, but after a little the hullaballoo died down and herself and Sean and the children settled down to the mundane task of making a livelihood and living their lives.

Fr. Williams stayed in Coleman but was shifted to another parish after a few years. His housekeeper, Mae, died. Iníon Ní Breathnach moved in, fulltime to supposedly replace Mae. When he retired some years later, he built a house where they both lived until he died in his sixties. He had lived most of his life in fear of being discovered and unable to reconcile the rules with his feelings. For a finish, his heart won.

Peter went on to represent Wexford in Dáil Éireann and married late in life.

It was the end of August before I sat down to write to Mel. I had put it off, I told myself, because I did not know what to write. I went to my bedroom and sat on the bed.

"Dear Mel,
I have bad news. Michael is dead."

What sort of a gobshite was I? – What way was that to write a letter?

"Dear Mel,
I have some bad news. You know Michael whom you used to be friendly with? Well ..."

(Shite!)

What was I going to write. It was like going to Confession. I stopped again. What did I want to say? I started again.

"Dear Mel,
The worst thing in the world that could happen has happened ..."

And then the sluice gates opened and I cried my heart out. I higged and sobbed for an hour but I finished my letter that evening. I never saw Mel again, but her mother wrote to my mother and said she had been very upset by the news. She sent me a Christmas card for the next three Christmases, but they stopped when her mother died.

I went down to Hiawatha before I went away to the boarding school. He cried when he saw me, but I did not get upset. It was shortly after I had written to Mel.

"We are so stupid and God is so wise," he said. "It took the death of an innocent little boy to shake us all up and become a community again."

"Do you think that is why it happened?" I asked.

"There are no reasons – and there are no explanations – that is just the way life is" he said.

Thomas Whitney Senior died two years later. The boycott broke his spirit they said. He was a decent man and had been grievously wronged. Nobody had ever said "Sorry" to him.

Hiawatha lived ten more years and that was the next time I felt like crying. Funnily enough, I could not cry then either. That only happened when I went to Larkin's grave to tell him about it. I stood there for five minutes bawling.

And so, one by one the people were all laid to rest, but the ghosts of the boycott still haunt the air. A lot of the people forgot, but more of them could not remember the details. The Bishop hid his files and the politicians followed suit. Little by little, the stories were revised and, little by little, fewer and fewer were involved. For my part, I grew up. I look back now on the little village and realise how old I have become. I am the oldest man of my age that I know for I have seen men right and wrong and live and die and so indeed am I.

Epilogue

This Epilogue is a counterpoint to the author's note. Difficult as it is to believe, it happened. On the day following the signing of the Agreement by my uncle Peter and Thomas Whitney Senior, thirty-six whales were washed up on the beach at Coleman.

It could have been taken straight out of Shakespeare's *Hamlet* (Act I, Scene I) – the bit where he said, "harbingers preceding still the fates, a prologue to the omen coming on," except in this case it was the Epilogue proceeding from events. It was as if, sickened to its bowels by events, the very sea around Coleman vomited up its most powerful citizenry – the whales. And there they lay beached – the powerful mammals of the sea, unfettered, unruffled, but yet their hearts were dying sadly deep within them. People came from far and near to see them. I came as well with my father. He remarked as we walked away that evening, "Isn't it all very strange – will we ever see the likes of it again?"

The boycott demanded a funeral and it got it.

When I was researching this book and read this account, the hair stood up on the back of my neck – it could have been an account of the people in the boycott but it wasn't. In fact, there was no account of the boycott, and its ending in the paper whatsoever or at all. The story of the boycott carried nationally but not locally.

In local lore and memory traumatic events that affect the community become etched into the folk mind. Instead of referring to dates, folk often refer to "the Night of the Big Wind" or "the Year of the Heavy fall of Snow", as being more definite and emotional hallmarks and watersheds than scientific calculations by date, month or calendar. In this mode, the local journalist from *The Free Press* had commenced his article on the Pilot Whales by prefacing his comments with these two paragraphs;

> I am sure it will be a long while before the whales are forgotten and I am equally sure that the memory of their visit will long be preserved in that locality, tickled by many a salty yarn.
> The whole incident of their coming and their ultimate fate make up the sort of rare happening that deserves to get a place in local lore.
> It might even become a minor sort of historic occasion and maybe for a decade or two to come 1957 will be recalled as "The Year the Whales Came In", and other occurrences in the area will be dated as having happened before "The Year of the Whales" or afterwards, as the case may be.

It wasn't, it was always known as "The Year of the Boycott."